THE LAST PASSENGER

THE
LAST PASSENGER

MANEL LOUREIRO

TRANSLATED BY ANDRÉS ALFARO

amazon crossing

Text copyright © 2013 Manel Loureiro
Translation copyright © 2014 Andrés Alfaro

Previously published as *El último pasajero* by Editorial Planeta, Spain, in 2013. Translated from Spanish by Andrés Alfaro.

Published by AmazonCrossing, Seattle
www.apub.com

ISBN-13: 9781477826539
ISBN-10: 147782653X

Cover design by Edward Bettison Ltd.
Library of Congress Control Number: 2014910661
Printed in the United States of America

For my son, Manel,
the axis upon which my universe spins

PART ONE

—

THE FOG

I

*The spray, the fog, the night. A moisture
that seeps into your bones with the boldness
of a rooting weed. Dark water, turbid.
Thousands of feet of abyss beneath
the ship and somewhere, below, monsters.*

I. Freskor

SS Pass of Ballaster
Somewhere in the North Atlantic
August 28, 1939
4:57 a.m.

Six hundred miles off the coast of Ireland the night was black like the depths of a mine, disappearing into the calm, opaque sea. It was there that the fog struck.

A knot formed in Tom McBride's throat as he tried to pierce the mist with his gaze. He spat and pulled his coat, emblazoned with a captain's insignia, tight. It had been nearly twenty-four hours since they'd been caught in the spongy mass. Moisture was seeping into every last crevice of the *Pass of Ballaster.*

"I don't get it," he murmured. "Fog in the middle of August. At this damned latitude."

Grumbling, he reached to his left without peeling his eyes from the horizon, which at that moment meant a distance of no more than ten or eleven feet. He picked up the cup of coffee that was sitting on the navigation table and took a sip. It was cold like everything else on board. Nothing stayed hot for more than ten or fifteen minutes since they'd been surrounded by this thick yellow haze.

At least the waves aren't too rough, he thought, spitting the coffee back into the cup with a look of disgust. *A storm is the last thing we need.*

McBride knew what he was talking about. The *Pass of Ballaster* had already seen its best years go by. The five-thousand-ton cargo ship was covered by a thick layer of rust, which mattered little since the rust was almost completely hidden by the sticky black powder from the loads of coal that were piled up in its hull.

The ship also sported a gigantic scar on one side, a souvenir left behind by an inexperienced tugboat captain who had miscalculated his distances in Halifax Harbor. The *Pass of Ballaster* was a ship that had been condemned to being scrapped, yet continued on in spite of itself.

I don't believe we'll make too many more journeys aboard you, old friend, thought McBride as he undid the top button of his jacket. *Maybe one or two more. Who knows?*

McBride had always thought of the ship like an old dame who had been stripped of her beauty and glamour but who tried to maintain her withered dignity until the very end. Now it was spending its final years shipping coal between Boston and Bristol.

Every member aboard was conscious of the fact that the vessel had very few voyages left in it. The *Pass of Ballaster* was just too old, the repairs were getting too costly, and above all, the coal market had practically dried up. It would only be a matter of time before the ship's owners decided to retire it from service.

The outbound journey, made in ballast, had been perfect. The summer weather was such that the crew could strut on deck shirtless. The loading of the cargo in Boston had taken place without a hitch, apart from whisperings of impending war. It was supposed to be a trip like any other.

Until they hit this damned fog bank.

First, the radio cut out, despite the fact that the communications officer had checked it thoroughly, swearing that everything was in order. It had just stopped working. All that could be heard was the screeching of static and a faint beat in the background, a sort of dull *tac-tac-tac* that repeated at random, every few minutes.

Sometimes the radio remained silent for hours until, as if suddenly realizing the ship was still there, it would hiccup out a series of low regular clicks, like a mad butcher whacking a cleaver against the chopping block. Then, silence.

On top of that, there was the cold. Sure, it was normal for it to be chilly within a fog bank, but this was different. This was an intense cold; frozen vapors formed each time you took a breath outside, and every exhalation tried to take a piece of lung out with it.

If that weren't enough, it had been six hours since the compass started acting up.

This had not been like the problem with the radio—unexpected—but rather had come on slowly, gradually. At first there was a slight tremble in the needle, subtle enough that the crew attributed it to the vibrations sent out by the ship's old and worn twin piston engines. After some time it became evident that the needle was becoming more and more erratic and unreliable.

McBride leaned over the compass again, though he knew he had just done so ten minutes prior. The needle fluctuated violently from east to west, unable to steady itself for more than a second.

The captain gulped. To navigate without a compass and with no visibility in the middle of a fog bank was an invitation for disaster. They could circle about for hours or, worse yet, lose their way completely. This was something that the *Pass of Ballaster*, with its asthmatic engines, could not risk.

As if reading his mind, the helmsman, a young man of no more than twenty, turned around upon hearing the creak of the command chair.

"Captain," trembled the young man's voice as the compass sitting on his right danced to the same broken rhythm as the one McBride had by his side, "what do you suppose I should do?"

"Stay the course," ordered McBride. *And don't forget to stay calm,* he added to himself. "If we haven't strayed too far off our last estimate, then we should be on course. As soon as we can get out of this fog bank, everything will be better, son."

"Yes, Captain," answered the helmsman.

Never let on to the crew that you are nervous, too, thought McBride. He could almost hear in his mind the old adage every captain of the merchant fleet memorized at the academy. How easy it all seemed on land, under the sun's radiance. There, in the middle of the strangest situation of his career, he figured nothing worse could happen that evening.

A gust of cold air, heavy with moisture, caused the edges of the navigation chart to flutter. Captain McBride raised his eyes to see Tom O'Leary, the *Pass of Ballaster*'s first mate, walking in backward and fighting against the wind to keep his coat closed as he shut the door to the command bridge.

O'Leary, a forty-something Irishman, red-faced and slender, shook off the water that had collected on his jacket and muttered under his breath. McBride greeted him with a tired motion. His first mate was efficient despite his nervous and irritable personality.

"Have you overseen the changing of the guard?"

"Of course, Captain," answered O'Leary as he approached the navigation table. "But this damn fog frays my nerves."

"It's only fog," replied the captain laconically, licking his lips.

"Yes, sir," he said, exchanging a nervous look with McBride that was much more eloquent than anything they could have said. "It's only fog, sir."

Both were lying and they knew it. But going from there to admitting it was a big step.

Between the two of them, they had more than forty years of maritime experience on these waters. They had come across fog banks thousands of times. Many had been much worse, more dense and dangerous than their present situation. Besides, it was August, and the possibility of encountering an iceberg along the way was slim. They had already gotten far enough away from Newfoundland that the danger of hitting some clueless Portuguese fishing boat was remote. In theory, it was simply another fog bank.

But somehow, this was different.

"This just keeps getting worse," said McBride.

He briefly entertained the idea of going to bed and leaving the first mate in charge tonight. Head to bed and trust that in the morning the sun would be out, the radio would be up and working, and the compass would stop acting like it had gone berserk.

Everything would be back to normal. But then he noticed something in the corner of the starboard window.

I'll be damned if I don't see ice forming in that window, he thought.

Ice in August? A strange tingle ran up his spine.

"Mr. O'Leary, sound the ship's siren every three minutes instead of every five. And send another two men with binoculars to the lookout on the bow. I have no intention of hitting any damned Turkish merchant ship whose crew's fallen asleep or some block of ice run adrift," he grunted, standing up. "Some polar ocean current must have come down this way. It may have brought a surprise with it."

"Not to worry, Captain," answered O'Leary as he gazed at the crystalline frost with an unusual look.

The first mate saluted and, without another word, strode off the bridge toward the staircase that led to the crew's quarters.

The *Pass of Ballaster* was a small ship that did not require a large crew. On this particular trip, the crew was comprised of the captain, O'Leary, and seven seamen from various countries.

•   •   •

When the first mate opened the door to the common area, a flash of light smacked him across the face. The interior of the ship might have been a few degrees warmer than the bridge, but it was still freezing. Although the ship's heating system was firing on all cylinders, not even the red-hot radiators could counter the icy sensation.

O'Leary entered the galley, where two of the crew on watch had come to take refuge in an attempt to get warm. Seated at a table, they were in the middle of a hotly contested round of cribbage.

"Men, the old man wants two of you to go to the lookout on the bow," he muttered, giving a friendly slap on the back to one of the sailors. "Any volunteers?"

"Come on, Mr. O'Leary!" one of them protested. He was a lanky, freckle-faced youth of eighteen with more acne than hair on his cheeks. "Tonight is dreadful, and besides, you can't see a thing out there."

"That's exactly why, Duff," he replied patiently. He poured himself a glass of brandy and turned around toward the other deckhand, a middle-aged man who was short and squat like a circus strongman. His face was crowned by thick black eyebrows that seemed to have a life of their own. "Stepanek, you and Duff can head up to the crow's nest with a pair of binoculars. Keep your eyes open. If there's any problem, radio the bridge."

"Yes, sir," replied Stepanek. He reluctantly picked up the deck of cards and packed it away in its box.

He was a weathered sailor with a distinct Slavic accent. He had served aboard many vessels and knew that, on occasion, however unpleasant the order, there was no choice but to obey.

"You will be relieved within three hours, but in the meantime I would like you to remain vigilant. If you fall asleep and we hit something, I swear to God I'll strangle the both of you before I see this ship go down. Is that clear?"

"Yes, sir," answered Stepanek as he buttoned up his heavy winter parka and looped the binoculars around his neck. He turned to the youngest sailor and ruffled his hair. "Come along, lad. Tonight we'll be counting seagulls."

"Seagulls? What seagulls, Step?"

"Sometimes I wonder how the hell you got aboard alone, kid." Stepanek shook his head and dragged the boy along behind him.

As soon as they got up on deck, the two men began to shiver. The fog stretched out in all directions, clammy and viscous. It made the ship's lights dull and lifeless.

"You can't see anything out here," complained Duff. "It will be no better in the crow's nest."

"Pleased to have your opinion on the matter, Excellency. Now quit your griping, so we can head up the mast before O'Leary comes back. If we hit something, they'll have our hides. Now move! Let's go!"

The crow's nest was a sort of basket set atop a tall mast, seventy feet in height. Besides holding the nest, it served as a good base for the radio antenna. Going up there was rare. And the only way to the top was by climbing a ladder attached to the steel post. The iron rungs of the ladder gleamed maniacally from the thin sheet of ice covering them.

"Watch where you step, Duff. If you fall, your brains will get to Bristol before your body."

All Duff could do was answer with a strangled groan.

It took one long minute to climb the ladder, grunting and kicking at each one of the metallic hoops before placing the weight of their feet on them. Finally, they climbed into the nest and squeezed into the small, cramped space. In one corner, attached to the mast, was a black telephone connected to its counterpart located on the bridge.

"See? What did I tell you? You can't see anything up here," moaned Duff.

"What would you have? Sunshine? Take those binoculars and cover your side, numskull," replied Stepanek, tossing the binoculars at him.

Stepanek knew the boy was partly right. Even seventy feet up, visibility hadn't improved a bit. It seemed the fog was doing nothing but getting worse.

From the crow's nest one could see neither the bow of the ship nor the deck. Even straining, one could hardly make out the faint lights coming from the bridge. For a moment Stepanek had the sensation they were alone in the world, suspended amid a spongy, dense mass the color of a dead man's bones.

Stepanek shook his head, troubled. Something just didn't feel right about it all.

He turned toward Duff to make sure he was holding on to the railing of the nest. Then, he picked up the phone to test the line.

It worked. The tone was faint but constant.

With his free hand he shook the base of the antenna to make sure it was properly attached. Everything was in order.

But something wasn't right. It took him a minute to realize what was wrong.

Silence.

All sounds had ceased. Neither the rumbling of the engines nor the crash of the waves against the hull of the ship could be heard.

It was like being in a coffin.

"I'm cold," said Duff in a low voice, shivering. A moment later he added, as if embarrassed, "And scared."

"Shut up." A feeling of urgency slowly crept across Stepanek. He felt as if his skin were crawling, and not just from the cold. *Something* was out there.

"Purgatory must be a lot like this," mused Duff, becoming restless. He had the binoculars in his hands, looking nowhere in particular. Despite saying he was cold, he was sweating.

Stepanek looked him over again and considered a reply. But at that very moment he seemed to spot something out of the corner of his eye. He turned to his right, then left. "Did you see that?" he asked Duff.

"See what?"

Then, they saw it. Or, rather, they guessed at it. Suddenly, it appeared in front of the bow of the *Pass of Ballaster* as if it had been waiting all along for the coal ship to pass by. It was a black shadow, enormous, elongated, and it swooped toward the vessel at full speed.

"Shit!" yelled Stepanek.

The sailor grabbed the phone and hit Duff, who had almost been turned catatonic by the colossal shadow.

"We're gonna crash!" he howled into the speaker. "Iceberg straight ahead! Veer away, quick! Steer clear!"

For a few unending moments the *Pass of Ballaster* stayed its course, seemingly immutable, heading straight for that shadow crossing its path. Then, slowly, very slowly, several things started to happen. The mast began to tremble, shaken by the vibrations from the ship's engines firing to change course. The faint sound of the roaring engines reached them as the bow of the ship began to slowly veer, little by little, away from the black patch that was growing larger by the second.

It's too slow, Stepanek thought to himself as he watched the shadow. *We're going to crash.*

"Keep turning," he shouted into the phone. His voice had turned into a stifled wheezing. "Keep turning all the way, or by God, we're going to die."

If the *Pass of Ballaster* had been any larger or had been going any faster, a turnaround with such short notice would have been impossible. The small vessel, however, responded, and foot by foot, inch by inch, it began to skirt the obstacle, which was now that much closer.

We're going to make it. Just maybe we're going to make it. Stepanek's mind was racing as the mass continued to grow larger. It was the biggest iceberg he had ever seen, at least twice as high as the ship's tallest point, and much, much wider. The fog had covered it up like a shroud, but its dimensions could be surmised from the light cast by the lanterns on the bow.

Finally, with the sluggishness of a waking cat, the front of the ship pointed toward the abysmal blackness of the night, avoiding disaster by no more than thirty feet.

"We just missed it," he shouted, slapping Duff on the back. "That goddamned iceberg was nearly the death of us all! By God, that was a mighty close call."

"Tell them to shut down the engines," replied Duff, wearing a glassy expression. His voice was strangely calm. He wasn't looking at Stepanek but instead behind him.

"What? What on earth are you talking about?"

"Tell them to shut down the engines," repeated Duff hoarsely. He sounded like he had a pound of cotton in his throat.

"Why do you want them to shut down the engines?" Stepanek asked. He felt his enthusiasm begin to wane and turn into something akin to panic. He knew he should turn around and look at what Duff saw. But he didn't want to.

"It's not an iceberg," came Duff's response, his eyes glued to the horizon.

Feeling as if everything was suddenly in slow motion, Stepanek turned around without letting go of the telephone gripped in his hand. Then, he opened his eyes wide and began to pray under his breath in Croatian, something he had not done since he was a child.

Floating, silent, shadowy, less than seventy feet away, the bow of an enormous ship rose out of the water, several times larger than the *Ballaster*. It was stopped dead on the water, completely immobile and without a single light.

Above the anchor, several feet overhead, the ship's name could be seen.

Valkyrie.

For the next ten minutes chaos reigned aboard the *Pass of Ballaster*. The crew rushed around from place to place, while Captain McBride and the first mate howled orders in three different languages. It took them nearly twenty minutes to completely halt the progress of the old coal ship. Meanwhile, the helmsman, trying not to drift too far from the *Valkyrie*, had his hands full zigzagging toward that great shadow without getting too close— that great shadow, which could only be sensed behind the dense mist. In the end McBride himself took control of the vessel, carefully approaching the enormous and silent floating mass.

"Mr. O'Leary, have you been able to make contact with the ship?" McBride asked his second-in-command.

"No, Captain," replied O'Leary, flustered. "The radio is still dead. Bernie . . . I mean . . . Mr. Cornwell, says we may have blown a vacuum tube. He's still working on it."

McBride nodded without taking his eyes off the fog. In the last twelve hours they had taken the radio apart three times and put it back together again without finding a single blown tube. He knew that couldn't really be the problem, but they had to try it anyway.

The situation was disconcerting. The ship sat completely motionless with no lights and no signs of life on board. It just didn't make sense.

"Mr. O'Leary, take the signal lamp and try to make contact with the *Valkyrie*. Identify us, and ask them if they're having some sort of problem or if they need any assistance."

O'Leary assented and went up on deck accompanied by a deckhand who would act as the signalman. Each stationed himself behind the lamp, but the light would not turn on. From where he stood, the captain could hear their hurried whispers.

"What's going on, Mr. O'Leary? Are you waiting for a goddamn invitation to turn on the lamp?" McBride noticed his voice was more tense than usual.

"No, Captain," came the officer's troubled response. "There must be an electrical problem. They were supposed to have it fixed in port, but the electricians said it would need an alternator that—" Suddenly, O'Leary realized he was jabbering and shut up.

McBride looked at him with a severe expression and kept himself to one question. "Can you fix it before we drift and crash into that ship?"

"Of course, sir. It will only take three minutes."

"Then, do so at once, goddammit," grumbled the captain, taking out a handkerchief and wiping sweat from his forehead.

If he hadn't been so preoccupied with the distance between the two ships—which was decreasing every second—he would have noticed that he was no longer shivering. Several of the crewmen had taken off their raincoats and were now in shirtsleeves. The frost on the portholes began to melt rapidly, making little trails that dripped down to the deck.

But nobody took notice. Everyone was focused on the enormous hull of the *Valkyrie*. It had been growing larger for some time now, taking up more and more of the horizon and dwarfing the *Pass of Ballaster.*

It's big. Very big, thought the captain. At least twenty thousand tons. But I don't understand what it's doing here. Or why nobody responds.

His gaze fell on the mast rig to see what flag it was flying. If the yellow banner was out indicating "Quarantine on Board," it would be imperative for the *Pass of Ballaster* to get as far away from there as possible, as quickly as its engines could carry it. But there was no such banner.

The *Valkyrie* floated lazily like a sleeping whale as the two ships drifted closer and closer. Just then the powerful signal light came to life with a bright flash, and they pointed it toward the ocean liner's hull.

"Finally," the captain snarled.

Flashes of white light bounced around in the fog, making everything seem that much more surreal. Each time the lamp flashed to life, millions of droplets danced in its beam of light, swirling madly as if confused. Meanwhile, the *Valkyrie* shimmered, practically within arm's reach, dark and wet like the skin of a sea monster.

Chik-chik-chik. The signal lamp blinked endlessly, each flash illuminating the *Valkyrie*'s hull, like a lightning storm.

Five lengthy minutes later, McBride shook his head.

"That's enough, Mr. O'Leary. They aren't going to respond."

"Should we try the bullhorn?" asked the first officer without taking his eyes from the ocean liner. "We're close enough."

"We might as well try everything," the captain grunted, wiping his brow.

A chunk of ice came loose from the rim of the porthole and crashed to the deck with a splash. The sudden rise in temperature had caused water to drip from everything.

The first officer picked up the brass bullhorn. He tried to swallow, but his throat was too dry, so he cleared his throat and licked his lips.

First, he tried in English. No response. He looked to the captain, nervous, but the captain gave no sign. He was absorbed by the *Valkyrie*, pensive. A few minutes later he tried again, this time in poor German. Still nothing.

It's like talking to a tomb, thought McBride with a shudder. Because that is what the ocean liner seemed to be—an enormous, silent, and wet coffin.

"Let's send out a raft," he declared with a sigh. "You and two men. I believe we've got a long cable in hold number three. There must be a grappling hook somewhere in the anchor room. Get up on that ship, and find out what the hell is going on."

"Yes, sir."

O'Leary turned on his heel, and his gaze fell on Duff and Stepanek, who had just come down from the lookout. Their weatherproof jackets were wide open, and both were sweating as if they had just finished running a marathon.

"Sir, the heat up there is hellish," Stepanek complained. "Not even in the middle of August—"

"I know, Stepanek," O'Leary interrupted. "Nothing is normal tonight. Come with me, you two. We're going to do a bit of sightseeing."

Duff was about to say something, but the Croat quietly stepped on his foot.

As they strode quickly carrying a huge roll of cable following the first officer, Duff managed to give Stepanek a fiery look. In his eyes, just one question: *"Why us again?"*

| | |

With the help of the stern-side davit, they lowered the *Pass of Ballaster*'s only raft down to the water. The sea was as glassy as a mirror—not the slightest imperfection could be seen on the pitch-black water. It looked like the heart of a slumbering lake.

Stepanek grabbed one oar, Duff the other. O'Leary took up the helm.

With a few powerful strokes the boat broke away from the *Pass of Ballaster* and began slowly approaching the ocean liner. Each time the oars plunged into the water, ripples shimmered across the surface, and the echo of each splash reverberated ominously between the two ships. Their only light was from the sodium lamps they had taken from the vessel.

"Maybe there was a fire on board or something," panted Duff between strokes. "The passengers and crew would have abandoned the ship, leaving it to drift."

"Can't be," murmured O'Leary. "All of the lifeboats are hanging from their supports, at least the ones on this side. If they've abandoned ship, it wasn't by lifeboat."

"I don't smell smoke," added Stepanek. "Plus, it doesn't seem damaged at all. I'd bet anything that damned ship doesn't even have a crack in the hull."

"Quiet!" ordered O'Leary. "We're getting close."

The raft was a few yards away from the *Valkyrie*. They were close enough to see the seams where the steel hull had been soldered and painted jet black. O'Leary tilted his head back and looked up toward the bulwark lost in the shadows, several feet above. After a quick mental calculation, he was discouraged to realize he would need to be much stronger to throw the grappling hook that high.

"Let's go around," he said. "It might be easier to get up on the other side."

The boat advanced slowly around the hull of the *Valkyrie* until reaching the bow.

"I can't see a fucking thing," grunted Stepanek. "Should we use the floodlight, sir?"

O'Leary nodded. He suddenly felt vulnerable. To one side was the mass of a ship, abandoned by all appearances. To the other, the immensity of the sea, wrapped in a thick layer of fog. Confined to their small wooden raft, he became aware of just how fragile he and his men were.

They began to track the floodlight over the side of the *Valkyrie* as they continued to row slowly. O'Leary's hopes faded as they approached the stern and saw the ship's bulwark was at least fifty feet high, definitely out of reach.

"I don't think we'll be able to get up from here." He turned to his crew and thought out loud. "If we go back to the *Ballaster* and bring her close enough, maybe we could launch the grappling hook from our bow."

Suddenly, a loud crack, like paper being ripped, and an intense pounding sounded above them. Then, a thunderous clang crashed against the hull of the *Valkyrie*, right above their heads. Pieces of broken planks and torn canvas began to rain down all around them.

"Fuck, we're gonna be crushed!" yelled Duff in a panic.

"Shut up and steady the floodlight, you idiot!" shouted O'Leary, trying to balance the raft, which wouldn't stop rocking.

Something huge fell next to them and sent an icy splash of cold water up and over the side, leaving the sailors completely soaked.

The floodlight swung with a life of its own, sketching strange arabesques across the metallic skin of the *Valkyrie*. Gradually, the shower of objects ceased and the raft steadied.

"Are you guys all right?" O'Leary asked, unable to see his men, who were obscured by a dark shadow. "Answer me, goddammit!"

A pair of scared voices replied, wavering. It was no wonder. O'Leary himself had a knot lodged in his throat.

"What the hell was that?" he murmured. He pointed the floodlight toward his men and cursed.

A smashed lifeboat hung a few feet above them. Having come loose from its support, the boat had shattered against the *Valkyrie*'s hull. Now it was barely hanging by one end.

"Shit! Look at the pulley wheel. It's given out," remarked Duff from the back, relieved. "That was close! We could have been crushed like ants."

"You'll always remember this as the day you were nearly flattened by a pulley that gave way," answered O'Leary without taking his eyes off the dangling lifeboat. *Unless someone sabotaged it,* he thought. He had no idea why this had occurred to him, but it triggered a flash of acid in his stomach. He wouldn't swear it, but he was fairly certain he had heard something just before the lifeboat came loose.

They maneuvered until they were able to hook the grapple on the bottom end of the broken lifeboat. With one end tightly secured, O'Leary turned to his men.

"Who's coming with me?"

The two exchanged glances. Neither moved.

"What if we all go up, sir?" came Duff's voice, almost pleading. "It's a very large vessel."

"Plus, I don't want to be left alone on this damned raft while you two walk around up there, sir," added Stepanek.

"All right," O'Leary conceded. "Secure the raft before we go up. If it goes adrift, the old man will have our heads, especially mine."

In less than a minute the officer and the two sailors secured the raft and began to crawl up the wreckage of the lifeboat. O'Leary tried to control his breath while he climbed. He stretched out his arm and grabbed the bulwark to climb aboard.

Then, several things happened at once.

First, O'Leary felt cold again, but this was a bitter cold that charged into his veins, cutting his breath short. The metal of the rail was so frigid that he had to suppress a yell of pain.

Second, the silence. Nothing could be heard aboard that mammoth ship.

Third, the overwhelming sensation he was being watched.

The three mariners clustered together on board the *Valkyrie*, unsure what to do next.

"Let's go to the bow and then to the bridge," said the first officer, trying to control his voice. "If there's nobody aboard, then we'll toss our cable over to the *Ballaster* and tow her to port. Rescuing a ship like this should make for a tidy sum!"

As they explored the deck, using their lanterns to light the way, O'Leary was overcome by a wave of excitement. Until now it hadn't occurred to him that the ship might be deserted. International maritime law dictated that a third party had the right to rescue any goods abandoned at sea. The abandoned ship's owner would have to fork over an enormous premium to recover the property.

"Did you hear that?" asked Stepanek suddenly, wrenching the senior officer from his reverie.

O'Leary pricked up his ears but could not detect anything unusual.

"What am I supposed to be listening for? I don't hear anything."

It took O'Leary a moment to catch on—he couldn't hear anything at all besides their footsteps. Neither the creak of metal nor the clang of a skylight closing. Not even a gust of wind whistling across a sail.

Nothing.

It's almost as if the entire ship is holding its breath. The idea, like a snake, slithered into O'Leary's thoughts. *We are being watched.*

"Quit fooling around," he whispered, unaware he had lowered his voice. "Let's work our way to the bridge and finish this as quickly as we can."

The *Valkyrie's* deck was lost in the darkness. Their lantern barely illuminated the few feet in front of them while the mist flickered in its light. As they walked, O'Leary took note of the lifeboat pulleys with an expert eye. Since the *Titanic* disaster some twenty-seven years earlier, every passenger liner in the world was required to be equipped with enough vessels to seat every passenger and crew member. The *Valkyrie* was much smaller than the *Titanic*, but even so, the number of lifeboats was unbelievable. Not a single one was missing.

They appeared to be fastened securely with weatherproof covers stretched across each one. There were no signs they had ever been moved. O'Leary would have wagered his life savings that the only boat not secured was the wrecked one, which dangled from the side of the ship some fifty yards back, without which they never would have been able to climb aboard.

A metallic thumping a few feet ahead broke the silence. The off-kilter click-clack started loud and became quieter. The three men seized up, not moving a muscle.

"Hello?" shouted O'Leary in a voice less firm than he intended. "Anyone there? Hello? Who's there?"

They heard a frenzied rustling and a raspy sound of something sliding around, but nothing more moved in the darkness.

"Zdravo Marijo, milosti puna, Gospodin s tobom, blagoslovljena ti medu ženama . . ." Stepanek prayed under his breath for the second time that evening as his eyes tried to penetrate the darkness.

"All right, that's enough." O'Leary suddenly felt very irritated. Not only was he shivering and exhausted, but he also found himself aboard an unknown ship with some twisted bastard who wanted to play a game of ghost. It was too much for one night.

"I am First Officer O'Leary of the British liner *Pass of Ballaster*," he shouted. "Whoever you are, there's nothing to fear. We are here!"

Nothing happened. No response.

Until they heard a whispering behind them.

Weeee're heeeere!

Stepanek turned around so fast that he bumped into a frazzled Duff, and the two of them stumbled into O'Leary. Before they knew it, all three were on the ground, a pile of arms and legs.

"Who's there? Who's fucking there? Who?" Stepanek's lantern spun around as he tried to get up.

"Let's get out of here! Let's get the hell out of here!" Duff's voice was hysterical.

"Shut up, you idiots," roared O'Leary, replacing his hat. He was so nervous he spat as he spoke. "We're not going anywhere! Got it?" His bloodshot eyes studied his sailors fidgeting like nervous schoolchildren. "What do you want to do? Return to the ship, and tell the captain we've just escaped from a bunch of ghosts? He'd dress us down and send us back. Now act like men. We just need to get up to the command bridge and find out if the ship is empty. If she is, we can throw a cable back to the *Ballaster* and tow her to port." Here, he changed his tone of voice, trying to be persuasive. "As soon as we're finished, we can go back to the *Ballaster* and get the hell out of this fog. Then, we can forget this ever happened until we get back to Bristol. Is that clear?"

The two sailors, accustomed to maritime discipline, agreed with more doubt than faith in their eyes.

"But that voice," said Duff.

"That was just an echo, idiot," replied O'Leary. "Some acoustic effect must have made it sound like it came from behind us. Probably the fog, or a thousand other things. I studied it at the academy, years ago."

Duff and Stepanek nodded again, somewhat more calm. But as they continued walking, O'Leary didn't exactly feel at peace. He knew his reasoning had been a tremendous lie, and that there was no explanation for such an acoustic phenomenon. Plus, there was one other small detail.

O'Leary was certain the voice of the echo had not been his own.

I V

The officer kept his thoughts to himself as they approached a wide open door.

"Do you think this door made that noise earlier?" asked Duff nervously.

"Maybe," answered Stepanek as he slowly swung the door back and forth, causing the hinges to squeak. "Or maybe it was the wind."

"It would seem so," said O'Leary, hardly convinced.

The three men crossed the threshold and ventured into the *Valkyrie* but not without one last dubious look back at the mist that covered the horizon.

The interior was completely dark, but apart from that, there was nothing out of the ordinary. They were in a long corridor, lined with wood panels, the floor layered with plush red carpet that muffled their footsteps. They stayed close together. The only light came from their lanterns, glimmering off the copper molding that framed the doors and the lamps in the ceiling.

The hallway led to an even longer one that was studded on both sides with doors. Every few feet they stopped to call out a loud greeting, but there was not the slightest movement within the ship's interior.

A great set of oak double doors ended the second hallway. After a slight hesitation, O'Leary placed his hand on the doorknob. He was convinced he felt *something*. But it was just an ordinary doorknob, cold and unassuming.

He threw open the two doors, and for a brief moment, they were breathless. They found themselves in a huge oval-shaped room decorated much more luxuriously than the corridors. It was very large, much bigger than any compartment on the *Pass of Ballaster*.

In the middle of the room stood an enormous staircase that split into two, as it ascended upward out of their view. The balustrades lining the staircase were crafted from thick sections of oak that formed scrollwork, which merged into handrails made of a darker grain. The white marble steps gleamed in the lantern light; the inscription on each stair alternated between "*Valkyrie*" and "KDF."

O'Leary noticed that each handrail began with an eagle, wings spread wide and a laurel wreath in its talons. The center of each wreath held a swastika that extended down to the floor.

Swastikas appeared almost obsessively throughout the hall, including along a trim that ran around the entire length of the ceiling, featuring the profile of the eagles, each grasping the Reich's most recognizable symbol. Most English and North American passenger liners had a timepiece or a classical statue surrounded by plump little cherubs at the head of the stairs. Not this ship. Instead, there were two flags: the red flag of the Reich with a swastika at the center and a similar blue one with the arms of the swastika formed by beams of sunlight that surrounded a cog with "KDF" underneath.

"Where are we, sir?"

"I believe this is the main lobby of the ship." He pointed his lantern upward, causing the crystal chandelier above to sparkle with infinite tiny reflections of light. "If I'm right, we can get to the main hall from here as well as access the bridge."

"And those flags?" asked Duff innocently.

"It's a German ship, you half-wit," Stepanek said, pushing him. "Don't you read the news? That's the Nazi flag. They've been waving it about with no end in sight for some years now. Sometimes it seems that's all they know how to do. Protest and wave that fucking flag."

"Let's not lose track of time," said O'Leary. "We have a lot to do."

They climbed the staircase quickly, paying no attention to the paintings on the wall. Reaching the upper landing, they found crystal doors that led to the main dining hall. When they entered, they were struck by a smell.

"What's that smell? Lamb?" said O'Leary.

"I think so," answered Stepanek, "and sausage if I'm not mistaken."

"Look at this, sir." Duff's voice could barely be heard.

He passed his lantern over one of the round tables located next to the door.

The table was luxuriously set for twelve diners. The crystal glasses and plates were engraved with small eagles on one side and "KDF" on the other. The napkins, red and blue, were folded elegantly. An enormous fruit bowl, filled with apples and oranges, artistically arranged, was in the center of the table. The lantern light sparkled off the finely polished silverware that was waiting for nonexistent diners.

Next to the glasses, small ceramic saucers each held a bread roll. O'Leary picked up one of the rolls and squeezed the pliable crust with his fingers, releasing a mouthwatering aroma.

"It's still fresh," he murmured with amazement. "It couldn't have been made more than an hour ago."

He could not tear his eyes from the table. The plates were spotless, and there was an enormous tray of meat waiting for someone to work up the nerve to dig in. One of the glasses was half-filled with red wine. O'Leary would have bet anything that he could see lipstick on the rim of the glass.

He paced around the rest of the dining room without realizing he still had the bread roll in his hand. There were at least some twenty or thirty other tables all set in the exact same manner. Some of the tables even had plates with leftover food, the chairs drawn back as if there had been a few early-bird diners who were forced to leave unexpectedly.

"We should have brought a weapon," muttered Duff.

"Shut up," said Stepanek.

The mood was silent and spooky. A few roasted piglets on trays smiled sardonically, as if they were keeping a secret from these three newcomers. A block of ice was slowly melting in a champagne bucket that held three bottles of Riesling.

O'Leary grabbed a bottle and held it up. "This bottle couldn't have been sitting here more than two hours. I don't understand any of this."

"Where is everyone, sir?" asked Duff aloud.

The same question had gone through all three of their minds since the moment they walked in.

"I have no idea," murmured O'Leary. "Obviously, they aren't here anymore."

"The ship is quite large. Maybe they're in their cabins," guessed Duff.

"Or maybe they've taken refuge in the storage compartments," added Stepanek as he ran his fingers over a roll of bread with an indescribable look on his face.

"Why the hell would they take refuge in storage?" O'Leary passed his light across the room. The band's instruments sat waiting for musicians to belt out some ragtime. "It doesn't make any sense."

The senior officer's mind was racing. Twenty minutes had already passed since they departed the *Pass of Ballaster*, and it occurred to him that the rest of the crew had no idea where they were and what they were seeing. It had been a mistake for the captain to send them here. The *Valkyrie* was too vast to be explored by only three exhausted men. He looked at the two sailors. They seemed to be no more than one screech away from shitting their shorts.

"We need to split up. I know that doesn't appeal to you, and it might seem like a bad idea, but it's all we can do." O'Leary turned to the younger sailor and tried to sound more persuasive. "Duff, go back down the hallway and head toward the bow of the ship. Signal our ship to throw us a guide cable, so we can tow the *Valkyrie*. Now move! Go!"

The boy ran out of the room with a relieved expression. Anything was better than being stuck in this room. At least by the bow he would be in sight of the *Ballaster*, even if that meant breaking his arms trying to tug the heavy tow cable.

"Stepanek, find the engine room. After we secure the ship, we'll need power and electricity."

"True. Without an engine it would be like towing a fucking iceberg," grunted the Croat.

"Find the engine room and memorize the route. I don't want our engine specialist aboard this ship any longer than necessary. I promise when we get to port, I'll buy you a pint of the finest beer you've ever had in your life."

Stepanek blinked a few times and exhaled. With the cold resignation that comes from years at sea, the weathered sailor tried to wrap his head around venturing into the dark bowels of an abandoned ship.

"Where will you go, sir?"

"To the bridge. I'd like to make sure the helm isn't stuck, or everything else will be useless. Let's go. Time's short."

O'Leary parted company from Stepanek by patting him on the back. Compelled by a sudden impulse, he turned around and muttered, "Be careful."

But O'Leary never found out if the sailor heard his words.

Taking a deep breath, he returned to the lounge that was decorated with eagles. Before becoming first officer of the *Pass of Ballaster*, O'Leary had served as a petty officer on many ships, including a yearlong stint in 1925 aboard the *Highland Chieftain*, a transatlantic vessel of the Nelson Line with service to South America. If the *Valkyrie* had the same layout as those luxury cruisers, then there had to be a staircase on that floor leading directly up to the bridge.

After five minutes of searching he found it. It was a metal door concealed by an oak laminate coating that covered the walls in back of the dance floor. He would have completely missed it had it not been for the visible wear on the carpet caused by the door being opened and closed. The door led to a service stairwell without any of the adornments that had decorated the spaces intended for passenger use. It was a quick route for communication between the bridge and the dance and dining halls. When the *Valkyrie*'s captain got bored of wining and dining the sweaty women who sat with him during gala dinners, he could duck out by fabricating a story that he was needed on the bridge. In the case of an actual emergency, this would also be the quickest way of getting to the bridge.

O'Leary's footsteps echoed metallically as he climbed several flights of stairs. Finally, he came to a landing with a set of doors. A placard reading *"Funkraum"* hung from one. O'Leary's basic German was enough for him to guess that this was the radio room.

Some gracious officer had tacked to the door an illustration of a technician fixing a radio with his hand inside the apparatus and all of his hair standing on end.

Without hesitating, he turned the doorknob and found himself on the bridge. Unlike the stairwell, the bridge was tenuously lit. O'Leary first thought Stepanek had somehow found a way of restoring power before he realized the light was being provided by two reflectors mounted on the *Pass of Ballaster*'s bridge.

He approached the window to the side of the helm and looked toward the bow where he could see the diminutive form of Duff. The sailor stood next to the mouth of the anchor and was sweating profusely as he tugged at the esparto rope, which was tied to the much thicker towing cable. Usually this was a job for three or four men, and the poor devil was stuck doing it all himself. But he didn't seem too unhappy. From the *Pass of Ballaster*, which had moved within half a cable's distance, Captain McBride continued to signal orders.

Suddenly, O'Leary felt very alone on the *Valkyrie*'s bridge. Nobody could see him, and an irrational fear struck him that his ship would take off and leave him in the middle of the ocean on this illogical floating castle. His heart skipped a beat.

The officer closed his eyes and tried to calm down. He was letting panic get the better of him. He looked around and saw that the bridge was impeccable. There was no sign of human life. He walked toward the navigation table, where the nautical map showed the ship's course. Evidently, the *Valkyrie* had left the Port of Hamburg only five days prior. Sitting atop the map was a grease pencil used to mark the ship's course. O'Leary held it between his fingers and scrutinized it. It was recently sharpened. Someone had sharpened it *after* making the last mark.

Out of the silence, a scream resonated with such force that O'Leary momentarily felt like his blood had stopped pumping. It was a violent shriek that rose up and down in intensity as if coming from a tortured animal. Then, a moment of silence, long enough for O'Leary to doubt whether or not he had simply imagined it. But as quickly as it stopped, the noise started up again, clear as before. It was an inhuman screech, one that reverberated exquisitely with a million distinct degrees of pain, like shards of glass being pressed into the palm. The voice was familiar.

Stepanek.

As O'Leary ran off the bridge, the light from his lantern created mad shadows in the room's corners. Just before crossing the doorway, he saw the ship's logbook to the side of the command post. He grabbed it on the fly, and although one part of his brain told him the log should have been in the captain's quarters, he clutched it tight and went down the metal steps two at a time, sending pounding echoes throughout the stairwell.

Stepanek's screams rose and fell as if he were a badly tuned radio losing its reception. Each time O'Leary stopped to catch his breath he listened closely, trying to detect where the cries were coming from. He crossed the banquet room in the dark and shouted Stepanek's name. The shrieking continued as if he couldn't hear O'Leary. Or wasn't capable of responding.

O'Leary found the opening of the stairwell leading down to the engine room and wavered. The darkness flooding that section of the ship seemed to possess its own density, like some sort of thick gel choking the air. He considered turning around and going back to the *Pass of Ballaster* for backup. But when Stepanek's cry scaled two octaves, O'Leary ran on with renewed vigor. Still holding the ship's log in one hand as if it were an improvised shield and his lantern in the other, he descended several flights, catching his breath at each landing.

Having lost count of the number of stairs, he arrived at an area that split off in three directions. Trembling, he thought he could see a bit of yellow lantern light at the end of one corridor. O'Leary made his way toward the light and felt as if the air around him were growing hotter, thicker. The space crackled with electricity. He spotted Stepanek collapsed on the ground, curled into a ball, with his back to him. As he moved closer, the unmistakable scent of urine stung his nostrils.

O'Leary placed his hand on the sailor's shoulder to turn him over and let out a scream of pure terror. Stepanek was shaking uncontrollably. His eyes rolled madly about in their sockets and blood streamed from his mouth and nostrils. Horrified, O'Leary realized the sailor might have bitten his tongue.

"Stepanek! Stepanek, wake up!"

He shook him by the collar, but Stepanek's mind seemed to be off in another especially cruel and horrific land. O'Leary decided he couldn't take anymore and wouldn't stay a moment longer on this cursed ship.

He shoved the ship's log down the front of his pants and lugged the sailor up on his shoulders like a cargo sack. He held the lantern in his free hand and retraced his steps up the staircase. As he walked he had the distinct impression that someone, or *something*, was behind him, but he did not dare look back to see.

Don't look, he thought. *Keep walking. Get the hell out of here. Don't look.*

The atmosphere was so electric that the hair on his arms stood on end as he climbed the stairs; his heart leaped into his throat. A monotonous buzzing echoed throughout the entire ship like the ringing of a dead tuning fork. The vibrations traveled up through the soles of his feet and hummed in his head. He wiped sweat from his forehead.

He found himself in the banquet hall again. The back door led to the dance parlor and its ornate staircase. He was almost out.

Then, O'Leary heard it. At first, between Stepanek's moans and his own heavy breathing, he had not detected a soft yelping that came from his right. He moved his lantern in that direction, scared of what the light would reveal.

But there was nothing except a pile of sheets haphazardly strewn across the dance floor. O'Leary swallowed, and a small spot of wetness spread in his underwear. The pile of sheets had not been there when he had passed by not ten minutes ago. He was sure of it.

The yelping sounded again and the pile moved. In an almost hypnotic state, O'Leary watched the sheets come toward him, and the noises around him multiplied. A chair fell and plates crashed to the floor. The buzzing grew louder and louder.

He reluctantly moved to meet the pile and directed his light toward it.

It was a baby, no more than a few months old, tossing about restlessly. He let out a muffled moan as if too weak or too tired to cry any louder.

O'Leary did not think twice. Despite the voice of terror in his head that insisted he leave that baby on the ground and get the hell out of there, the officer crouched down and placed him in the crook of his arm like a package. Staggering under the weight of Stepanek and the child, he crossed the room as quickly as he could until he reached the giant staircase. With all of his attention focused on getting off the ship, he walked toward the door and felt the sharp corners of the logbook as they poked him in the groin.

He finally reached the last hallway. Suddenly, a dark shape materialized before his eyes. O'Leary felt a stifled groan stick in his throat. He was so close. The figure raised a lantern to his face; it was Duff.

"Sir! What's going on? The whole ship is rattling! What happened to Stepanek?"

O'Leary felt so relieved he thought he might faint. "Help me with this," he said, passing Stepanek's limp body to Duff. "We have to get out of here right now."

"You don't have to tell me twice, sir," answered Duff with a panicked expression as he held his shipmate.

O'Leary took the logbook out of his pants, placed it under his arm, and cradled the baby in his arms. Following Duff's light, they made it outside, and yet again on this night that refused to end, they were forced to keep from gasping.

The fog that enveloped the *Valkyrie* funneled into the mouth of an enormous vacuum. Wisps of steam twisted and turned around the ship as if a tornado were forming. The *Pass of Ballaster* had turned around, dragging behind it the tow cable Duff had secured. From the front rail, O'Leary could see the worried captain, who was signaling to them.

Without hesitation the two men climbed down to their raft and rowed toward the *Ballaster* as if trying to break a world record. Water splashed up into their faces as the oars hit the surface, but they never took their eyes off their goal. The *Pass of Ballaster* loomed before them.

As they secured the raft to the ship and climbed aboard, O'Leary couldn't stop wondering about the little boy he held so close to his chest.

And more to the point: *What the hell had happened aboard the* Valkyrie?

PART TWO

—

KATE

V

Present-day London
6:30 a.m.

The incessant ringing of the alarm clock sliced through Catalina Soto's head. The young woman tossed in bed and tried to break the bonds of a dream that still held its grip. She turned off her alarm with a dull thud and rolled over again without opening her eyes. Her left arm slid to the other side of the bed, which had been empty and cold for weeks.

Catalina made a heroic effort to not go back to sleep again. Sleeping let her get away from it all and not have to think. Not have to remember him. Sleeping hurt less.

She had spent the first week in a state of constant but fitful slumber, conscious yet dazed, first from the shock and then from a fistful of colorful pills someone had placed in her hand. Perhaps that person feared her collapse would be imminent without the pills. She figured things would get better with time, but the second and third weeks were hardly any better.

Robert was no longer there. She had to admit it outright. But it was very difficult to accept. Since she had left her parents' house ten years ago, slamming shut the door to her past, Robert had always been by her side. Sometimes close, other times distant, but never too far. Robert had first been a summer fling, then the man she was in love with, and then, quite simply, the core of her existence, the axis on which everything turned: the sun, the moon, the planets, and her world. Then, one day, he disappeared. Poof. Bye-bye, Kate.

She vividly recalled the day she stopped being Catalina Soto and became Catalina Kilroy. Kate Kilroy. They had married just outside Barcelona. It was almost as if they had feared that if they didn't do so, the spell would be broken. Perhaps it had been a good idea, because the magic lasted for five more years.

Kate—nobody called her Catalina anymore except her mother—got out of bed feeling stiff. She tripped over the kitchen chairs on her way to turn on the coffeemaker. As the coffee brewed, she took a long cold shower that managed to drive away the final remnants of sleep. Twenty minutes later when she stepped out of her apartment and onto Cheyne Walk, located in the heart of Chelsea, nobody would have suspected that the impeccable woman who was getting into a taxi dressed like an executive was the same disheveled, puffy-eyed young woman from thirty minutes before.

The offices of the *London New Herald* were only fifteen minutes from her house in light traffic. When she arrived, she passed her ID card over the electronic turnstile and rode the elevator to the twenty-fifth floor. As they went up she noticed how some of the men gave her sidelong glances. This was normal. Barely twenty-seven years old, tall, thin, and with thick red hair that fell in curly locks down her back, Kate was the type of woman who could cause a traffic accident if she really wanted to. Only the empty, drained expression in her grayish eyes betrayed her sadness.

When the elevator finally arrived at her floor, the din of the newspaper staffroom enveloped her like a gentle, comforting lullaby. The clicking of keys, the ringing of phones, and the murmur of conversations: all of it was painfully familiar yet alien at the same time. Kate wondered for the umpteenth time that morning if it had been a good idea to come to work.

She stood next to the front desk, nervous. One of the secretaries looked up at her and opened her eyes wide. When Kate looked over, the secretary looked away and leaned over to her coworker and whispered something in her ear. Another furtive glance. More whispering.

Some people had stopped working and were staring at her. By their expressions and movements, Kate realized many of the women were gossiping, about her and Robert, of course.

She couldn't take it. She thought she could be strong, but she couldn't. It had been a mistake to come to work. She turned around to leave and stumbled into a dark woman around fifty, dressed in a beautiful pearl-colored suit and carrying a briefcase.

"Kate! What are you doing here?" asked Rhonda Grimes, the newspaper's editor in chief. Her voice, legendary for making hundreds of reporters and interns tremble over the years, was now imbued with concern. "Did something happen, sugar?"

"Hi, Rhonda," answered Kate, trying to control the volume of her voice. "No, nothing's happened. It's just that . . . I thought I'd be able to, but . . ." Tears began to well up in her eyes.

"Oh, honey." Rhonda rested her hand on Kate's arm and leaned in to whisper, "Don't let them see you cry. Come to my office."

Kate nodded as she dabbed a tear that was threatening to escape. A secretary and a pair of assistants hastened to converge on Rhonda at that very moment, each one convinced that the messages and calls they had to relay were of the utmost importance. Rhonda, who had not become the newspaper's chief editor by coincidence or from lack of character, sent them away with a motion of her hand. They scattered like frightened doves.

The two women passed through the bullpen and entered Rhonda's office. Rhonda closed the door behind them and turned toward Kate, who had dropped to the sofa. Kate looked dejectedly out the window at the fantastic view sprawled before her.

She is so young, thought Rhonda. *Yet she's seen so much tragedy in so few years. She doesn't deserve it.*

"I thought you were going to take a couple more weeks off before coming back," she said as she offered Kate a box of tissues. Kate waved it away. If she had had a moment of weakness, it had passed. She again projected the image of a ruthless executive.

"I can't take being at home anymore, Rhonda."

"I understand," she replied. "A lot of thinking."

"Too much," Kate countered. "I can't stand doing nothing. It makes me feel useless. And every time I turn my head, I see something that reminds me of him. It's too much. Even for me."

"Have you thought about getting help?" asked Rhonda cautiously.

"Help isn't what I need. What I need is time to put my affairs in order," answered Kate in painful consideration. "I don't want to be popping Valiums and whatever else, like I'm eating popcorn. You know what happens to people who abuse that crap. You end up a zombie, totally unmotivated. That's not me, Rhonda."

"I know, dear."

Both women kept their silence for a beat.

"We all regret what happened to Robert," murmured Rhonda. "We all miss him."

Kate gulped and didn't answer. Anything she had to say at that moment would sound empty.

"Do you know what you want to do yet?"

"I need to go to the United States. His parents will want to have his ashes."

When she uttered the word *ashes*, a shadow fell over her face.

"Why?" asked Rhonda.

"Because it's the right thing to do. Because it's what he would have wanted. Because I don't know what else to do." A devilish glow, fleeting as a spark, crossed Kate's eyes. "Plus, I don't think being in a tin on top of the mantel, between his two Pulitzers like a fucking cocky cat wagging its tail, is exactly how Robert envisioned eternity. You know how proud he was."

The two women laughed quietly, at ease for a while.

The old Kate was back, joyfully irreverent, if only for a brief time. *Easy now, world. I'm still just as screwed up.* The thought popped up with such force that Kate almost jumped.

Rhonda looked at her thoughtfully as if she had just had an idea.

"Kate, I may have something of interest to you. Something to keep your mind off things and help you move on. Not to mention you'd be doing me a huge favor."

Rhonda began rifling through the folders on her desk, pushing through piles of papers awaiting review.

"Rhonda, thank you, but I'm not in the mood to cover a fashion show. If I have to interview some stupid celebrity who is full of herself, I just might kill her."

"It's nothing like that," murmured Rhonda, pushing a huge dossier to one side. "Where the hell did I put it? I swear I had a copy around. Ah, here it is!"

Rhonda's coral necklaces rattled as she held up a purple folder with a look of triumph. Kate's face lit up with a flicker of interest. Purple was the color that was used for feature stories, the pieces that had made the *London New Herald* famous and were assigned to only the most reputable reporters. The biggest names in journalism had fought in these hallways to take home one of these folders. Now Rhonda was holding one in front of her and flashing an intriguing smile, like a drug dealer loitering at the entrance to a school.

"Are you serious?" asked Kate without taking her eyes off the folder. For the first time in weeks, she was thinking about something besides Robert. "Until now I've only covered the society and culture beat."

"*Until now* is the correct expression, sugar," replied Rhonda, opening the folder. Kate stood up from the sofa, but all she could see was a photo of something that looked like enormous scaffolding. "I believe you're ready for something like this. I'm not the only one. Robert believes—believed—you could do more than just interview Justin Bieber or Madonna. Truthfully, this story should have been his, but he was planning on working on it with you."

Kate's eyes clouded over. Robert had held that same folder. His eyes had passed over its same contents. The final hours of his life could have been consumed with thoughts on how best to tackle this story. Suddenly, reading everything in the folder seemed more important to her than anything else in the world.

"I need details."

"Does the name Isaac Feldman ring a bell?"

"I don't know. I don't think so." The reporter inside her suddenly felt mortified for not recognizing his name. "Should it?"

"Unless you spend a lot of time betting in online casinos, it shouldn't."

Rhonda took an image from the folder and handed it over to Kate. It was a photograph of an elderly man around seventy. He had great shocks of white hair and looked surprisingly hefty for a man his age. His unshaven face along with his look of surprise made him appear quite unhappy to be having his picture taken.

"So you want me to investigate online casinos?" Kate suddenly felt disheartened.

"Nothing like that, dear. You're too late. Feldman is an Israeli with a British passport, or English with an Israeli passport, depending on the person you ask, and the owner of at least five of the largest online betting houses. Obviously, he's made tons of money. But it would seem he hasn't paid his taxes for the past three years, and now he's under investigation by the Treasury Department." Rhonda smiled. "You see, it's not exactly an investigation you can take part in."

"So what's the angle?"

"Feldman is clearing out his accounts in the United Kingdom, or at least that's the word on the street. But he's invested huge amounts of cash in the last five months in a bizarre project that's about to become public. They say he's obsessed with it and he doesn't care if he loses everything as long as it goes ahead."

"What is it? Funding a church? Building another Vegas in Dover? Hunting UFOs?"

"It's much more mysterious than any of that. Robert thought it would be the story of the year. Have a look for yourself."

Rhonda turned the file over in her hands and passed it to Kate. It was open to a page showing a color photo of a ship in terrible condition, surrounded by scaffolding in the middle of a shipyard. Like ants, dozens of workers were polishing the ship's hull. A piece of the bow was in the air, and looking closely, she could make out the ship's name in spite of the fact that its lettering was faded and covered in moss.

Valkyrie.

V I

An hour later, Kate got into a taxi and headed to London Victoria station with the purple folder clutched in her hands. She'd been surprised by how light the documents felt, but the sparse amount of information presented a challenge for her avid mind.

She had accepted the assignment without much hesitation. It would give her more than enough to keep her mind occupied for at least a couple of weeks, and that time would be good for figuring out what to do with the shattered remains of her life. In the meantime, she would flesh out the story from scratch with nothing more than a loose end to work from.

She took out Isaac Feldman's picture and carefully looked it over for the third time since leaving Rhonda's office. He had rugged features and an expression of determination. There was something magnetic about this man, but she couldn't unravel the riddle he had tucked away. She went over the notes that had come with the photo.

Isaac Feldman, son of Abraham and Lisa Feldman, born and raised in Merseyside, close to Liverpool. His father was a Jewish tanner from Kraków, and his mother was a housewife. The junior Feldman grew up in a tough neighborhood and was arrested twice before the age of sixteen. After a short, two-week stint in jail, he and a partner began a small battery-recycling company and, two years later, opened their first betting house. After some time, it grew into a network of online casinos that extended throughout the world. He was a millionaire by the time he turned fifty. He became a dual citizen of Israel and the UK, suspiciously. He was also suspected of having transferred vast amounts of money from Eastern Europe to the more secure fiscal havens of the Caribbean. That was all the information she had to go on.

Why would a mobster bookie—with an economic empire—dedicate nearly all of his efforts to launching a ship nearly seventy years old? It simply didn't make sense. The more she thought about it, the more confused Kate got about the matter. The pieces didn't fit together.

The young woman sighed, disheartened. Getting an interview with Feldman was completely out of the question. By all appearances, he hated anything that was remotely related to journalism. The only lead she had was the photo of the ship.

Before he'd died, Robert had traced the *Valkyrie*'s location to the naval harbor of Denborough, close to Liverpool. Kate had to hold back tears as she looked over her late husband's spidery, tight scrawl. His notes, always hurried and marked with a small asterisk in the bottom left corner—*my lucky star,* he'd say—were all over the dossier. Kate could almost imagine his hand dragging across the paper while he listened to some obscure jazz group in the background. Just Robert being Robert.

Kate was en route to Denborough. From the editorial office she had confirmed an interview with the commander in charge of public relations at the military base where the *Valkyrie* was in dry dock. She was in dire need of information about that ship.

Kate glanced at her watch. If all went well, she would be in Liverpool in a few hours.

She took advantage of the train ride to sleep. In fact, she fell into such a deep sleep that she did not awake until she arrived. The sky was coated dark gray as she left the station. Curtains of rain were falling, propelled by powerful winds.

Another taxi drove her to the base's front gate. As the guard checked her credentials, Kate looked out the window. Illuminated by two magnesium lanterns that stained everything yellow, an enormous sign announced that she'd reached "Military Depot No. 19" of the Royal Navy.

Kate was surprised to note that this was more of a repository than an active military base. The guard at the gate possessed an air of boredom, and the fence surrounding the compound didn't look capable of stopping anyone truly determined to break in. When the taxi finally rolled onto the base, she understood why security seemed so lax.

The place was practically a junkyard.

Parked side by side, huge rows of trucks from the 1960s were slowly rusting in the rain, their tires deflated. Rectangular shipping containers were piled up in uneven pyramids as if some giant kid had decided to leave his Erector set scattered around the base. God only knew what they held. Crates could be seen everywhere. There were vehicles that had been out of service for years and huge spools of cable all covered in ivy. An air of neglect permeated everything.

As the taxi rolled slowly forward along the macadam surface and headed toward the buildings located by the dock on the bay, Kate could make out the twilight silhouettes of more than a dozen docked military vessels. Getting closer, she could see streaks of rust splintering away from the portholes. It didn't look like any of the ships had much of a chance of setting sail in the near future.

The taxi stopped in front of the main building's entrance. A uniformed serviceman was waiting, holding a wide umbrella.

"Welcome to Denborough Naval Depot!" The man's voice sounded loud enough to project over a hurricane. "I'm Commander Collins. I believe we spoke by phone this morning."

"I'm Kate Kilroy." Kate extended her hand to the officer, who grasped it with surprising gentleness for a man of his size.

"I don't detect any Irish accent," he remarked.

"Kilroy is . . . was my husband's surname. My maiden name is Soto. I'm Spanish. From Barcelona."

"Ah," murmured Collins. He didn't require any further explanation for the time being. "Please, come inside. It's a terrible evening out."

The interior of the office was an unexpected change from the outdoor chaos. Everything was pristine and in order, as if at any moment the Queen herself might stop in for an inspection. A coffeemaker gurgled in the corner, a delicious aroma wafting through the air. The room was equipped with a few tables and filing cabinets but little more. The bluish glow of computer screens melted into the white light cast from the ceiling fixtures.

"Please, have a seat." Collins graciously drew out a chair for Kate to sit down. "We don't get many visitors here in the Junkyard, so please forgive our lack of comforts."

"The Junkyard?" Kate raised an eyebrow.

"Just a nickname we've given the base," replied Collins. "I suppose you've already guessed why."

"The truth is it's very . . . quaint." Kate chose her words carefully and took off her coat.

"It's disgusting is what it is," confessed Collins with a wide grin. "This is the Royal Navy's dumping ground. This is where all the rubbish ends up that nobody wants. That includes me. I always liken it to that drawer we all put our useless junk in. But we dare not throw any of it away lest we have a need for it in the future."

Kate smiled, captivated by the officer's sincerity and merriment. "I'm getting the picture. I also have a junk drawer like that in my house."

"Ah, but this is the largest junk drawer in all of England!" He raised his hand and signaled out the window. "At this very moment I must have eight destroyers docked here that saw action in the Falklands, nearly a dozen patrollers from the 1960s, three minesweepers, and if I'm not mistaken, about twenty other kinds of ships. That's not even counting the tons of obsolete equipment strewn about."

"You're the head of a small army, Commander," Kate laughed.

"I have enough materials to declare war on a small country." Collins shrugged, then smiled. "That, of course, is if any of it works. Would you care for some coffee?"

Kate realized she had not eaten anything since lunch. Next to the coffee machine was a box of doughnuts. Her stomach rumbled. Embarrassed, she felt the blood flow to her cheeks.

"I like it when a person can get to the point," joked Collins with a hearty laugh. He passed Kate the doughnuts and coffee. "Now let's dispense with the pleasantries. You're here because you want to know about the *Sinful Siren*, right?"

"The *Sinful Siren*?" replied Kate with half a doughnut in her mouth.

"The *Big S*, the *Crusher*, *Hitler's Vixen*. It's had many names over the years."

He removed a manila file from his desk drawer and opened it to the first page. It was an old black-and-white photo of the *Valkyrie*. The foreground showed two men in uniform posing in very different ways. The older of the two, wearing the captain's stripes, seemed quite comfortable, whereas the younger man standing at his side wore an expression of worry and fatigue.

"The ship's official name is the *Valkyrie*. It was built in 1938 by the Blohm und Voss shipyard in Hamburg for an organization called KDF." He looked up at Kate. "Do you have any idea what that might be?"

Kate shook her head and took a sip of her coffee.

"As stated in the report, it made its inaugural voyage on the twenty-third of August in 1939, with two hundred and seventeen passengers and fifty-five crew members aboard. Five days later, a coal liner called the *Pass of Ballaster* came across the luxury cruiser adrift at sea. Neither the ship nor its engines had power when it was found eight hundred miles off the coast of Newfoundland."

"Adrift? Was there an accident?"

"That's the peculiar thing," answered Collins. "No one knows. They found nobody on board."

"Nobody? But that's impossible. What about all the passengers and the crew? All those people don't just vanish without a trace!"

"I agree," Collins said, furrowing his brow. "But we do know that before the *Pass of Ballaster* towed the ship back to Bristol, they spent twelve hours searching the area in which they found the *Valkyrie* without finding a clue. There wasn't a single lifeboat missing. It's quite the mystery."

"OK, let me see if I've got this straight." Kate set her coffee on the table and laced her fingers together. "A coal liner finds an empty cruise ship floating in the middle of the ocean. There's no trace of anyone. The ship gets towed to port, and nobody opens an investigation? How did this not make headlines in every major newspaper? Shouldn't this story be better known?"

"The fact is a few days later Germany invaded Poland, sparking the beginning of the Second World War. England and France declared war on Germany, and before anyone knew about it, the newspapers had much more interesting headlines. There was no room for a strange story about a ship found abandoned at sea. A German ship, mind you."

"I see." Kate was taking notes as the colonel spoke. "So I take it there was never any kind of official investigation."

"Are you kidding?" Collins smiled sadly. "During the next twelve months, Hitler's submarines nearly finished off England's navy. In the span of fifteen weeks, hundreds of transport ships were sunk, ships that had supplied raw materials to the islands. Thousands of Allied sailors disappeared at sea. Nobody even considered mounting an investigation regarding the *Valkyrie*. The story lost all importance before it was even born."

"What happened to the ship during all this?"

"The *Valkyrie* was internalized. That's military jargon for civil ships that are captured from an enemy nation." Collins rifled through the pages of the report. "However, there was a bit of a legal snafu. Since the ship had been seized four days *before* the war started, it technically couldn't be considered an internalized ship. But it also couldn't be categorized as a rescued ship because it sailed under the enemy flag. A sort of bureaucratic tangle, you see."

"I suppose it was no favor to the owner of the towing ship, the"—Kate consulted her notes—"*Pass of Ballaster*. Did he get his finder's fee?"

"Oh, I don't think so." Collins raised up a packet that was taking up nearly half the dossier on the *Valkyrie*. "He spent nearly four years in litigation against the Royal Navy in pursuit of the reward money, but it was in vain. During the war there were bigger fish to fry. Facing a scarcity of ships, the Admiralty decided to commission the *Valkyrie* for the transportation of soldiers, and well, this is where things get strange."

Kate leaned forward. She was enthralled with the curious nature of the colonel's story. A flash of lightning lit up the room.

"What happened?"

"For starters, nobody could get the engines to work. The best mechanics from London were called in. They took the motors apart piece by piece and put them together again, but to no avail. The engines simply refused to work. They tried replacing them with British engines, but the setup of the cams the Germans had used was so specialized that it proved impossible. Eventually, they realized the ship would not be leaving Liverpool, so they turned it into a floating antiaircraft vessel."

"A floating antiaircraft vessel?"

"Yes, to defend the port against shelling from the German Luftwaffe. Eight antiaircraft cannons were installed on deck and assigned a crew to oversee them, and the navy anchored the *Valkyrie* near the port's refinery. That way it would be as close as possible to the resources it was meant to protect. But in case the German forces did manage to fly over unimpeded, the ship could be cut loose and allowed to drift away with the tide."

"So what happened?"

"The dark legend of the *Valkyrie* began taking shape." Collins was holding an old draft of a report that looked fragile enough to disintegrate in his hands. "In August 1940 a German bomb fell on one of the cannons, killing all servicemen in the act. Unbelievably, the *Valkyrie* sustained little damage. The following month a powder keg exploded in cannon number four. Sixteen sailors that had been loading missiles were killed in the blast. Again the *Valkyrie* escaped nearly unscathed, only losing a couple of bulkheads. The cause of the explosion was never discovered."

"Sounds like a ship with a curse on it," Kate said, scrawling down every word. "I suppose nobody wanted to be stationed there."

"Just wait. It gets better." Collins looked at her seriously. "The twenty-first of November in 1940 was the worst night of the German Blitz on Liverpool. Hundreds of people died that night alone. However, according to reports, at two forty in the morning, at the height of the bombing, the cannon on the *Valkyrie* ceased firing. At first it was believed that the ship had received a direct hit and had been sunk. But from the refinery it was confirmed that it was still there, floating in the dark, and that the artillery had simply quit working. Now take a guess."

Kate suddenly noticed how dry her mouth was. This was all too bizarre to be true. "That would mean—" she stopped short.

"Exactly. When they went aboard the *Valkyrie*, they found that the crew assigned to oversee the cannons had completely vanished. As if they had never existed."

V I I

"People don't just disappear like that," murmured Kate. "I suppose they were found later, right?"

"They most certainly were not. At least that's not what the report says," answered Collins.

"Are you saying the ship swallowed them up like it did the passengers?" Kate's voice was skeptical.

"Not at all. Are you familiar with Occam's razor?"

"I believe it states that when there are two or more competing hypotheses regarding a single event—"

"The simplest one has the highest probability of being correct," Collins finished the phrase.

"So what is your theory?"

"First, the artillerymen were a part of Home Guard. That means they weren't even trained military." Collins set the file on the table and began listing on his fingers. "Shop owners, attorneys, and milkmen dressed in uniform and put in charge of a few little cannons to defend against the Luftwaffe? Put yourself in their shoes. They were last seen at night aboard a dark ship with a reputation for being cursed. A vicious bombing campaign was unfolding, and they were stationed next to millions of gallons of combustible fuel. I propose that, very simply, facing the risk of being scorched to death, the sailors on duty that night shit their pants and got the hell out of there as fast as they could."

"You think they deserted?"

"In those days everything was in chaos, and there was little oversight, especially with the men from Home Guard. They probably hurried home and reenlisted the next day. Or maybe they ended up in the army. It's hard to say. In any case, would you agree my theory makes more sense than thinking they were swallowed by a ship?"

Kate nodded, reflective. The story made sense. "What happened afterward?"

"Very little." Collins shuffled his papers as if he were looking for some hidden order in the dossier. "By the end of the war, the company that owned the *Pass of Ballaster* no longer existed. The same can be said of the Nazi government, the original owner of the *Valkyrie*. No one laid claim to the ship. While things were being resolved, the ship was towed temporarily to the naval depot at Denborough. It was placed in dry dock until they figured out what to do with it. But given its nature and origin, the navy decided not to make its location or existence public, in case Communist Germany wanted to reclaim it. It was the Cold War, you understand? So here it has stayed for the past sixty-eight years."

"No one's discovered the *Valkyrie* for nearly seventy years?" Kate lifted her head up from her notepad, stunned. "How is that possible?"

"It was a civil ship docked at a military base in the middle of a nation fresh from war. Plus, in the fifties, commercial flights started between America and Europe. That left passenger liners like the *Valkyrie* with little relevance. After so much time exposed to the elements, the *Valkyrie*'s hull has deteriorated substantially, making it too expensive to repair. In the sixties, some thought about using it as a floating target, but they abandoned that idea for some reason. It was easier just to leave it where it was and take care of other business."

"So it's just been sitting there all of these years? Hasn't anyone gone aboard?"

"All the hatchways except a few were sealed to keep thieves from breaking in and stealing the wiring or other valuable materials. Plus, that helped keep the moisture from filtering in and ruining the remaining furnishings. Early on, they made monthly rounds through the ship. But after a while, even those stopped."

"Why's that? More disappearances?"

"Nothing that creepy." Collins laughed out loud. "The guards began suffering dizziness and vomiting from nothing more than going aboard. Some even became seriously ill. A committee ruled that the condensation from the toxic gases emanating from the bilge was to blame. They decided to seal up the ship entirely."

Just then the door opened, and a heavyset man walked in wearing a military raincoat. Grumbling, he shook off the water that was sliding down his jacket and pulled it over his head.

"Blasted weather! Stupid, shitty rain," he sputtered from beneath a thick gray mustache, without noting Kate's presence. "I've got two years till retirement, and that next day, I swear, I'm going anywhere you can't see a single fucking cloud anywhere. I've had it up to . . . Oh, dear!"

"Miss Kilroy, I'd like to introduce you to Sergeant Major Lambert." Collins stood up as the portly sergeant blushed clear up to the edge of his receding hairline. "He's usually a little more polite in front of a lady, but it seems today is not his day."

"Please, forgive me. I had no idea we had a visitor," he said in embarrassment. "Here at the Junkya—I mean the depot—we don't get many visitors. At least we didn't use to."

"Don't worry about me," said Kate, smiling. The sergeant relaxed a bit. "I suppose that's normal when you spend too much time in a place like this. Are there many stationed here?"

"Five guards on the perimeter, two assistants to Sergeant Major Lambert, and the two of us," answered Collins. "More than enough to keep this place out of God's hands."

"Miss Kilroy is a reporter from London," Collins explained while the sergeant major poured himself a cup of coffee. "I was just telling her the story of the *Big S*."

Lambert nodded before saying, "I was glad to see them get that thing out of dry dock and take it away. I waited fifteen years to see it go."

"Who took it?" asked Kate, feeling she had begun to approach the crux of the matter. "Why? How?"

"Its new owners took it. You see, next year the Royal Navy will be terminating half of the Trafalgar-class submarine fleet," answered Collins. "They're monsters built in the eighties, filled with asbestos and so many other pollutants that it's going to be a major headache to scrap them. Someone in the Admiralty realized they would need a quiet, remote place to do the dirty work. Naturally, they chose here."

"For the first time in sixty years, we've been ordered to make space," added Lambert. "It came down from London that the dry dock holding the *Valkyrie* along with three other old ships had to be cleared out, and those ships were put up for auction to the highest bidder."

"In other words, after sixty years outside the public eye, the *Valkyrie* suddenly resurfaced from oblivion." Kate began to grasp why Robert had thought there was something bigger to this story.

"Essentially, yes." Collins took out the topmost file from the folder and handed it to Kate. Its brilliant white contrasted starkly with the yellowed pages contained within the rest of the folder. Apparently, it had not been there too long. "A public statement announcing the auction was released six months ago. It ran in print ads and on the ministry's website. Not to mention the other usual media. I think it even appeared in your newspaper."

"I see from this that there were three bidders." Kate's eyes fell on one of the names. "Garrison and Sons . . ."

"That's a scrapping firm that has over thirty years' experience," explained Collins. "Normally, they're the only ones who bid when one of these old ships comes up for auction. They're close by, which makes transport cheaper for them. But in this case, they didn't win. The other two bidders made exorbitant offers for the *Valkyrie*."

"I see." Kate scanned the other two names. "Feldman Inc. is obviously Isaac Feldman's company, but who is this other one? Who is Wolf und Klee?"

"I believe that would be a German company, and it would appear they had been determined to make off with the *Valkyrie* at all costs. Before the auction they sent a group of technicians to inspect the ship and take tons of photos. They were all German and all quite keen on the *Valkyrie*."

"It's true," added Lambert. "They ran around her like headless chickens. They acted like it was some marvel instead of a cursed heap of junk from the thirties."

"But in the end Feldman won," countered Kate. "How did he pull it off?"

"He had the highest bid." Collins's eyes sparkled playfully. "He must have wanted that old ship more than anything because he paid dearly for it. He only managed to make the Germans acquiesce once he entered a bid of one hundred and fifty million pounds."

Kate's eyes grew big. "That's an incredible sum for a broken-down ship."

"It's an incredible sum even for a new ship," remarked Collins. "Yet our pal Feldman paid the tab without a peep. His pockets must run deep."

"I can see that." *No wonder Feldman is bankrupt if this is how he spends his money,* she thought.

"They came to inspect the ship five months ago." Collins closed the file and pushed away his empty coffee cup. "Feldman arrived in person along with a group of around fifty employees and a few extremely expensive Dutch floating cranes. I'd risk my neck to wager that all of them were either ex-military or naval experts. They looked like hardened and resourceful men."

"They managed to remove the *Valkyrie* from dry dock in only thirty-six hours," added Lambert. "Considering the ship hadn't budged for seventy years, I think that's quite a feat."

"Do you know where they took it?" asked Kate, hopeful.

"I haven't the foggiest idea," answered Collins. "It stopped being my problem the moment it left the dock. Believe me, I have no desire to see that ship ever again."

"Nor do I," agreed Lambert. "I must say, Feldman's men were quite gruff. They were in such a hurry to remove that ship they practically kicked out me and my boys. And on our own base."

"Why do you think they were in such a hurry?"

"They looked nervous, like they were scared someone might wrench the ship from their grasp at any moment, which is odd." Lambert brushed an imaginary speck from the lapel of his uniform. "Who would want to quarrel over an old ship with a bad reputation?"

"Perhaps the runners-up?" Kate suggested. "The people from Wolf und Klee?"

"Could be. But it doesn't matter anymore. No one here is going to miss the *Valkyrie*."

"Except old man Carroll," said Lambert thoughtfully.

"He's a raving old lunatic who used to sneak on base all the time," said Collins, exchanging a reproachful look with the sergeant major. "He's been the biggest security threat in the last twenty years, which isn't saying much for our surveillance system."

"He's an old crackpot!" Lambert burst out as he stood up. "He used to sneak about like a rat, and he always made his way onto the *Valkyrie*. He'd spend hours on the bridge, spinning around, muttering strange things."

"Do you know where I can find him?" asked Kate.

"Carroll? He lives maybe ten minutes from here," answered Collins with a glimmer of interest in his eyes. "How did you know I was going to suggest you talk to him?"

"I didn't." Kate shrugged and stood up. "It seems like he would be a good source for the article I'm writing. That's all."

The two men exchanged a look.

"It's OK," said Kate, smiling. "Why were you going to suggest him?"

"Because old man Carroll," Collins replied, "claims to be the same man who discovered the *Valkyrie* in the Atlantic."

VIII

Half an hour later a taxi dropped off Kate in a blue-collar neighborhood of Denborough. The quiet little houses were swallowed up by the pitch-black night and torrential rain. She wondered for the thousandth time if it had been a good idea to come. She was tired and wanted badly to find a hotel. Instead, she found herself standing in front of an old house that looked haunted.

She shivered as a particularly strong gust of wind blew past. Her return train was scheduled to leave early the next morning. If she didn't take advantage of this opportunity, she might not have another chance to talk with the old man. Most likely, he was just senile and had confused the *Valkyrie* with some obscure merchant ship from his time as a cabin boy fifty years earlier. But she had to try. Something in her stomach—the fluttering of fruit bats, Robert used to say—told her that this was a good lead.

"Wait for me here, please," she told the cabdriver. He was a sallow-skinned Pakistani with a bushy beard who was looking around nervously.

"This is very bad neighborhood, ma'am. Very bad. Drugs, whores, and bad people. You shouldn't be here. Me neither," he said with urgency.

"I'll just be ten minutes. Maybe less," she said, trying to appear confident as she handed the driver two fifty-pound notes.

The driver took the money and muttered something under his breath. Still, he appeared more at ease. Kate couldn't help but notice the man had a club within arm's reach underneath the dashboard.

Approaching Mr. Carroll's house, Kate noticed that it had seen better days. The paint was peeling and parts of the eaves were missing. Graffiti covered an entire side of the house, and plywood shuttered one of the first-floor windows. Empty beer cans and cigarette butts littered the front steps.

Kate hesitated before ringing the doorbell. Nothing happened. After a moment's wait, she tried again. Finally, she gingerly knocked on the door a few times with little hope. Disappointed, she turned back around to the taxi. But then, she heard several deadbolts unlock. A wrinkled, hunched man with suspicious eyes opened the door slightly and peered at her.

"You can't work here," he grumbled. "Go find another corner to show your tits, but don't come to my door! Go away or I'll call the police!"

"It's not what you think," she said, rifling through her bag for her press badge. She looked up to see the man closing the door.

"A gun," he howled. "She's got a gun."

"It's just my badge," Kate yelled, trying to show it to him through the gap in the door. "I'm a reporter. I just want to talk."

"Reporter? I don't want to talk to you. I've been blowing the whistle on all those junkies from Compton Road for years now. I've called the papers dozens of times and for what? They never listen to me. Never!"

"I'm not here to talk about Compton Road." Kate could tell the man excelled in holding a grudge. "I'm here to talk about the *Valkyrie*."

The change in the old man's expression was so unexpected that Kate realized she was holding her breath. The earlier confusion drained from his face, and he even straightened up a few inches. Kate caught a glimpse in him of the former sailor of yesteryear.

"Hold on." The man closed the door, and Kate heard him undo the chains. He opened the door again. "Please, come in. This area isn't safe at these hours."

Kate crossed the threshold and walked into the entrance hall of a modest but tidy home. Though the wood floors were worn and the wallpaper was faded, everything had been placed in careful order, and the house held a pleasant fragrance.

"Years ago, this was a good neighborhood to live in," said Mr. Carroll. "But about two decades ago, under Thatcher, the area began to turn into what you see today. Still, it's my home. At ninety-three, I can't very well be starting over, now can I? Can I offer you anything?"

Kate shook her head politely, but the man ignored her and went into the kitchen to put a kettle on to boil. In the corner of the living room was a small television that had been muted. A lively television presenter with a dress that fit too snugly was greeting the audience and inviting them to do something silly. A half-finished newspaper crossword puzzle and a carefully sharpened pencil lay side by side on the table.

Her eyes scanned the walls. They were covered with pictures, nearly all of them black and white. In a few, a youthful Mr. Carroll was pictured with a woman and two small children. But the majority showed him aboard various ships. Kate slowly took in the living room, thinking about the photos. They were hung

in chronological order, and it was like taking a fascinating journey back in time. The first few pictures were of an older Carroll
dressed in his captain's uniform. Then, as the pictures went
along, younger versions of the sailor were pictured, looking som-
ber in one or defiant in another.

Kate paused to look more closely at the last photo. It was so
ancient that one edge of the yellowed paper was torn as if it had
been handled often and kept in many places.

The photograph was of a group of sailors on the deck of a
ramshackle ship. In the center, an imposing captain with a white
beard stared ahead gravely. He was flanked by a group of officers,
who in turn were surrounded by the rest of the crew. It took Kate
a moment to pick out Carroll from the other sailors. He couldn't
have been more than twenty, with a puckish face. He wasn't
looking ahead at the camera but was focused instead on two
seagulls perched on the rail. The birds had become frozen in
time alongside the mariners. In shaky scrawl across the bottom
of the photograph, it said, "*Pass of Ballaster*, 1938."

"That was my first vessel." Carroll's voice startled Kate out of
her thoughts. He had returned from the kitchen with a cup of
tea, quiet as a mouse. "The *Pass of Ballaster*. In those days, I was
a cabin boy, and everyone called me Duff. It was a dumb nickname, but then again I was a dumb kid, so I guess it fit."

"This man looks straight out of a how-to guide for captains,"
Kate said, pointing at the captain.

Carroll nodded. "Captain McBride was a good man, and I
learned a lot from him. He died in '41, or maybe '42, when the
Germans torpedoed his ship in Newfoundland. In fact pretty
much everyone in that picture died during the war." His hands
shook as he took a sip of tea. "The *Valkyrie* wanted no survivors,
and it's slowly been taking care of them all, that's for sure. I'm
the only one left."

"I've just been to the naval base, and they told me you have quite a history with the *Valkyrie*."

"Indeed. I found the damn thing in the middle of the ocean. But I wish I never had."

"Why's that?"

"Because that ship is cursed. She devours people's souls and spits them back as something dark. And every time is worse than the last."

An awkward silence ensued. The only sounds came from the babbling rain as it poured down the gutters. Carroll gestured for Kate to have a seat.

"What I'm about to tell you happened at the end of August 1939, just before the war broke out," he said, sounding distant, almost as if he had returned to that very day.

Kate frantically took notes—she cursed herself for not having the foresight to bring her recorder—as Carroll told the story of finding and boarding the *Valkyrie*.

"Officer O'Leary nearly ran me over when we met in the doorway. He had been trying to get out of there as quick as he could, and he was carrying poor old Stepanek on his shoulders like a sack of potatoes. Stepanek looked about a thousand years older. His mind was gone. And O'Leary had that little baby in his arms."

"Baby?" Kate's head perked up, and she stopped taking notes. "What baby?"

"The little boy we found on the dance floor, of course." Carroll looked at her fixedly, changing the tone of his voice to one of grave concern. "Didn't you hear about that?"

Kate shook her head. She had reviewed the file Robert had left behind, and there was nothing that referenced any baby.

"Are you sure?" she asked cautiously. "Could you be mistaken?"

"Miss"—Carroll began to count on his hands—"I've been torpedoed twice, I've crashed into a reef, I've sailed through typhoons, and I've even battled Malay pirates on a couple of occasions. But I promise you, only once in my life have I encountered a passenger liner adrift with a baby on board. So, yes, I do believe I'm sure."

"What happened to the baby?"

"I have no idea." Carroll shrugged. "I suppose he was taken to an orphanage or some kind of facility. The day we arrived back was the day the war started. Within a few weeks Europe was filled with thousands of orphaned babies. He was abandoned on a German ship. Just imagine the attention he'd get."

"Indeed," Kate murmured. "What about the other two men who climbed aboard with you? O'Leary and Stepanek? What happened to them?"

"O'Leary was a good man. Too good." The old man's voice was starting to sound weak. He had been talking for some time now and was beginning to look fatigued. "They called him up for duty, and he went into the Royal Navy. But that damned *Valkyrie* left him wrong in the head. He'd say he was hearing things or that he could see—" Mr. Carroll did not finish his sentence and shuddered. "I have no idea what was going through his head. But I do know he left something of himself behind on that ship, and she left something of herself in him. He shot himself in Gibraltar six weeks after we ported with the cruise ship in tow. They say he left his cabin filled with writings he'd done."

"My God," whispered Kate, "that's awful."

"Stepanek spent the next seven years in a mental hospital in Croydon. He was reduced to a helpless vegetable." Carroll's breathing sounded more labored than before. He was trembling, on the verge of collapse.

"We don't have to keep going," Kate said, taking his teacup before he dropped it. "We can pick this up another day."

Carroll shook his head. His eyes glimmered with fierce resolve. "Someone has to know about all this," he wheezed. "Please, listen. There's still more. The mental ward helped Stepanek's body but not his mind. He ate, drank, and slept but did nothing else besides babble and stare off into space. I went to visit him a couple of times, and he didn't even recognize me. One day I got a phone call that he had jumped out of a window."

"Jumped out of a window? But didn't you say he was like a vegetable? How is that possible?" A chill ran through Kate.

"It was May 15, the same day they moved the *Valkyrie* from the port in Liverpool to here." On the verge of desperation, Carroll clung tightly to the edge of the table, his knuckles white. "Do you understand?"

"Understand what?"

"The move threw the curse for a loop. Stepanek took advantage of that fact and managed to get away. Somehow, the ship loosened its grip long enough for him to jump out of the window at the psychiatric hospital." Carroll placed his bony hands on Kate's arm. The heat emanating from his body was not normal. He was burning up.

"That's crazy, Mr. Carroll. Nobody was trapped aboard the *Valkyrie*."

"That's where you're wrong, Miss Kilroy. That's where you're wrong." He coughed hoarsely and doubled over. A bit of blood trickled out of the corner of his mouth. He wiped it away with the back of his hand and continued, despite the fact that his lungs sounded like the wheezing bellows of a foundry. "Come closer."

Nearly in a trance, Kate acquiesced and leaned closer. His breath was hot and dry next to her ear.

"They're still trapped inside. Dozens of people," he whispered. "I broke free because I didn't spend long enough for it to take hold. But that thing did something to me because I can see them."

Kate moaned and tried to free herself from Carroll's grip. The old man was completely deranged.

"Ah, yes. I can see them all right. And talk to them." His eyes were ablaze, and he gripped Kate's arm tighter. "They're still there. Dozens of them. It's a place worse than hell. Stay away from that ship."

Carroll finally let go and Kate pulled away. He tumbled back in his chair and panted heavily, nearing collapse. Kate stood up and took two steps toward the door. Her legs wobbled as she picked up her notes and bumbled out a hasty farewell. She wanted to get the hell out of there. But just as she made a motion to grab the doorknob, Carroll's feeble voice stopped her.

"The boy," he huffed. "The boy was important. The Jewish boy was important."

Kate paused at the door, thinking she'd misheard him. She turned around and walked back into the living room.

"The boy was Jewish? Jewish? Why do you say that?"

"The boy . . . he was circum . . . circumcised, and . . ." His breathing sounded like a whistle filled with dead skin. "He had a star . . . the Star of David . . . hung around his neck. He was wrapped in a Jewish thingy . . . used to cover . . ."

"A *tallit*," muttered Kate. A Jewish boy aboard a Nazi ship. It didn't add up. Unless, perhaps, he was a stowaway.

Carroll motioned weakly with one hand. He had said all he needed to say and had closed his eyes, exhausted. Kate placed a pillow under his head, so he could breathe more easily. He raised his head in thanks and grasped her hand.

"Be careful." His voice was almost inaudible. "There's something about that ship . . . a . . . something . . . Please be careful. I beg of you!"

Kate nodded to placate the elderly gentleman and began to tiptoe out of the living room. She began piecing it all together. If the boy was Jewish, Isaac Feldman's involvement in all this made more sense. Feldman was Jewish and even had Israeli citizenship. What if Feldman was somehow related to that boy? In fact, maybe he *was* the boy. Why not? They were close enough in age.

Lost in thought, Kate walked down the house's front steps without noticing the headlights that were fast approaching from her right. A car thundered straight toward her at a tremendous speed.

"Look out," shouted the cabdriver.

Kate was startled back into reality mere seconds before it was too late. She looked up to see the nose of an SUV with tinted windows hurtling like a rocket toward Carroll's house. Without thinking, she leaped to her right and landed in a pile of cardboard boxes a bum had probably planned to use as a mattress.

As the vehicle sped by, the side mirror hit Kate's arm. The car continued forward, and the mirror dragged across the front of the house and broke off in a burst of metal and glass. The SUV managed to uproot the mailbox, sending beer cans and trash cans flying. The sound of metal grating against cement chilled Kate as she crawled frantically across the ground to get away from the car's back wheels.

The driver of the SUV hit the brakes, unsure how to proceed. The taillights cast a red glow over Kate as she desperately gasped for breath on the ground, trapped between the SUV and the front of the house. If the driver put the car in reverse, she would be crushed like a grape. The cabdriver ran toward them, club in one hand, phone in the other, screaming frantically.

It was enough to make the mystery driver step on the gas and tear away at full speed. Before the cabdriver reached Kate, the SUV had already rounded the corner and disappeared into the night.

"Are you all right?" shouted the driver, a nervous wreck. "I told you this was a bad neighborhood. Bad neighborhood."

Kate got up, trembling, her head whirling.

Someone had tried to kill her. She had no idea why.

I X

Thirty minutes later, Kate was in her hotel room standing beneath a jet of hot water as steam clouded around her. Her left arm had an enormous bruise that was slowly taking on a sickly yellowish hue.

Who would want to kill her?

She dried herself with a wide cotton towel and put on pajamas while she considered the possibilities. The only reason that came to mind was her newfound interest in the *Valkyrie*, and she could think of only one person who would care: Isaac Feldman.

Any other reporter might have given up the story right then and there. In fact, Kate considered it several times as she brushed her teeth and got ready for bed. But the very idea of going back to the office with her tail between her legs made her dismiss that thought.

This had been Robert's story. Thinking about him made her heart cave under the weight of her sorrow. Robert had never given up when something good came along. She would do as he would have done. Not only for him but for herself, too. If she truly wanted to make something of herself in this profession, she couldn't let herself be rattled.

But they had tried to kill her.

It suddenly dawned on her that she had almost been run over by a car just an hour earlier.

Run over.

Like him.

It hit her harder than the SUV ever could. Her legs began to shake, and she had to sit on the bed to hold back a swelling flood of hysteria. Her emotional floodgates burst open, and she began crying uncontrollably, inconsolably. Her tears were a mixture of the tension from the fateful afternoon and the throbbing pain that had burrowed into her weeks ago, never letting go. Until now it had not been afforded the luxury of being let out.

Tears streamed from Kate's eyes. Lights swirled through her mind; the SUV's headlights fused together with the morgue's fluorescent lights from a month ago, when she had identified her husband's broken body.

She had almost suffered the same fate. Cold. Dead. Displayed on the mantle next to Robert in an urn.

Her fears slowly spun into a cold, merciless anger. She would not be deterred, nor would she let someone scare her away. If, for some strange reason, Feldman wanted to keep her away from the *Valkyrie*, she would not let him. Suddenly, she felt much better.

That night she slept surprisingly well. The next morning she woke up and put on a blue tailored suit with long sleeves to cover the bruise on her arm. When she was ready, she went down to the lobby and waited for a taxi.

Thanks to the file Robert had left behind, she knew Feldman lived in a mansion forty minutes away. Although the gambling tycoon never gave interviews, Kate figured she could improvise. She had no appointment and no plan, but the worst he could do was turn her away. Plus, if she didn't manage to talk to Feldman directly, someone nearby might be able to give her a clue as to the whereabouts of the *Valkyrie*.

Since the ship had been taken from the navy yard, there had been no sightings of it. As if the earth had swallowed it whole.

One thing was certain: there was no way it could be in a junkyard. Nobody pays that kind of money for a ship just to scrap it for steel planks and kitchen rags. The photo of the small army of technicians working on the ship right there at Denborough proved that Feldman was absolutely determined to make the passenger liner seaworthy, at any cost.

Still, it was also evident that those basic emergency repairs had not been enough for the ship to return to sea on its own. The *Valkyrie* had to be in dry dock somewhere or anchored in some harbor, awaiting Feldman's decision to launch. Kate was determined to find it.

Adrenaline pumping when her taxi arrived, Kate vowed to get the full story that afternoon, if she had to strangle it out of Feldman with her own two hands.

Her plans, however, quickly began to unravel.

Feldman's residence, Usher Manor, was in the countryside. Long before the cab could even approach the front door, it encountered an iron gate flanked by an enormous brick fence that stretched out of sight on both sides.

"We can't go any farther," said Hussein, the same driver who had taken her to Carroll's house the night before. Kate felt attached to him since he had saved her from being run over. "Either they open the gate, or we'll have to turn around. Would you like me to use the intercom, ma'am?"

Kate shook her head. She knew calling the house would do no good. There had to be another way.

"This is the main entrance to Usher Manor," she mused. "But I'll bet anything that an estate this large has another way in. There must be a service road somewhere. Let's have a look."

Hussein groaned and wondered why on earth he was doing this. Allah had placed a nut job in his path. He touched the *hamsa* hanging from his mirror and looked imploringly at the beautiful young woman in the backseat.

"Come on, Hussein." Kate gave him an encouraging slap on the back and flashed her most charming smile. "It won't be so bad. We'll be fine, you'll see."

In response, the Pakistani muttered something in his native tongue and shook his head.

They coasted along a stretch of country road lined on both sides with tall hedges until they reached a fork in the road. In one direction, a muddy-looking dirt road carved its way toward the mansion.

Kate used her most persuasive tone to convince Hussein that the cab wouldn't get stuck going up the road. Five minutes and a hundred quid later, they were bouncing down a bumpy road that made the car's shocks creak ominously every few feet.

More suited to pavement, the taxi hit a thick patch of mud as it headed up the hill. Hussein stepped on the gas repeatedly, but he managed only to spin the tires in place, sending mud flying through the air.

"Leave it. I'll walk from here. The house can't be far."

"Walk?" Hussein's eyes became saucers. "In those shoes?"

Kate looked at her feet and cursed. He was right. She was wearing high heels. She looked at Hussein's shoes. He was short, and his feet seemed about right. A sinuous smile crept across her lips.

"No. No way."

A few minutes later Kate was treading cautiously up the road, wearing a pair of sneakers that were too large. An irate Hussein stood barefoot next to his taxi, fifty pounds richer but all the more nervous.

At the top of the hill Kate stopped to catch her breath, not from fatigue but to take in the view. Usher Manor was an impressive Victorian-style mansion, reminding Kate of Howards End, but subtly altered.

The gardens and fountains had been ignored, or forgotten. Weeds grew on the terraces, and the fountains were dry. Rancid water filled the ponds, and bramble choked the pathways. Kate got the impression nobody had visited the area for some time.

Planted in the flower beds, satellite dishes of different sizes pointed in all directions. A huge telecommunication tower loomed imposingly on one side of the house, casting its shadow over a wing of the mansion. A group of people milled around what looked like a truck generator connected to the house.

The place resembled a company's headquarters more than a summer home belonging to a wealthy millionaire.

Something to her right caught her eye. Two men driving ATVs headed straight for her, looking extremely unfriendly. This was private property. She stuck her hand in her purse and blindly felt for her press card as the ATVs grew louder. They skidded to a stop next to her, speckling her suit with mud.

"Hello," she said with a nervous smile as the two men dismounted. "I'm a reporter with the *London*—"

She was silenced by a set of cold eyes fixed behind the dark barrel of a rifle pointing straight at her. Kate asked herself if she had taken things too far.

They put her on the back of one of the ATVs with her hands bound behind her back by a hard plastic cord, and then they took off at full speed, heading toward the mansion. Kate struggled not to fall off the vehicle each time they hit a bump in the road. The cord dug into her wrists, and her hands tingled from lack of circulation. The two men had thoroughly tied her up without a care for diplomacy. They seemed like they were ex-military, and Kate suspected one of them did not speak English.

When they reached Usher Manor, they crossed the outside encampment, attracting curious looks from the workers lingering about. Clearly, visitors were rare.

It dawned on Kate that Hussein was the only one who knew where she was. Given the treatment she'd received, she was certain he, too, had been taken into custody.

The ATVs stopped by one of the mansion's side doors. One of the men leaped off and bounded inside while the other waited with Kate, smoking a cigarette and giving her sidelong glances every so often.

She then realized that during the rough ATV ride her skirt had hiked up, revealing her lacy black underwear. The guard smoking the cigarette was practically cross-eyed.

Flustered, she tried to compose herself as best she could, knowing full well this had become a disaster. The cabdriver's shoes were no more than two pieces of felt hanging from her feet, her hair was covered in mud, and her suit looked straight out of a thrift store. Still, she managed to straighten up and calmly inspect her surroundings, as if all of it were simply a routine task.

Just then the door opened, and the guard appeared with three more men. Two of them were a part of the security team, but the third was an older gentleman, perhaps seventy, looking resolute and authoritative. It was Isaac Feldman.

The first guard handed Kate's press badge to Feldman, and as he looked it over, the guard methodically emptied her purse and recorded all of its contents. Upon finding her iPhone, he tossed it to the ground and gave it three powerful blows with the butt of his gun, smashing it to pieces.

Kate started to protest but let the sound die in her throat. It was only a phone, and she had bigger fish to fry at the moment. Feldman looked at her with an impenetrable gaze. Horrified, she reflected on all of the terrible stories she had read concerning his reputation as a mobster and realized her destiny lay in his hands.

"She was up on the hill watching the mansion," the first guard said. "She didn't have any cameras that we could find, but she had a partner, a Muslim guy in a taxi a little ways back. He's being brought here right now."

"Muslim?" Feldman, himself a Jew, began to smile malevolently. Kate realized a paranoid maniac like Feldman would not understand that Hussein was there only by coincidence.

"It's not what it looks like . . ." She heard herself babble, her composure withering before Feldman's hawkish look. "I'm a reporter from the *London New Herald*. I wanted to talk to you about the *Valkyrie*. I think we could—"

"Take her back to town," Feldman cut her off. "Her and her associate. Turn them in to the police, and report them for trespassing and harassment. Let's step up security and find out how they got in. This is totally unacceptable, Moore."

The man called Moore paled upon being reprimanded and clenched his jaw. He looked at Kate with such hatred that she thought he might burst into flames.

"Yes, of course, sir," he muttered. "It won't happen again."

A pair of hands like claws grabbed Kate and dragged her toward a parked van. Feldman turned around and, without another glance at Kate, headed into the house.

"Wait!" she shouted. "Wait! I have to talk to you!"

Feldman paid no attention as he walked through the doorway. This was her last chance.

"I know about the child!" she yelled with a sudden burst of inspiration. "The Jewish baby found aboard the *Valkyrie*."

Feldman stopped in his tracks. The guards had already placed Kate in the van despite her kicking and screaming. The elderly man took in the scene for a moment. He looked down at the press badge still in his hand.

"Let her go."

The guards immediately obeyed, and Kate wriggled away from them furiously. She looked directly at Feldman, who returned her gaze.

"I know about the little boy," she repeated. "I know it *all*. I'd like to talk to you about it."

Feldman shrugged and, for the first time, smiled openly.

"All right, Miss Kilroy. Since you want to talk about me, let's talk," he said enigmatically, although Kate detected a threatening undertone. "I hope the conversation proves stimulating. For your sake."

X

Usher Manor's interior offered such a stark contrast to the exterior that Kate blinked in disbelief. Thick Persian rugs covered the floors. Beautiful, priceless oil paintings hung from every wall. Kate could have sworn the painting above the fireplace was a genuine Constable. As the two took a seat, Kate's eyes fell on an elephant's head hanging on the wall. It watched them with a look of fury.

"This house belonged to the same family for four hundred years," Feldman said, noticing Kate's surprise. "After the Second World War, it was ruined and nearly demolished. I decided to buy it some fifteen years ago along with all of its belongings. Lovely, isn't it?"

Feldman's tone was proud and satisfied. His skin was surprisingly smooth for a man who had to be close to seventy years old. His eyes, deep blue, watched Kate almost without blinking. His magnetic gaze was renowned in the world of gambling. If the rumors were true, on one occasion he had completely unnerved a rival without ever blinking. He was tall with a sharp nose and confident demeanor. His snow-white hair fell gently over his ears. Everything about him exuded authority. He was a self-made man who had utilized hard work and perseverance to make something of himself. Not to mention the occasional corpse, Kate was forced to remind herself. Isaac Feldman was a dangerous man.

Feldman turned Kate's badge over with his long fingers, which were crowned by perfectly round fingernails. After a few moments he set it down on the table and leaned back in his seat without taking his eyes off the badge.

"How do you know about the child?"

"Where is the *Valkyrie*? What do you plan to do with it?"

"The *Valkyrie* now belongs to me," answered Feldman emphatically. "I've spent years searching for it. Some idiot from the Ministry of Defense registered it under a code name. It took decades of shots in the dark just to find it. For a while there I even thought it might have been scrapped. But now it's mine."

Feldman uttered his last words with such force that Kate jolted in surprise.

"Why is that old ship so important to you, Mr. Feldman?" asked Kate coolly, feeling like she was prodding a sleeping lion.

"I don't remember anything about the orphanage. I was barely there three months. The Blitz had yet to begin, and the war in Europe was still a distant echo. The number of orphans was normal for peacetime." He smiled bitterly. "Not at all how it would be just a couple of years later."

"You were the baby boy they found on the dance floor of the *Valkyrie*."

"My parents, the Feldmans, were good people. He drank too much but worked like a dog in the leather trade. She couldn't have kids, which nearly destroyed her entirely. When I was placed up for adoption, it was a blessing for them. They weren't first on the list, but they were the only ones who had checked

'Jewish' on the adoption form. So I was placed with them. That's how I grew up and became what I am today."

"How did you find out where you came from?"

"When my parents adopted me, they were given all of my personal effects." Feldman reached under his shirt collar and pulled out a gold Star of David. "This pendant, a high-quality *tallit*, and the blanket someone benevolently wrapped me up in so I wouldn't freeze my little butt off on that dance floor. That was all I had. The blanket had the KDF logo and the name *Valkyrie* stitched on the edges. From there, I began to follow the trail. But it was cold."

"KDF?" interrupted Kate. "What's KDF?"

"Initials that stand for Kraft Durch Freude. Do you know what that means?"

Kate spoke German quite well and nodded. "Strength through joy. What I don't get is what it means."

"That was the Nazi organization in charge of planning vacations and leisure activities for those loyal to the Reich. Believe it or not, it was the largest and most important travel agency in the world in the thirties." Opening a drawer, Feldman took out an old book and set it on the table. He flipped it open to a page that showed a flag. In the middle was a swastika surrounded by a cog and sun rays. "That was their symbol. They planned trips, organized private parties."

"Cruise ships like the *Valkyrie*."

"The *Valkyrie* was one of the first ships owned exclusively by the organization. It was built in Hamburg, but almost all documents that mention the ship or the KDF were destroyed during the Allied air raids during the war. Almost nothing is known about that cruise liner except that they found it floating in the middle of the ocean with no sign of any passengers or crew. It's a mystery."

"An empty ship. Then it's true."

"Not completely empty," Feldman corrected her, a flash in his eye. "A Nazi ship with a Jewish boy as its only survivor. Me. Now do you see why that ship is so important to me?"

Kate nodded, seeing Feldman in a different light. The man had seemed like he was haunted by some sort of fever. Now she realized Feldman had spent his entire life racked by doubts and fears about the true nature of his origin. As if the pairing of a Jewish baby with a Nazi cruise ship wasn't bizarre enough, Feldman was also the only survivor of the largest disappearance of people at sea in history. Yet only a handful of people knew about this ghost ship.

"Now that I have told you my story, Miss Kilroy, I believe the time has come to hear yours."

Kate took a deep breath and wondered whether or not she could trust this man. She realized she had no choice. She opened her purse, removed the purple folder with the *Valkyrie*'s file, and handed it to Feldman. As he looked through it, Kate began relating the interview she had conducted with Collins and Lambert at the naval base. When she got to the part about Duff Carroll, Feldman looked up in shock.

"A sailor from the *Pass of Ballaster* is still alive?" His voice betrayed his torment. He sprang up, and the folder and its papers fell to the floor. "Where? How?"

Kate was puzzled. She remembered that the men at the base had said Feldman's employees were rude and arrogant when they came to take away the *Valkyrie*. Perhaps they had not mentioned anything to Feldman about the old man and his strange obsession with the ship.

As she told him about her conversation with Carroll, Feldman's apprehension increased. He took wide strides across the living room, pacing past the mounted animal heads with a look of distress.

"I must talk to that man. Where does he live?"

"I'll tell you if you let me go with you and allow me to take notes for my story."

Feldman stared blankly at her for a few seconds. Then, almost imperceptibly, he nodded.

"All right, Miss Kilroy . . . Kate." Feldman started toward the door. "You're in. Now let's go see Mr. Carroll."

•   •   •

Ten minutes later a caravan of five vehicles departed Usher Manor. Kate and Feldman sat in the backseat of an Audi SUV with tinted windows. The four other vehicles flanked the Audi: two in front and two behind. Seated with them were bodyguards like those who had captured Kate earlier. Richard Moore, head of security, sat up front and spoke by phone to the other cars as the convoy sped down the highway.

Kate and Feldman kept quiet in the backseat, each lost in thought. Kate wondered what might be going through the head of the man by her side. As if by reflex, Feldman moved his hand toward the gold pendant around his neck and held it tight. He seemed to be lost in the throes of a memory.

Kate tried to imagine what Robert would have done in her position. She was sure he would have been chatting effortlessly with Feldman, calm and relaxed, dissipating any tension as if by magic. Robert had possessed an innate ability to make everyone around him relaxed and comfortable. Kate cursed herself for not having the same gift. All she could do was look out the window as the scenery whipped by.

When they arrived in Denborough, Kate could sense the tension rise. Dozens of prostitutes and junkies wandered near trash piles and ruined houses, regarding the convoy with the same empty expression before returning to their dark lives. In the daylight, the neighborhood looked even more dirty and downtrodden than it had last night. Kate shuddered. She had almost been killed.

She looked at Feldman. His surprise at discovering Carroll had been genuine, of that she was sure. Feldman had never heard of the man, let alone where he lived.

So if Feldman hadn't put a hit on Kate, then who had? Her head buzzed as she racked her brains for a clue.

The caravan came to a halt in front of Carroll's little home. The bad scrape across the front of the house was still visible from the night before. Kate and Feldman got out of the Audi and climbed the two front stairs that led to the entrance. But before they could reach the front door, Moore ran up, looking grave.

"One moment," he said in a low voice. "Something's not right here."

Kate did not understand until she saw that Carroll's front door was ajar. The door's wood trim was cracked, and the frame was damaged in one corner.

Immediately, half a dozen armed guards surrounded Feldman and Kate, each pointing his gun in a different direction. The lost souls who were milling about on a nearby corner had the sudden urge to be anywhere else but there, leaving the entire street deserted.

"Wait here," Moore ordered in a grave tone.

Three of Feldman's men entered the house cautiously, guns ready, while the rest waited outside impatiently. After two minutes, one of the guards returned with a strange and somewhat pallid expression. He leaned against the doorway and vomited on the doorstep.

"Clear," he croaked and wiped his mouth with the back of his hand. "No one's inside. But I warn you, it's a butcher shop in there."

Kate felt her legs begin to shake. Feldman, cold and ruthless, lived up to his reputation and did not bat an eye.

"You don't have to go in," he told her, placing a hand on her arm with surprising gentleness.

"I'm going in," she said, taking a deep breath, wishing her voice had sounded firmer.

The hallway was just as it had been the night before. Beyond that, it looked as though a tornado had hit.

The first thing that struck her was the smell. It was slightly sweet and sticky, with a touch of ocher to it. But underneath was another scent. Burnt hair.

As they entered the living room, Kate grabbed Feldman's arm to avoid collapsing. It looked like a mad butcher had decided to decorate the walls with human remains. On the table lay Mr. Carroll's body, or at least what was left of it. His hands were tied to his feet with wire, and every one of his fingers was broken or severed and scattered on the floor. Horrified, Kate noticed that nearly all of them were missing fingernails. The body had been torn open. His organs had been extracted and placed in neat piles as if some forensic specialist had simply done his job. Blood was streaked across the walls in crimson designs. But the most striking thing of all was Mr. Carroll's head was nowhere to be seen.

"But who? How?" Kate stuttered.

"Who could have done this?" Feldman responded, somberly. "Someone hell-bent on getting answers."

One of Feldman's men found a scalpel and blowtorch underneath the coffee table. It was a cheap blowtorch, the kind that could be bought at any hardware store. From the foul stench in the air, it had been used for a very different purpose than its manufacturer had intended.

Kate glanced at the wall in disgust. She realized something was off. The pictures chronicling Carroll's life at sea were still hanging there except now they were spattered with blood. But one was missing.

An empty yellowed piece of wallpaper occupied the space where the picture of the *Pass of Ballaster* had once been. Someone had taken it.

"This is barbaric," Kate said in disbelief. "He was a charming, polite man."

"He chose the wrong neighborhood to live in," replied Moore, who seemed to be the only one unaffected by the slaughter, apart from Feldman.

"This wasn't done by any old crack addict," answered Kate, pointing toward the television, which was still on. Instead of a busty young hostess on-screen, however, a movie was playing. Next to the television was Mr. Carroll's open wallet with a few ten-pound notes visibly protruding.

"I must agree with Miss Kilroy," Feldman said icily. He was undoubtedly thinking something, but it was hard to say what that was. "This was the work of a professional. Someone motivated enough to behead a man."

"There's also one picture missing," Kate pointed as she tried to avoid stepping in a pool of blood. She wanted to vomit, but she refused to give Feldman and his men the satisfaction. "The picture with Mr. Carroll aboard the *Pass of Ballaster*."

"That's not all that's missing," Moore chimed in with a strange note in his voice.

Intrigued, everyone turned around to look at Moore, who was standing beside the corpse.

"His heart is gone," he said, pointing to the pile of organs. "Someone's taken it."

X I

Moore shoved them out of the house before the police could arrive. Kate tried to protest, but one look from Feldman quieted her down immediately.

"There's a decapitated body on the living room table. Parts are missing, and we've made a thorough search of the house," Feldman reasoned as they climbed into the Audi. "I don't want to spend the whole day in a police station, trying to explain why we were there in the first place."

It occurred to Kate that she had been in the house less than twenty-four hours ago. Her fingerprints were probably everywhere. She shook her head as she reached to open the car door. "The police will want to talk to me. We should stay."

"I don't think that's a good idea," Feldman said as the Audi started up. "Things are about to get hot around here. And fast."

Kate looked at him blankly before noticing a subtle movement in his eyes. She turned around and looked out the back window. Without realizing she was doing it, she let out a cry of horror as flames burst from the windows and the front door of the house. Thick clouds of smoke billowed out, enveloping that entire stretch of road.

"You set the house on fire," she cried.

Feldman nodded as the convoy rounded a corner en route to the highway. In the distance, the wail of sirens could be heard, but they were not heading toward the fire. Denborough wasn't a high-priority neighborhood. By the time emergency crews arrived, the house would probably be nothing but ash.

"Why?" asked Kate, still not understanding what had happened.

"To avoid potential problems," answered Feldman. "Going in there, we left footprints, hair, and God knows what else. Half a dozen junkies watched us go in, and even if their word isn't worth shit, they could lead the police to us if they found any forensic evidence. Our license plates are fake, so that won't be a problem, but I don't want anything that might lead to a criminal investigation. Not now that we're so close." Feldman stopped as if he had said more than intended.

"So close to what?" asked Kate with a knot in her stomach, sensing the danger of the situation. Feldman's sinister reputation took on a whole new meaning.

"Nothing you need to worry about, Miss Kilroy," Feldman grunted hoarsely. "Nothing you need to worry about."

"You mean that the house and the body were just loose ends that needed tending?"

Feldman confirmed her accusation with a single nod.

A long silence ensued between the two of them as the convoy merged onto the highway.

"Am I just another one of those loose ends?" she whispered, the knot in her stomach turning to ice.

Feldman's blank expression slowly transformed into one of respect. He nodded. "It's true. You're another loose end, Kate."

"Where does that leave us?"

"In a complex situation for the both of us. You're a strange variable in my equation. I'm not sure what to do with you."

Kate shrunk into her seat. She looked out the window and immediately discarded the possibility of jumping out of a moving vehicle. They were traveling well above the speed limit, weaving between heavy traffic. A man like this paid no mind to things like traffic tickets.

Feldman looked at Kate, and a sudden look of understanding crossed his face. He let out a thunderous guffaw. "Do you think I'm going to kill you? Who do you take me for?"

"You're Isaac Feldman," she said weakly. "You're a gambling tycoon. They say you enjoy watching your enemies get slaughtered. You have your own private army at your disposal. You're a man who just set fire to a crime scene without batting an eye."

Feldman laughed harder than before. "Some of those things are certainly true, and others not so much. But rest assured. I do not intend to harm you."

Kate noticed that when Feldman let himself smile, his face became calm and peaceful.

"So?"

"So we have a complex situation on our hands. You know too much about the *Valkyrie,* which is not good these days." He motioned outside in reference to Carroll's house. "And you know too much about me. Plus, you're an accomplice to the destruction of a crime scene."

Kate opened her mouth to protest the accusation, but Feldman raised a hand to silence her.

"On the other hand, you're a smart woman who seems to ask the right questions. You want to write a story on the mysterious ghost ship that comes to life after seventy years."

When he said the words *ghost ship*, Kate noticed that Feldman made an effort to utter them calmly, but his eyes betrayed him.

"We cannot forget that you were the last person to talk to the only survivor of the *Pass of Ballaster*. All of that makes you quite valuable."

"I would like to go aboard your ship, Mr. Feldman. I want to tell that story."

"You can't do that until the voyage is over, and you will let me read your story before it's published."

Kate would rather die than allow Feldman to censor her report, but she agreed. She would cross that bridge when she came to it.

"All right, Mr. Feldman." Kate extended her hand and, for the first time that day, felt like everything would be OK. "Do we have a deal?"

"Deal," he said. "Welcome to the crew of the *Valkyrie*."

X I I

The Elba River was dark gray that morning, concealing innumerable secrets as it splashed softly against the piles of Pier 74b. In the cold morning air a few seagulls squabbled over a piece of trash floating downstream as the river rolled toward its final destination in the North Sea, some sixty miles away.

Kate stood at the edge of the pier and zipped up her jacket, craning her neck in an effort to warm her face in the few rays the sun had to offer at that hour. Around her the people of Hamburg were shaking off sleep and getting ready for a new day.

Pier 74b was located in the heart of the port, near the city. It was one of the oldest sections in the entire port complex. A nearby set of low, run-down warehouses made the area appear even older than it was. During World War II, the Allied forces had thoroughly razed the port, which meant the warehouses couldn't be more than fifty years old. Still, they looked older than the river itself. The dark windows loomed imposingly as if watching, and being utterly bored by, Kate and the two dozen or so people scampering about the docks.

Some one hundred yards away several enormous cargo ships from some of the world's most unlikely places were docked. Cranes were lifting and lowering huge, colorful metal containers. The noise of the engines and the clanging of the containers was deafening, even from afar.

More than a half mile away, the upper edge of the *Oasis of the Seas* was visible through the fog. The enormous cruise ship had a maximum capacity of more than six thousand passengers. Its white body blended together with those of three or four other cruise ships in the vicinity. They were nearly as massive as the *Oasis* and were docked at the beautifully modern passenger terminal.

This is not that terminal, Kate thought to herself as she blew into her hands for warmth. *Now we're on this bloody awful pier waiting for Feldman.*

Despite being the middle of August, it was actually quite chilly. In the distance Kate could see the cafeterias and restaurants in the passenger terminal. They were most likely serving the first breakfasts of the morning. Her stomach growled in protest. But she ignored it completely. She had eyes only for the ship immediately to her right. Floating. Silent. As if out of a dream. Or perhaps a nightmare.

The *Valkyrie.*

Kate had arrived in Hamburg barely twenty-four hours earlier. Feldman had arranged for a private jet to fly her. Parting with Feldman had been truly bizarre. Instead of taking her back to Usher Manor, he'd insisted on taking her directly to her hotel in Liverpool. Once there, Feldman and his men waited patiently as she went up to her room, showered, changed, and came back down again. From there they drove her to the train station, where she almost died of embarrassment when their cavalcade screeched to a halt in front of the station entrance and several men in suits surrounded the perimeter.

"Tomorrow I will send one of my associates to meet you at your apartment," Feldman said from the Audi window. "That person will accompany you to Hamburg. The *Valkyrie* and the rest of the team are there."

"Hamburg? Germany?"

Feldman nodded.

"Will you be there?"

Feldman smiled astutely. Kate recalled that Feldman was being investigated by the Treasury Department and a judge had revoked his passport. Theoretically, he was not allowed to leave the country.

"I'll be there, Miss Kilroy. But I'll have to make the journey solo. Not to worry, though. We'll see each other in Hamburg."

Then, with a wave of his hand, the caravan started up again, and Kate was left alone in the middle of the sidewalk, confused and somewhat frightened.

That was how things were done in Feldman's world.

Several hours later Kate was home, talking on the phone with her editor while she frantically packed a suitcase with her free hand. Finally, she did not feel trapped in the tomb known as her apartment. Kate realized the story of the *Valkyrie* had enthralled her because it gave her a way to escape the black hole she had wallowed in since Robert's death. But there was something else. Something deeply disturbing about the whole thing held her inexplicably spellbound. She was hell-bent on finding the answer.

As she decided what clothes to pack, her gaze crossed to the mantel and the ceramic urn containing Robert's ashes sitting on top. Kate had not passed by the fireplace for several days in an effort to avoid the agonizing evidence of his absence. On a whim she picked up the urn.

For the first time she was able to look at it without bursting into tears, though her heart still felt a lash. She closed her eyes and tried to imagine the musk of his flesh, the feeling of their embrace, and the vibrant force of his body. She shook her head to drive away the memories. Robert was gone forever. Hit by a drunk driver who fled the scene. Now he would walk on the dark banks of the River Styx for eternity.

On another whim she placed the urn in her suitcase. She didn't know exactly why, but it suddenly seemed unbearable to be separated from him. If Kate were going to board the *Valkyrie*, the urn would have to come, too.

That night she dreamed of Robert. Her husband was aboard an empty ship and held a parcel, a parcel that was crying and had two chubby little arms flailing out of it. She tried to chase him, shouting his name but to no avail. She sprinted through the corridors, compelled by an infinite urgency. When he finally got to the dance floor, he gently placed the baby in the middle of the room. Then, as he turned to Kate, she saw that the man was not Robert, just someone who looked a great deal like him. Something dark, voracious, and evil had set a trap for her. She awoke screaming and soaked in sweat.

The next morning Kate, looking slightly pale, was dressed and ready when they arrived to pick her up. A black car with tinted windows parked in front of her apartment and drove her directly to Heathrow Airport. From there, Feldman's private jet flew her to Hamburg. She arrived just as the sun was setting.

Another black vehicle—Kate wondered if Feldman had dozens of identical cars scattered across the world—took her to the Port of Hamburg. Kate's surprise upon passing the cruise ship terminal turned to unease when they ventured into a forest of cranes, semis, and enormous ships in the industrial section of the port. Eventually, they came to an area cordoned off by security guards: Pier 74b.

The guards at the entrance would not allow the vehicle or its driver to enter. From that point, security became even more ironclad than the system at Feldman's mansion. Kate was the only one allowed in, but only after extensive questioning. Once cleared, she had to walk the final stretch, dragging her suitcase over the rough cobblestone. Kate cursed Feldman under her breath for his paranoia and excessive affinity for secrets and security. As she walked along the pier, Kate tripped on an iron bollard, and she cursed aloud. Rubbing her ankle, greatly irritated, she looked up and saw the ghost ship. She gasped, and her eyes grew large as she took in the spectacle that stood before her.

The *Valkyrie* had been restored to its former glory. A team of welders, restoration specialists, mechanics, woodworkers, and painters had labored tirelessly for weeks to restore the *Valkyrie*. The ship looked like it had just been built instead of being over seventy years old.

Kate estimated it to be more than five hundred feet in length. The bottom half of the hull was painted black in the style of the 1930s, while the greater superstructure was completely white. Two tall smokestacks were painted red with a white circle in the middle. Kate found the combination strange until she recalled that, in its original design, the white circles had contained two huge swastikas.

The lifeboats hanging from the sides were of a design Kate had seen only in old photographs and movies. They were made of wood crossed by two long planks for seats. A waterproof canvas covered each one. From the pier, she could not tell what the walkway had in store, but she bet anything the floor was wood and the hammocks were netted. The ship looked exactly as it had in the thirties, with the exception of the missing swastikas on the smokestacks.

A gangplank ran up the side of the *Valkyrie*. Two armed men stood guard at the bottom, while a group of Feldman's men loaded wooden crates, barrels, and mountains of baggage. A column of steam had already begun to rise from the smokestacks, mixing with the smog of the port. The *Valkyrie* was ready to cast off into the open ocean.

She almost looks alive, Kate told herself, immediately wondering why the thought had occurred to her.

Kate gave a shiver that had nothing to do with the temperature and wondered if it would be wiser to just let the story go. Go back home, back to working on culture and society stories, and forget about everything else. Go out, get drunk, meet new people. Flirt with a guy, or maybe even several guys. Live.

But the *Valkyrie* called to her, and Kate yearned to get on board. Then, she could begin to unravel the ship's mysteries and finish the story Robert had started. In doing so, Kate hoped to discover peace once and for all, something that was sorely lacking in her life and holding her back.

"Impressive, isn't it?"

The voice startled her. Kate turned around to find a young woman, not more than thirty, looking at her carefully. She was tall, lean like an athlete, and undeniably Slavic in appearance. Her blonde hair was tied back in a ponytail, and she was wearing cargo pants. A knapsack was at her feet.

"Senka Simovic," said the woman, extending her hand without smiling, looking attentively through intense blue-green eyes. She spoke with a singsong accent that Kate couldn't identify. She was probably from one of the countries that had come out of the chaos in Yugoslavia.

"I'm Kate Kilroy," she replied, shaking Senka's hand, surprised by the strong grip.

"You must be the journalist," Senka said. Kate waited for her to say something else, but Senka's silence felt strategic.

Just then, a delivery van from a meat shop drove up. It clattered over the cobblestones and came to a stop next to the two women. Kate had no time to wonder how the van had slipped through the iron grip of pier security before the rear doors swung open and Isaac Feldman jumped out.

"Good morning, ladies," he greeted them cordially. "I see you two have already met. Hello, Senka. It's a pleasure to see you here."

The blonde gave a hint of a smile as if the mere act of arching her lips upward was taking a great toll. Still, she was clearly quite friendly with Feldman.

"Everything is ready, Mr. Feldman," Senka said. "The scientific team is already on board and so is the crew. The only ones yet to board are the security detail and us."

"Perfect," Feldman answered. Seeing Kate's confused expression, he took her by the arm and began walking with her toward the gangplank. "As you can see, I've had to travel an unbeaten path to get here. Not to worry, Kate. As soon as we're on board, I promise I will explain everything about the research team, among other things, all in great detail."

As they walked along, Kate could feel Senka's gaze boring a hole in the back of her head.

They came to the foot of the ramp. Feldman stopped and turned to Kate with a look of severity. "OK, this is your last chance," he said, his voice quivering with nervous excitement. "If you walk up this ramp, there's no going back. If I'm right, this will be the most amazing story in history. But I offer no guarantees for that or for your personal safety. I don't know if it's a fair deal, but it's all I have to offer. What do you say?"

Kate smiled and tightened her grip on her suitcase. Without a glance back she stepped forward and walked up the gangway.

All aboard the *Valkyrie*.

PART THREE

—

VALKYRIE

X I I I

If the ship's exterior had surprised Kate, the inside left her speechless. It looked like a movie set, only real.

It was not Kate's first time aboard a cruise ship. For their honeymoon, she and Robert had taken a Mediterranean cruise from Venice to Istanbul. Robert had enjoyed the trip so much that he was instantly converted into a lover of cruises and displayed the same brand of childish wonder Americans tend to express when they take an interest in something. In fact, Kate was curious if perhaps his interest in the *Valkyrie* had begun there.

On that particular trip their ship had been identical to the ill-fated *Costa Concordia*, an enormous, modern-style cruise ship that was a cross between a hotel, water park, and Las Vegas casino. Kate had greatly enjoyed the cruise and all the attendant luxurious comforts. Robert had splurged, booking a suite for the two of them. Those days on board had been magical, golden times, though she was fully aware of the hollow, shallow splendor so often associated with cruises. Like props on stage—rocks made of cardboard and the glitz of tinsel on the high seas.

Nevertheless, the *Valkyrie*'s interior did not look like any other cruise ship Kate had ever seen. Every last detail was a re-creation from the ship of the 1930s. Everything was decorated in art deco style. The furniture appeared to be excellent reproductions of the original furniture from that era. At least that was what Kate thought until she passed by a table on the terrace. She found, to her great surprise, that they were not reproductions at all.

Feldman had been watching her. "Nearly 80 percent of the furniture and decor you see here consists of original pieces," he said. "Much of it comes from the *Valkyrie* itself. When they converted it into a warship, they emptied out everything and sent the contents to a warehouse in Scotland. I found them and purchased everything nearly twenty years ago. My experts have restored everything in its original place, using original photos that survived the war as a guide."

Kate nodded, impressed by how Feldman had not spared a single expense or compromised any of the details. A lamp screwed into one of the tables on the terrace caught her eye. She was no antiques expert, but she was certain that one little piece had to be worth thousands of dollars, and there were hundreds of objects like that throughout the *Valkyrie*. It was extraordinary.

"After you've settled in and had a chance to relax in your cabin, I'd like you to come to a scheduled meeting to meet the rest of the team," Feldman said. "We have a fairly small crew for this voyage since we have no passengers. While we won't have many companions for the voyage, you'll find at least they're interesting."

It was then that Kate noticed Moore, the head of Feldman's security team, board the *Valkyrie* with a dozen other men. They were loading heavy wooden crates, and even from that distance, Kate could tell the crates held guns and ammunition.

"Is that really necessary?" she asked, pointing at the men.

"You can never take too many precautions, Kate," Feldman replied and motioned her to walk with him. "I don't expect any problems, but we'd be idiots not to prepare ourselves."

Problems? Prepared for what? Questions piled up in Kate's mind, but for the moment, she chose to keep them to herself.

They came to an entryway and walked into a wide, softly lit hallway. The carpet on the floor was blood colored, and music floated in the background. They had to step aside a few times to let Feldman's personnel pass as they were busy stowing the equipment and putting the final touches on the ship before departure. In some places it still smelled like fresh paint and sawdust. The deck shook slightly. Somewhere in the bowels of the ship enormous diesel engines had rumbled to life. The *Valkyrie* was ready to cast off.

"This is the entry to first class," Feldman explained as he stepped aside to let two crewmen carrying wine pass. "At the moment, the second- and third-class sections have not been restored. We'll be stowing supplies on those levels instead of in the original cargo hatches as they are still sealed."

"I thought you had renovated the entire ship," Kate said as she took pictures of the cigar lounge.

"I will," answered Feldman defensively. "But there hasn't been enough time to prepare all the details before our trip. Not if we want to stay on schedule."

Kate nodded even though she had no idea what he was talking about. She figured he would explain everything more thoroughly at the meeting. In the meantime, she kept snapping pictures.

Next, they entered a wide oval-shaped room that was absolutely breathtaking. A giant crystal chandelier cast a blinding array of sparkles throughout the room. The marble and oak staircase that Kate recognized from one of Carroll's stories rose before them. The stairs were etched with "KDF" and the name of the ship. The eagles that stood at the foot of the stairs had spread wings, and each one held a laurel wreath in its talons, but the center was empty, devoid of the swastikas. The Nazi flags that had once decorated the main landing of the staircase were also missing, replaced by an enormous palmlike plant that made for a strange contrast.

"They destroyed the staircase when the ship was converted. The marble and oak were excellent quality but were marred by the Nazi themes." Feldman laughed. "Thanks to the pictures in the shipyard's archive, we've been able to make a faithful reconstruction, minus the swastikas. There isn't a single one on board the entire ship."

"I thought it was supposed to be a faithful reconstruction?"

"It is. Nearly everything is exactly the same as when the ship was found at sea, more than seventy years ago. In fact, practically everything here is original. We've had to renovate only a few things that were damaged over time, like the staircase. In the process we eliminated the swastikas."

"I see."

"We haven't done it just because Nazi imagery is banned here in Germany and we happen to be in Hamburg," Feldman continued. "I'm Jewish, and on my ship I will not have a single swastika, unless—" Feldman cut himself off.

Before Kate could ask what he meant, an older woman, perhaps in her fifties, entered wearing a classic maid's outfit with her hair in a bun. She glared at them over her beak-like nose.

"I thought you'd never get here," she said. "From the minute those scientists stepped on board, all they've done is whine. 'My room is too dark, or too sunny, or too hot, or too cold.' It's like they were born to complain, Isaac."

Isaac? A smile crept across Kate's lips. The woman was the first person who was not afraid of the almighty Isaac Feldman. In fact, he seemed uncomfortable in front of her.

"Mrs. Miller has been Feldman's housekeeper for over thirty years," Senka whispered from behind. Her mouth was right next to Kate's ear, close enough that she felt Senka's warm breath drift over the back of her neck, causing a sudden surge of hostility. "She's the only person who dares to call him by his first name. Sometimes they even get into shouting matches."

"Are they lovers?" Kate asked curiously.

"It's rumored they used to be years ago," Senka answered in a seductive voice. "But I don't think they are anymore. He respects her, though."

"Kate." Feldman turned toward the two whispering women with the look of a man who was trying to outrun a pack of wolves and had suddenly found a tree to climb up. "Mrs. Miller will take you to your cabin. Senka will accompany you down to the Gneisenau Room at noon sharp. Our first meeting will take place there. I strongly suggest you stay in your cabin in the meantime. There are still areas on board undergoing renovation, and I wouldn't want you to wander into danger. It's for your personal safety."

"Should I ask Moore to leave one of those rifles for me?" asked Kate. "For my personal safety, you know?"

"Please don't be angry, Kate. As soon as we're at sea, you're welcome to wander throughout the *Valkyrie*. But we're still trying to close off all of the dangerous areas, and I wouldn't want you to suffer an accident before we leave."

Kate was certain that Feldman was lying to her again. But she kept quiet. It was not the time to pick a fight, especially with Senka and Mrs. Miller standing right there, watching her closely.

"All right, Feldman. See you at noon then."

Kate followed Mrs. Miller down another hallway until they reached an elevator that looked straight out of a museum. To enter it, the outside gate had to be opened by hand. The inside was lined with velvet. Along the back wall was a bench where a weary traveler could rest during the short ride.

"It looks magnificent," said Mrs. Miller in a friendly tone, "but it's slower than a snail. This elevator gives you time to get old, and that's just in the time it takes to move past the three floors in first class."

"What about in second and third class? Are there elevators?" asked Kate.

"I'm not sure." Mrs. Miller shrugged. "I've never been down below. Only a few have, but workers are sealing the entrances to those areas until they're ready to be reopened. From what I've heard, though, the mess deck in third class doesn't have an elevator. And I think the elevator for second class doesn't work. It hasn't been used for seventy years, you know?"

After what felt like an eternity, the elevator stopped with a tremble, and Mrs. Miller opened the gate. They stepped into a hallway not unlike the one they had come from, only the carpet was blue and imprinted with "KDF." There were at least twenty doors along the walls.

"First class used to be quite small on this ship," Mrs. Miller explained as they walked along. "Three floors with a total of forty-five cabins and eight suites. They're quite roomy." They stopped at a door with a golden plaque that read "Room 23." "This is your room."

She opened the door. Kate held back a gasp of astonishment. The room looked like it had been modeled after an old, elegant black-and-white movie. The wide queen-sized bed was covered by an antique bedspread, and the walls were lined with inlaid teakwood. Art deco lamps sat on the nightstands. A splendid

Persian rug covered the floor. The sun shone through two windows. The room was made complete by a sofa with wide arms, an end table with stationery, and a mahogany dresser that had to be worth a fortune.

"It's beautiful," Kate said, taking note of the lack of a television or telephone. Nothing to remind her of the twenty-first century. There was only one ancient-looking outlet. She wondered if the voltage would be the proper amount to plug in her laptop without getting a shock.

"You haven't seen the best part yet," Mrs. Miller said with a smile.

She opened up a sliding door and revealed the bathroom. Kate covered her mouth. Along the wall closest to her was an enormous sink with ornate brass faucets set below a mirror. In back was a gigantic square bathtub decorated on the bottom with small mosaic tiles, just like the colorful ones that adorned the walls. The combination reminded her of a Roman bath.

"Enjoy your stay, Miss Kilroy." Mrs. Miller bid Kate adieu with a smile and exited the cabin.

Alone, Kate fell back onto the bed. Kicking her shoes off, she took in her surroundings. The *Valkyrie* was amazing—a piece of history afloat at sea. As she lay there in the sunlight and listened to the voices on the pier, all of the horror stories regarding mysterious disappearances seemed completely ridiculous to her. *Occam's razor,* she repeated. Sunlight beamed through one of the windows, and specks of dust danced in its glow. Exhausted, she closed her eyes and fell right asleep.

A faint vibration woke her up. Her camera, which was on the table, was buzzing on the marble surface. Curious, she got up. The entire cabin floor was shaking. For an instant she experienced something akin to panic. But then she remembered she was aboard a ship. She looked out the window and watched a pair of workers winding up the mooring lines as the pier slowly shrank away.

The ship had cast off. The gangplank had been brought aboard, and now there was nothing tying them to land.

The *Valkyrie* was at sea once again.

X I V

Kate's patience lasted all of twenty minutes. After pacing around her cabin like a caged lioness, she decided to take a little walk. This, of course, meant that she was directly disobeying Feldman's orders, but she figured it would be worth the risk. If she came across anyone, she could explain she needed to take pictures of the *Valkyrie*'s departure for her report, which was actually quite true. Still, she also wanted to wander around to get a better idea of the ship's layout.

She opened the door carefully and poked her head into the hallway. No one was in sight. Briefly, she thought Feldman might have placed a guard at her door for her "security," but it seemed everyone was busy with the ship's departure. She made as little noise as possible as she closed the door behind her and walked down the hall in the direction of what she thought was the bow.

Most of the hallways were deserted, but as she turned a corner she bumped into a couple of Moore's security guards. Recalling how Feldman's men had reacted when they caught her prowling the grounds of Usher Manor, she panicked, but they passed right by her as they chatted and only gave her a brief glance. One of the men even gave her a little nod as if they were old friends.

As soon as they had gone, Kate realized she had been holding her breath. Then, she noticed where the two men had come from.

There was a wide entrance leading to a staircase that wound down into the heart of the *Valkyrie*. The stairs were old and worn compared to the rest of the ship. The varnish had disappeared, and the edges of the steps were scuffed up. Four or five steps down, someone had welded together some heavy sheets of steel into a door that sealed off the staircase. The ugly joints the welders left behind jutted out of the door like lumpy tumors, a stark contrast with the high-quality wood lining the hallway. The guards had placed a red sticker on the door with enormous black lettering:

"Danger!
Area Under Construction
Do Not Enter. Risk Of Fatal Fall"

Kate assumed the staircase led to the unrestored second- and third-class sections. Dubiously, she made her way down the stairs until she reached the makeshift door. The stairs creaked lightly with each step. Kate thought about how the wooden stairs had not been used for more than half a century. She leaned forward and placed her hand on the door.

A gust of cold air ripped through a poorly sealed joint and gave Kate a jolt. The air had come from somewhere down there, and it smelled awful. It was a strange smell, a mixture of dust, stagnant water, and rot. The stench also carried a hint of some metallic odor Kate could not pinpoint. She gently pushed the steel door and felt it budge slightly. The welder had done a rush job, and the steel sheets of the door were joined only at four points. She pushed again, fascinated, trying to figure out what was down there.

Kate . . .

A woman's voice called from behind her. Startled, like a little girl caught in the act of mischief, Kate flinched and turned around, muttering some hurried excuse.

No one was there.

She tiptoed toward the hallway. It was deserted in both directions. She ran around the corner the guards had turned earlier, but no one was there, either. Confused, she retraced her steps back to the staircase. She examined the ceiling to see if there were any security cameras or loudspeakers, but the only thing hanging from the ceiling were the bronze light fixtures, with *Valkyrie* etched into their bases.

She listened closely. All that could be heard was her heavy breathing, the soft buzzing of the hallway lights, and in the background, the dull, distant rumbling of the engines.

But she was certain someone had said her name. She did not like the tone.

It had sounded violent. Dirty.

Needing some fresh air, she walked away from the staircase, feeling stiff.

After a few minutes wandering through the hallways, Kate came to a doorway that led to the walkway along the bow. The gust of fresh air, dense with the smell of the sea and engine smoke, that greeted her upon stepping outside was the most marvelous sensation she had ever felt.

In the distance, some fifty yards away, she could see the silhouette of a tugboat slowly pulling the *Valkyrie* toward open sea. From where she stood she could make out the tugboat's name, *Vintumperio*, and she could even distinguish the shapes of the sailors in red uniforms loafing about on deck. On the poop deck was the captain, a heavyset man with a goatee, and a member of the port authority, who was tall with gray hair. Both were looking back toward the *Valkyrie*, sipping coffee and chatting with one another. Suddenly, Kate had the urge to be with them, among those trustworthy men, and not aboard the *Valkyrie*, with its strange voices and mysterious past.

But it was too late. The North Sea was already visible in the distance. The tugboat released the *Valkyrie* and bid it farewell with two toots of its horn. The tugboat slowly receded into the distance, and finally, they were alone.

Kate leaned on the railing and took a deep breath. The morning was luminous, and out there, it seemed like nothing could go wrong.

What the hell, she thought. *You're on a fucking luxurious cruise ship from the thirties. You're going to write a fucking story, and in the meantime, you're going to drink all the champagne you can and relax in the sun. You're going to stop thinking about Robert and take control of your life once and for all—*

"Kate." A woman's voice startled her from her thoughts, and the blood drained from her face. She spun around like a top, certain nobody would be there, but there stood Senka, staring at her.

"I didn't mean to scare you," she said.

"It's not that. It's . . ." Kate blushed and became quiet.

"It's not wise to disobey a direct order from Feldman." Senka stared at her with a disquieting gleam in her eyes. "He asked you not to leave your cabin."

"It didn't sound like an order to me," Kate replied, holding up her camera. "It sounded more like a suggestion. Plus, I need to take pictures for my story."

"If I were you, I'd follow every single one of Mr. Feldman's suggestions to a T. This ship can be misleading. Even deceitful."

"What do you mean?" The hair on the back of her neck stood on end.

"During these past few weeks on board the *Valkyrie*, strange things have happened. Things that are hard to explain. There have been accidents. Do you believe in ghosts, Kate?"

"No. The truth is I don't," she answered, her heart wrenching in pain as her thoughts turned to Robert. "When someone dies they're gone forever."

"Good," Senka responded with a strange smile. "That which you do not believe can do you no harm, right?" She looked toward the horizon and took a deep breath as if she was collecting her thoughts. "I think you should go back to your cabin. I'll go with you. This time make sure not to leave until the time we agreed on."

"Hopefully, it will be worth the wait."

Senka crinkled her eyes. "Trust me. The meeting is going to blow your mind."

X V

At noon, Kate entered the Gneisenau Room accompanied by Senka. Once more she was in awe. The room looked like a re-creation of an Italian palazzo from the Renaissance. Travertine marble columns rose from floor to ceiling, some fifteen feet in height. On the ceiling an enormous fresco portrayed an ancient Teutonic battle. In another panel, a pair of gigantic Valkyries held a dead warrior while a pair of horsemen brutally stabbed each other.

Between tall venetian windows that looked out over the sea, classical sculptures stood on ornate stands. The floor, made of wood and stone, could barely be seen as several thick, enormous rugs covered it. Stepping on them, Kate thought that if she were to drop a dime, it would probably never be seen again.

Several luxurious couches and chairs were haphazardly spread throughout the room. A huge wooden table with large legs occupied the center of the room, and an enormous, unmoving clock hung on the rear wall right above a grand piano.

The rest of the passengers were sitting around the wooden table. Kate was surprised to see how few there were, perhaps fifteen or twenty people, mostly men. A few of them stood up upon seeing the women enter. The others hardly noticed, too ensconced in passionate conversation.

Feldman sat at the head of the table; Moore was to his left, and there was a vacant chair to his right. Senka led Kate to her seat and, in doing so, kept her hands on Kate's shoulders a little longer than necessary. Then Senka swaggered over to the seat at Feldman's right and sat down, attracting the attention of most of the men.

They were all there. Feldman coughed and the table quieted down. Kate discreetly switched on her tape recorder.

"Ladies, gentlemen," began Feldman in a polite but passionate tone. "Allow me to welcome you to the *Valkyrie*. Before we present anything, I'd like to thank you from the bottom of my heart for accepting my invitation to participate in this voyage."

Several people nodded in recognition of his appreciation.

"First, let's talk about the ship. The *Valkyrie* was built in 1938 by Blohm und Voss, a shipyard in Hamburg. As you may have guessed, there are few ships still sailing from that period. In fact, this is the last survivor of the golden age of 1930s cruise liners. All of its rivals from those times have sunk, been scrapped, or were destroyed during the war. Only the *Valkyrie* has made it to the present day, for reasons you already know." He nodded toward someone at the table. "Mr. Corbett . . ."

Mr. Corbett cleared his throat and stood up.

"My name is William Corbett. I'm the chief engineer . . . ahem . . . the one in charge of general maintenance aboard the *Valkyrie*." He nervously shuffled some papers. "The fact of the matter is the repairs have not been too hard. We'd expected the ship to be in much worse condition, but its time in dry dock seems to have preserved the ship extraordinarily well. The hull had no evident deterioration at all. We found no fissures or cracks that needed repairing."

"That's incredible," muttered one man, who appeared to be of Asian descent.

"We've only had to give it a new coat of paint." Corbett pushed up his glasses, which had slid down his nose.

He reminded Kate of a mechanic explaining why the bill was so high in spite of having done nearly nothing.

"After sixty years covered by canvas and out of the water, the ship was in superb shape," Corbett continued. "Practically like it never went to sea until now."

"Was it difficult to repair the engines?" Kate asked.

Every head at the table swiveled in her direction. Kate felt the blood rise to her cheeks.

"Hi . . . this . . . I'm Kate Kilroy," she stuttered. "I'm documenting the entire voyage and, well . . ."

She saw Feldman smile at her to calm her down. *Do your fucking work, Kate,* she told herself.

"Records from 1939 show that it was impossible to repair the ship's engines." She took a copy of the military record from her purple folder and read aloud:

Both engines present some kind of malfunction that is impossible to identify, both in the ignition and combustion systems. They are absolutely inoperable, and this technical department does not know of any solution or method of repair. We recommend it be scrapped immediately.

She raised her eyes and looked at the engineer. "So I repeat: Was it difficult to repair the engines?"

Corbett looked about, somewhat disconcerted, and then responded, "It was not necessary to repair the engines, Miss Kilroy. Both engines started on the first attempt after we had them fueled up. They weren't damaged. In fact, they were in superb condition."

Hushed whispers swept across the table. A few nodded heartily while others shook their heads in protest.

"The ship's overall condition is quite good considering its age," Corbett went on. "The entrances were sealed after the war and practically nobody had entered the ship for some sixty years. There haven't been any leaks or humidity to speak of, especially in first class, where the temperature seems to have been held at a constant sixty-two degrees Fahrenheit. It's like a gigantic time capsule. Only some areas internally appear to be somewhat worn."

"That's fantastic," Feldman applauded. "How is the renovation going?"

"All of first class, the machine rooms, the bridge, and essential services like the kitchen, laundry, and the infirmary have been completed. However, all of the second- and third-class sections have yet to be restored, in addition to many of the hallways." He shook his head. "Generally speaking, I think we've managed to restore about one-third of the *Valkyrie*, give or take. When we arrive in New York, we can finish what remains."

Voices whirled around the table again.

"Nobody said anything about New York, Feldman," shouted a heavy man with a scraggly beard and a Russian accent. He sat two seats down from Kate. "I don't even have my visa in order."

"Not to worry, Cherenkov," Feldman replied, with a hard tone that silenced the room like a poisonous whip. "I've already taken care of it."

Feldman rose. Every one of them watched him with anticipation.

"Today is August twenty-third," he began. "On the twenty-third of August, nearly eighty years ago, this ship launched its inaugural voyage with two hundred and seventeen passengers and one hundred fifty crew members on board. It departed Hamburg from the exact same dock that we took off from just a few hours ago at the exact same time we did. It launched out into the North Sea just as we did and at the same time we did." He took out an old navigation book and held it up dutifully. "We know all those facts because the ship's logbook was recovered by the crew of the *Pass of Ballaster*, the ship that discovered the *Valkyrie* adrift at sea." He opened the book to a page he had marked and displayed it for all to see. The page was blank. "On August twenty-eighth, five days after departure, the *Pass of Ballaster* found the ship. Not a single crew member or passenger was found on board. The only exception was someone who didn't appear on the list—me."

Kate was hit by a wave of excitement for what he was about to say.

"We're retracing, nearly eighty years later, step by step, the same voyage made by the *Valkyrie*," Feldman exclaimed, quite seriously. "Five days from now, following the same trajectory as recorded in this logbook, we will know once and for all what happened that night back in 1939."

X V I

A flurry of voices swept across the table. Everyone suddenly had something to say. The only ones who kept quiet were Feldman, Moore, and Senka, who scornfully watched as the meeting devolved into pandemonium.

"This is bullshit," a young man proclaimed, smiling like the whole thing was a psychiatry discussion. He was around thirty and seated directly in front of Kate. He had long hair, and his thick-rimmed glasses made him seem somewhat absentminded. Kate was struck by the fact that his floral shirt was adorned with a pin of a cartoon raccoon.

"That's impossible," shouted one woman, who was somewhat older and very stern.

"We should have made the trip with a test ship and no crew," yelled another man, who was sitting next to Kate, looking as if he had just eaten a restaurant out of all its food.

"We're running an enormous risk, Feldman," roared the scraggly bearded man, who had been called Cherenkov, bellowing over everyone with a thunderous voice. "The chances of reproducing the event without a support team—"

"Not to worry, Professor Cherenkov. We'll be counting on a support team." Feldman raised his hands in a conciliatory fashion, and Kate watched in fascination as he once again utilized his unsettling charm. Slowly, the voices around the table hushed. "Now if I may continue."

Everyone listened, intrigued.

"I've spent more than half my life trying to piece together my past. I do not know who I am or where I come from. My story begins on the dance floor two decks below us, some seventy-four years ago. A Jewish boy abandoned in the middle of an empty ship. This ship."

Feldman stood up and placed his hands on the table and leaned forward. Kate was reminded of a feverish messiah leading his flock.

"For years I let those concerns stagnate in my mind. You know my reputation. I dedicated my heart and soul to carving out a place for myself among all the other sharks. There are those who say I'm a mobster." He burst out laughing. "That's nothing but an old wives' tale. I've become rich thanks to the casinos I own in Europe, Asia, and the United States. But I'm no mobster, though I don't mind the reputation," he sighed and became quite serious. "In a way, I should be a happy man. But I've been missing one piece of the puzzle: Who the hell am I, and how the hell did I get here?"

"That's all very well, Mr. Feldman." The man with the floral shirt and the raccoon pin spoke in a soft American accent. "But perhaps it would have been better if you had hired a few private detectives to trace your history instead of wasting a fortune replicating the goddamn scene of the crime, if you'll excuse the expression."

A few soft chuckles could be heard around the table, but they were quickly snuffed out like a bonfire in a rainstorm when Feldman answered.

"I did, Dr. Carter. I did. But your grandparents' generation and their B-17s made damn well sure Hamburg suffered. Every KDF record on file concerning the *Valkyrie* was burned to ashes, along with half the city, in 1943. Nothing survived. All that remained was the ship. This isn't a replica of the crime scene. This is the original scene in every way. Whatever happened, it had to have happened here, between these very walls. We're going to find out what it was."

"Mr. Feldman, I'm a physicist," answered Dr. Harvey Carter as if he were speaking with someone who did not speak English. "A scientist, the same as nearly all of us here at this table. I do not believe in magic or in anything that cannot be explained or proved by the methods of science. Time travel is impossible. If you think we're going to be able to travel back to 1939 in this old ship—"

"I'm not stupid, Dr. Carter." Feldman's poisonous whip cracked again, leaving Carter cowering. "I have no intention of traveling through time. That's impossible."

"Then, what is it? What are we doing here?"

"We're conducting a scientific experiment. Retracing the route step by step. Finding out what could have happened. Gauging the situation and, if possible, trying to understand it. We might discover a clue."

"What if we find nothing?" Kate asked. "What if we get there, and the trip just keeps going without incident?"

Feldman shrugged. "I'll keep trying as many times as necessary," he said. "Either way, you'll have a marvelous story for your newspaper, and I'll be the owner of a 1930s luxury cruise ship with a mysterious past."

Kate immediately understood what he meant. In an age in which all of the cruise ships were clones, enormous white mountains that traversed the seas and were crammed with tourists obsessed with the shows, casinos, and restaurants on board, the *Valkyrie* stood out like a poppy in a weed patch. Delicate and elegant, it recalled the golden era of glamour and luxury. Plus, the shadow of its cursed destiny only intensified its allure.

Kate issued a low whistle. People would come to blows for the honor of boarding this ship. Cruise fanatics would pay huge sums to travel on an authentic 1930s-style cruise. Kate's story in the *London New Herald* would be the perfect promotional piece to attract publicity. Feldman, the great manipulator. She had no doubt he had planned this from the very beginning.

The young physicist, Carter, was not going to give up so easily, however.

"Nothing will happen," he insisted. "Even if we retrace the ship's course under the same conditions, there are a million other variables. We have no way of knowing the reason why everyone aboard the *Valkyrie* disappeared or what the seasonal patterns were like at the time. This will prove completely fruitless, Mr. Feldman. Seriously."

"We've controlled the main variable, Mr. Carter," Feldman replied, "which we believe was the cause of all this."

"The *Valkyrie*," murmured Carter thoughtfully.

"Not exactly."

The walkie-talkie Senka Simovic was wearing on her waist interrupted the conversation. She turned away to listen more closely and then turned to Feldman and whispered something in his ear.

"I have word that our support team has finally arrived," he announced with excitement. "Would you like to step outside a moment to see them? This is an ideal time to take a short break."

They flocked outside to one of the terraces, where there were some potted plants and comfortable lounge chairs. They were on the upper level of the ship, and Kate thought that the command bridge could not have been far away.

They had left land far behind, and in every direction there was nothing but ocean. Not far from the *Valkyrie*, Kate caught sight of a small ship approaching that was painted a vibrant red with two white stripes along its side. When the group appeared on deck, the ship gave two loud toots of its horn to which the *Valkyrie* immediately responded, nearly leaving them deaf.

"The *Mauna Loa*! Our support ship," Feldman shouted over the horns.

"Its design looks familiar," Cherenkov said with a half smile.

"I'll bet it does," replied Senka. "It's an old spy fishing boat that the Soviet Union used in the seventies. From the outside it looks like a harmless tugboat, but the vessel is loaded with radars and other surprising technological devices. We bought it at the end of the nineties for the price of a junker."

"I was on the team that developed some of the electromagnetic-interference gadgets that little ship is carrying," added Cherenkov with a wisp of nostalgia.

Kate could not pull her eyes from the ship. It did not seem like much compared to the *Valkyrie*. As far as support went, it hardly inspired confidence.

Suddenly, a blinding flash appeared on the stern of the *Mauna Loa*. The sound of the explosion reached their ears less than a second later, along with a shock wave. The column of smoke was accompanied by screams coming from members of the crew.

The *Mauna Loa* was jittering like a rabbit being chased by a dog and yawed nearly ninety degrees. Several sailors were running on deck toward the stern, where flames had begun to appear.

"What the hell is going on, Moore?" Feldman asked. "I want to know what's happening right now."

"Right away, Mr. Feldman." Moore grabbed his walkie-talkie and began barking out orders. Minutes later, a dinghy pushed off from the side of the *Valkyrie* with two armed guards aboard. As soon as they touched the surface of the water, they took off like a shot toward the *Mauna Loa*, which was listing badly to starboard. Several men worked furiously to stop the flames from spreading over the stern, filling buckets with water that had flooded the deck.

"Is it going to sink?" asked Kate with apprehension.

One man who was badly hurt had been pulled from below deck. He was bleeding profusely and barely moving. Kate wondered if he would die.

"I don't think so," Senka answered somberly. "If she were going to sink, she would have already. But there must be a hole in the hull. I don't think she can keep pace with us."

They watched as another man was brought up to the deck, covered in burns. Even from that distance it was obvious he had suffered grave injuries.

"The curse of the *Valkyrie*," whispered one man at Kate's side in an accent she couldn't identify. When he realized Kate had heard him, he held out his hand. He was short, husky, and around forty years old, and his upper lip bore a mustache of Homeric proportions. "I'm Will Paxton. Geologist and specialist in underwater formations. But I'm afraid that won't be much use to those aboard the *Mauna Loa* right now."

"There's no curse," grumbled Senka, waving her walkie-talkie. "It was sabotage. Someone planted a bomb on the *Mauna Loa*."

XVII

Upon hearing the word *bomb,* Moore began shouting orders like crazy. Before they knew it, a dozen armed guards surrounded the passengers and directed them toward the interior of the *Valkyrie.* A few of them protested with the same annoyance of a passerby being asked to leave the scene of a horrific traffic accident, but most obeyed immediately. Kate took a few rushed photos before she returned inside as well.

Moore was on the verge of a fitful rage. His pupils had shrunk down to the size of two tiny black marbles as he kept issuing orders. He approached his boss and relayed a piece of information that caused Feldman to nod gravely.

"Attention." Moore raised his voice. "This is an emergency. Return to your cabins while we run a security check on board the ship. Don't move until we advise differently. Exiting your cabin is strictly forbidden until we say otherwise. Anyone who disobeys will be removed from the ship, after having some quality time alone with me."

"Look, buddy," said Carter, the American with a lazy Southern accent, as he listened nonchalantly. "You don't have to show such poor manners. It's not like we've signed up for the army, so far as I know."

Moore cast a furious look at him. Carter, indifferent, proceeded to wipe his glasses with the edge of his shirt, unperturbed. He thoroughly cleaned them before holding them up to the light with an expression of impatience before bringing them down to wipe them again. Finally satisfied, he put them back on.

"Since I've been on board I've spent more time locked up in my cabin than out of it. The last time I looked at my passport I was a free citizen. I think, at the very least, we deserve an explanation."

Moore approached Carter until their noses were nearly touching. The Brit was a mountain of muscle and a head taller than the American. Still, Carter seemed unflustered.

"Listen to me," said Moore, his voice raspy and threatening. "This is not an invitation or a suggestion. It's an order. Anyone unwilling to go freely back to their room will be escorted back by two of my men. You have ten minutes. It's your choice."

Without another word he turned to Senka and left the Gneisenau Room followed by three of his men.

The fifteen passengers looked at each other, confused and disoriented. They had left Hamburg barely five hours ago, and it was already beginning to seem less and less like an eccentric indulgence.

Feldman walked toward them in silence, and Kate caught a hint of worry on his face. It was a tiny inkling, no more than a light shadow, yet it was the first crack in the hard granite shell he had erected to keep his feelings from being exposed. This scared Kate. If Feldman was worried, the situation had to be serious.

"I beg you to listen to Mr. Moore," he said in a conciliatory fashion. "At times he can be quite curt, but he knows what he's doing."

"What's going on, Feldman?" asked Kate. Somehow, she had become the spokesperson for the entire group. *Let the reporter do the talking* seemed to be the common sentiment.

"An object has exploded in the engine room on the *Mauna Loa*, and at least two crew members are dead and one is seriously injured. The ship has also suffered serious damage and is drifting as we speak. We think someone may have infiltrated her while we were docked in Hamburg. If so, they could have planted a bomb with a timer set to explode at sea. Worse yet, in spite of all our security, there is still a chance someone has planted a bomb aboard the *Valkyrie* as well."

A hushed panic swept through the group. Almost by instinct, they huddled closer together.

Kate and Feldman locked eyes. The incident with the SUV, the death of Carroll, and now the explosion. Someone definitely did not want the *Valkyrie* project to move forward.

"We need to talk," Kate said in a voice low enough that only Feldman heard.

"We will." Feldman nodded. "But for now, please return to your cabin."

Kate turned around and walked inside. As she entered she gestured toward Carter. The American, who seemed like the rebellious type, reluctantly followed Kate. The rest of the group, like lost sheep, crowded together and babbled to each other as they followed orders.

"What are we doing?" the physicist whispered as they walked down the hallway together. "If there's a bomb, it could be anywhere."

Kate gave no response and continued walking. Eventually, she turned to Carter and gave a sly smile.

"You were brave back there with Moore. Almost reckless," she said.

"I don't stand for bullies."

Kate smiled as she recalled the scene. Moore could have whipped him like a wet dog, but Carter had not been scared. Or, at least, he had not let it show.

"Feldman's right. Moore as well, in his way," Kate finally said. "If someone has planted a bomb somewhere, they could have only done so in the restored areas. The rest of the ship has been sealed off since we left, and before that only Feldman's most trusted confidants were allowed on board. If we're not getting in the way like drunken ducks, Moore and his men can finish the search sooner."

Carter chewed on something while he mulled over Kate's thoughts. Finally, he nodded.

"So what's Feldman got up his sleeve, then?" the physicist asked. "Do you know something he hasn't told the rest of us?"

"No," she answered, thinking of Carroll.

Carter grinned. "Hey, you're all right, Kate Kilroy. I suppose that's because you're the only one who doesn't look at Feldman like he's Zeus. Or perhaps I should say Yahweh?" he said with a chuckle.

"He does command a certain reverence, I'll agree with you there," Kate answered with a smile. "What can you tell me about yourself and all these people, Carter?"

"I really don't know much about what's going on here. Two weeks ago I was working as a physics professor in Georgia when someone called and asked if I'd be willing to participate in a scientific expedition. Of course, I agreed. They're paying me a small fortune for a two-week voyage, but they haven't filled me in on anything else. I think all the others are in the same boat." Carter laughed at his pun as he pointed a thumb back at the rest of the team. "There are astrophysicists, mathematicians, a geologist, two meteorologists, and even a guy I think I've seen on TV before. Everyone here is blind. Nobody knows much except Cherenkov. He's in charge."

"Cherenkov?" Kate turned around to look at the Russian, who was conversing with another scientist and waving his arms about wildly. "Why him?"

"He's the only one who is up to speed on Feldman's master plan. He recommended all of us and recruited this team. I guarantee this is no easy team to unite. I've heard of several of these scientists and their reputations. I'd bet anything they haven't left their laboratories for anything less than a fortune."

"But what exactly is the project?"

The pair had arrived in the hallway where their cabins were located. The guards, looking nervous, were urging everyone to get in their rooms as quickly as possible.

"I'm not sure," answered Carter just before stepping into his cabin. "But I'd bet the farm it has something to do with the Cherenkov Singularity."

"The *what* Singularity?" asked Kate, but Carter had already closed his door.

X V I I I

Kate entered her cabin with unanswered questions whirling in her mind. As she took her shoes off and let her hair down, she tried to put together what facts she had: the *Valkyrie*, its scientific research team, the unknown person who had tried to kill everyone.

The voice she had heard in the hallway.

The memory spread through her mind like poison ivy, but she pushed it out as soon as it entered. It had not happened. The tension, the idea of being aboard a haunted ship, the nerves. There were a million possible explanations. Occam.

She sat down on the bed. For ten minutes she sat without taking her eyes from the same point on the carpet. Her thoughts explored what had happened so far that day.

She decided a bath would do her good. She went to the huge bathtub and turned on the water. It rushed out from the bronze faucets. After only a few seconds, the bathroom had filled with steam, making the place look like an ancient and decadent hot spring bath.

She dipped into the water and gave a slight gasp. The steam traced strange shapes in the air. Kate closed her eyes, relaxed.

She noticed how the small ceramic tiles pressed into her butt without being uncomfortable. To her right was a large jar of bath salts. She took a handful and sprinkled the crystals into the water. Immediately, a delicious fragrance permeated the entire room. She closed her eyes again and sank back into the cozy little spa she had created for herself. She breathed deeply, satisfied.

But then something almost imperceptible crept in. Kate nearly overlooked it and continued relaxing, but underneath the smell of the bath salts stirred a much more subtle scent. Something metallic and oily.

Boom.

Kate sat up in the bathtub, completely alert. The door separating the bathroom from the bedroom was slightly ajar, exactly as she had left it. Steam flowed out of the cracks of the doorway and swirled lazily through the air. Someone was moving on the other side of the door, dragging something heavy. Then, she heard a dull thump as if someone were fluffing the biggest pillow in the world. She heard a peculiar and labored breathing. Almost like a death rattle—deep, desperate gasps and quick panting, over and over. Kate shivered as her skin sprouted goose bumps.

Sitting in the bathtub completely naked, she could hear her heart pounding as adrenaline rushed through her body. Someone was in her cabin.

Or something, Kate. Or something.

She looked around for something that could act as a weapon. She grabbed the heavy ceramic bath salt jar and tried to stand up in silence. As she rose, a small splash of water betrayed her movement. The noise on the other side of the door ceased. Kate cursed herself. Without bothering to cover herself, she slowly tiptoed toward the door. Her skin felt like it was receiving an electric shock.

She quietly placed her hand on the door and then burst forth, wielding the ceramic jar over her head.

Nobody was there. Even so, an icy knot formed inside her stomach.

The room was absolute chaos. Her suitcase had been moved from the sofa and placed beside the desk. The bed was unmade as if some angry person had torn off the sheets and then decided to repeatedly stab the mattress with a large knife in a mad effort to remove all of its stuffing. A pillow was at her feet. Kate picked it up and discovered, much to her horror, that it was soaked in some foul-smelling liquid. There was a dark mud-like stain all over the back of the sofa, which had also been gutted like the mattress.

Kate suddenly felt very vulnerable standing there naked. Without turning around she stepped slowly back into the bathroom as her heart struggled to leap out of her chest. Once inside she grabbed a towel and covered her body.

Easy, Kate. Go into the hallway. Call security. Be quick.

She walked back into her cabin ready to rush through, but she stopped, aghast. Her knees shook, and the blood drained from her face.

"This isn't possible. It can't be."

The bed was made without a single wrinkle. The upholstery on the sofa was immaculate, and her suitcase was back where she had placed it hours ago. Feeling as if she were trapped in a dream, she went to the bed and uncovered the pillows.

They were all dry. Completely, utterly dry.

She felt dizzy.

I know what I saw. I am not crazy.

She walked around her cabin feeling numb, like a bag of cotton was stuck between her ears. Her eyes jumped about erratically in search of some clue. She realized she was still holding the ceramic jar. She shivered and knew it had been no dream.

She began to hyperventilate. Something had been there with her in that cabin. Standing on the threshold between the bedroom and the bathroom, she turned back and forth over and over again, feeling more scared each time.

Two loud bangs sounded, and Kate dropped the jar to the floor and screamed. The banging became louder, more urgent.

Only then did she realize she had a caller at the door. Voices could be heard in the hall.

Knees aquiver and trying to regulate her breath, Kate wrapped the towel tighter around her body and opened the door. It was Senka accompanied by one of Moore's guards.

"I hope I'm not interrupting," said Senka, tossing back her blonde hair and giving a sly smile as she noticed Kate was only wearing a towel. "We're just doing a quick inspection of all the cabins. It will only take a minute."

They barged in without asking permission. While the guard methodically took inventory of the entire room, Kate sat on the sofa with her legs crossed, clutching the towel closer to her skin and trying to keep from shivering.

"Are you all right, Kate?" asked Senka. "You look pale."

Kate shook her head and muttered yes. She did not want them to think she was crazy. But she wasn't quite sure of her state of mind.

"I take it that's your luggage?" Senka pointed to Kate's unopened suitcase sitting on the sofa. "I need to inspect it. Do you mind?"

Kate shook her head. All she wanted was for them to get out as quickly as possible.

Senka opened and began pushing Kate's belongings to one side. When she got to her underwear, she paused before a smile began to show at the corner of her lips.

"This is quite seductive," Senka said, holding a tiny black thong with red trim. "Is all of your underwear like this?"

Kate shook her head, feeling nervous. She had no interest in playing games.

"What's this?" Senka asked, stiffly holding up the urn that contained Robert's ashes.

"That's my husband," answered Kate. "What's left of him."

"Do you always travel with your husband's ashes?" Senka looked at her in disbelief as she undid the top to have a look inside. A puff of ashes was sucked out and floated down to the carpet, leaving a small gray mark on the design.

"Put the urn down. Now." Kate's voice was glacial. But underneath, the fury was so intense that Senka's playful expression melted into an uncomfortable grimace.

Watching Senka with fiery eyes, Kate's temples were pounding. All the panic and fear she had felt only minutes before were boiling into a rage that made her want to rip out someone's throat. Barely thinking, she walked toward Senka and yanked the urn from her hands. Her towel nearly came loose from doing so, but her wrath was such that she hardly noticed.

"Don't play games with this," Kate hissed, "or you'll regret you ever met me. That's your only warning."

Senka took a step back. She had a strange gleam in her eyes. It was a mixture of fear and respect. Maybe even excitement. "Kitten's got claws," she finally said. "I'll have to keep that in mind."

The guard who had accompanied Senka poked his head out of the bathroom door and shook his head. The inspection was done.

"It's been a pleasure, as always. See you soon," Senka said and raised an eyebrow.

As soon as they were gone, Kate shut the door. She shook with rage. Tears welled up in her eyes, but she was determined not to cry. With trembling hands she placed the urn containing Robert's ashes on the table and kneeled down on the rug, trying to recover the tiny amount that had spilled out. There was so little that she could hardly pick it up. Sweeping her hands over the floor for a second time, Kate lost the majority between the rug's fibers, leaving behind a dirty streak in the fabric.

Plop, plop. The first two tears fell like drops of rain. Then, slowly, the rain became a storm, and Kate tried to break free from all the pain and fear she was carrying deep within her. Once again she felt terribly alone.

X I X

The inspection of the ship took longer than Kate expected. Mrs. Miller, hair in a bun, came to her room after some time. She was accompanied by a server pushing a meal cart. Kate tried to exchange pleasantries with Mrs. Miller, but all she got in return was a warm smile and the promise that "this little fuss" would be over shortly. Kate didn't believe a single word of it, especially since the waiter pushing the cart had a holstered gun hidden beneath his white uniform. He looked tenser than a taut bowstring.

Kate still felt edgy and disoriented after the earlier events. She had searched the room top to bottom—even after Senka's little inspection—but found nothing that could explain what she'd seen.

What had happened?

Kate was certain it hadn't been a dream. The jar of bath salts, her wet footprints on the rug—it had all been real. But she was still trying to work out which parts were fantasy and which were not. No answers came to her.

Night had arrived. In the circle of light surrounding the ship, she could still make out the whitecaps that frothed up all around the *Valkyrie*. Beyond that, darkness.

Someone knocked on her door. A uniformed crew member handed her an envelope. Kate watched him knock on other doors along the corridor. Several passengers lingered in the hallway with a look of boredom or fatigue while others were half-asleep. All of them, however, had one of the envelopes in hand.

Kate opened hers. It was a formal invitation to attend dinner that night. The card included the KDF logo in the corner, minus the swastika, of course, and a beautiful sketch of the *Valkyrie*. In the middle, written in elegant German, was the menu. As Kate read through it, she deduced that the menu had to be the same as the one offered the first night of the *Valkyrie*'s inaugural voyage. Feldman was attentive to detail.

She glanced around at the other guests in the hallway. She immediately wondered if one of them might have also had a similar experience to hers. If someone had, would the passenger be willing to say anything? She studied each person. Most acted relieved to see an end to the confinement, but a few just looked groggy. None of them had the appearance of having seen anything unusual during the last few hours.

She would talk to Carter. The talkative physicist would be able to help her, of that she was sure.

She checked the time and cursed. Dinner was in half an hour. She would have to hurry to get ready. She used only a minimal amount of makeup but made an effort to style her hair. She wanted to look attractive without looking like she was dressed up for a cocktail party. Truth be told, she had no idea what was on the agenda that evening. As she was doing her hair, she began thinking, somewhat cynically, about all the gala society dinners she used to cover just a few weeks ago. How different things were now.

Ten minutes later she found herself strutting down the hall accompanied by two middle-aged chemists who were thrilled to escort a beautiful young woman to dinner. Trying to impress her, they battled each other in a game of witticisms. But all Kate wanted was to be alone.

Each new hallway they passed through elicited renewed gasps of awe. Luxury and good taste were on full display everywhere on the *Valkyrie*. Its original designers had conceived the ship, or at least first class, as a great neoclassical mansion in which passengers would be able to mingle and dine in a refined atmosphere. The gaming floor equipped with roulette and card tables, the cigar lounge, the library and all its books—every space was incredible. Kate stopped to peruse the shelves in the library and found that they had replaced the original books with newer ones. There were tons of bestsellers and a selection of magazines and newspapers from that very day.

She was unsurprised to find a couple of copies of the *London New Herald* among the many newspapers in half a dozen languages. Still, as much as she looked, she could not find a single copy of *Mein Kampf* or any of the other books that had first occupied the shelves. Apparently, Feldman's rigorous adherence to historical accuracy had its limits.

Finally, they entered the dining room by crossing the great hall and ascending its beautiful balustrade staircase. To Kate, it was thrilling. She knew she was entering the same hall Carroll and his shipmates had entered several decades before. They had crossed those same floors in the dark, only to find a vast, empty ship and a baby abandoned in the middle of the dance floor.

Kate and her two companions were the last to arrive. The rest of the guests were already seated around cocktail tables in the back of the hall, near the bandstand, sipping drinks. In another corner Kate could see a table already set for some twenty diners; the cutlery and china sparkled underneath the lights. The delicious aroma of roasted fish wafted around the room, and Kate's stomach growled with hunger.

Feldman greeted her amiably, but he was engrossed in conversation with Cherenkov. The Russian gesticulated wildly as he spoke and, on occasion, sent little pearls of spit flying at Feldman's jacket. Enthralled by what Cherenkov was saying, Feldman paid no attention.

"Kate!"

She turned around to see Carter signaling her from his table. He was sitting with Paxton, the geologist with the epic mustache. She excused herself from her two escorts and walked toward their table.

"Please allow me to say that you are the loveliest lady on board," Paxton said with a slight bow.

Kate loved his deliberately antiquated style. She smiled and pointed to Senka, who was standing in a corner alone, her blue-green eyes narrowed as she watched everyone like a wolf near a chicken coop.

"I think she's much prettier than me," Kate said. "She could be a model."

Paxton shook his head, aggrieved. "She is also lovely, no doubt, but I do not believe she wants much to do with me. We do not play on the same team, unfortunately."

"What do you mean?" Kate asked, confused.

"I believe Mr. Paxton is referring to the fact that Senka is a lesbian, Kate," Carter chimed in, laughing. "I figured you already knew."

"Oh!" Kate stuttered and blushed. At times she lacked the social skills necessary to avoid embarrassing moments like this.

"Well, either way, that is a very kind thing of you to say, Mr. Paxton."

"Either way, he's just telling it like it is," added Carter, enjoying Kate's discomfort more than anyone.

"How was the afternoon for you two?" Kate asked. "Have you noticed anything strange in your cabins?"

Carter and Paxton exchanged glances and shrugged.

"No," they responded nearly in unison.

"Actually, I slept the afternoon away," Paxton said.

"I was on my laptop going over one of my students' thermodynamics projects," Carter said. "Actually, I can't remember if I finished or not. I must have fallen asleep as well. A room with no TV or radio can become somewhat tiresome."

Kate was about to share her experiences with them when dinner was announced.

Fuck, Kate. Get your act together. You've got to tell someone what you saw, or you'll go crazy. That is, if you're not already crazy.

There were no assigned seats, so everyone began sitting down in the groups they'd already formed during cocktails. Kate was about to take a seat next to Carter and Paxton when Feldman motioned for her to sit by him. She gave her companions, who looked quite disappointed, an amusing look before walking over to join the expedition leader.

"How's the *Valkyrie* treating you, Kate?" Feldman asked as she sat down.

"I haven't had much time to see it. But I must say it's a spectacular ship. There's nothing like it in the world."

"Indeed. Of that, I am certain." Feldman took a sip of his wine and looked thoroughly satisfied.

"You still owe me an explanation, Feldman. About the bombs. And Carroll. You know who's behind it all, don't you?"

Feldman nodded thoughtfully before taking an enthusiastic bite of the tuna appetizer. "I will tell everyone when the time is right, after dinner."

Famished, Kate resigned herself to eating. She saw that nearly a third of the diners, including Carter, were vegetarians and had received special meals.

As they ate, the conversation around the table was light and entertaining, but in that superficial, nervous way typical of an elevator. Everyone was anxious to finish what they had started earlier that day. Everyone wanted answers.

When Feldman proposed an after-dinner coffee in the dance hall, everyone agreed, relieved. The diners rose from their seats nearly in unison and left behind half-finished desserts.

As Kate walked in, it was clear to her that Feldman had considered the moment very carefully. Apart from a round table surrounded by comfortable chairs for everyone, someone had placed a podium beside a big screen. A projector was humming. On the table, a gadget that reminded Kate of a cross was set between a satellite telephone and a computer.

They all took their seats and waited as Feldman went to the podium. Giving a half smile and exuding energetic confidence, he began his speech.

"Good evening. I hadn't planned to have us meet so late. But considering what happened earlier, I think you'll understand."

A murmur of assent swept around the room. *Feldman's animal magnetism in action again,* thought Kate, intrigued to see what he had in store for them.

"First, a brief explanation of what happened this morning. Everything was an unfortunate accident. After sending out a team of technicians, we have confirmation from Hamburg that the explosion in the *Mauna Loa*'s engine room was accidental. A worn-out pressure valve burst and caused the short circuit that sparked the fire. The engine on that ship was more than thirty years old. It would seem that quality control wasn't everything it could have been back then. I've been told corrosion of the steel in the engines is to blame." He looked down at some papers before continuing. "This is a problem not uncommon of old Soviet ships."

Kate listened to him in amazement, unable to believe what she was hearing. Feldman was blatantly lying. She had seen the fire from the explosion. She was no expert on the matter, but she was certain the fire had not been caused by a steam valve bursting. She furtively glanced around to see the majority of the scientists breathing a sigh of relief upon hearing there was no terrorist in their midst. Only Carter looked as dubious as Kate did.

"Our inspection of the *Valkyrie* has confirmed that we run no risk aboard this ship." Feldman was cut off by a wave of applause.

Cherenkov stood up. "I believe I speak for all of us when I say thank you for your efforts in keeping us safe. Now we can begin work on our project as soon as possible."

"Certainly, Professor," answered Feldman, "we shall not waste another second. Lights, please."

The lights in the room dimmed. The projector turned on, and a black-and-white image of the *Valkyrie* popped up on-screen.

X X

"On the twenty-eighth of August in 1939, at 4:57 a.m., this ship, the *Valkyrie*, was found adrift in the middle of the ocean at approximately 53 degrees, 94 minutes and 17 seconds latitude north, 18 degrees, 47 minutes and 15 seconds longitude west. We don't know the exact position because the crew that found the ship logged the position a few hours after the fact. I'm guessing they were too busy trying not to keel over in awe."

A surge of laughter swelled throughout the room, and Feldman went on.

"I know I'm not saying anything new when I say there were no passengers on board except me. Everyone knows that. But although it may seem quite strange, the *Valkyrie* is not an isolated instance. It's not even a first. Such an event has happened before. Many times, in fact."

The projector clicked and a map of the world appeared, showing dozens of red dots throughout the oceans of the world.

"Since the dawn of recorded history, tons of ships have been documented as disappearing and reappearing without the crew aboard. Herodotus, the ancient Greek historian, recorded three different cases in his writings. He calls them the 'ships without a soul.' Strabo, Pliny, Agricola, Manetho—dozens of writers and historians of antiquity reference the obscure histories of ships found adrift. Often, they are missing no cargo, there are no signs of violence or damage, and the crew has vanished. If we look at sources from China, India, or Japan, we find the same phenomena. The history of 'ships without a soul' is found throughout ancient texts from the Old World."

"I suppose each and every one of those cases has an explanation." Carter's voice sounded from the darkness.

"Many of them do, no doubt. Pirate attacks, epidemics, ships overturned during storms, human error. The possible causes are numerous. But there's something important that distinguishes the case of the *Valkyrie*."

Feldman pressed a button. On-screen, old manuscripts in several languages flashed by in between images of old ships. Galleys, galleons, liburnas, and xebecs cast their glow across Feldman's face. Kate was reminded uncomfortably of a dark wizard conjuring up shadows that should be left alone. Shadows capable of destroying a room and leaving it new again.

"The problem with ancient sources is that they are often incomplete and imprecise. Historians tend to adorn cases like these, anomalies as they like to call them, with epic or death-defying backstories. Finding the real story behind something cloaked in so much folklore and legend has proven exhausting. Fortunately, we've found a team willing to work on the case for the past three years."

Feldman took a sip of water and continued.

"Throughout the centuries, these cases have occurred again and again. It's even been partially documented how, in 1660, five galleons from the Spanish treasure fleet suddenly vanished, only to be found adrift a week later with the cargo untouched but no signs of the crew. Only the cats and dogs remained on board."

"That's fascinating," Kate interrupted. "I grew up in Spain, and I don't remember ever hearing that story, not even in school. That story's strange enough to be known."

"Two English vessels were the ones to discover the ships," Feldman said. "At that time, England and Spain had just finished thirty years of war, and the British throne had no interest in letting the rest of the world know that they had captured five ships laden with gold that didn't really belong to them. So they covered it up. Only later do we learn anything about this event from inquiries made by the British Admiralty."

Carter mumbled something unintelligible. Kate was only able to make out the word *fantasies* and couldn't help but smile in spite of his bad mood.

The next image to flash up was a brigantine. The ship had two masts and looked graceful with its British flag fluttering off the stern.

"Eventually, we get to the nineteenth century, and the cases begin to be documented more properly. This here is the *Mary Celeste*."

Kate was taken aback. She knew the name of this ship.

"This is possibly the most famous ghost ship. Arthur Conan Doyle wrote a short story about it. On the fifth of November in 1872, she sets sail from New York with a crew of seven. Captain Briggs is accompanied by his wife and their two-year-old daughter. Seemingly, the voyage begins without a hitch. Yet, a month later, another ship called the *Dei Gratia* finds the *Celeste* in the middle of the Atlantic Ocean under full sail. The captain of the *Dei Gratia* becomes suspicious when, after two hours of observation, nobody appears on deck. Thus, he decides to send a crew out to investigate. They find that, despite the ship being in full working order and missing none of its original cargo, nobody is on board. The last entry made in the logbook is from a week prior, yet they find a hot meal on the table, just like on the *Valkyrie*."

A wave of murmurs swirled around the table. Cherenkov was nodding and looking serious. Feldman took the opportunity to go to his next slide. It was another ship, this time a photograph.

"February 28, 1855. The *James B. Chester* is found adrift in the middle of the Atlantic with all of its cargo intact and fully seaworthy. Only the compass and the ship's log are missing. The crew's belongings are piled at the base of the masts. No life rafts are missing, and there are no signs of violence. Its crew is never heard from again."

A new picture. This time, a steamship.

"Bahamas, 1905. A little more than thirty years before the incident of the *Valkyrie*. A merchant ship called *Rossini* is found sailing adrift with its boilers off and no one on board. Its cargo of wines, fruits, and silk is untouched. The only things alive are the cat, a handful of chickens, and a pair of starving canaries. The ship had been derelict for nearly two weeks."

A new image flashed up of another smaller cargo ship.

"An even more striking anomaly crops up just a few years before that incident. The ship you see here on-screen is the *Ellen Austin*. She's sailing near where they found the *Valkyrie* when she came across a three-masted schooner. Captain Weyland of the *Ellen Austin* sends a search crew out to investigate the schooner. They find no one alive on board, and yet the ship is unspoiled. Still, they are unable to locate the ship's logbook, the captain's log, or anything specifying the ship's name or its place of origin.

"Forty-eight hours later, as they are sailing in tandem toward Gibraltar, a thick fog bank envelops both ships." Feldman raised his eyes from his notes, and his tone became grim. "The *Ellen Austin* loses sight of the schooner. When they finally find her again, a day later, none of the replacement crew is on board. That anonymous ship was empty once again with no marks of violence or any trace of its occupants."

With all eyes on him, Feldman went on.

"So Weyland decides to send out another search crew to board and operate the ship, which almost causes a mutiny aboard the *Ellen Austin*. The two ships continue sailing in tandem until, two hundred miles from Gibraltar, another terribly thick, cold fog envelops both ships. They lose sight of the schooner again, but this time it ends up being for good. When the fog dissipates, the ship without a name is nowhere in sight, and the crew who had been sent to sail her is never heard from again."

The room was dead quiet. The only sounds came from the buzzing of the projector and Cherenkov's heavy breathing.

"That can't be," said Carter with a touch of doubt in his voice. "I mean, that has to be fake, or a legend."

"It's all documented. The British Admiralty conducted an inquiry, and the insurance backed by Lloyds Bank was forced to pay substantial damages to the families of the missing sailors. There's no doubt, Carter. It happened. What we still don't know is why."

Feldman turned to Cherenkov and made a gesture toward him. The Russian stood up and walked up to the podium, which the stately Feldman graciously relinquished.

"There have been more than thirty incidents in the past one hundred years," Cherenkov rumbled. "They cannot be explained. I'm a physicist, and my field is electromagnetic radiation. I came across these incidents in 1972 when one of our Golf-class ballistic submarines, the *K-94*, disappeared for seventy-two hours and reappeared again with no crew on board. We managed to find it thanks to its emergency beacon, which was coming from nearly one thousand feet below the sea with its reactor at half power and all of its locks secured. Not one drop of salt water was found inside the submarine, and yet, of the eighty-three men aboard, officers and sailors, not a single one was found."

Someone took a noisy sip of coffee. Cherenkov had the group hanging on his every word.

"The rescue operation was a true logistical marvel that, for obvious reasons, never became public." Cherenkov sounded proud. "We were able to get back a nuclear submarine from the United States' very own territory without anyone knowing. Not even the Americans."

He pressed a button, and a diagram of electromagnetic waves appeared. To Kate, it might as well have been Chinese, but it still made for an arresting image. For the physicists in the room, however, the diagram proved extremely interesting. Most leaned forward and began to take notes.

"The data the submarine sent out right before its disappearance was extremely odd, but it indicated, more than anything, the existence of a strong electromagnetic disturbance. The instruments had gone wild, and it seems they lost electromechanical control of the nuclear reactor for a few moments. I spent the next twelve years studying that data, and my research led me to other similar cases like those described by Mr. Feldman. It hasn't only happened to ships, either. It's also occurred with planes."

"Like the squadron of torpedo bombers that was lost in the Bermuda Triangle?" someone asked from the back of the room.

Cherenkov nodded patiently. His look of resignation indicated he had guessed the example might come up during the course of the conversation.

"Yes and no," he answered. "This has nothing to do with the Bermuda Triangle or anything of that nature. Forget all about that. The Triangle, which isn't even a triangle, is pseudoscientific garbage with no foundation. We're not talking about aliens or Atlantis or any of that newfangled bullshit."

The silence in the room at that moment was absolute.

"This is serious," Cherenkov went on. "There are two types of movements in the water of the oceans. Surface movements, which are influenced by the wind, the temperature, and other factors related to climate. And then there are deep-water movements, largely governed by ocean currents. A difference in the movements of two currents can cause important differences in pressure and static that wind up generating powerful electromagnetic storms."

"Like hurricanes," said one of the meteorologists.

"Exactly, only much more intense and harsh. Whereas an atmospheric storm might last a few days—or say, a couple of weeks in the case of a hurricane—an underwater storm can last for months. Its movement is much slower, and the energy it emits is much stronger. Its electromagnetic field can be powerful enough to disturb ships sailing above."

Cherenkov pressed another button. The odd-looking gadget Kate had noticed earlier sent out a beam of light, and as if by magic, a 3-D representation of the earth began revolving above the table. Gasps of awe came from the passengers. Kate was reminded of the image produced by the tape Princess Leia inserts into R2-D2 at the beginning of *Star Wars*. The technology had to be brand new. Clearly, Feldman had spared no costs.

"This is where the *Valkyrie* disappeared." A bright-red dot lit up on the surface as the planet spun on its axis. "Here is where the submarine disappeared in 1972." Another red dot appeared as soon as Cherenkov spoke. "These are the places where similar anomalies have occurred according to records from the past one hundred years, like those cases Mr. Feldman discussed."

Dozens of red dots began peppering the surface of the oceans as if the hologram were suffering a bad case of the chicken pox.

"Now for the most interesting point," Cherenkov said like a magician about to perform a particularly difficult trick. "Take a look at this."

The points on the projected image began to be joined by straight lines that crisscrossed the planet. The lines crossed and overlapped each other, covering the earth with an intricate framework, and Kate struggled to follow the logic in the chaos, like a child's drawing. After some careful observation, though, Kate was amazed to realize there was a pattern, a game of lines repeating over and over but only crossing at the sites of the disappearances.

"That's unbelievable," she whispered.

Cherenkov heard her and turned to her, smiling.

"I've christened it the Cherenkov Singularity. Right now we are heading straight for one of those points where the Singularity exists. Soon, we'll discover if I'm right or wrong."

X X I

An explosion of shouting filled the complete silence that had swallowed the room in the wake of Cherenkov's declaration. All at once, everyone was trying to say something or ask a question. The normally reserved scientists were suddenly acting like a hive of killer bees had been put in their trousers.

Feldman raised his hands and tried to bring order to the commotion. Everyone began to settle down, but the mood in the room couldn't be contained. A current of pent-up energy buzzed throughout the group like a live wire. Everyone wanted to say something, and even the typically skeptical Carter looked excited. Each and every one of them saw scientific implications in the project that were beyond Kate's understanding. Nevertheless, she was able to pick up on one thing for certain: the information was credible, and they thought Cherenkov might be onto something.

"We have only four days until we reach the Singularity, and we have no idea what might happen when we do. During that time, all of you will be able to study these documents," Feldman said.

Senka began to walk around the room, placing a thick red dossier in front of each of the participants, with the exception of Kate.

"The evidence points to the fact that in every incident there have been climatological, electromagnetic, and other types of anomalies," noted Feldman. "You will work in your assigned field and coordinate your efforts with Professor Cherenkov. He will be the lead on the scientific assessments. Miss Simovic will head up all organizational duties and will make any materials or equipment you might need available in the course of your investigations. Finally, everyone will ultimately answer to me."

"We should have been told this beforehand," Paxton said, shaking feverishly. "In my lab I have journals and studies that could have been helpful."

"Do not worry about that," replied Feldman. "It's all been taken care of."

Feldman turned to Senka, who switched on a bizarre-looking computer hard drive. It was a silver rectangular box the size of a briefcase and was connected to a keyboard and monitor.

"This computer is directly connected to Sonora, the data center located in Usher Manor. There are twenty people working there twenty-four hours a day. They are capable of gathering any information you might need. All of you will have access to a terminal for as long as you need in the Gneisenau Room, where we met this morning. Senka, if you don't mind."

Senka pushed a series of keys, and the screen lit up with a string of numbers. Then, the screen blinked and a beautiful young woman flashed on-screen. She was twenty-something with brown hair down to her shoulders, dark eyes, and a contemplative expression on her face. She was in an office crowded with computers and screens. Behind her, people were bustling about, carrying papers, books, and boxes.

"Good evening, Anne," Feldman said. "I'd like to introduce everyone to Anne Medine, coordinator of the Documentation Division at Usher Manor. Any information you need can be requested from Anne. Any experiment you would like to perform that cannot be performed aboard the ship can be entrusted to her. Anne and her team will be our eyes and ears on the ground."

"Good evening to all of you," answered Anne. Her voice came in clear and without any delay despite the fact they were thousands of miles apart. She was slightly taken aback at being in front of so many people even though it was from such a distance. Obviously, she was not used to public speaking.

Anne started to explain the procedures for requesting experiments and analyses that could be sent through their own satellite network. Kate almost choked when she heard "own satellite network." It explained the plethora of antennas that occupied the flower beds at Usher Manor. Kate suspected that Feldman was stretching his pocketbook to the limit with this project. Perhaps even enough for the Treasury Department to flag his account.

Discreetly, Feldman got up from the table. He seemed somewhat fatigued after the presentation, but Kate was not about to let him leave. He walked away, supported by Senka, revealing just how exhausted he was. A pair of dark rings framed his hawkish eyes, which looked duller than before. It occurred to Kate that Feldman was paying a higher price than anyone else by making this voyage on the *Valkyrie*.

But she could not let him go without some answers. She got up from the table and ran after him as he and Senka were exiting the dance hall through a door leading out to the deck.

"Feldman," she shouted. A strong wind kicked up, and a layer of clouds lined the sky, obscuring the stars from sight.

Feldman turned around and looked at her with tired eyes, though something in them twinkled. Regret, perhaps? Senka stepped between them, but Feldman brushed her aside.

"Kate Kilroy," he said her name slowly as if he was relishing it. "The woman who always knows the right questions to ask. I suppose there's something you'd like to know?"

"Just the truth, Feldman," answered Kate. "Tell me what really happened to the support ship. And at Carroll's house. I know that was no accident."

Feldman leaned against the railing and sighed. He motioned her over. Senka watched them warily, but Feldman signaled her to leave the two of them alone. Reluctantly, she walked away, but not without casting a dubious look at them.

Kate sat down on a wicker chair and waited for Feldman to do the same. He took a small tin from his pocket and offered up a cigarette, which she declined. Feldman shrugged and fought against the wind to light his. When he finally managed to do so, he took a few drags while he arranged his thoughts.

"I'm not the only one who's been looking for the *Valkyrie*," he began. "I didn't know its location until a few years ago when I discovered the Royal Navy's warehouse, where the majority of the ship's furniture was stored. When I made my bid, I found out there was a company offering a huge sum for the whole lot. I assumed they were antique collectors or something along those lines. But when the bid surpassed market price, I realized they were looking for something more. Maybe the same thing I was." He took a long drag and looked out at the dark ocean. "The company was a partnership with headquarters in the Cayman Islands. I had them investigated, and the trail led us to three or four more companies, all of them located in fiscal havens. Whoever they were, they had a lot of money and were dead set against anyone finding out their true identity."

"But you managed," guessed Kate.

Feldman nodded. "It wasn't easy. It required a considerable effort and a great deal of money, but it paid off. The trail ended at a Swiss firm with a German name: Wolf und Klee. Does that ring any bells?"

"I heard the name in Liverpool," she answered. "Collins said they had vied to make off with the *Valkyrie*. Who are they?"

"Wolf. Und. Klee." Feldman uttered the words slowly, almost spelling out each sound. "The wolf and clover. I didn't have the faintest notion of who they were when I heard it the first time. It took my people several months to trace them down. Have you ever heard of Werwolf?"

"I don't think so."

"In 1944, it was quite apparent that Germany was going to lose the war and that the Allies would invade the Reich. SS *Obergruppenführer* Hans Prützmann was charged with organizing a clandestine group that would operate behind Allied enemy lines. Its mission would be to carry out covert acts of sabotage and assassinations. Nearly five thousand men were chosen for the task. Some of them were grizzled veterans of the SS. But most were just kids from the Hitler Youth, kids barely capable of picking up a rifle.

"Werwolf was a failure from the beginning. They were disorganized and lacked material goods. Germany was simply stretched too thin by the war to sustain a clandestine movement of that magnitude. They managed to assassinate a few Allied officials and blow up a couple of bridges, but that was about it." Feldman wrapped his jacket around him to ward off the cold. "Nearly all of them were arrested or deserted, especially the youngest ones, by the time the war was over. Peace is much more enticing when compared to the possibility of an ugly, insignificant death in a dark alley somewhere."

Senka poked her head out to check on them. She was carrying two cups of steaming coffee, which they accepted with a nod of appreciation. Feldman waited for Senka to return inside before he continued his story.

"One sect of Werwolf never disbanded, though," he said after taking a long sip of coffee. "The hard-core, most fanatical members refused to give up. But they weren't dumb. If they had been, they wouldn't have survived. They knew the world was changing and that guerrilla action was no longer possible. So they changed their tactics. No longer did they worry about saving the Third Reich, which died at the end of the war. Instead, they focused on saving everything they could for the seeds of a future Fourth Reich. They became the guardians of the Nazi legacy."

"So Werwolf became Wolf und Klee," Kate deduced.

Feldman nodded. "The wolf and clover," he whispered. "The Prützmann family crest was turned into the new organization's logo. As the years passed, they placed their members in key positions in the German government. The de-Nazification of Germany was quite superficial, and many top officials went on with their lives. In those times, the Soviet threat had become much more pressing."

"But what does it mean to uphold the legacy? What does the *Valkyrie* have to do with that?"

Feldman looked her over and made a plea for patience. "Over the years, Wolf und Klee has become extremely wealthy and powerful. And secretive. They had funds at their disposal left behind by the Nazi regime, and they'd also managed to infiltrate important strata in German society. They dedicated part of those funds to financing neo-Nazi movements in Central Europe. But the majority went toward acquiring relics."

"Relics?"

"Symbols. Nazis were the first to appreciate the power symbolism can have on the masses. They knew that sooner or later Europe would undergo a similar socioeconomic disaster as the one that had brought about the rise of the Nazis in the first place, and they wanted to be prepared. They wanted to have symbols that would help unite the malcontented. Symbols that would help revive National Socialism."

Kate's mouth went dry. She had not anticipated any of this.

"By buying, stealing, murder, and extortion, they managed to put together a genuine museum of horrors over time. They have Himmler's and Goebbels's ashes, Hitler's skull, and God knows what else in some armored vault in Switzerland."

"That's disgusting," whispered Kate.

"In some ways, they never stopped being a gang of old, loony antique collectors. That's fairly harmless." Feldman let out a bitter laugh. "I even took advantage by selling them a diary that supposedly belonged to Hitler. I managed it through a clueless Dutch art dealer. It wasn't real, of course, but it was an extraordinary forgery, perhaps one of the finest ever made. They paid me a fortune, and I used part of that money to buy the *Valkyrie*. Plus, I knew they wanted the ship, and I was hoping to drain their funds before the auction."

"Did it work?" Kate asked.

"It did, but they never gave up on the *Valkyrie*," said Feldman, suddenly very serious. "At first I figured that a Jew owning the last Nazi ship on the face of the earth was something they couldn't tolerate. But that wasn't all. I didn't realize the true reason until I found out that Mikhail Tarasov, a former member of Cherenkov's research team, was working for them."

Kate sipped her coffee and thought about the implications of this detail.

"That means they have access to the same data we do concerning the singularities and anomalies but with a different perspective," Feldman continued, leaning forward and visibly shaken. "They're willing to kill anyone and do anything to get the ship. I'd stake my life on it."

Terrified, Kate did not want to hear what Feldman might say next.

"Those with Wolf und Klee and Tarasov believe the singularity points are actually able to produce spatiotemporal disturbances. It's wildly difficult to explain, but . . ."

"But . . ." Kate repeated.

"The difference is they believe that if this ship is in the right place at the right time, we will wind up in the year 1939."

"What?"

"If they can go back in time, they'll be able to help Hitler avoid making the same mistakes that led to his defeat. Stalingrad. Normandy. None of it will have ever happened." Feldman's voice had become distraught. "Don't you see, Kate? Germany will win the war. The Jewish population will be completely exterminated, and the course of history will be altered. Forever."

X X I I

For an instant the only audible sounds were the rushing of the wind across the main deck of the *Valkyrie* and the dull hum of the lights. Kate looked at Feldman in dismay.

"You can't be serious," she finally blurted out. "Time travel isn't possible. You said it yourself."

"I know what I said," Feldman replied. "I stand by that. I've had many conversations about this with Cherenkov and continue to do so on a daily basis. We both think Tarasov's approach is completely off. One cannot travel through time just as one cannot fall up. The laws of physics are intractable."

"So what's this all about then?"

"The question is not what *we* believe but what *they* do." Feldman shook his head, looking dog-tired. "As long as those lunatics at Wolf und Klee are convinced that the *Valkyrie* is their ticket to a fucking interview with their beloved Führer, we will have serious problems."

"So there really was a bomb on the *Mauna Loa*," Kate said in a hushed voice.

Feldman nodded and waved his hand toward the interior of the ship. "If we tell everyone we have a band of lunatics on our heels, what do you think will happen, Kate?"

"Total chaos. The end of the voyage. Everybody would immediately demand we return home."

"That's right," Feldman nodded. "And for that reason I ask you not to say a word to anyone. If Wolf und Klee has gotten to anyone on board, Moore will take care of it. Meanwhile, time is on our side."

"All right, Feldman," she said after a slight hesitation. "But in return I want full disclosure from you. No more secrets. Deal?"

"Isaac," said Feldman, smiling.

"What?"

"Isaac. Call me Isaac. Everyone calls me Mr. Feldman, and it gets old. And yes, we have a deal. No more secrets. You have my word, Kate."

She nodded, satisfied, and they shook hands. Feldman's hand was extremely frigid. Kate had the horrible sensation she was touching someone marked by the shadow of death. She tried to push the thought from her mind.

"So what about the hit-and-run attempt on me? Or Carroll?" Kate asked.

"Right. The incident with that poor old man from the *Pass of Ballaster* was their work as well. What I still don't get is why they wanted his head and heart. That has me completely puzzled."

Recalling the walls covered in blood and the stench of burnt flesh made Kate tremble. She couldn't shake the feeling that the same thing had happened to someone else in another time.

"It certainly doesn't seem very scientific or rational," she said.

"We're not dealing with rational people here, Kate. We're dealing with fanatics. They'll do whatever it takes to seize this ship and prevent us from arriving to the Singularity first."

They were both sitting silently when Moore appeared, as if by stealth, and approached Feldman. He leaned over and whispered something in his ear.

Kate watched them with unease. Knowing what she did now, the presence of Moore and his men on board the *Valkyrie* didn't seem like such a bad idea. She remembered the crates of weapons that had been brought aboard. Maybe Feldman was right after all.

"Kate." Feldman's skin had taken on an ashen color. "We should go to the bridge immediately. We may have a problem."

      •   •   •

The bridge of the *Valkyrie* was a work of art in naval engineering. Its designers had provided the captain and the bridge crew with the best possible visibility for that time—the entire front wall was nothing but a giant window that overlooked the bow. Feldman and his staff had restored this area of the ship to be identical to how it was in the thirties, with the exception of the back wall, which was crowded with modern navigation equipment. Next to that same wall, a radar screen was connected to a chart plotter, two backup computers, sonar, and half a dozen other gadgets Kate was unable to identify. All of the twenty-first century technology contrasted oddly with the rest of the command bridge, but it made her feel a little more at ease.

Passing by the radio room, Kate peeked in to see the communications operator sitting lazily in front of a modern console containing several monitors. Most of them showed various scenes being recorded by security cameras on board the *Valkyrie*. Others monitored all forms of communication arriving via satellite. Finally, one of the monitors played an NBA basketball game. The operator showed more interest in the game than in any of the other screens. Kate smiled. At least one place on the *Valkyrie* still lived in the present. Her smile faded, however, when she looked out the front window of the bridge.

Immediately in front of them, an enormous fog bank hovered on the horizon, no more than a couple of nautical miles away. It extended far and wide in its thick dirty-yellow cover. The outlines of the waves blurred at the brink of it, like a painting forced to end at the edge of the canvas. Kate had lived in London long enough to know something about fog, but she had never seen anything as thick and sticky as this. From time to time a lazy eddy swirled to the surface, almost as if an enormous prehistoric beast stirred below. A few wisps of fog were advancing over the water's surface like long, rapacious fingers.

Kate thought the fog had a certain look about it, ominous and disagreeable. Or maybe she was simply too open to suggestion after everything that had happened that day. Perhaps it was nothing but a common, everyday fog bank.

She looked at the captain. He was a tall man with a kind face, gray hair, and a carefully trimmed goatee. Maybe fifty, he was dressed informally in a sweat suit, giving the impression that he'd been torn from slumber before he threw on the first clothes he could find. She noticed worry lines around the captain's eyes.

"Mr. Feldman," he said turning toward him and extending his hand.

"This is Captain Steven Harper, Kate," Feldman said, introducing the two. "He has more than thirty years' experience at sea with the last twelve captaining cruise ships."

Harper bowed slightly but looked tense. He did not have time to engage in social niceties.

"What's going on?" Feldman asked.

"There's a fog bank ahead," answered Harper as he held out a pair of binoculars. "It appeared on the horizon sixteen minutes ago, and God knows where it came from. Given our course, I don't think it will be more than a half hour before we run into it."

"It looks like any other fog bank," Feldman said.

"The forecast didn't mention any fog," replied Harper in a muffled voice. "In fact, we're in the middle of a high-pressure front. It's night, the middle of August, and it's sixty-eight degrees Fahrenheit. These aren't the right conditions for a fog bank. Certainly not one of this size."

"Sometimes predictions can be off," grumbled Feldman like a grouchy dog, looking out with disdain. "It's only a bit of fog."

"Predictions can be off," said Harper, "but technology usually doesn't fail in these situations. Have a look."

He turned toward the back with all its modern equipment and punched some commands into one of the consoles. After a few seconds a screen showed a satellite image of a small section of the ocean with a blinking dot in the middle.

"That's the *Valkyrie*. Do you see what I mean?"

"I don't see anything," said Feldman.

"That's the problem," answered Harper. "Neither the satellite nor the radar is picking up the fog bank or anything about what's inside. It's like it's not there."

A few moments of excruciating silence ensued.

"That's impossible," Feldman finally blurted out, signaling toward the window. "It's right there."

Captain Harper opened his mouth as if to say, "I see it, you idiot," but he closed it and pursed his lips instead. Even though the captain was usually the leader of a ship after God, in the case of the *Valkyrie*, Feldman occupied the space between the two.

"The fog stretches out in both directions as far as the eye can see," Harper said. "We won't have sunlight for another six hours. The only way to avoid it would be to steer off our present course."

"We'll stay the present course, Captain." Feldman pointed to the navigation table. Kate saw a yellowed, ancient-looking book on top. It was the original logbook of the *Valkyrie.* The same logbook that had come to an abrupt halt after only four days of sailing.

"With all due respect, Mr. Feldman, we cannot compromise the security of the ship and its passengers," Harper said. "If we just make a quarter turn portside—"

"We will not veer from our course, not one fucking inch," Feldman roared. "We will follow the course indicated in this book. If you don't like it, tell me right now, and I will begin an immediate search for your replacement. Have I made myself clear, Harper?"

The tension on the bridge was as heavy as the approaching fog. All eyes, including those of the helmsman, were on Feldman and the captain.

"Of course, Mr. Feldman," answered Harper rigidly after a few moments of insufferable silence, "at your service. But I delegate all responsibility for what happens to you. Everyone here is witness to that."

Feldman made a vague gesture of assent that could have meant "all right" as much as it could have meant "I don't give a shit."

"Then, we keep on," murmured Feldman.

"Forward two-thirds speed, no change in course," the captain barked at the helmsman.

"Forward two-thirds speed, no change in course," the helmsman repeated mechanically.

Like an enormous sea creature spewing smoke, the *Valkyrie* closed in on the fog bank. Slowly, the ship penetrated the thick mist. For a fraction of a second, if the passengers had been paying close attention, they would have heard a watery gurgle like life being snuffed out under water.

Then, there was nothing.

Only silence.

X X I I I

Valkyrie
Day two

When Kate woke up the next morning, she immediately realized
two things that were both quite unusual. The first was the complete silence that encompassed the *Valkyrie*. The only sounds
came from the sea as it pushed past the ship's hull. Nothing
more. Not the wind across the rigging or the squealing of sea life
or the splashing of waves. Nothing. Only silence.

The second thing she discovered was the temperature had
dropped at least ten degrees. The previous night she had been
sipping coffee with Feldman on the deck of the ship in no more
than a simple sleeveless silk dress. She had been neither hot nor
cold. That morning, however, as she walked across the starboard
deck toward the first-class dining hall, she was practically shivering in her wool sweater.

The fog had wrapped around the ship like a shroud over a
dead man. Visibility was no more than thirty feet in all directions. As she walked Kate could make out the shapes of empty

lounge chairs as they slowly materialized before her eyes like dark shadows from the mist.

Halfway down the corridor she spotted a man in a plaid suit sitting on one of the lounge chairs. He was smoking a cigarette and had a book in his hands. Before she could get close enough to see who he was, the man got up, flicked his cigarette over the railing, slapped a wide-brimmed straw hat on his head, turned away from her, and began walking in the direction of the bow.

A straw hat? Who wears one of those in the middle of a fog bank? Something about it didn't make sense. She quickened her step, but by the time she got to the chair where he'd been sitting, he was out of sight.

Suddenly, she realized someone was running toward her. She almost panicked until she realized it was Carter.

"Good morning, Kate," he said as he approached. The physicist was wearing a sweat suit, as if he had just run a marathon. "If it even is morning. With this damned fog you don't even know what time it is."

"It seems quite thick," answered Kate. *And someone's wearing a big straw hat in spite of it,* she thought to herself.

"Our three meteorologists are going bonkers," Carter said, wiping the sweat from his forehead with a sleeve. "They do nothing but pace back and forth between the weather station at the bow and the bridge's radar. They're so revved up I'm sure Captain Harper would love to toss them overboard. It's a fog of intrigue, so it seems."

"The captain thinks so, but Feldman doesn't," Kate replied as she looked off into space. "By the way, who was that man you passed earlier? The one in the plaid suit."

Carter looked straight at her and blinked as if he had not heard correctly. "I didn't pass by anyone."

"That can't be. He was heading right toward you."

"I've been jogging this deck for twenty minutes, and you're the first person I've come across," said Carter. "I suppose it's not a great day to go for a stroll. Nearly everyone's inside. What did this guy in the suit look like?"

"I don't know. I didn't get a good look at him. He was probably just a figment of my imagination," Kate answered, flustered.

"Could be," Carter said suspiciously.

Mortified, Kate noticed the physicist watching her with that "you-are-not-right-in-the-head" look, usually reserved for those who hear voices or believe themselves to be alien ambassadors. Or those who see things that aren't there.

"I'm going to get some breakfast," Kate said, trying to change the subject. "Would you care to join me?"

"I can't. I need to shower. I'm getting together with Cherenkov in fifteen minutes. I'm hoping he'll show me his Singularity calculations. They looked promising yesterday."

"I'll see you later then."

"If you see the man in the plaid suit, don't forget to let me know." Carter bid her farewell with a burst of laughter and began running down the deck.

Kate was left alone on the walkway and felt thankful that, at the very least, the fog was hiding her blush.

Congratulations, Kate. You've acted like a complete fool, she thought to herself.

Infuriated, she continued toward the dining hall.

Because of the fog, she nearly passed it by. But there it was stuck between the lifeboat stanchions and the deck railing: the straw hat with a blue sash around the cap. It was as if someone had stuffed it there so the wind would not blow it away.

Seeing it startled Kate. She looked around to see if anyone was trying to play a joke on her. For a second she thought about Carter, but he did not seem like the practical jokester type.

Carefully, she leaned out and grabbed the hat. It was surprisingly cold like it had been left outside all night. She held it in her hands, squeezing it to make sure it was real and not a product of her imagination. She turned it over and noticed there was a name embroidered on a label stitched inside the hat: Schweizer.

She repeated the name several times.

It did not ring any bells. But on the other hand, she had yet to learn all of the scientists' names let alone all of the names of the crew. In total, there were some seventy people on board, and she barely knew a dozen of them. It could belong to any of them.

With the hat in her hands, she entered the dining hall and served herself breakfast from the buffet. Barely a dozen others were dining at that moment, and nearly all of them were crew members apart from a couple of scientists. There was no trace of Feldman, Moore, or Senka. Of course, there was nobody in a plaid suit.

Kate was tempted to ask if anyone knew a Schweizer, but she restrained herself. She had already acted foolish enough in front of Carter. She would have to find the owner of the hat another way.

She finished her breakfast as quickly as she could and then headed toward the Gneisenau Room. They had pushed the couches and rugs to one side and arranged a long table with several computer terminals. It looked like a cybercafe from the 1990s.

Only two people were using the stations, a middle-aged woman and one of the chemists who had wooed her so gallantly the night before. Each was absorbed in the numbers and readouts on their screens and taking furious notes. They hardly looked up when Kate took a seat to connect to Usher Manor.

The screen blinked a few times as a series of numbers rushed across the bottom. A few minutes later, little had changed.

Confused, Kate figured she must have made some mistake. Then, the screen flashed to life, and Anne Medine appeared with Usher Manor in the background. The young woman looked somewhat shy but also exhausted.

"Good morning," she said. "We've been having some communication problems for a few hours now. I apologize for the wait. What can I do for you, Miss Kilroy?"

Kate blinked, surprised that the woman knew her name, but she supposed Feldman had supplied her with a complete file for each one of the participants on board.

"Good morning, Anne," she said, adjusting her headset. "I need a favor. Could you tell me who Mr. or Mrs. Schweizer is? I have to speak with him or her about something. But I'm not sure if they're one of the scientists, crew, or security."

The video distorted and then cut out for a few seconds. When the signal returned Anne had a full passenger list in her hands.

"Schweizer, you said? Could you spell it for me?"

Burning with impatience, Kate spelled out the name. The connection cut out again, and the screen went black. She could hear a kind of distant banging in her earphones, almost like a hammer against an anvil wrapped in rags.

". . . not on record," Anne Medine said, reappearing. "I'm sorry, Miss Kilroy. There is no one aboard the ship by that name."

"Are you sure?"

"No one on board has that last name."

Kate thanked her and ended the call, dejected. As she left the room, hat in hand, she glimpsed a tiny detail. A small rust-colored spot marked the edge of the hat's sash. It was like a smudged fingerprint, as if someone had quickly picked up the hat with something on his fingers before setting it down for the last time.

Kate was not sure why, but she would have bet anything the spot was blood.

She could have sworn it had not been there a moment ago.

X X I V

Tom McNamara's troubles were piling up. For starters, he had lost one hundred quid the night before playing poker with the boys. Afterward, he had decided to drown his sorrows in more liquor and ended up passing out. For that reason, he overslept the next morning and proceeded to get lost twice in the hallways of the ship before arriving late to the changing of the guard, panting and distraught. To top things off, Moore had been waiting for him with fury in his eyes.

Tom was a veteran of the war in Afghanistan, as were most of the men Moore had recruited. Of course, the pay was much better than in the army. Plus, the chances of getting blown up on the side of a dusty road or coming across a town bustling with hate-filled, bearded fanatics were far lower. Overall, working for Feldman was a fairly cushy job as long as you did not rub Moore the wrong way. Oversleeping was one of the many ways to do just that.

That was how Tom ended up pulling guard duty and how he found himself draped in shitty fog like a thick puree that seeped to the bone while everyone else leisurely strolled inside the *Valkyrie*, warm and sheltered.

Tom fished out a wrinkled pack of cigarettes from his pocket. He lit one, but after a few puffs thousands of microscopic droplets of water infiltrated the tobacco until it no longer stayed lit. Furious, he tossed it overboard. As he was about to turn away, he noticed something move out of the corner of his eye.

He turned back, more fascinated than scared. A young woman of around thirty was walking on the deck, heading inside. She was wearing a black skirt that went to her knees and a red sleeveless blouse. Her hair was elaborately styled, reminding Tom of the actresses from the old black-and-white movies his mother used to watch when he was a kid. The woman wrapped her arms around herself. She looked as if she were freezing. She was walking quickly yet absentmindedly, as if lost in thought. Her high heels clicked rhythmically as she walked on the wooden planks of the deck.

"Hey," Tom shouted. "Hey."

The woman stopped and looked in his direction. The guard could see her eyes were puffy and red like she had been crying. Her mascara was running, and she had dark streaks down her cheeks. She watched him closely as if wondering what the hell he was. Her expression was blank like a tomb. Then, as if she were making a colossal effort to remember how, the woman's smeared lips curved up in a tragic imitation of a smile.

The effect was horrifying. With her makeup-streaked face and an amorphous, blank smile, she looked like a demonic clown.

Then, the woman tilted her head like she could hear something he could not. Tom thought of how the kids in his neighborhood used to drive the local mutts crazy with a dog whistle. The woman suddenly seemed to lose all interest in Tom and turned in the direction of the superstructure of the ship.

"Hey," he repeated. "Stop. Stop or I'll shoot!"

The woman ignored him and disappeared into the fog. Without another thought Tom began running after her while he undid the safety of his AK-47. The woman was walking quickly toward an entrance on the bow, and she was about thirty feet ahead of him. Tom instinctively reached up to his shoulder where his walkie-talkie should have been to call for backup.

His fingers, instead, swiped at the air. Only then did he remember that, in the rush of the morning, he had forgotten it in his locker.

"Warning," he shouted, hoping someone might hear him. "Here on the bow!"

The fog swallowed his shouts. Like trying to shout under water, the sound was muffled and died out after only a few feet. Tom cursed under his breath. He was alone in this, and it was his fault.

If he had not been so tired and hungover, he would have remembered to carry a whistle in his pants pocket. If he had not gotten so drunk the night before, his head would have been clear enough to realize that if he fired off a couple of warning shots, he would have immediate backup from half a dozen of his cohorts. If he were smarter, he would not have sprinted toward the dark door the woman had opened, and he certainly would not have gone in without first thinking it through.

But Tom was not that smart.

The doorway led to a hallway in the first-class service area. Those same hallways had been used by the crew in the thirties to attend to the needs of first-class passengers without them needing to spend more time than necessary in their areas. To one side, Tom noticed a staircase that led to the top floor. He hesitated a moment over which way to go, but then caught a glimpse of the woman rounding a corner just down the hall from where he stood. He ran after her.

They were in a part of the ship that had been restored but was not in use. On this particular voyage, there were not enough crew members aboard to justify using this section of the ship. He sprinted past empty cabins, a small lounge, and some bathing facilities. The air was rife with a heavy metallic scent, like that of an engine warming up.

Rounding a corner, Tom stopped. In the middle of a landing was a staircase that went down to second class. He knew there must be a makeshift steel door blocking the way. Tom himself had been there just the day before, putting the finishing touches on it by placing a sticker that warned anyone from breaking the seal.

But the door wasn't there. There was no trace of it. Not one mark from the welding on the walls or a single scratch on the floor. Nothing.

It was like the door had never existed.

Tom swallowed and, for the first time, wavered. This was unsettling even for someone with as little imagination as Tom. But then he was reminded of how angry Moore had been that very morning and began thinking about the possible consequences of letting a rogue element loose in the depths of the ship.

He shuddered at the thought. Perhaps this was just an elaborate test Moore had set up to make sure he was alert. A sort of trick. That bastard was capable of stranger things.

Reassured by those thoughts, Tom began descending the staircase toward second class. Each step creaked beneath his boots with a sound that gave him away, but Tom remained unaware of that little detail. Just as he remained unaware that the metallic odor had become stronger and that the walls had begun to throb with a monotonous rhythm as he continued forward.

A cloudiness, like the fog outside, entered his mind. He was unable to think straight. He felt like someone was forcing a thousand images into his head at once.

This is not a good idea. *Nein.*

He stopped, perplexed. Had he just thought something in German? He did not speak a word of German. What the hell was going on?

Dizzy, he leaned against the wall. The vibrations ran up his body in waves, first through his hands and then up his arms and up into his skull, where they buzzed and reverberated with homicidal rage. A drop of black liquid fell on his forearm. He wiped his hand across his face and found his nose was bleeding profusely as if someone had turned on a faucet of blood.

Tom.

The woman's voice was soft, sensual. Tom spun his head around slowly like he was trapped in a movie. The woman from the deck stood in the doorway of a cabin that was brilliantly lit and in perfect order. She beckoned him toward her.

Come, Tom. Come with me. Let's have a good time together.

Almost catatonic, Tom stepped forward. One part of his mind was screaming in horror for him to get the hell out of there. He was vaguely aware that this area of second class was in perfect condition, not at all like the other areas he had seen in that sector. Had someone renovated without telling him?

Come, Tom. We can be alone down here.

The woman continued to beckon him forth, and he tried once more to come to terms with the travesty of a smile that was spread across her face. It was even more terrifying up close.

Fear finally took over. Tom made a herculean effort to step backward, and he shook his head in defiance. Before he realized it, his gun fell and clattered to the floor.

No. *Nein. Nein.*

He turned around and began walking toward the staircase, each step quicker than the last. The walls began to pulsate more quickly, and that was when Tom knew there was something behind him. Something dark, malevolent, and voracious, watching him intently.

"Nooooooooo," he shouted with a mix of desperation and anger as he tried to run.

The doors were a blur as he ran across the carpet. Darkness pursued him, getting closer by the second. Tom felt a cold, wet breath grazing the back of his neck. The mere touch made every hair on his body stand straight on end.

It was then that something happened. *It* was still behind him, but Tom felt as though he were gaining some distance. Perhaps it had decided to stop for some reason. Hope flickered in him, however dimly. He was going to escape. He was going to get out of there.

Turning the corner, he ran headfirst into someone. Both fell to the floor in a tangle and ended up rolling a few feet. When Tom looked up he was at the foot of a polished bronze clock running slow.

Hysterical, Tom let out a bloodcurdling scream as he braced himself and tried to protect his body. He looked over at the person he had run into and breathed a deep sigh of relief that echoed from the depths of his soul.

"It's you, thank God!" he said choked with emotion. "You can't imagine how glad I am to see a familiar face."

The other person helped him up and looked at him carefully.

"What happened?"

"Didn't you see?" Tom shook his head in excitement. "The hall was shaking and that . . . that thing was chasing me, and the noise. Fuck, tell me you saw it!"

"I didn't see or hear anything. I just heard some screams, and so I ran to see what was going on. That's when I ran into you."

"But I swear—" Tom stopped, furrowing his brow. "Just a second. What are you doing in this section? Nobody's supposed to be down here. Mr. Feldman has strictly prohibited it."

The other person shrugged and gave an ambiguous smile.

"We have to go. I need to tell Moore what's happened," he said, turning around and heading toward the staircase.

For that reason Tom did not see his companion remove a small, sharp scalpel from a pocket.

When the blade slit his neck and severed Tom McNamara's carotid artery, the last thing to go through his mind was a feeling of profound dread for dying in that narrow hallway at the hands of another human being.

With that shadowy thing on the loose below.

Waiting.

X X V

Kate was in the middle of a particularly torrid dream when a knock at her door startled her awake.

Since her husband had died, she had yet to remember him in such a vivid and explicitly sexual way. In her dream Robert had undressed slowly, removing the clothes from his magnificent body garment by garment until he was standing in front of Kate completely nude. The two were alone in her cabin, and Robert was looking at her with that playful half smile she knew so well, mischief dancing in his eyes. Without a word he approached her for a long, marvelous kiss. His tongue executed a complicated dance with hers that left her quivering. Then, he threw her down to the bed and began to undress her. First, he removed her top, exposing her breasts. He paused to enjoy her nipples with rhythmic movements of his tongue. Then, with a practiced hand, he began to undo her jeans while she breathed faster. He brought them down to her ankles to reveal a little thong that he loved. She took delight in Robert's hard body rubbing against her own. He grew larger as his hand slowly moved down her abdomen, lower and lower, until he reached the thin lacy edge of her underwear.

Then, someone began to pound on the fucking door, and Kate woke up, bathed in sweat and breathing hard.

With the agility of a drunkard, she stumbled to the door and attempted to tie her hair back. She had fallen asleep rereading her file on the *Valkyrie* for the hundredth time, trying to get a head start on her story.

Still dazed, she opened the door and found Senka with her fist in the air, about to knock once more. Senka looked very serious, but upon seeing Kate, a sweet, mischievous smile danced across her face.

The bitch knows, thought Kate as Senka puckered her lips in a sensual pout. Kate's flushed cheeks, her heavy breath, and the sweat on her neck—they were all clear signs to Senka, who was clearly delighting in the situation at hand.

"Hi, Kate," she purred in a playful tone, looking over Kate's shoulder into the empty cabin. "Did I interrupt something important? Maybe I could be of service?"

The innuendo hung in the air, thick and lewd, but Kate shook her head.

"I'm just a bit groggy, that's all. What's up?"

Senka shrugged, clearly disappointed. "Mr. Feldman would like to see you. Now."

It sounded more like an order than an invitation. Kate liked the idea of changing, but that was out of the question with Senka there, so she quickly put on her shoes and strode out of the cabin following Senka.

Feldman's cabin was a suite located on the stern of the ship. It had enormous windows that would normally offer its occupants a magnificent view of the ocean. But given the density of the dark-yellowish fog, only a weak light filtered into the room and stained everything a sickly color.

Feldman was seated. He looked worried. Moore was at his side with a jaw so tense he might as well have been chewing granite. His expression was a mixture of anger and embarrassment.

Kate noticed that Feldman looked older, as if some of his energy had fled his fragile body in search of a better home in which to nest. A flicker of vitality twinkled in his eyes when he saw Kate enter. He gestured for her to have a seat, and Senka closed the door behind them. This was a meeting for just the four of them. The tension in the room swelled up like the tide.

"Can I trust you, Kate?" Feldman asked.

"You know you can, Isaac. We made a deal."

"I know, dear, I know." Feldman shook his head. "The question is whether or not I can add one more secret to the list of little arrangements you and I have."

"My lips are sealed," she said without hesitation, her pulse quickening. "But if it's got something to do with the *Valkyrie*, I want to know everything."

"We have a serious problem," Feldman said. "Twenty minutes ago one of Moore's men was found dead, murdered."

"Murdered? Are you sure?"

"Unless he decided to cut his own neck, I'm quite sure, Kate," Feldman replied.

"How did it happen?"

"Moore has the details, but I believe it would be best if we go see it with our own eyes. We were waiting for you," Feldman said, rising from his seat with great difficulty.

"Why?" she asked.

"Why what?" Feldman said.

"Why tell me this? Why me?"

"Because we trust each other. Because you're a smart, sensible woman, and because I gave you my word to keep you up to date on all that happens on board. But primarily, because the four of us are the only ones on the ship that know about Wolf und Klee and the threat they pose. We are going to need the help of everyone to try to find out what the hell is going on . . . and stop it from happening again."

They left Feldman's cabin and walked quickly through the internal maze of first class without running into a soul. It was lunchtime, and most of the crew members were busy taking care of service. When they arrived at a flight of stairs leading down, two of Moore's men, heavily armed, were awaiting their arrival.

Without another word they began to descend the staircase. They came to another landing, which had several hallways forking off of it. There was also another flight of stairs that led to the *Valkyrie*'s mechanical facilities. A pair of heavy steel plates that had been fashioned into a door stood blocking the path to second class, but Kate noticed one of the plates was somewhat damaged. Someone had undone the soldering joints with a blunt object, and the steel plate was bent back far enough to allow a person to crawl through the space.

"We're in the first-class service area. This section is unoccupied for our voyage," Moore explained and pointed toward the steel door. "The door at the end of the hallway leads to the bow-side deck where Tom, er, I mean where the victim was standing guard. I have no idea why he came down here. Perhaps he heard something or found someone trying to sneak in."

"We have to go down and see," Senka said, taking several high-powered flashlights out of her shoulder bag. "Be careful and watch your step. These stairs are quite old and have not been restored."

As Kate crawled through the open space between the steel plates, she noticed the steel had left a deep gash in the delicate varnish of the hardwood floors; the mark reminded her of an infected wound.

On the other side the staircase receded into the darkness. Below, a symphony of drips and creaks could be heard each time the *Valkyrie* encountered another ocean wave.

"Surely, there are leaks in the hydraulic system," explained Feldman as they went down the stairs. Moore and one of his men led the way while Senka and another guard made up the rear. "So that's what you are hearing."

They entered a dark hallway that smelled stagnant and putrid. The carpet was no more than a complicated, frayed patchwork that had been destroyed by humidity. The paint on the walls was peeling in large, uneven chunks as if an especially virulent leprosy had attacked the ship and was consuming it from the inside out. In some places the wood floor bulged from water damage, making strange, grotesque shapes. The flashlight beams crisscrossed the walls as the visibly nervous security guards swiveled around looking for some threat in the darkness. Even Moore looked on edge.

"This way," he said, pointing to his right. "It's not far."

They walked a bit farther down the dilapidated hallway and tried not to trip over the rotting wood debris cluttering the hallway. The doors, defeated by their own weight, had fallen off the hinges and were now no more than moldy pieces of lumber, revealing desolate cabins.

Finally, a blinking light could be seen at the end of the hallway, exposing the shadowy outline of a body on the floor. A wall clock, which had not worked for decades and was on the verge of crumbling, presided over the scene like a voiceless witness. A large rust-colored bloodstain had spread across the floor from beneath Tom McNamara's body.

Kate tried to keep herself from heaving. Luckily, she had not eaten lunch yet.

Tom's face was twisted into a bizarre expression, a strange mixture of unbounding terror and bewilderment. His throat was slit from ear to ear in the fashion of a second smile, toothless and malicious. In the shadowy lantern light, the effect was absolutely petrifying.

"He was killed here," Moore said as if that were not already clear. "Someone came from behind and slit his throat. It had to be someone he knew. There's no way Tom would have been caught off guard. He wasn't the smartest guy, but he was good at what he did."

"Where's his gun?" asked Senka. "I don't see it anywhere."

They swept their lights over the floor, but there was no AK-47 to be found.

"Just what we need," sighed Feldman. "Now whoever did this has a weapon. It just keeps getting better."

"Wait a second, there are some drops of blood this way," said Kate, pointing to a big round drop of blood the size of a dime. Not far away was another, at the edge of the darkness.

"His face is covered in blood," Senka said in a shaky voice. "It's like he was bleeding from his nose or mouth."

They followed the droplets deeper into the heart of the ship. A heavy weight settled in Kate's head, almost like she had a terrible hangover. Her temples were pounding incessantly. She noticed she was not alone. Moore was rubbing his eyes, and his men were shaking like they were each carrying two hundred pounds.

Straight ahead, something glinted in their beams of light. Moving closer, they saw that it was the dark barrel of the AK-47 resting on the floor like another of the ship's leftover relics. The trail of blood ended there in front of a bleak, lonely cabin just like all the others.

"Whatever happened, it happened here," Kate said in a very matter-of-fact tone.

The others remained quiet, wrapped up in their own thoughts. Contemplating the gun and wearing his usual poker face, Feldman was the only one who seemed to be unaffected.

"Nobody can know about this," he finally said. "Take the body, put it in a bag, and keep it in one of the freezers. Moore, you're in charge."

The head of security still had his head tilted down as he stared blankly into the empty cabin. He looked a million miles away.

"Moore," Feldman raised his voice. "Did you hear me?"

Moore turned his head slowly as if a dozen rusty gears controlled it. His look was darker than normal, and his nose had begun to bleed.

"I don't think that's a good idea, sir," he finally uttered, in perfect German, much to the terror of the others. "I believe it would be best if we contact Berlin immediately."

X X V I

"What the hell are you talking about, Moore?" Feldman grunted threateningly. "Do what I say. Now."

"Moore? Who's Moore?" sputtered the head of security, shaking as he talked like he was having trouble staying upright.

It was all too much for Feldman. He walked straight toward Moore and shoved him against the wall with all the might he could muster. It was like moving a mountain of meat, but Feldman was undaunted.

"Come on, Moore! Wake up," he shouted. "What the fuck has gotten into you?"

In slow motion the English bodyguard brought his hands up to his eyes as he was racked by a ferocious attack of trembling. He rubbed his face and looked all about with confusion. Moore looked at Feldman as if his sudden proximity were a surprise.

"Of course, Mr. Feldman." He turned to his men and furrowed his brow as he tried to figure out what was going on. "We'll take the body to a freezer immediately. Let's go, boys. Be careful."

Kate watched as two of the men gingerly lifted up Tom McNamara's body. One of the guards absentmindedly used the sleeve of his uniform to wipe away a bit of blood that was running from his nose. The other guard was humming a soft melody, repeating the same line over and over. A heavy odor in the air lay hidden under the stench of dried blood. It was giving Kate a terrible headache.

"Let's get out of here," commanded Feldman.

He did not have to repeat himself. McNamara's body was placed into a body bag that someone had brought down, and the group practically raced out of second class. Nobody wanted to be the last to leave. Moore brought up the rear and looked back anxiously every few seconds as if he had heard something behind him.

Something that scared him.

As they were climbing the stairs, Kate noticed her head clearing up as if the vise that had been compressing her temples had suddenly loosened a little. She saw that the same was true of the others. Even Moore no longer had cloudy eyes, although he still appeared to be dizzy.

When they got to the service hallway, they parted ways. Moore and his two men went toward the enormous industrial freezers in the kitchen. They would store their macabre package there while Feldman, Senka, and Kate headed toward the upper deck.

Outside on the deck the temperature had dropped another three or four degrees, and the difference between that and the warmth of the ship's interior was immense. The yellowish fog enveloped them completely, and as soon as they had taken a few steps forward, Kate had the sensation they were suspended in a cold, wayward vacuum with no points of reference or cardinal directions.

"What happened down there?" she asked.

"I suppose an agent from Wolf und Klee caught our man by surprise," Feldman said.

"That's not what I mean," Kate interrupted with a slight tremble in her voice. "You know what I'm talking about, Isaac. I mean Moore talking nonsense in German. That strange feeling."

"I felt it, too," Senka added. The Serbian, normally so level-headed, looked extremely pale. "It was like I could suddenly hear dozens of people all at once inside my brain. It *hurt*."

"I have no idea what you're talking about." Feldman looked truly baffled by the discussion taking place. "I didn't feel anything, and I didn't hear anything, either. You were probably just spooked."

Senka and Kate looked at each other with surprise. Had Feldman really not noticed that wave of numbness that had rushed over them? Had he not been affected? Or was he right, and the two of them had simply behaved like two impressionable young women?

"But Moore told us to contact Berlin," Kate ventured.

"Mr. Moore hasn't been getting much sleep in the last forty-eight hours," Feldman countered. "He has fifteen, make that fourteen, men to keep watch over an enormous ship that is five hundred feet long and twelve levels high, eight of which are sealed up. Or they were. Fatigue makes people say strange things."

What Feldman was saying made sense, or at least it made more sense than the vague notions Kate was cooking up in her head. *Occam, Occam,* Kate repeated to herself. *The simplest explanation is probably the correct one.*

They continued slowly inside. Lunch had already passed, and the three of them were famished. When they arrived at the dining hall, nobody was there except a group of crew members seated around a table in the corner. They had their heads down and were murmuring to each other in low voices. Kate noticed that many of them looked extremely pale. They hardly resembled people accustomed to life at sea.

Feldman excused himself by saying he was exhausted and needed to rest in his cabin. Kate imagined Mrs. Miller would personally take charge over all the magnate's needs.

Sharing the intense experience earlier had eased some of the antagonism between Kate and Senka. Kate was not a woman who kept many friends, but the last thing she wanted at that moment was to eat alone. She wondered where Carter and the others might be.

The two women tried striking up a conversation, but they were too shocked to discuss trivialities. Kate felt a deep pang of nostalgia tinged with sorrow. If Robert were there, everything would be *different*. He'd always known what to say and how to act to make her comfortable. But Kate's only company was another frightened woman stuck on this ship, hundreds of miles away from safe haven.

She suddenly had a great urge to speak with someone who wasn't on the ship. She wondered if Captain Harper would let her use the communications center to call the newspaper and talk to Rhonda. She wanted to explain how her story was going and ask for advice. But more than anything she simply wanted to hear the voice of a friend.

Something told her that the guard's death had much bigger implications. Since boarding the *Valkyrie*, everything seemed to be spiraling out of control. But she figured there might be a hidden pattern behind it all that she had not yet discovered. She suspected that if Tom McNamara's throat really had been slit, then it must have been for something he saw. But what?

Maybe Anne Medine could give her more facts about the ship and the hallway in second class? A different perspective.

She got up from the table hurriedly, knocking over a glass of water. It fell to the floor and shattered, but no one turned their heads at the noise. Everyone was too lost in thought to care.

She bid farewell to Senka and beat a hasty path toward the Gneisenau Room. When she entered she did not see a single person. There was no hint of Cherenkov's research team; the chairs were vacant, and the computer screens idly flashed Feldman's company logo. The room was totally empty.

She sat down at one of the terminals to begin the connection process. She entered her user ID and waited. A series of numbers flashed across the screen before going blank again. Kate waited five long minutes with no success. Suddenly, a blinking cursor appeared on the monitor.

STANDBY COMMUNICATIONS SYSTEM
CBX7800000AAA879000// SONORA// *VALKYRIE*
SIGNAL INCOMING . . .

ANNEMEDINE// SONORA: GOOD AFTERNOON, MISS KILROY. WE'RE HAVING SOME DIFFICULTIES WITH THE SIGNAL RECEPTION. THE SATELLITE HAS BEEN DOWN FOR TWO HOURS NOW. WHILE THE TECHNICIANS ARE WORKING ON IT, WE'LL ONLY BE ABLE TO COMMUNICATE VIA CHAT. I HOPE THAT WON'T BE A PROBLEM :-)

Slightly taken aback by the message, Kate began typing.

KKILROY*VALKYRIE*: THAT SHOULD BE FINE. WILL IT BE POSSIBLE TO RECEIVE INFORMATION THROUGH THE COMMUNICATIONS SYSTEM LIKE THIS?

AnneMedine// SONORA: OF COURSE. THE DATA FLOW
GOES THROUGH A DIFFERENT CHANNEL THAT'S STILL UP
AND RUNNING. WHAT DO YOU NEED?
KKilroy*VALKYRIE*: INFORMATION ON SECOND CLASS.
THE LIST OF PASSENGERS ON THE ORIGINAL VOYAGE.
THINGS OF THAT NATURE.

Kate stopped. She was not sure if she should ask for information on Wolf und Klee. She had no idea how involved Anne was
in the grand scheme of things.

AnneMedine// SONORA: OF COURSE. I'M SENDING
THAT NOW. IT'S A LARGE FILE, AND WITH THE LIMITA-
TIONS OF THIS CONNECTION, IT WILL TAKE A WHILE TO
DOWNLOAD. I THINK YOU SHOULD HAVE IT IN ABOUT AN
HOUR.

Kate nodded, appeased. She was taking steps in the right
direction. She was about to say good-bye when the screen lit up
once more.

AnneMedine// SONORA: ALSO, I'VE FOUND YOUR MR.
SCHWEIZER. IT TOOK ME A WHILE, BUT THE NAME
SOUNDED SO FAMILIAR THAT I DECIDED TO DO SOME DIG-
GING. I FOUND HIM. HE WAS ONE OF THE PASSENGERS.

Kate didn't understand.

KKilroy*VALKYRIE*: ONE OF THE PASSENGERS? HOW IS
THAT POSSIBLE? I THOUGHT NONE OF THE SCIENTISTS OR
CREW HAD THAT LAST NAME? JUST YESTERDAY YOU
SHOWED ME THE PASSENGER LIST.

The cursor blinked a few moments that stretched on forever.

AnneMedine// SONORA: I'M SORRY. I SHOULD HAVE CLARIFIED. MARTIN SCHWEIZER, SINGLE, AGE FORTY-SIX, CABIN 172. HE WAS ONE OF THE ORIGINAL PASSENGERS ABOARD THE *VALKYRIE*. IN 1939.

XXVII

Kate blinked and stared at the screen. She felt like she had just been punched. It was simply impossible. The year 1939 was decades ago. They were *not* in the fucking 1930s.

Her hands trembled. She was about to type again to ask how the hell a passenger who vanished more than seventy years ago could be strolling about the ship when the screen started to flash several times, and the chat box disappeared. A message popped up.

Signal lost
Please wait . . .

Kate slapped the table in anger.
Not now, goddammit. Not now.
She waited around awhile, but it was in vain. The signal was gone. She looked around to see if there was a technician to help users, but the room was still completely empty.

Kate sat back in her seat as her mind began to race.

Her first thought was that the straw hat must have been aboard the ship the whole time. It was the most logical explanation. But that did not explain why nobody had seen it in the middle of the ship's walkway while the restoration work was being carried out. Plus, it was in far too good of shape to have been sitting around the ship for seventy-plus years.

Another explanation was that someone had placed it there on purpose for her to find. But that didn't make sense, either. When she had stumbled upon the dumb thing, it was stuck on a stanchion, about to blow into the sea. Nobody could have planned something that precisely.

The final explanation, as ridiculous as it sounded, was that the owner of the hat had traveled from 1939 only to bump into Kate on the walkway of the *Valkyrie*.

Occam, Kate. Occam.

Sitting there, stunned, she couldn't believe that the last explanation was the most likely one even though it sounded like complete madness. A week prior she would have burst out laughing at such a notion. But after everything she had experienced since boarding the *Valkyrie*, suddenly, nothing seemed impossible.

She realized she needed to tell Feldman and Cherenkov about it immediately. Maybe it had something to do with the anomalies surrounding the Singularity. She wanted to discuss it with Carter as well to see what he thought about the matter. He would be able to give her an injection of his logical, scientific skepticism, but she had not seen him at all since they had run into each other that morning.

Feeling resolute, she decided to head toward the bridge. As she crossed through the doorway, one final hypothesis occurred to her with such force that she stopped immediately. Kate told herself that it had to be impossible and stored away the thought in a little, dark mental compartment. Still, as she did so, a more primitive part of her began to fill with profound fear.

Perhaps Schweizer and his hat had been aboard the *Valkyrie*. All along. Together with the rest of the missing passengers. Waiting.

She shook her head, angry with herself. She did not believe in ghosts. Robert would have laughed hysterically at the mere thought. He would have come up with half a dozen bad jokes to tease her.

But Robert was not there, and fear is an invasive species not easy to eradicate. The more she tried not to think about the idea, the more difficult it became to avoid it.

She climbed up toward the bridge, her heart racing. Captain Harper was there, dressed in his peculiar style: dress pants and a floral shirt. She was not surprised. Someone had mentioned at dinner the night before that Harper, after twelve years of wearing an impeccable uniform on each and every cruise, had developed a visceral hatred for the outfit. To him, his voyage aboard the *Valkyrie* was to be an experience of liberation.

"Hello, Miss Kilroy," he greeted her matter-of-factly. He had a glass of water in one hand and was about to take two tablets held in the other. He flicked both pills in his mouth, took a long drink of water, and then set the glass on the navigation table beside the *Valkyrie*'s original logbook.

"I need to contact Mr. Feldman and Dr. Cherenkov," Kate said as she tried to control her breath. "I need to speak with them. It's very important."

Harper massaged his temples and looked irritated. He seemed to be afflicted with a severe headache.

"I don't like to bother passengers in first class unless it's warranted," he answered after a slight pause. "I trust that your reasons are such?"

Kate stared at him as if she had sand in her ears. *Passengers in first class?*

"It has to do with what's happening on this ship. So, yes, I suppose my reasons are indeed warranted," she replied a little more roughly than she wanted.

"In that case you should direct it to me, first." Harper fell back in the captain's chair, stretched his hand out over the navigation table, and began gently stroking the ship's logbook. "Company policy is very clear in that respect. I am the captain, after all."

Kate had to make a considerable effort not to strangle Harper. Nothing was turning out how she had envisioned.

"I beg of you, please, Captain," she implored, placing special emphasis on the word *captain*. She hated the tone of her voice when she had to beg. "It's very important I see Mr. Feldman and Dr. Cherenkov. It is directly related to their project and has nothing to do with the ship's security or that of the crew. I promise. I don't know where they are, and if you could call them over the loudspeaker that would save me having to run all around the ship looking for them."

Harper coughed and continued to massage his temples vigorously. His headache must be one of colossal proportions. Exhausted, he nodded.

"All right. Hanisch, page passengers Feldman and Cherenkov to the command bridge." He turned to Kate and pointed to the door. "Wait there, next to the radio room. Passengers are not allowed to be on the bridge while we are at sea."

Kate opened her mouth to snap back at him but immediately shut it. Either Harper was a greasy bastard, or she was losing her mind. She hoped it was the former, but she would gain nothing by confronting him.

She turned around and went into the radio room. The radio operator was sitting in front of the monitors as before, but this time, even though another basketball game was on and in its final minutes, he paid no attention. The Knicks were crushing another team in blue uniforms that Kate couldn't identify. Static clouded the reception, blinking in and out.

Perhaps that was why the operator had his headphones on and appeared to be focused on transcribing what he was hearing over the radio. As Kate entered, the man gave her no more than a quick glance and arched his eyebrows in recognition of her arrival.

Kate waited for fifteen long minutes and chewed on her nails to pass the time. Finally, the door opened, and Cherenkov and Feldman walked in one after the other.

The rings under Feldman's eyes had grown darker. It had barely been two days, and he looked like he had aged ten years. Cherenkov, in turn, just looked angry.

"This had better be important," he barked in his Slavic accent as soon as he walked in. "I have tons to do, and my team is very limited. We can hardly keep up."

"I won't take much of your time," Kate said as she motioned them toward a corner of the bridge where they would not be heard. There, she began telling them the story of Schweizer and his straw hat.

She had taken her time to closely consider how to relate the story. In the end she decided to present the facts in a cold, methodical way like an informant would, without hunches or conclusions. Let the two of them decide for themselves.

By the end, Feldman and Cherenkov were hanging on her every word. Each seemed intrigued by the story for different reasons judging from their expressions. Feldman looked on the verge of collapse while Cherenkov's eyes lit up with excitement.

"Did you say you have that hat, Kate?" Feldman asked feebly. "Do you really have it?"

"It's in my cabin, on my bed," Kate said. "We can go get it right now."

"Yes, I'd like that," Cherenkov said. "I'm very much looking forward to seeing it with my own eyes. May I take a sample from it?"

"I'll give you the whole damn thing, Professor," Kate laughed, relieved, "if you'll promise to take it right away."

They headed for the cabins. As they came into the main lobby, Kate could hear upbeat music coming from the stage. She would have liked to see who was playing, but time was short.

They came to Kate's cabin door, and she unlocked it. Her confident expression became an open gape of confusion.

The straw hat had disappeared.

"So?" asked Feldman. "Where's the straw hat?"

"I don't know," Kate stuttered in shock. "I left it right here."

Cherenkov snorted in exasperation.

"Are you sure, Kate?" asked Feldman. "Maybe you put it somewhere else?"

"I am absolutely certain."

"The hat must have grown legs," Cherenkov chided, visibly angry. "Or maybe its owner from seventy years ago took it on a little stroll down the hallway. Or, more likely, you dreamed it up, honey."

"I did not dream it up. It was real. I had it in my hands. It had a blue sash with a stain on the edge." Tears welled up in her eyes, and she had to make a tremendous effort not to cry. "I swear."

"Kate, the hat is not here," Feldman said.

A knot twisted in Kate's neck, and she didn't know what to say.

"I know the last forty-eight hours have been very emotional, Kate." Feldman squeezed her shoulder affectionately, looking at her with sympathy. "I imagine this is too much for everyone. It's natural to think we've seen something or to mix up our facts. It can happen to anyone. It happens to us all."

"It wasn't a dream." Her voice was at its breaking point. "It wasn't a dream."

"Kate, let me give you a piece of advice," Feldman said. "Get some rest. Sleep it off. If you can't, Dr. Scott in the infirmary can prescribe something to help you do so. You'll see things more clearly in the morning. This awful fog will be gone, and the sun will sweep your doubts away. Don't worry."

Kate shook her head, on the verge of weeping. She was telling the truth, and they did not believe her. Cherenkov grumbled something in Russian as he took long strides down the hallway. Feldman gave Kate one last look and left with feet dragging and a hunched back.

When Kate was alone in her room, she scoured every corner in search of the hat, possessed by an energy that was charged with fury. By the end, it looked as though a rock band had trashed the room, but she did not find the hat. It was as though it had never existed.

Feeling completely hopeless, she fell back into a pile of blankets that had been tossed to the floor. She tried to calm down and control her breathing, but a single tear rolled down her cheek.

Ha, ha, ha, ha, ha, ha!

It was a feminine laugh, cruel and derisive. It came from *within* the cabin despite the fact that Kate was alone. The laughter reverberated off the walls, generating diabolical echoes. It stopped as quickly as it had begun and left an ominous silence in its wake.

Wrenched by an icy grip on her heart, Kate curled up in a corner and began to sob out loud. This was terror in its purest form.

Whatever had laughed had been laughing at her, feeding off her suffering and fear.

Even worse, the malevolent laughter made it clear that its fun was only just beginning.

X X V I I I

Two hours prior

At first it was subtle. A nearly imperceptible odor beneath the aroma wafting up from her dish of goulash. Senka looked up and thought it was coming off the redhead sitting across from her, but if it was, Kate had no idea. She was lost in her own world.

Senka felt a twinge of excitement pulse through her body, but she managed to pull herself together. She had been completely abstinent for four months. To her, *completely* meant that not even a date with the showerhead was allowed, and it was getting harder and harder to clear her head, especially now that a woman as gorgeous as Kate sat so close to her. Their knees brushed below the table, and with each touch, Senka fell victim to waves of desire that nearly choked her. But Kate did not seem tempted to dip into the pleasures of Sappho. At least not yet.

Senka took a deep breath and smiled, hiding her true feelings. It was something she had done very well since she was a little girl.

She had grown up in a small town, primarily Serbian, in Bosnia. One day, the Bosnian brigades launched an attack against Mladić's paramilitary Serbian forces, which had besieged Sarajevo. Nobody guessed that the Bosnians, battered and on the brink of defeat, would be capable of organizing such a powerful incursion. But they did, and it was the reason why the Serbs were not able to defend Senka's hometown. During the twelve hours in which her small town was in Bosnian hands, her village morphed into a microcosm of all the horrors of war. The darkest sides of the human soul had risen to the surface, unfettered and unchecked. A desire for revenge coupled with anger invaded the souls of those men.

Little Senka watched them line up and shoot her father and twelve other men from the village. Later, the Bosnians chucked the villagers' bodies down a well. Senka would never forget her father's blank expression when his body toppled over the edge. Only minutes beforehand, her father had been telling her a story.

Next, she watched a handful of soldiers systematically rape her mother and three other women on the hood of their truck as the rest of the platoon cheered them on and hooted. Only after they had gotten their fill did they slit the women's throats and toss them down the same well. By then, Senka's tears had stopped flowing.

Finally, four militants who were jacked up on booze and cocaine grabbed seven-year-old Senka and slammed her down on the hood of the car. They ripped off her pink bunny rabbit pajamas and brutally had their way with her for two hours as the village burned to the ground.

She never understood why they hadn't killed her. Maybe they had felt a shred of compassion for the little girl. But in all likelihood the Serbian counterattack had more to do with it. What is certain is that when they found her there alone in the middle of the square, blood running down her naked legs, she was the only person left alive in a place once teeming with life.

No different from dozens of towns and villages on both sides of the war. Hell on earth.

She spent the next ten years in an orphanage. She became a quiet child with a broken soul who felt terrified whenever she met a man. Her anger at the world slowly transformed into ferocity, and that was how she wound up getting arrested when she was seventeen and was offered an ultimatum: the Serbian army or a cell block.

So Senka continued to fight. She soon discovered she had a real talent for inflicting pain on other human beings, and in doing so, she managed to eradicate some of the pain that had built up within her. After a little more than a year, she entered the intelligence division and from there a special counterespionage unit. She had developed into a stunning woman, the kind of idealized Slavic woman men fantasize about. Still, her pain lingered on, incessant, and bored a hole inside of her that seemed to have emptied her.

One evening she found herself in a hotel in Vienna. A woman she hardly knew was lying in her bed after a particularly wild fuck. Senka was holding a bottle of whiskey and looking down the barrel of her gun, wondering why she did not simply pull the trigger and end the pain once and for all.

But then Feldman entered her life. Her unit, by request of Interpol, had been investigating Feldman's investments in Belgrade and his contacts with the Russian mafia. When she first found herself face-to-face with him, his magnetic eyes captivated Senka in a way she was unable to understand. Each of them was like a mirror of the other. They were two tortured souls who were searching for answers to unanswerable questions.

So Senka left the military and began working for Feldman. He was always able to guess her heart's desires. He was, to Senka, like a surrogate father. For Feldman, Senka's profound sorrow and self-destructive tendencies, along with her uncanny ability to ascertain information and procure results no one else could, constituted an important asset. He felt all the tenderness a grandfather might feel for a particularly gifted granddaughter.

She had been working for him for five years. It was enough time to have allayed her grief. It finally looked as if one of them would be able to confront the fears and doubts that had been lurking for so long. Feldman had found the cure to his anguish in the *Valkyrie*. As for Senka, she knew she could never escape from atop the hood of that truck.

Kate got up and bid her a hasty good-bye, pulling Senka back to the present. The reporter seemed nervous, as if she needed to get somewhere urgently. As she left she knocked over a glass of water. Senka hardly noticed. She was too busy watching Kate with curiosity and lust. She could not help it.

Senka finished her meal and headed for Feldman's cabin. The old man had not looked well after finding the body. That was no surprise. Even she had been affected. And then there was Moore. What the hell had happened to him? She thought it would be best to check on Feldman to see if he needed anything.

Walking down the hall, the sweet scent she had detected earlier returned stronger than before. She sniffed in all directions like a hound searching for a trail. Just then, a sharp, stabbing pain attacked her temples. It was as if someone had stuck a red-hot needle into her head just above the ears and decided to slowly push it deeper and deeper. The pain came in mounting waves that made her so nauseated she had to lean against a wall to keep from stumbling over.

I should go to the infirmary, she told herself. *This is the second time today.*

She turned around and tried to remember how to get to the ship's clinic. Her mind was heavy as if jammed with ten thoughts at once. Attempting to shake off the pain, she managed to focus on the hallway, and remember where to go. She needed to turn right, pass three doors, go down the stairs, and find the second door. Infirmary.

She began walking there, but then a gust of rain struck her face, causing her eyes to open wide. Dazed, she blinked several times. Her entire body was soaked. To wipe the water out of her eyes, she would first have to put the screwdriver in her pocket.

Screwdriver?

She was unable to move. She clutched it tighter in her hand and reflected. The run-of-the-mill screwdriver was made of steel, and its handle was red plastic. The bottom had some marks on it like it had been pressed against something hot.

She had never seen this tool before, and she had no idea where it had come from.

She glanced up and could not choke back her panic. Senka dropped the screwdriver, and it rolled on the floor slowly before coming to a stop at the toe of her boots.

She was on the upper deck, above the command bridge. Less than five feet from her was one of the *Valkyrie*'s enormous smokestacks belching smoke into the air. A little farther, a forest of antennas stood out in the fog, the radar whirling to no end.

What am I doing here?

She took a couple of shaky steps forward before noticing the fistful of different colored copper wires in her other hand. The plastic insulation was frayed at the ends as if the wires had been torn out of something.

How did I get here? What's happening?

She dropped the wires like they were nettles. She wiped her hands on her shirt and looked around anxiously. No one was in sight. The yellowish fog was still thick. The only difference was that it was now raining. She was soaked as if she had been in the rain for an hour.

She walked a little farther, like a disoriented sleepwalker. Her stomach lurched, and she vomited her lunch across an air vent. She spent a long time heaving until all that came out were strings of spittle. When she righted herself she was shaking uncontrollably.

I must be going insane.

Her head was buzzing, incapable of taking in everything that was happening to her. She felt dizzy, lost, and above all, frightened. Her eyes fell upon a ladder leading down to the crew's quarters near the bridge. To have reached this point, she would have had to climb up from that way, but she had no recollection of scaling that ladder.

She went down carefully. The descent was complex because, apart from her tremors, every rung was slicked with something slippery like oil. When she finally made it down to the bridge, she sneaked about discreetly. She was not sure what she would say if she encountered someone. They would see her soaked, pale as a corpse, and shaking out of control.

She needed to get to her cabin to change. Then, she could think over what had happened. She tiptoed across the cigar lounge in first class, leaving a trail of droplets behind on the rugs and teak tables with their fitted bronze ashtrays.

Senka.

She stopped cold like a deer caught in headlights when she heard the voice.

Senka, I'm right here. Look at me.

Senka closed her eyes tight, unable to move a muscle.

This is not happening, this is not happening, this is not . . .

Senka!

The voice was louder, and as if controlled by an invisible hand, Senka turned around.

A woman who looked to be around thirty was on top of one of the tables. She wore a black frilly nightgown that didn't cover her knees. The low-cut neckline revealed a pair of large firm breasts. Around her neck a long pearl necklace fell to her waist. She was blonde, just like Senka, with restless green eyes that stared out with great interest as she coolly took a long drag from her cigarette.

Hi, Senka. Come sit with me.

Unable to object, Senka sat next to the woman with the hypnotic gaze. Senka could not look away.

My poor Senka. You are soaked and trembling from the cold. You have to get those clothes off. We can't let you catch a cold.

"Who are you?" Her voice sounded like gravel. "What's going on?"

I'm your friend, Senka. Nothing bad is going on. I've come to help you.

The woman reached out and took Senka's hand. She had a warm, gentle hand. As soon as it grazed her skin, Senka had to fight the urge to moan. She was no longer cold.

You're lovely, Senka. Intelligent and beautiful. But you're so alone. Do you like being alone, Senka?

Senka shook her head as delightful warmth moved down her chest toward her pelvis. All of the fear and confusion she had felt a minute ago melted away like it had been a terribly realistic nightmare. Although one part of her mind continued to struggle, aware that none of this was normal, the objections were drowned out by the rest of her thoughts.

I figured. I don't like to be alone, either, and I've been alone for so, so long.

The woman leaned forward and stroked Senka's cheek with the back of her hand. The touch set off a blaze beneath Senka's skin. Suddenly, all her needs subsided, replaced by a more pressing and intense desire. It was an oven between her legs.

The woman pursed her lips, and Senka realized that although she had been talking, the woman had not opened her mouth. But the voice of logic was becoming so weak that it wasn't worth paying attention. The blare in her skull was deafening. Voices blended together in excitement.

I'm going to kiss you. Would you like me to kiss you, Senka?

As if in a dream she nodded and leaned forward slightly, without loosening her grip on the other woman's hand. In turn, the mysterious woman slowly moved closer and pressed her lips gently against Senka's.

She was sweet with a metallic aftertaste. Her mouth was hot—too hot—but her playful tongue glided inside Senka's mouth.

Senka moaned and felt dazed. The fire in her crotch was out of control and sent a tide of desire swelling throughout her.

Come, Senka. Let's go somewhere cozy. Wanna come with me?

Senka nodded, completely at this stranger's beck and call. She realized for the first time in a long time that the agony in her heart was distant and frail.

The two of them stood up, still holding hands, and walked out of the cigar lounge. Somehow, the blonde knew the way to Senka's cabin. When they got there Senka sluggishly fished around in her pocket for the key. She watched herself with a blank, detached look. She was unable to summon enough coordination to perform this menial task, yet she was unconcerned. It was like watching another person.

The woman smiled seductively. She turned the knob, and the door opened easily, like it had never been locked in the first place. Senka's warning sirens, already silenced and defeated, remained mute. The bed gleamed in the soft lamp light, tempting them forth.

They entered the cabin and closed the door behind them. The woman began kissing Senka again, this time with much more passion and fervor. The woman's hands cupped Senka's breasts, lightly pinching and twisting her nipple until it became hard. Senka moaned in pleasure and pulled the blonde against her, holding her tightly.

Still locked in their passionate embrace, Senka began to undo her soaked pants, which fell easily to the floor. She kicked off her boots and was suddenly left in no more than a shirt, still damp, and a pair of panties. The woman ran her hands up and down Senka's body. With every brush of skin, Senka moaned, prey to fresh, electric torrents of pleasure.

She leaned back to take her shirt off. The wet blouse fought to stay glued to her body, and it took a moment to peel it off.

The mystery woman had let her nightgown fall down to her ankles and was completely naked, smiling seductively. Her golden skin looked delicious enough to lick. Her nipples were large, dark circles, and she had a sexy little patch of blonde pubic hair that almost looked white.

The blonde reached out her hands and pulled Senka onto the bed without a word. They fell down side by side, and the mystery woman skillfully slipped off Senka's panties. Her mouth ran ravenously toward Senka's breasts and began licking her nipples with deliberate desire. Each time the woman's lips pressed against Senka's breasts, every last nerve exploded with pleasure. After a minute Senka began moaning faster. She watched as the woman kissed back and forth between her breasts with a rhythm that grew faster as her hands continued to caress her body up and down. To Senka's great surprise, she exploded in a long electric orgasm that felt like freedom. She moaned in ecstasy and dug her nails into the woman's back. The mystery woman was breathing in a deep and rhythmic fashion. Senka tried to turn her over, but the woman would not allow it. Instead, she continued down, tracing complex designs on Senka's skin. At Senka's navel, she paused briefly before kissing down to Senka's sex, which was begging for attention.

The blonde teasingly licked everywhere around Senka's clit before focusing solely on it, nibbling and sucking that little bit of pulsing flesh. Senka let out a long cry of pleasure. She felt as if all the energy in the universe were being focused through that little nub between her legs. She saw that the blonde woman's hair was spread out over her abdomen as her face remained buried.

Every part of Senka's body was on fire. Her legs quivered uncontrollably, and she felt another orgasm building up, this time a wave even bigger and more powerful than before.

Do you like it, Senka? Do you want more?

Senka could only whimper yes before she climaxed for a second time, this time with the force of a flood. She screamed out in total bliss as her back arched. Waves of pleasure traveled rhythmically down her body from head to toe in powerful bursts.

Soaked in sweat, she continued to shake uncontrollably. The blonde, leaning on her elbow, watched her lustfully.

Did you like that, Senka?

Grinning like a Cheshire cat, Senka nodded, still unable to speak. A heavy, inevitable drowsiness had overcome her. It was getting more and more difficult to keep her eyes open. Her mind was clouding up and going dark like a city experiencing a blackout.

Before completely surrendering to sleep, she heard the woman get up from bed. A pungently sweet, tinny odor permeated the entire room. Senka was bleeding from her nose, though she did not know it. She was sprawled out on the mattress, naked and reeking of sex.

We love our friends, Senka. You've behaved yourself and did as we asked. This is a little present. We'll take care of you.

Forever.

X X I X

Valkyrie
Day three

The loud steps outside Kate's door woke her. It sounded like a group of people racing down the hallway. Over the noise she could hear excited voices but could not quite make out the topic of discussion.

In the cabin's semidarkness Kate blinked and felt numb. She glanced at her watch, feeling disoriented. It was past midnight. She was still curled up in the corner where she had fallen after Feldman and Cherenkov left her room.

After she had heard that sinister laugh.

She had passed out after exhausting herself of all the tears she'd been storing up since boarding the ship. She was completely beat, miserable, and crippled by fear. But above all she felt terribly alone. With every passing moment she regretted more and more accepting this assignment. There was something intrinsically perverse about the *Valkyrie*, something that seeped through both crew and passengers like the stench of rotting fish. Out here in the middle of the ocean, there was nowhere to hide.

She got to her feet and winced. Her leg was asleep. She paced awkwardly around the room to get the blood flowing. Massaging her thigh, she heard two voices, one male and one female. The rhythmic jangle of jewelry accompanied the conversation, which was slowly fading as they walked farther away.

Kate looked at her watch again. It was late, but perhaps there had been a second round of dinner. All those crew members had to go somewhere. Her stomach grumbled with hunger.

She went into the bathroom, brushed her teeth, and washed her face. Then, she combed her hair and styled it, so it didn't appear like she'd been asleep on the floor. Looking at herself in the mirror, she couldn't help but notice the distressing dark bags under her eyes.

She went back into her room and put on slim-fit jeans and a blouse, over which she wore a corduroy jacket. It seemed to be getting only colder outside the *Valkyrie*. Once she was satisfied with her appearance, she slung her camera around her neck and, after double bolting her cabin door, walked down the hallway.

The corridor was softly lit, and a light hint of perfume floated on the air. As she walked toward the dining hall, she thought about how best to broach the matter of the straw hat with Feldman. Kate worried that he had lost some of his confidence in her. Perhaps Carter would be able to advise her on a different approach. Either way, she would have to talk to Feldman and Cherenkov again. She wanted to make it clear she was still worthy of trust and not mad as a hatter. She did not want to be left out of the loop under any circumstances.

As she neared the dining hall, the murmur of voices and music became louder and clearer. Someone was playing a tune not unlike what she had heard earlier that afternoon, only this time it sounded even better. Kate wasn't sure, but it sounded like a Charleston.

When she entered the hall, the enormous chandelier was fully illuminated, casting blinding diamonds of light over the polished marble staircase. Three women Kate had never seen before were dressed like flappers and advancing up the stairs. One of them said something that made all three explode in laughter.

Kate stood there, stunned by the vague sensation of being trapped in an absurd nightmare. Looking around the room, her eyes landed on two men dressed in old-fashioned tuxedos who were smoking as they leaned against a wall, watching her closely.

Kate closed her eyes tight. She was dreaming. She had to be dreaming. She opened her eyes again, but nothing had changed. The lights, the noise, the stench of tobacco, the murmuring of voices leaving the hall. The taller of the two men leaned over to the other and whispered something into his ear. The shorter man laughed and then glanced back at Kate, watching her unabashedly.

Kate started walking, but her legs felt weak like they might give out at any moment. She was also short of breath. When she made it to the foot of the staircase, she noticed that the enormous potted palm was no longer on the landing, and in its place were three flags: two had swastikas set against a red background, and the third was the KDF flag.

Horrified, Kate stumbled back into one of the enormous wooden eagles standing guard at the foot of the staircase. Its open beak screamed out an eternal call of silent defiance. Kate's gaze dropped to the wreath that the eagle clutched between its talons—an enormous wooden swastika sat in the middle.

"This can't be happening," she whispered in confusion. She sat down on the first step.

A waiter with a tray filled with glasses passed her by and gave her an inquisitive glance before moving on.

Feldman must be playing a joke on me. There has to be a hidden camera in here.

But the eagle was real. She ran her hands over the edge of the swastika. It was not glued or nailed into the wreath. It had been carved as a single piece. In order to alter the carving, they would have needed to tear out the entire staircase with an industrial crane. But before they could even do that, they would have needed to remove the roof just to get the crane in there in the first place. It was simply impossible in the middle of the ocean.

Kate dug her nails into her palms, and the pain was intense and distinct. It was no dream. She was awake.

"Are you all right, Fräulein?" The voice startled her. A waitress dressed in a black uniform and cap was leaning down, looking worried. "Would you like me to bring you a glass of water?"

Kate took a couple of deep breaths to calm her nerves. A woman who was either dead or had disappeared more than seventy years ago was offering her a glass of water. Or maybe it was a ghost. Kate forced herself to choke back the hysterical laughter that was threatening to erupt.

"Nein, danke," she answered in perfect German, automatically switching languages. "I'm just a bit dizzy. I'll be all right in a moment. Really."

"Are you sure?"

"Positive," she said, trying to give her best smile even though she knew it was a tragic substitute for a genuine one.

The woman nodded and left, but not without one last sidelong glance at Kate.

The noise in the hall became completely raucous when the band started a new song. It was an all-out celebration. Kate stood up and steadied herself on the carved swastika before starting up the staircase. She stared long and hard at the flags as she passed them but did not dare touch them. She was certain they were real, just like everything else around her.

The doors of the dance hall, which was usually closed off and dark, were open wide, and the space was packed with people. Couples were dancing the foxtrot while other groups of passengers moved back and forth on the dance floor, attended to by a small army of waiters and maids. On stage a seven-piece band was playing as if possessed. The party had swung into a groove. Champagne was flowing, and the passengers were red-faced and lively, wrapped in the cacophony of the celebration and the dense clouds of smoke. The laughter was uproarious, yet to Kate's ears, slightly off, like everything was out of tune.

A woman with a blank look passed by her side, sending a chill through Kate's body. Everything seemed so real. But there was *something* that did not fit even if she couldn't put her finger on it. Despite the obvious fact that none of it could be real.

Kate considered the possibility that some vein had burst in her brain and that she had lost her mind. She wondered if she might not be lying in her cabin bed at that very moment, no more than a vegetable, declared by the ship's doctor to be certifiably insane.

Kate grabbed a glass of wine from a tray as it was carried past her. She took a sip, tasting a fresh and bubbly white Riesling. If this were a hallucination, it was the most perfectly realistic one of all time.

A familiar face in the crowd caught her eye. It belonged to one of the chemists, and he was dressed in a fancy two-piece suit. Her heart beat faster. Seeing someone she recognized in the midst of this ghostly celebration made the wheel of unreality she found herself trapped on spin a little slower. Kate dug deep in her mind to recall his name. He was Finnish; it was something euphonious and exotic. It started with "Lau." Laukannen. That was it. He and another chemist had joked around with her the day of the first meeting. He was a kind, innocent-looking man with deep blue eyes.

Kate began walking between groups of revelers. As she passed through she noticed how conversations were coming to a halt and that cliques of groups had begun to talk in whispers. Dozens of eyes were on her.

Something was wrong.

She caught a glimpse of her reflection as she passed a mirror, and it dawned on her. Kate's casual outfit stood out like a sore thumb in the middle of this formal 1930s party. Likely, none of those present had ever seen a pair of jeans in their lives. That is, if they were truly alive.

Ignoring the stares, she closed in on the chemist and his group. He was chatting in German with two women and a man. As Kate got closer they abruptly became silent.

"Hello, Mr. Laukannen," Kate said in German. She leaned closer to him and switched to English, whispering, "To the lounge, quickly."

The Finn was taken aback and looked exceptionally baffled. "I'm sorry, Fräulein," he whispered back in German. "I do not understand you. I do not believe I speak your language."

"Laukannen," she murmured, shaking her head. The icy grip within her tightened.

"What's wrong, darling," asked one of the women, placing her hand on Laukannen's shoulder as if asserting ownership. "Who is this woman?"

"I have no idea, love," he replied, looking at Kate with mistrust in his eyes.

Kate stumbled away without a word and felt their glares pierce the back of her neck. If they assumed she had been drunk, her inglorious departure did nothing to counter that theory.

She was in the middle of the dance floor. People parted as she passed, as if they could smell that she did not belong. The sweetness in the air was almost suffocating, and yet, on this occasion, there was a hint of decay underneath. The hall smelled like everything in it was rotting. Kate was dizzy. She needed to get out of there.

As she left she saw Harper chatting with a group of passengers. The captain was dressed in his formal uniform and had a thick mustache on his face, which had not been there earlier that morning. Showing no sign of recognizing her, he suspiciously watched her pass.

He whispered something to a man at his side and then made a subtle gesture to the waiters standing along the wall at the back of the hall. Kate watched as two of them began walking toward her, making their way through the crowd.

With a gasp of terror she turned around and moved through the hall, trying to widen the gap between her and the waiters. Harper's intense blue eyes hovered in her mind. It wasn't just their cutthroat, merciless appearance. It was Kate's certainty that earlier that day Captain Harper's eyes had been brown.

X X X

Kate bounded down the staircase two steps at a time. On a whim she took hold of her camera and began snapping pictures in all directions. If this nightmare should ever end, she wanted to be sure it was real and that she hadn't dreamed it. Or perhaps she needed definitive proof she was indeed crazy.

As she took the first shot, the automatic flash went off with a blinding blue light, which filled the entire hall and attracted a few curious glances. But Kate had better things to think about, as the two waiters who were after her had just reached the top of the stairs.

The young journalist caught sight of a door leading to a little hidden hallway. She made sure the waiters could not see her from the top of the stairs, and without a moment's hesitation, she ventured into the hallway, closing the door behind her.

Laughter. The laughter of children came from the end of the tunnel. Kate ran forward and tried to find the source of the sound. The hall led to a room she had never seen. The wood-paneled walls rose to a height of a little more than six feet. Children's frescoes depicting farmers, deer, and snowmen were hanging on all four walls.

A little antique carousel was spinning in the middle of the room. Horses, rabbits, pigs, and cats turned ceaselessly around the wrought-iron center. The saddles were marked with the KDF symbol. Each one of them had a little boy or girl on top, screaming joyfully. All around the carousel ran a waist-high rail, and to the side was the ride's operator, who lackadaisically handled the controls as a military march blared from a gramophone. On a bench in the back, a group of middle-aged women were gossiping among themselves. Periodically, they would stop to look wearily at the children.

Kate glanced back. The door she had come through was still closed. She crept back and pushed the door ajar. She saw that the two waiters were still in the lobby, looking in every direction for her. Eventually, one of them ran off toward the bridge, and the other headed into the dining hall.

They had lost her. But she did not have much time.

Think, Kate, think. What are you going to do?

The obvious choice was to go back to her cabin and wait until the delirium subsided. That is, if it ever did. She wondered if Tarasov and his team at Wolf und Klee had been right all along. What if they had somehow gone back to 1939? Feldman, Cherenkov, and Carter had maintained that it was completely impossible. That it would violate the basic laws of physics. None of them was here now, however, seeing all of this.

Getting back to her cabin was not going to be easy. To get there she would have to cross through the lobby. The well-lit, crowded lobby with those two waiters chasing her. Not to mention her outfit would attract unwanted attention. She needed to find an outfit appropriate to the period.

As she took in her surroundings, Kate noticed a little girl who was sitting at the back of the nursery, completely alone and set apart from the noise of the rest of the children. She seemed focused, looking in Kate's direction with contempt like kids do when something greatly displeases them. Brow furrowed, she began swinging her legs in her seat. It was not just her attitude that was different. Her clothes were much simpler than those the others wore. Instead of shiny leather shoes and a lace dress, she was wearing sandals and a gray linen dress that looked like it had seen better days. It was one or two sizes too big for her like she had inherited it from an older sister.

The girl lifted her hand and pointed straight at Kate. She remained unmoving, with her arm raised and eyes fixed on Kate. The effect was so shocking that Kate had to stifle the overwhelming urge to scream. She was on the verge of running away, but if she retraced her steps she would come across the two waiters and however many other people were now searching for her. The little girl lowered her arm before she cocked her head to one side like she was listening to something coming from far away. Despite the fact that Kate's mental alarms were blaring, something drew her toward the girl.

She approached and managed to avoid the curious mothers, who remained seated on the bench. Kate kneeled down next to the girl, who stared at her without blinking.

"Hello," Kate said. "May I sit beside you?"

The little girl nodded, legs still swinging beneath her seat.

"Why were you pointing at me?" Kate's voice cracked, and her mouth was completely dry.

The little girl remained silent for a while and looked absently at the floor. Kate noticed that she looked malnourished and her left arm had a huge, ugly yellow bruise.

When Kate repeated the question, the girl turned to her.

"You shouldn't be here," she said very simply, her voice imbued with abject sorrow.

It was unnatural to hear such a small child use that tone of voice. It spoke of suffering, horrors, and unabated hardships. It spoke of lost innocence.

"I know," Kate managed to utter. "I'm lost and I just want to get back to my cabin. You wouldn't happen to know . . ."

The girl shook her head and looked sullen. "I don't mean here," she finally answered as she lightly stroked her bruise. "I mean now. You aren't from here. You cannot be here. She will be very mad if she sees you."

"She? Who? Why will she be mad?" Kate babbled out. "Who are you talking about?"

The little girl reached out and touched Kate's plastic watch with pictures of animal heads and colorful beads. Her niece, Andrea, had given it to her as a present. The little girl looked at it with dreamy eyes as if she were imagining herself wearing it on her own wrist.

"Do you like it?" Kate asked, taking off the watch and handing it to the child.

The little girl took it in her hands with reverence as if she could not believe something so beautiful could exist. She ran her hands over the beads, enjoying the feel of the plastic like it was something exotic. Suddenly, her knuckles went white, and her fist shut tight. She looked up in terror.

"We have to go," she said full of fear. "She's coming."

"She? Who do you mean?"

"She's coming! She's coming!" She stood up, clearly shaken. "The others will follow. We have to go."

Without a glance back the little girl ran toward the door at the back of the room. Thinking about what to do, Kate noticed the same sweet, metallic odor that had become familiar to her. The smell alone made her stomach turn. The carousel had come to a stop, and all of the children silently stared at Kate with empty eyes. Their mothers had stopped their chatter to fix their attention on her. One had dropped her eyes to the floor, while another woman, who had been knitting, held her hands frozen in midmotion, like a statue.

Every one of the women had something in her eyes. Something alien. Something dark.

Kate's blood turned to ice. Not waiting a second longer, she got to her feet and walked backward toward the door the little girl had used. Her right hand drifted toward her camera, which hung around her neck. A loud click-click-click echoed throughout the room as Kate snapped a flurry of pictures.

It was enough to set the chaos in motion. All of the children simultaneously began shouting at the top of their lungs. These were not normal screams, however. They were deep, savage shrieks, far too cruel to come from the mouths of children. They were rough and bestial. They were howls of warning.

There she is. There she is. There she is. There she is. There she is. There she is. There she is. There she is. There she is. There she is. There she is. There she is. There she is. There she is. There she is. There she is ...

The screams reverberated with such force that Kate thought her head might explode like a live grenade. She put her hands over her ears, but the collective noise sounded *inside* her head.

It hurt. It was painful.

Kate turned around and sprinted out of the room. A loud noise came from behind her like something being ripped, but she didn't stick around to find out what it was. Her life, or perhaps her sanity, was at stake.

The door led to a long service hallway that was much simpler than the hallways in first class. At the end of the hall, she caught a glimpse of the girl and her terror-stricken face before she disappeared around a corner.

Kate sprinted up the hall, her camera bouncing hard against her chest. Something was chasing her, rounding each corner with what sounded like a watery gurgle.

This part of the ship was like a maze. The ceiling was a complex filigree of thick cables and metal pipes instead of the beautiful wood paneling adorning the other corridors. Every so often the hall forked, and it did not take long for Kate to be completely disoriented. Her only saving grace was the little girl running a few feet ahead. Kate knew that if she lost track of the girl, she would be hopelessly lost and at the mercy of whatever was after her.

Something heavy fell to the floor behind her with a tremendous clatter. Whatever was chasing her, it was getting closer. The hall lights were becoming dimmer as whatever it was began absorbing every ray of light, like a vast black hole of wickedness. The lights flickered and slowly went out. Gradually, the entire hallway was being swallowed into darkness as if the electric current had lost its intensity. Kate was blindly running, somehow panting and gagging simultaneously. Ahead of her the girl's gray dress blended into the darkness. The long blonde hair that seemed to float above the ground acted as her only guide.

If you trip, you're fucked, Kate. Watch your damn step.

She ran into the opening to a staircase that led to the lower decks, and Kate knew where she was. It was one of the points of access to second class. The little girl moved down the stairs with difficulty, her sandals clapping as she clung to the handrail.

"Wait," Kate shouted as she tried to catch her breath. "Don't go down there. It's dangerous."

The little girl ignored her and continued her descent. Kate hesitated, but the sounds of whatever was chasing her were becoming louder. She placed her weight on the first step. The staircase was completely black like the depths of a cave. There was no light at all, and the shadows seemed to be moving restlessly, waiting.

Another crash sounded closer. She could wait no longer and began to move down the stairs.

Into the darkness.

X X X I

Once when she was little, Kate had been trapped in an elevator. In those days she was known as Catalina Soto, and she lived with her parents in Barcelona. Although she couldn't recall how old she was at the time of this incident, she remembered being alone. She had been going up when there had been a power outage, and the elevator came to a halt. From there things only got worse.

The worst part had been when the lights went out and little Catalina was alone in the dark, her only companion being the heavy dread crawling up her legs.

Too young to be rational, she did not even consider that the blackout would only last a few minutes at most. Terrified, she began screaming. It was Sunday, however, and very few of her neighbors were home. Those twenty minutes trapped on the elevator constituted one of the most traumatic experiences of her life.

As a souvenir from that experience, Kate Kilroy had developed a profound fear of the dark.

Now each step down into the darkness required a colossal effort on her part. The hallway light was dimming, and it didn't take long for her to be immersed in total darkness. Anxiety impeded her breathing. She gasped for air but felt like she was drowning.

She looked back up, yearning for the rectangle of dim light that marked the stairwell's opening. Without realizing it she took a few steps back up, toward the light and fresh air.

But then she saw it.

She was not sure what to call it, but something created a silhouette at the top of the stairs. Kate could only make out a vague shape that looked remotely human, but it was definitely *not* a person. At least it did not move like one. It somehow glided along the walls and floor at the same time. Darker than the surrounding shadows, it was a black hole absorbing all light that dared to pass by.

She gritted her teeth and continued down the stairs. She could no longer see the little girl, but she could hear her footsteps and her labored breathing ahead. Kate's camera strap dug into her neck like barbed wire. She lifted it over her neck, ready to throw it on the ground before having a much better idea. She raised it above her head and took a picture.

The flash went off and filled the entire stairwell with a surreal light. Briefly, Kate saw the little girl's figure a few feet ahead, concentrating on her next step.

"Wait up," Kate shouted, more to hear her voice than to make the little girl stop running.

Kate continued snapping pictures to light the way. Each time the light died out, she was submerged in darkness again, but at least she was able to see enough in that half second of flash to help her along and widen the gap between her and the shadow.

When her feet fell on plush carpeting, she knew she'd reached the hallway below. She took a series of pictures, so she could orient herself with the aid of the flash. She nearly fell over in fright when one of the flashes momentarily lit up the face of

Adolf Hitler standing right over her. She began screaming until she realized it was only a painting.

The hallway branched in several directions. The girl had chosen her path and stopped long enough to motion Kate toward her.

Kate took another picture and glanced at the camera's LCD screen. The bitter taste of bile settled in her mouth as her stomach churned.

Shit. Shitshitshitshitshitshitshit.

In the moment the flash lit up the hallway, Kate had been able to see soft carpeting, wood-paneled walls, and perfectly white cabin doors.

On her screen, however, the same hallway was completely ravaged by the passage of time. The carpeting was only a decayed semblance of what it had been, and the wood paneling was rotting, discolored, and warped. The picture even showed the rusted iron plating that ran along the bottom. The paint on the doors was peeling, and a few of them had even fallen down.

Another watery gurgle like a sink being cleared sounded right behind Kate. She exhaled, and a cloud of vapor formed in front of her face. Little specks of frost began to cover the walls.

Come here, bitch. Listen to my voice.

The pain inside Kate's skull became intolerable, a hot searing burn. Screaming, she stumbled away. The little girl was waiting for her around the corner, near a cargo elevator with an interior light casting a dim clarity over the room.

A metal gate divided the room in two. A sign in German warned that third-class passengers were not allowed in second class. Nevertheless, the door was wide open, swinging on its hinges. Kate blinked. The room looked just as ruined and decayed as the unrestored second-class section Kate had seen the day before. She rubbed her eyes in disbelief.

When she opened them again, the room was as pristine as the day it had left the shipyard. Kate choked back her fear. Just a moment before, the room had been in ruins. Suddenly, the image *skipped*.

Kate could find no other word to describe what happened. It was like she was watching an old, worn-out VHS tape that displayed a distorted picture. In a flash, the two images, the old and the new, had overlapped like two radio stations broadcasting on the same frequency. The overlap did not last long. Maybe a few seconds. The elevator's lights began to flicker and threatened to die out completely. Then, it stopped. The room again looked as immaculate as it had in the thirties.

"We need to go down to third class. They can't get us there," the girl whispered.

Kate got into the freight elevator, and the girl pulled the gate shut and hit a button. With a jolt they continued their descent into the depths of the *Valkyrie*, jerking and creaking the entire way.

As the elevator went down, Kate examined her camera. The red low-battery light had turned on. Kate cursed. Her liberal use of the flash had drained the battery, and she would be lucky if she could get a few more shots.

The little girl looked up, scared. Something slammed into the gate on the floor they had just passed, and Kate fell back against the wall, bashing her head hard enough to see a tiny constellation of stars dance before her eyes. The elevator jerked along like someone was shaking it.

She got up and grumbled to herself. The little girl moved close to her and placed her hand on Kate's. She pressed back in relief and appreciation. Her skin was smooth but surprisingly cold.

"What's your name, darling?" whispered Kate.

"Esther."

"Where are we going, Esther?"

The elevator stopped. Kate concluded they had to be below the ship's Plimsoll line, probably near the cargo holds. She and Esther left the elevator and came into a wide recreation room in third class. Moisture and time had wreaked havoc here. Mold covered broken chairs, and the air smelled like stagnant water and rotting wood. Where there had been light fixtures once, brass wires gnawed away by rust hung from the ceiling.

During their descent, the image had skipped again.

Esther looked considerably more relaxed, as if that dark shadow could no longer bother her. Kate saw an antique oil lantern in the corner of the room. Its glass cover was cracked, and its copper base was a sickly green color. When she went over and shook it, she could hear that there was still fuel inside. She searched her pockets until she found an old lighter Robert had kept as a good-luck charm. It no longer ignited, but it still sparked. She brought the lighter up to the candlewick, and within seconds a warm and comforting source of light traced a magical protective circle all around her, vanquishing the shadows.

They walked down an ugly hallway with huge communal dormitories on both sides that could accommodate about forty people each. The *Valkyrie* was able to transport many more passengers in second and third class, and the majority of its passengers would have traveled in the latter of those two.

Following her reporter's instincts, Kate's hand automatically reached for her camera to take a picture. It was then she realized she was alone.

Esther had vanished.

Kate searched several rooms and called out for the girl, but it was as if she had evaporated. There was no sign of her anywhere, and Kate had no idea how to get out of third class. She looked around, confused.

Then, she heard the voice.

"Kate."

It was only one word, but her whole world stopped spinning with its utterance. Her heart skipped a beat, and her emotions fought for attention as they all suddenly wanted to be heard.

"Kate," the voice repeated.

She began trembling incessantly as fat tears fell down her cheeks. That voice. She knew it so well. She had missed it so much. That voice.

She whirled around, propelled by disbelief and hope. She was ready to see the body from which that voice originated. Ready to be drunk on happiness.

Smiling, he watched her as he leaned against a door frame, his hair uncombed. Vibrant, confident, charming.

It was him.

As he had always been.

Kate wiped the tears from her cheeks with the back of her hand and broke into her first genuine smile since he'd died.

"Hello, Robert."

XXXII

They stared at each other for what seemed like forever. Robert grinned, his eyes crinkling with the familiar fan of wrinkles around his eyes that she'd always covered with kisses. Kate wept openly, caught between the most intense extremes of pain and joy.

Robert was within her reach, but she knew he couldn't be real. He'd been dead for a month, and his cold gray ashes were in a ceramic black urn in her cabin.

"It can't be," Kate said, shaking her head as her insides tore apart. "I know you can't be here."

"I'm here, Kate. Right in front of you. I'm as real as that silly camera around your neck, which is actually mine, or at least it used to be. We bought it together in New York. Remember that day we thought the world might end because it was raining so hard?"

Kate could hardly see through her tears. Of course, she remembered that day. On a walk through the city, Robert had laughed elatedly about his new camera, just like a little kid. They'd stopped to watch a mime in Central Park before the rain drove them back to their hotel. While the downpour outside threatened to wash the city away, they made love for three hours.

The people in the next room had complained about the noise, and in response, Robert made outlandish excuses to the concierge while she remained in bed mortified and holding back waves of giggles.

She remembered it all so vividly that it hurt.

"You're gone, Robert," she sobbed. "You were hit by a fucking drunk driver who sped off."

"True," he answered seriously. "But somehow, I'm here for you, Kate. I'm here. I don't really know why or for how long, but I'm here."

"How do I know you aren't a hallucination?"

Robert sighed. Kate saw that he was dressed in the same cream-colored suit that he had put on the day he was killed. Even his tie was the same. With a spark of tenderness, she noticed that the knot of the tie, which she had tied herself, was exactly the same. When she'd arrived at the hospital to identify his body, emotional and screaming his name, the tie was gone. The paramedics had removed it, trying to save him. They returned it inside a plastic bag, a wrinkled ball that was stained with blood—his blood. But the knot had still been tied just as she had always done it. Just as she had learned from tying her father's tie as a little girl.

"Well, I guess there's only one way to find out, right?" Robert said with a playful half smile.

The expression was so familiar that Kate shook like a tree branch.

It was him.

"Have you come to take me away?" she asked. "What's it like? Will it hurt?"

"Kate," sighed Robert, shaking his head patiently. "You are not dead. Now are you going to spend the whole morning being the clever little reporter, or are you going to kiss me?"

Kate heard herself laugh like an enthusiastic little girl before a giant iridescent soap bubble, wanting to touch it but fearing it might burst.

"I'm not going to disappear, Kate."

Her feet, which had been soldered to the floor, came to life. Pressed up against him, she breathed in his aroma, the same combination of cologne and musk that she remembered so well. He felt hard, smooth, and hot, just as she remembered. She ran her hands up his body and around his neck, while he laced his hands around her waist before lowering them to her ass.

Kate closed her eyes in bliss as an animalistic growl, of both liberation and submission, escaped her throat. The mixture of relief, pain, joy, and excitement she felt was unbelievable. Robert scratched his stubble against her cheek, and instinctively, she looked up and parted her lips.

The passionate kiss was long and intense. Kate couldn't stop caressing her husband's face. It was like this was their first time again, and she eagerly devoured what was in front of her. Their two bodies fused together as if they were simply extensions of a singular entity that was impossible to pull apart.

After a few minutes they parted, breathing hard. Kate's eyes burned with the bright flame of excitement that had been extinguished.

"Robert, why here?" Kate asked, her cheek nuzzled against his chest so she could hear his heart. "Why now? Why is this happening, love?"

Robert kissed her on the forehead and rubbed her back. "I have no answers to your questions, Katie. Some things can be explained, and others can't. There are rules. Rules that cannot be broken. Just know I've been allowed to come here for a reason. To help you."

"I don't like this place." She buried her nose in his chest to breathe in his musk. "It's probably teeming with rats."

"Oh, there aren't any rats. That's for sure."

"How do you know?"

"Because if there were rats, every last one of them would have poked its whiskers out to have a look at your amazing ass."

Kate playfully slapped his shoulder and was taken aback by the sound of her laughter. It was lighthearted, carefree, and full of life. In this dark, dirty part of the ship, it sounded completely out of place and somewhat disconcerting.

"I've missed you so much," she whispered. "I don't ever want to let you go, Robert. Stay with me."

Robert let her go and sighed. "I don't want to leave you, either," he said. After a moment of hesitation, he added, "There's something important you need to know. Don't ask me how I know it or who told me because I can't explain that."

"Rules," Kate said.

"Rules." Robert nodded. "But listen closely. There's something evil on this ship. Dark, voracious, and evil. It's ancient and very dangerous. It's wrathful. You and I, for whatever reason, don't fit into its plans. We shouldn't be here. If it manages to catch you, it will take you somewhere even I can't get to. I will lose you forever."

"All of this is so scary. I need you."

"I'll be with you, babe. But you need to get out of here. Now. We both play a part in all this."

Kate shook her head and clung to Robert harder. The very notion of returning to the top deck of the *Valkyrie* and leaving her husband was unbearable.

"I don't want to leave you. Not after all this time." She shook her head. "No way."

Just then a tremendous vibration pulsed through the *Valkyrie*, breaking their embrace and knocking them to the ground. A second later the dull blast of a distant explosion seeped down into the depths of the ship. Seconds later the far-off sound of alarms could be heard. The ship lurched as if a torpedo had struck it.

"What do you think that was, Robert?" She turned back toward her husband, but he was gone.

She screamed his name until her throat hurt, but Robert had vanished just like Esther. She briefly wondered if she had hallucinated the whole thing, but even her clothes smelled like him. She could still taste him.

It had been real. She had been with him.

"Robert," she whispered.

A soft light came on to Kate's right. The service elevator had opened for her.

"Thanks, babe." Kate smiled as she got into the elevator. "I'll come back for you. I promise."

XXXIII

As the elevator creaked and groaned its way up the shaft, Kate tried to collect her thoughts. After the euphoria of reuniting with Robert, the sense of dread at being aboard the *Valkyrie* had returned once again. She couldn't get her husband's words out of her head.

There's something evil on this ship. Dark, voracious, and evil.

As the elevator rose, the blare of the alarm system became shriller. The stench of smoke and burning plastic became stronger. Something had gone awry upstairs.

The elevator stopped with one final jerk. Kate pulled the gate open and found her path blocked by a steel plate. She realized she was in first class, and the elevator had been one of the access points sealed off by Feldman's team. Her anger at being blocked out quickly turned to relief. The steel plates were tangible objects belonging to the real world in which she lived.

She pushed against the steel. It gave way slightly. When they had made the door, it was only to impede anyone from accessing the restricted area from the outside. Kate kicked the steel door with all her strength. It was like kicking a granite wall. Her foot hurt like hell. She tried again, but this time she attacked one of the welding joints. It was in vain. Without a lever it would be impossible to make the steel budge.

She was trapped there like a rat. So close and yet so far away. She wasn't exactly sure what awaited her on the other side, but at least there would be light. Nonetheless, she had no other choice but to go back down into the depths of the *Valkyrie* and try to retrace her steps.

The stress of the situation paralyzed Kate; she could do nothing but lean against the elevator wall. Loud cracking broke the silence. To her amazement the metal sheets began to bend as if being hit by an invisible force. The metal heaved repeatedly until the door finally crashed to the floor.

I'll be with you, babe, Robert had said.

"Thanks, honey," Kate whispered, feeling better than she had since first boarding the ship.

Cautiously, she leaned out of the elevator and found herself in one of the first-class service corridors. The pale light of morning pushed weakly through the small circular portholes. The light was tinged with the ghostly color of the fog that surrounded the *Valkyrie*. Gusts of wind lashed rain against the glass.

The smell of smoke was very strong now. Kate walked down the hall until she came across a staircase and suddenly found herself back in a part of the ship she recognized. It was then that Moore and several of his men appeared from around a corner. A couple of them wore firefighter suits and carried firefighting equipment. The others were holding fire extinguishers and an enormously long fire hose.

"Make way, Miss Kilroy," Moore bellowed before roughly pushing her aside.

Kate was flattened against the wall, but she was oddly happy. Moore had recognized her. The world was spinning in the right direction again. She followed the men out into the rain. It did not take more than two minutes for Kate to be soaked to the bone. The heavy rainfall limited visibility to almost nothing. She caught sight of a few people to her left, at the foot of a staircase that led to the highest point of the ship, a deck that passengers typically couldn't access.

She joined the group, but no one said a word. Feldman was there wrapped in a yellow poncho as his men began to climb up the stairs with their gear. Feldman looked so fragile that Kate worried a gust of wind would carry him away. When he saw her, he nodded as if she were just another piece of the puzzle.

"I was wondering where you might be hiding, Kate," Feldman said, pointing up and looking serious. "I figured you wouldn't want to miss this."

His tone made Kate frown, but she said nothing and began climbing the staircase with Feldman right behind her. She looked back to check on him, convinced that he was going to be blown out to sea, but Feldman seemed to have some hidden reservoir of energy in his feeble body.

Battling the rain, they eventually made their way to the upper deck. When they did, Kate couldn't believe what she saw. Near the bow and just above the bridge, where before there had been a multitude of antennas, it was now nothing more than a few steel joists all twisted and bent.

"What happened up here?" Kate asked.

"We've lost our entire communications system," growled Moore, who looked very pale.

"How? Was it an accident?"

Moore shook his head, enraged. "Someone came up here and cut the main power supply to the communications network. The system was designed with an emergency backup to avoid losing power in case of an outage." He pointed to the center of the destruction, where two of his men were cleaning up the debris. "Fifty high-capacity generators."

"Were the generators not working properly?"

"The generators worked fine," Moore replied. "There was a power surge, and fifty fucking generators exploded at once because someone made a bridge that connected them all."

"Any idea who did it?"

"Not yet, Kate," Feldman's voice came from behind her. "But we'll get to the bottom of it soon. By the way, where have you been?"

"Are you implying I was involved in this?"

"I'm not implying anything," Feldman replied coldly, the shadow of mistrust fluttering in his eyes.

Feldman looked as if he had undergone chemotherapy or was suffering from some strange disease that was eating him from the inside out. His face was shriveled and covered with little veins, erasing his previously smooth, healthy skin; his trademark hawkish look had been replaced by a dull, confused expression, like someone on the verge of dementia. The change was so devastating that it made Kate sick, and she was unable to shake the memory of the shadow that had chased her earlier—whether it had been an hour or seventy years ago, she couldn't really say.

"Someone has done my ship harm," Feldman barked. "My poor *Valkyrie*. Anyone who attacks her attacks me."

"It wasn't me, Isaac," she said in slow, clear speech. "I've been inside the whole time."

"You weren't in your cabin," Moore shouted without turning away from the damage, "and you weren't in any of the common areas."

"Where have you been, Kate?" Feldman asked.

Kate hesitated and both men took note.

"It wasn't me, Isaac," she repeated. "You'll have to believe me whether you like it or not."

"That won't be necessary," Moore grumbled. One of his men had just whispered something in his ear. "In five minutes there will be no doubt. Let's go to the control room."

Feldman nodded with a maniacal grin. He was losing his mind, skidding into a darkness filled with suspicions and imagined threats.

They went down toward the bridge. When they entered Kate noticed a few changes that made her feel that much more uneasy.

First, the back wall was empty. All the modern navigation equipment was gone. Where the sonar and satellite had been was now occupied by a few wires hanging out of the wall and a few sad metallic brackets. Kate could understand that the radar and communications system might not be working, and that, of course, this would constitute an enormous problem, but what she couldn't understand was why the sonar and meteorological station had been removed.

Harper was there, without the bushy mustache and with his eyes brown again. But he still had on the same uniform Kate had seen him wearing in the dance hall. When he saw them he clicked his heels to the floor and saluted them.

"Guten Tag, meine Herren," he spat. "I trust all of our troubles will soon end. We cannot have a relaxing cruise if these incidents continue. Someone has to take responsibility for this mess."

"Not to worry, *Herr Kapitän,*" Moore replied. "We're on it. We'll soon smoke out that Communist agent."

Communist agent? Kate thought it better not to ask. She had bigger problems. Two of Feldman's men stood at the door holding assault rifles across their chests, and they were looking right at her.

X X X I V

They entered the radio room, where the security screens were. The same operator was seated as usual, but this time he had his headphones on and looked to be deep in concentration. Kate noticed a new sign on the door with an illustration of a technician fixing an old radio; his hand was inside the device, and all of his hair was standing on end as if he were getting shocked.

The operator looked at her and arched his eyebrows in a gesture of recognition. Kate sighed in relief. At least he had not gone crazy.

"Hello," Kate said, hoping for a friendly smile. "How did the Knicks do yesterday?"

He looked at her perplexed. "The what?"

"The Knicks." She pointed to the television screen, which was off. "The basketball game."

"Basketball?" The man looked at her like she had just asked him to plant a field of barley on the moon.

Kate tried to choke back her growing sense of dread. She was in her own reality, that was for sure, but it was a reality composed of dozens of subtle changes. The whole scenario was maddening.

"Do we have the images?" Moore demanded.

Harper was at his side, imposing and princely in his uniform. Feldman, hunched over, leaned against a corner and gave a deranged, breathless laugh.

"Yes, sir," the operator answered. He punched in a series of commands, and one of the screens blinked to life.

It was a closed-circuit black-and-white video. In one corner, numbers furiously ticked as the video advanced. It showed the deck where the antennas had stood.

"This is from yesterday afternoon," the operator said, fast-forwarding the recording. The numbers went wild as the rain formed complex patterns through the speeding images. Suddenly, the operator paused the video. "It's here," he murmured with the satisfaction of a professional marveling at a job well done. "Look closely."

All that could be seen was the bridge until a dark figure walked into the frame from bottom left. It was Senka. She was unmistakable with her long blonde hair and cargo pants. But she was walking strangely, as if someone were pulling invisible strings to make her move.

Senka stumbled forward a few steps, tripping over her own feet. Suddenly, she stopped, tilting her head to one side like a cat trying to hear the rat inside a cupboard.

Then, she began to walk again with more confidence. She headed toward the staircase leading to the upper deck. In her hands she held a tool kit and a roll of cable. She paused at the foot of the stairs to stuff a few things in her pockets. It took her an eternity as if the instructions she'd been given were not being clearly communicated to her hands. Finally, when she managed to put the last item in her pocket, she took hold of the banister and began climbing up the stairs, exiting the frame.

"This is one hour and ten minutes later," the operator said, pressing another button that made the image jump to the instant Senka's feet appeared again on the stairs.

This time she was totally soaked. She was no longer clumsy like before. Her face was completely exposed. She looked scared, and her body was trembling uncontrollably.

But most of all she looked confused. And terrified.

Looking all around, she crouched down to avoid being seen, and sneaking off the bridge, she disappeared from the screen.

Kate was horrified. *Senka?* She couldn't believe it. That woman adored Feldman to no end. Kate had gotten the sense that he was like a father figure to her. There was no way she was a spy for Wolf und Klee.

"Very good," Moore said with satisfaction. "It seems we've found our traitor. Do we know who she is?"

Captain Harper cracked his knuckles, and another crew member came over with a heavy book in his hands. He began leafing through it. Kate watched as color photographs of all the passengers flipped by page after page.

"Here we are," Harper said in triumph. "First-class passenger Senka Simovic, Serbian nationality. Cabin fifteen."

"Serbian, eh?" Moore mumbled as if he had never heard of the woman he had worked with side by side for several years. "We're going to have to talk with our little Communist immediately."

From where he stood in the corner of the radio room, Feldman heaved out bizarre, asthmatic laughter. Kate noticed with disgust that he was drooling.

"She might have accomplices on board," the old man murmured, throwing a homicidal glare at Kate.

"Not to worry, Herr Feldman." Moore looked sadistic. "We'll know shortly. *Kommen Sie!*"

He made an abrupt sign to his men, and all of them, except Harper and his crew, filed out. Feldman stayed on the bridge and looked out of the window. His mind seemed to be wandering further from reality.

Kate ran after the group, certain that everything was just a silly misunderstanding. The recording had to be fake. Perhaps the ship itself had created it. If it could make hundreds of passengers appear out of thin air, then it could certainly make a fake tape. Still, there was nothing she could say to convince Moore and his men. Hopefully Senka could.

They ran down the hall toward Senka's cabin. When they got to the door, Moore's men stationed themselves on both sides of it. The muscular Brit planted himself in front and knocked with such force that the hinges creaked.

"Senka Simovic! Open the door!"

There was a moment of silence before a muffled voice came from inside. A few seconds later they could hear the lock being undone. The door opened and there was Senka. She looked groggy, like she had just awoken from a particularly intense dream. She was wearing only a T-shirt and cotton panties. A streak of dried blood ran from her nose down to the collar of her shirt.

"What's going on, Moore?" she said sleepily.

The head of security smiled and then brought his hand back and slapped Senka. She was caught unaware, and her head smacked the door frame. She fell to the floor, and her nose started bleeding again.

"Senka Simovic, you are under arrest in the name of the German Reich on charges of sabotage, conspiracy, and destruction of property belonging to the Reich," Moore snarled. "Take her away."

Senka blinked, far too confused to respond. Her eyes, full of fear, darted from face to face in hopes of finding some semblance of understanding.

"Moore. What the hell are you talking about?" she stuttered from the floor. "It's me, dammit. I don't know what the hell—"

Moore kicked Senka in her ribs with all the force he could muster, and she doubled over on the floor, gasping for breath. Moore's men grabbed her and yanked her to her feet.

Senka's horrified eyes fell on Kate, and the two exchanged a panicked look of understanding.

"Kate," she gasped. "Help me—"

This time Moore closed his fist before hitting her. Blood began openly pouring from her mouth.

"Quiet, bitch," Moore snarled. "Take her to the brig."

"You can't treat her like that," Kate shouted.

"She's a traitor," Moore said, eyeing Kate with the look of wanting to pick a fight. "As far as I know, you might be one, too, missy. Maybe fucking Communists work in pairs." He pointed his thumb at Kate and looked over at his men. "Lock up this one in her cabin until we figure out what to do with her. She's to have contact with nobody until I say otherwise."

X X X V

Will Paxton, the geologist whose expertise was submarine formations, felt off.

He was in his cabin, lying in bed in his dirty shirt and boxers. Racked by emotion, he was trying to emerge from the mists of the most extraordinary and powerful dream he'd ever had.

The dream had been about a gala dance in the *Valkyrie*'s main hall. All around him were women dressed like flappers, while the men who weren't in uniform wore tuxedos.

Paxton was in the middle of a group, holding a glass of champagne and laughing hysterically at something someone had said, though he could not recall what. When he'd looked in the mirror, he remembered being surprised that, instead of his usual wrinkled blue suit, he was wearing the impeccable and handsome uniform belonging to a captain of the Wehrmacht.

A band was playing in the background as a few couples danced feverishly, as if lit by an inner fire to shake and sweat across the dance floor. The place was hot and humid, like a room being heated in the middle of August. But nobody cared. The air had a thick, sweet scent with subtle undertones of burnt oil and something like rotting flesh.

Someone at the back of the room raised a glass. Paxton could have sworn it was a tipsy Cherenkov, wearing a snug tuxedo with buttons about to shoot off at any moment.

"Long live the Thousand-year Reich," Cherenkov bellowed in German, flushed, and without the slightest trace of a Russian accent. "To Greater Germany and our beloved Führer, Adolf Hitler!"

Everyone raised a glass. Even the dancers were pulled out of their hypnosis momentarily to turn and smile at Cherenkov.

"To our Führer, Adolf Hitler! *Sieg Heil!*" the entire hall shouted in unison.

"*Sieg Heil!*" Paxton followed suit, overcome by an inexplicable wave of excitement. "*Sieg Heil!*"

With a single gulp he downed the champagne and grabbed another one from a passing waiter. Adrenaline made his entire body tremble. He brushed an imaginary speck off his uniform and had another look in the mirror as he straightened his jacket. Never in his life had he felt so alive and powerful. A heavy buzz reverberated in his mind and impeded his thinking. His emotions, however, were loose and fought among themselves to be let out. Paxton was happy, anxious, excited, and nervous all at once. It was wonderful.

Strolling through the hall, he took in all of the details. Flags decorated with swastikas hung over the tables as dozens of waiters carrying appetizers and cocktails continued to file in and out of the elevators that shuttled between the kitchens. The civilians he came across let him gallantly pass by and offered up toasts and deferent smiles, all while admiring the gleaming medals on his chest.

It was then that Paxton felt as if a tiny hand were clenching part of his head and squeezing as hard as possible. He stopped, dizzy and incapable of taking another step under such intense pain. He fell back in a seat and gasped for breath.

Then, he saw her: the nosy reporter Feldman had brought on the expedition. She was in the middle of the dance floor, clearly terrified, her head swiveling in all directions. She could not see him as he was seated. But the geologist had a moment to delight in the way she was dressed. She was wearing a pair of jeans—the ones that leave nothing to the imagination—and a tight blue blouse that showed off her breasts. Paxton was certain she was doing it to get attention. They always wanted attention. They were all whores.

The pain in his mind sharpened, and he heard a voice. It was as clear as someone whispering right in his ear.

You see that little slut, Willie? You see how she sways and tries to be the damned star of the show?

Paxton nodded, unable to breathe. He undid the top button of his uniform.

She shouldn't be here, Willie. This is not her place. She befouls this immaculate setting.

"No," he droned, his mouth dry as sand. "She should not be here."

There's no room in the Great Reich for little Jewish sluts like her, right, Willie? I'm sure she's a Jew. Only a Jewish whore would come dressed like that to a place like this. She's trying to distract healthy and rational German men from their duties.

Beaded with sweat, Paxton gurgled out his approval. He was starting to see double. A waiter handed him a handkerchief while making an indistinct motion. Paxton accepted it before realizing that the waiter was pointing toward his nose. He dabbed his nose, and when he examined the handkerchief, it was wet with blood. Trying to stanch the bleeding, he heard a distant voice in his head inquire whether this seemed odd. But he did not listen to that voice. He only had ears for her. For her voice.

So, Willie? What are you going to do? Are you going to let her laugh at you like all those other little whores in your life, or are you going to teach her a lesson?

A sense of wrathful hatred, strong and pure, was growing inside Paxton, nearly drowning him. Simultaneously, a formidable erection had sprouted in his pants.

"I'll teach her a lesson all right," he said, stumbling to his feet. "I'll teach that bitch a lesson she'll never forget. She'll scream, she'll scream good."

Kate looked up as if alarmed, and Paxton turned around and saw the ship's captain—what the hell was his name? He knew it, but it refused to be found in the mush that was his mind. Whatever his name, the captain was instructing two waiters to go after Kate, who was one step ahead and hurrying out of the main hall.

Go after her, Willie. Make sure she never bothers you ever again.

Paxton began pushing his way across the dance floor. His bloody nose had begun to run down his uniform, tracing sinuous designs over the verdigris fabric, but that was of little importance. The only thing that mattered to Will Paxton was getting ahold of Kate.

Making his way to the main staircase landing, he scanned the crowd and felt disoriented. He didn't see her. At the bottom of the stairs, next to the wooden eagles, the two waiters looked equally confused. One of them decided to head in the direction of the bridge and the other in the opposite direction. Paxton punched the balustrade. The Jewish bitch had gotten away.

He remained standing there a few minutes more, brimming with anger and a squall of other emotions. Although he did not know it, hundreds of small veins were about to burst in his head, unable to withstand the pressure any longer.

The nursery, Willie. Run.

Paxton frowned as a whisper of doubt crept slowly into the back of his mind. The voice sounded worried.

Paxton shook his head and tried to think clearly. He'd never felt this bad, even after the time he'd gone through an entire bottle of tequila. Sweating, he began running down the stairs as fast as he could.

At the bottom, as if out of nowhere, a tall man dressed in a handsome cream-colored suit blocked his path. Paxton tried to go around him, but the man prevented him from passing. The geologist looked up and felt a surge of hatred. The man, probably in his thirties, with angular features and dark hair, was looking at him with a strange glint in his eyes. There was something odd about him.

"Get out of my way," Paxton spat.

"Where do you think you're going? Don't even think about touching my girl, you bastard," said the man before punching Paxton in the face.

The geologist fell backward, hitting his head against one of the stairs. Colorful little stars danced before his eyes and burst into utter darkness as he lost consciousness.

And then, he woke up.

He was lying in bed. The strong stench of smoke was in the air. The ship's alarms were blaring, making for a hellish racket.

He sat up in bed feeling dizzy and confused. He looked down at his plump legs and the blood-stained shirt pulled taut against his bulging belly. It looked nothing like the handsome uniform he had been wearing moments before.

With a shaky hand, he reached out for the flask on the nightstand. The liquor was hot as it slid down his throat before exploding in his stomach with that same feeling of comfort that it always brought. He rubbed his eyes and tried to figure out his next step.

It was just a stupid dream, Willie. Just a dumb dream.

He stumbled to his feet and went into the bathroom. When he finished emptying his bladder, he stood before the mirror and turned pale. His eyes were bloodshot, but that was not what had scared him.

He brought a hand up against his jaw, where an enormous bruise had begun to take on an ugly shade of purple.

"This can't be," he moaned.

With his other hand he felt the back of his head and found a bump the size of an egg.

It had really happened. It had not been a dream.

It had been here.

He knew it was time to act.

It was time to complete the mission Wolf und Klee had spent so long preparing him for.

X X X V I

He got dressed as fast as he could, taking care not to move his head too much as he put on a sweater. Once he was dressed he grabbed what he needed and went out into the hallway, where the alarms had finally been turned off. Two weary crew members were walking down the hall. One of them was covered in soot as if he had been dipped in ashes.

"What happened?" Paxton asked, grabbing one of them by the arm. "Why are the alarms going off?"

Dumbfounded, the sailor looked at Paxton. "Didn't you hear the explosion? Someone's planted a bomb or something on the communications tower. We've lost the satellite, radar, and God knows what else."

"A bomb?"

The other sailor misinterpreted Paxton's look and said, "Don't worry. It's all under control. The ship is in fine shape, and we've just sustained a bit of damage on the upper deck. It's nothing dangerous. Plus, they've already found the person responsible." The sailor issued a strange, dissonant cackle. "Moore is going to make a drum out of the skin on her ass."

Paxton nodded and looked lost. The crew members excused themselves and went on their way.

The awful pain in his head returned as the welt began throbbing violently.

Someone had planted a bomb, and it had not been him.

There must be another spy aboard, Willie. There's no other explanation.

He felt a wave of relief come over him followed immediately by one of irritation for not being told about the alternate plan. The Elders had specifically chosen him. They had provided him with the best training in Syria, Venezuela, and in some shitty Russian republic whose name he couldn't recall. They had molded him and supplied him with funds. They had given him a mission. He thought they trusted him.

But now he discovered that some other fucking agent was aboard the *Valkyrie*, and nobody had said a word about it to him.

Paxton gritted his teeth in rage as he walked down the hallway. He knew it was unwise for two agents to operate together. But not informing him of the other's existence was simply irrational. They could have easily killed one another. He stopped in his tracks like he had run up against an invisible wall. What if the other spy knew of his existence? What if he was no more than a Plan B in case Plan A failed?

Paxton had believed Wolf und Klee was offering him the recognition and respect he had always deserved but been unfairly denied. As the third of four siblings, he was certain his parents did not love him as much as they loved the others. Throughout his life he had accumulated a long list of offenses, real and imagined, that he vowed to someday exact revenge for. They would all pay: his neighbors; colleagues; the board that had denied him tenure; the women who, inexplicably, had not fallen for his obvious charms; those girls who attended his classes, dressed in miniskirts, but never accepted his crude advances. They would all have to answer to him.

Wolf und Klee had lavished him with the reverence and appreciation he had always wanted. *Wolf und Klee.* The wolf and clover. He was a wolf, a field agent, a fucking obtainer of things. That was why the Elders had considered him so valuable. Or at least that is what he had thought, until now.

His wrath continued to surge as he walked down the hall, forcing the pleasant expression that had been carefully practiced for the voyage. Will Paxton, amiable geologist. Will Paxton, full of fun little anecdotes. Will Paxton, absentminded, kindhearted, and harmless. Innocuous as a field clover. *At least until the wolf bares its teeth, hungry for blood.*

A flurry of voices coming from the end of the hallway rattled him out of his thoughts. A woman was shouting, and a bang followed. He stopped, his senses alert. Two of Moore's men were walking toward him, dragging Senka, who was dressed in no more than panties and a blood-spattered T-shirt. Her face was swollen like she had been hit by a truck.

They passed by him filled with hateful determination. Paxton stepped aside as he looked sidelong at the unconscious blonde.

Paxton never would have suspected Senka Simovic as the other agent. Ever since boarding the ship, he had believed her to be the greatest obstacle in carrying out the mission. She was watchful like a hound and did not seem to trust anybody. The perfect cover, no doubt.

But she had gotten herself caught, and that was a fatal flaw. The mission's objective was crystal clear. They were to stop the *Valkyrie* from completing the voyage, without doing irreparable harm to the ship, and make it turn around and head back to port. Once there the Elders would take over. They would arrange for the authorities to seize the ship from Feldman. The Elders had pulled many strings to get the Treasury Department on his back. When the time was right, the Elders planned on ruining him and leaving him penniless. When the *Valkyrie* went up for public auction again, the Elders would be there to buy it. It was the perfect plan, which had been spoiled by the incredible swiftness with which the Jew had managed to launch the ship. Old Feldman was no fool.

But he could not know everything.

.   .   .

Paxton walked distractedly toward the ship's kitchen, whistling a television jingle. He was surprised by the lack of people walking around on the ship. The *Valkyrie* was huge, and there were very few crew members on board, but normally, he would have come across at least a few others along the way. The entire ship was in utter somnolence as everyone waited for something to happen. The empty hallways would make his mission all the easier.

The spacious kitchen was sweltering. Hundreds of pots, pans, and plates all gleamed, hanging from long bars attached to the ceiling. There were enough ovens to accommodate a dozen chefs, but on this voyage there was only one along with half a dozen apprentices. They were working in a corner, busily skewering whole chickens. One of the prep cooks noticed Paxton and waved at him amiably. Paxton responded with his own friendly gesture as he rubbed his stomach with one hand and flashed a playful smile.

From the very first day, he had made a daily round through the kitchen, striking up friendships with the personnel and taking an interest in their work. He'd hinted that he was a serious glutton, and occasionally, he would like to sample whatever they were preparing at the time. The chefs were always fretting over their culinary innovations and were happy to have Paxton stop by. He'd made it a point to make his presence in the kitchen totally normal.

He leaned against a wall and tried a dish of crispy shrimp scampi. He was waiting for the proper moment, like a wolf stalking its prey.

He didn't have to wait long. One of the kitchen staff tripped, sending a seasoned chicken flying into the air. It fell to the floor and slid a few feet amid a chorus of yelling, screaming, and cursing.

Nobody was looking at Paxton. The geologist reached for a valve connected to the sprinkler system above the stove. As he turned the valve, several sprinklers began spraying large amounts of carbon dioxide over the stoves.

A stray chicken on the floor was now the least of the kitchen's problems. It turned into pure chaos. A harsh-smelling white cloud enveloped the cooks, who quickly began shouting even louder and stumbling into each other. Paxton took advantage of the confusion and slipped into the pantry without anyone noticing.

He walked deftly between crates of dry goods and mountains of canned food until he got to the stairs leading to the wine cellar. That door was locked, however. Before boarding, he'd been given the key that opened the lock, and he took it from his pocket. He sighed with relief as the lock opened with a click. For the time being everything was going according to plan.

He quickly walked down the stairs into the narrow climate-controlled space, which stored the prized wines. On one side, from floor to ceiling, a long rack filled with bottles stretched all the way to the back of the room. On the other side, dozens of wooden crates filled with more bottles of fine wine sat waiting for space on the racks to become available.

He walked down the corridor, looking for a particularly special wine. Upon locating two cases of 2005 Pingus, he smiled. It was a delicious wine that retailed for around $2,000 per bottle. But that was not what he had come for.

He brought the cases to the floor and pried them open with his Swiss Army knife. Under the storeroom's soft light, the magnums glowed temptingly. Paxton took them out one by one and lined them up single file like a battalion of guards. Then, he took out the straw that covered the bottom of the case and finally found what he was looking for.

They looked like clay tablets wrapped in cellophane. With a triumphant smile the geologist leaned in for a closer look. Twenty units of Semtex plastic explosives per box, and there were quite a few boxes. He would not need all of it yet, but it was there just in case.

From beneath his jacket he took out a green cloth bag and filled it with enough explosives and detonators for now. He glanced at his watch nervously. He had to get out of there before someone found him.

He zipped the bag shut and retraced his steps after he arranged everything just as he'd found it. When he got back to the pantry door, he stood watch for a second before fully emerging. The cooks had managed to shut off the gas line, but the kitchen was wrecked. That day's food was covered in a fine layer of white dust that was still dripping out of the sprinklers. At that moment there was a terrifying argument under way between four of the cooks, covered in white powder. *It is not a good day to be a chef,* Paxton thought derisively.

He slipped out of the kitchen and made his way down the same hallway by which he'd entered, whistling, with his bag slung over his shoulder. This was the riskiest part of the plan. If someone stopped and searched him, he was a dead man. Luckily, he passed only one sailor, who was bleeding profusely from his nose and muttering to himself. It looked to Paxton as if the man were on drugs.

Passing the library, he noticed that someone had knocked down a whole shelf as if possessed by some spirit of destruction. Books were strewn all over the ground with many of them ripped or lying open haphazardly. A partially dressed man was murmuring amid the ruins.

Paxton looked both ways cautiously before entering. The scene was too strange to pass up.

It was Cherenkov. The Russian physicist was on his knees; his hair was ruffled, and streaks of dried blood ran from his ears down to his neck. Surrounding him were pages filled with calculations in little Cyrillic characters. Most of the pages were ripped or crumpled. Cherenkov looked up when he heard Paxton enter, but he did not seem to recognize the geologist. His eyes were foggy, and his mind was a million miles away. He turned his head back and continued focusing on his work, which consisted of balling up his papers and tossing them into the fireplace. Paxton noticed that dozens of books and several notebooks were already in the fire.

Paxton opened his mouth to speak, but he thought better of it and silently exited the library. Clearly, the Russian was disturbed. The wacky professor. *Let the doctors on board deal with him.*

Still, the image of Cherenkov cheering on the Reich in the dance hall lingered in Paxton's head. Maybe he was one of the faithful. Paxton decided that once his plans had been carried out, he would return to the library and check on the Russian.

He went down the stairs toward the service sector and was finally able to put his bag down and rub his sore shoulder.

He checked all around to make certain no one was in the hall. He was next to one of the sealed entrances, an entrance not monitored by security cameras. He had memorized the security system's distribution thanks to a copy of the plans he'd obtained a month ago. It was incredible what one of the restoration members had been willing to do to ensure his wife never saw pictures of his private parties with other women.

Paxton took one of the chairs found in the hallways throughout the ship and placed it underneath a section of the ceiling that had been marked with a pencil. It was nearly invisible unless you were looking for it. He got up on the chair and gave the ceiling a hard push. A light click indicated the piece had come out. He reached up and blindly groped about until his fingers hit upon something that felt like hard rubber. He grabbed it and took it down. It was a pair of shears equipped with batteries. That little wonder would be able to cut through steel the same way regular scissors cut paper. Plus, it had a little engine that made the work effortless. He put the ceiling tile back in place and went back to the sealed entrance. He switched the shears on and brought the blades up to the welding joints. They sliced through the metal easily, like a knife through a ripe banana.

When he was finished he kicked at what remained of the door in order to make enough space to crawl through. It had to be quite a large hole. Paxton weighed more than three hundred pounds, and he was neither slim nor trim. After a good while he succeeded in making the hole wide enough, and he slipped through to the other side.

Immediately, he found himself surrounded by total darkness. He didn't like the idea of visiting such an isolated and dangerous area of the ship. The time before he'd nearly broken his neck, stepping on a rotten step that had given way under his weight. Then, that stupid guard came running and yelling like a madman about ghosts. The idiot shouldn't have been there, and he definitely should not have seen Paxton. It had been necessary to cut his throat. Paxton did not have the luxury of leaving behind loose ends.

He had two more hallways to cross through in second class before he reached his destination, but it felt eternal. The air down here was foul. It was almost as if some vat of oil filled with rotting fish was hidden somewhere. He also felt the need to yawn ceaselessly. His ears were ringing, and his mind seemed like it was turning to mush.

Behind him he heard a noise. He whipped around like a cobra. One of the cabin doors creaked open as if propelled by an invisible breeze. Paxton knew there were no air currents down here. He must have bumped it by mistake.

What are you going to do, Willie?

The voice in his head spoke gently yet had a poisonous, wicked overtone.

It doesn't exist. That voice doesn't exist, Paxton repeated to himself.

He walked toward the end of the hallway and consulted a map of the *Valkyrie* that had cost two lives and a tidy fortune, although Paxton was unaware of this fact. The Elders were quite skilled at dividing labor—one mole must never know what the other mole is doing.

Paxton reached a dead end. The wood paneling had taken on a sickly green color, the result of satisfied mold. Using his bare hands, he began tearing off huge panels, which crumbled in his fingers like dry cheese, leaving green streaks on his hands. After a bit, a new hole in the wall appeared right where it was supposed to be. The original designers of the *Valkyrie* had thought it best that the ship's crew have quick access between the passenger and service areas in more than one place. Paxton had uncovered one of these access points.

He pulled open the door. After decades of disuse the loud creaking hinges had rusted dry, and Paxton had to strain just to get the door open wide enough so he could enter. On the other side hot bright lights were awaiting his arrival.

He was happy to leave the ruins of second class behind for a maintenance room adjoined to the engine room. He was practically in the heart of the *Valkyrie* and nearing his goal.

He carefully advanced and looked around. He had been told there was almost never anybody down here. The way he had come had allowed him to avoid the control room and its entrances, where at least two guards were always on duty. Paxton chuckled. He was certain that not even Feldman or the chief engineer knew of the route he had taken. The *Valkyrie* held many secrets.

He walked past two huge blocks of modern steel that were pressed against the side walls of one of the ship's most spacious rooms. Paxton caught his breath and opened his bag. He began taking out the packages of Semtex, piling them at his feet, and then he searched for a good place for the explosives.

All modern ships have lateral stabilizers, a pair of engines mounted to their sides that help in docking and sailing maneuvers as well as preventing the vessel from bobbing side to side like some circus attraction. Until the invention of such a system in the 1970s, cruise ships that encountered rough waters would begin swaying back and forth like a cocktail waitress. Such experiences ruined what was supposed to be a luxury vacation for first-class travelers and resulted in passengers, rich and poor alike, being seasick, which was not good for business. Thanks to these mechanical beasts, however, balancing on the waves became easy. Modern cruise ships were able to remain stable, even on choppy waters.

When Feldman had renovated the *Valkyrie*, he'd taken the liberty of modifying the original design to include these motors. Because of them, the *Valkyrie* was steady as a boulder amid such turbulent waters.

But Paxton wanted to change that.

He began strategically placing the explosives and detonators. He set the timer, so they would explode in exactly one hour, which was more than enough time to sneak back to his cabin. Or to the kitchen, where he could eat some more food. As soon as he pressed the button, red numbers began ticking down on the tiny LCD screen.

XXXVII

Paxton still had some explosives in his bag as he leaned out into the hallway, at the end of which was the ship's engine room. Three engineers had their backs to him and were attending to the multitude of dials, gauges, and indicators that dotted the control panels.

The noise was infernal, and most of the area was covered in a shadowy darkness. The magnesium lamps were pointed toward the engine room, leaving the hallway's edges extremely dark. It was not hard for Paxton to sneak past the engine room and slip out through a service tunnel.

He was close to the ship's stern, and the tunnel was slightly bowed. Consulting his map from time to time with the help of a flashlight, Paxton continued forward as the shaft narrowed. He paused, took out his Swiss Army knife, and undid the screws on the grate that was now in his way. When he finished he wormed onward. He left his jacket carefully folded in the gap of the grate to hold it open. It was too hot in there, and Paxton figured it would help facilitate his getaway should he need to leave suddenly.

The tunnel gradually dwindled down to a circular crawl space. Paxton was forced to crawl forward while pushing his bag in front of him. The floor was trembling beneath him, and the vibrations shivered through his entire body.

Don't do it, Willie. It's not a good idea.

The voice pummeled his head as if a hammer had just driven several nails into his skull. Paxton stopped and groaned as his two nostrils became faucets of blood. The intense pain in his head only got worse, and his facial muscles began twitching uncontrollably.

"Shut up," he cried, rubbing his temples. "It's my mission."

Where Senka had failed he would triumph. For the first time since his dream, he knew what he needed to do. He would be the one to bring the *Valkyrie* to a halt and stop Feldman, that piece-of-shit Jew. When the *Valkyrie* was at sea once more, filled with wolves and clovers, Paxton would be first in line to receive praise. The Elders would undoubtedly recognize his worth.

Like a beacon of understanding, it came to him. He'd been on the other side. He'd seen the flags and shouted *"Sieg Heil"* in a room filled with those just as passionate as he. Paxton had been surrounded by true patriots. They had shown him what would be in store for him upon completing the mission—it was his destiny.

He was the chosen one.

He could see himself sailing on the *Valkyrie* toward Germany. Then, at the chancellery, an honored guest of the Führer, he would explain what had happened the first time the ship sailed and how to avoid making the same fatal errors as before by sharing the exact movements of the enemy. They would win the war and reestablish the Thousand-year Reich.

Rubbing elbows with the Führer.

The notion was so intoxicating that it managed to overpower the voice. Even her influence had withered under his burst of ambition so powerful and pure.

Stop, Willie. Don't be stupid. You shouldn't do it.

"It's . . . my . . . destiny," panted Paxton, breathless.

The upper ceiling of the tunnel was already starting to graze his back, and he hardly had enough room to propel himself forward with his elbows and knees. Everything was dark, and the only light came from a shaky flashlight inside of the green bag.

No, Willie.

The pain was a hundred times worse than all the other times put together. Paxton shouted aloud, unable to restrain himself, but his howl was drowned out by the noise of the engines.

Touching his face, he became distantly aware that, besides bleeding from his nose, blood was also pouring out of his ears. What Paxton couldn't be aware of was that a part of his brain, unable to fend off the dark force being exerted on it, had begun to die. Thousands of tiny veins were bursting, one after the other, like a house of cards collapsing.

Paxton shook his head and reached a tiny doorway that opened up to a room below. Awkwardly, he reached out and opened it. The noise behind the door was deafening. He pointed his flashlight down and could see the steely reflection of the *Valkyrie*'s propeller axle.

The axle was as wide as the human body. Paxton knew the explosive would not be enough to destroy it. But mangled by the explosion, the axle would stop turning, and the engines would choke from the sudden blockage. The *Valkyrie* would be rendered motionless at sea like a big, sleepy whale. End of voyage.

With no way of sticking the blocks of Semtex to the axle, Paxton began stacking them around the giant cylinder. It took him a long time to insert the timer wires into the waxy gray

explosive. He'd not even realized that half his body was no longer obeying his brain's orders.

Stop!

The voice became a hurricane-force roar. Paxton's mind,
already in a weakened state, had about as much resistance
remaining as an old wooden fence does before an avalanche.
Several arteries burst at the same time as blood began pouring
through the geologist's cranium, inundating every cavity. In
shock, he realized for a fraction of a second that he was about to
die. The thought struck him suddenly, and he brimmed with
anger. Once again he was going to be denied the glory he
deserved.

His final reflex was to stretch his fingers out toward the
timer. But he never got there. Blood had pooled extensively in his
head, and Will Paxton died before he was able to complete his
mission.

Darkness grew and devoured him. This time it was for good.

X X X V I I I

Valkyrie
Day four

Kate shook her wrists, angrier than she'd ever been in her life.
The duct tape they had wrapped around her joints prevented her
from moving her arms. She could feel the circulation being cut
off as her hands began to tingle.

She was lying on her bed, where they had tossed her before
leaving and slamming the door shut. She'd been there two hours,
and all of her attempts to undo the restraints had been in vain.
When she tired of floundering about like a tuna in a fishing net,
she tried to relax and put her mind at ease. She needed to calm
her anxiety and, above all, think of a plan.

She tried to recall everything that had happened, but it was
impossible to follow the course of events. In some strange way it
seemed like the reality in which she lived and the reality of 1939
were trying to occupy the same space. The *Valkyrie.*

For some reason the two worlds seemed to be bleeding into
one another and creating a new reality that was dark and menac-
ing, one in which something very dangerous was after her.

And then, there was Robert, of course.

She looked to the shelf, which held the urn containing Robert's ashes. That was the actual Robert, what was left of the man she'd known. Yet, a few hours ago, several decks below, she'd been kissing that same man, who she had thought was gone.

She was completely incapable of understanding how it was possible. She had a sneaking suspicion that the ashes being on board had something to do with it. But the rest of the story was so complicated that she was baffled.

"That's very feminine," a familiar voice said from behind Kate. "Instead of just accepting a gift from heaven no questions asked, you have to try to understand why it's happening. With you there's always a next question. You'll never change, Katie."

Kate smiled for the first time in hours. Adrenaline pumped through her veins, and she felt it spread like a fire throughout her body.

"That's very masculine," she replied, incisively, but with tears of joy in her eyes. "Sitting on your ass and talking about how annoying your wife is instead of freeing her when she's handcuffed."

She rolled over, so she could see him. Robert was smiling brightly on the sofa, one arm outstretched along its back. The knot in his tie was loose, and his blazer was folded at his feet. He looked relaxed.

"You really want me to untie you?" he asked with a grin. "Seeing you like this is the best. Remember that one time with those handkerchiefs from Hermès?"

"Robert!" Kate cut him off. She was still crying with joy but now feigned a look of anger. "Help me or you'll pay!"

"Really?" Robert laughed as he got up and walked toward Kate. He sat on the edge of the bed and began slowly undoing the tape. "What can you do to me? I'm dead. Remember?"

"Just maybe I'll throw you and your conceited smile in that urn once more," answered Kate, emotionally scattered. But she was lying. Never in a million years would she throw away a chance to spend time with him, even if he left her tied up there until she died.

Robert finished freeing her wrists, and Kate threw the tape to the floor. Then, he began massaging them until, little by little, the circulation returned to her fingers.

Kate looked at her husband's hands with fascination as he continued to rub her wrists. His touch was firm, steady, and warm. He still had the small paper cut on his right ring finger that he'd gotten a couple of days before the accident.

It really was Robert Kilroy.

Her Robert.

It was all too much for Kate. She'd built gates to control the pain and sorrow of Robert's death, and the torrent of emotions that had been bottled up for weeks pressed against those barriers before toppling them over with tremendous force. Kate freed her wrists from Robert's hands and laced her fingers behind his neck. Her mouth searched anxiously for his, and the two melted into a long kiss, slow and passionate. They were like two people who'd discovered an oasis after traveling across a desert for weeks.

The kiss was electric. All of Kate's physical urges and needs were suddenly unleashed. She felt her underwear become wet as her skin charged with electricity. She needed physicality.

And Robert did, too. His fun-loving, confident smile had disappeared, replaced by an anxious, excited expression of urgency. He had the face of a small child who'd been lost in the mall all day only to come across his parents after all hope had been lost. The face of a man who had just been pardoned from death row.

The face of someone with renewed hope.

Robert pushed her onto the bed without separating his lips from hers. He pushed Kate's arms above her head and pinned her down under the weight of his body as she twisted with pleasure beneath him. Robert grabbed both of her wrists with one hand and slid his other hand slowly down her neck and began tracing long circles. His fingertips caressed Kate in such an alluring way that she arched her back and let out a soft moan.

Robert began licking Kate's neck as his hands pressed down her body to her breasts, touching them lightly before moving to her zipper. Before Kate knew it, Robert had already undone the zipper and brought her pants to her ankles. With a deft move of his foot, he caught the jeans between his toes and sent them flying across the cabin in one swift motion.

Kate could take no more and reached toward Robert's shirt. She began unbuttoning it and kissed his chest with each new opening. Robert had always been particularly sensitive on his chest, and she knew she could drive him crazy, nibbling and licking. Robert groaned as she finished the last button. Kate threw it off without taking her mouth from his body. She'd been inching down his abdomen to his navel. Her tongue playfully swirled inside it, and Robert, unable to take any more, grabbed her in his arms and brought them back to the bed with her on top.

Kate smiled lasciviously. She knew the game. Straddling Robert, she pulled her blouse over her head and undid her lace bra, leaving only her thong. Robert breathed deeply. He looked up and down from her breasts to her waist and back up to her eyes, memorizing every last detail of her body. His hands found her ass and squeezed with delight.

Kate leaned forward and, without taking her eyes from his, began tonguing little circles all over Robert's chest. Then, she went lower, down to his waist, and undid the top button. It was his turn to rip off his pants, leaving him in only underwear.

She ran her hand over the enormous bulge that had grown. She could feel it pulsing, waiting on the other side of the fabric. She began kissing it through his underwear, and Robert was unable to contain a low groan. His entire body was tense, supercharged.

Robert placed his hands on Kate's head and, with another groan, buried his fingers in her thick, soft hair. In response Kate grabbed the waistband of his boxers, lowered them, and eagerly licked down his groin. Robert's member was swollen, and she grabbed it and rubbed it on her cheek. With patience that was almost painful, she began kissing it with her eyes closed, enjoying its familiar scent. Gently, she brought her lips to the head and pushed it into her mouth, sucking rhythmically and passionately.

Robert gasped, out of control, and his hips tightened. Kate enjoyed the immense feeling of power she had. Her head bobbed up and down on the shaft as she held the base with one hand and fondled his testicles with her other. She felt it pulse on her tongue, and she went deeper, leaving him slick with her saliva.

Kate continued for several minutes that were too short to her. Robert could take no more, and he pulled her hair back. She licked up his body, past his neck to his lips, and received the most wonderful, deep kiss she'd ever experienced. Robert's hands fondled her breasts, brushing over her nipples until they hardened like two pointy bullets.

He turned her over on the bed—it was his turn to lick. He started around her breasts and lightly bit her nipples, giving Kate a wave of pleasure. The feeling was so overwhelming that she was already moaning loudly.

Robert moved his hands down to Kate's hips and hooked a finger under the string of her thong. Automatically, in a gesture of total surrender, Kate raised her legs, allowing Robert to remove the tiny garment.

Robert spread her legs apart and came closer. Slowly, he rested his member on her lips and began rocking back and forth without entering her. The move was enough to rouse a moan of impatience from Kate.

Then, very gently, he entered her, filling up every last bit of space inside her. She dug her nails into her husband's back as her own moans became more rhythmic.

Robert began thrusting faster. With each move of his hips, Kate screamed, taking pleasure in the mix of joy, desire, and disbelief. Two bodies, united, in sync, their sweat mingling. The bed creaked underneath them.

Then, she felt an immense sensation begin to build in her pelvis. She buried her face in Robert's chest as an overwhelming orgasm rushed through her body. She screamed as waves of pleasure shook her to the core. It was a long, explosive, and deep orgasm—one of the most intense she'd ever had.

Robert responded by driving faster and harder—a staccato of delight. He gripped Kate's hips and pinned her into complete submission. As he did so, his face twisted into pure ecstasy immediately before he climaxed inside of her.

Feeling her husband's release, Kate experienced a new, surprising orgasm. The floodgates within had been opened, and she felt a deluge of pleasure fill her body.

Both collapsed on the bed gasping, their sweaty skin still touching. Kate snuggled closer to Robert and put her head in the crook of his neck. He gently caressed her back with smooth strokes.

"I love you, Robert Kilroy," she whispered. "I'm willing to do whatever it takes to keep us together. Even if that means staying aboard this stupid ship forever."

Robert propped himself up on one elbow and suddenly looked serious. "Don't say that. Don't even joke about that. This place is cursed, Kate. You have to get out of here as soon as you can."

"Only if you come with me, Robert," she answered and cuddled closer. "I can't imagine living the rest of my life without you. The world is too dark without you."

Robert pursed his lips, struggling against a severe internal conflict. He opened his mouth to say something but closed it right away. He hugged Kate tightly and buried his nose in her hair, taking in her wonderful fragrance.

"I'll always be with you, Kate. No matter what you do or where you go. Never forget that."

Kate detected profound sadness in Robert's words, but she closed her eyes and clutched him tighter. She wished the moment would never end.

"Now listen to me carefully," said Robert, sitting up in bed. "You need to move quickly. Only a few hours remain."

"A few hours? Until what?"

"To stop the *Valkyrie*, Kate. If you don't stop this ship, it will be too late. We'll be trapped forever."

"I can't leave here, Robert," Kate said. "There's a guard at the door, and Moore, Feldman, and everyone else seem to have gone mad. What can I do?"

Just then, more than two hundred feet below them, a small digital clock ticked down to its final second. A row of zeroes blinked across a screen before sending a tiny electric signal to several packages of Semtex that had been fastened to the lateral stabilizers.

The explosives went off in rapid sequence, and a roaring fireball propelled by a wave of destruction swept through the room, blasting the stabilizing engines into a thousand pieces. A bulkhead, held up with rusted rivets that were decades old, could not withstand such a violent force and was blown up, followed by a cloud of tiny steel splinters.

The three engineers in the adjacent room did not stand a chance. A volley of shrapnel passed through and ripped apart their bodies, scattering their remains across the engines. They were dead even before the floor gave way.

The rumbling shook all of the *Valkyrie* as if a giant had decided to kick the ship. The table lamps trembled, and the bed moved a few inches. All around the ship, the noise of hundreds of items falling to the ground and breaking could be heard as security alarms began sounding once more.

"What was that?" Kate asked.

Robert raised his head and kept his eyes closed for a good while. He seemed to be listening to an inner voice that only he could hear. He reminded Kate of a Tibetan monk in a state of deep meditation. His face was relaxed and peaceful, and he looked like he existed in some mystical realm beyond good or evil.

When he finally opened his eyes, he looked extremely worried and even slightly afraid.

"The lateral stabilizers have been blown up," he said.

"The what?"

"A modern addition Feldman made. Something foreign to the original design of the *Valkyrie*. That's why she allowed it."

"Will that stop the ship?"

Robert shook his head. "No, although it will make everything more difficult. There's still a way to stop the ship, but you'll need backup."

"I have you." Kate held him close, worried he might evaporate into thin air again.

"I can't help you with this. But Senka Simovic can."

"Senka?" Kate thought of Senka, who had been sent to the brig by Moore. She had no idea where that could be. "Why can't you help me? I don't want to leave you. Not again!"

"Kate, when we are together she can't see us, but only if we stay in a cabin. That is all I can do. I already told you that there are rules. If we move about the halls, she'll find us. This time she'll really be mad."

"So what do we do?"

"I'll try to distract her. Make her angry. Divert her attention." Robert got up and began getting dressed with confident, deliberate movements. His entire life he'd exuded an air of confidence. He acted like he was about to go out for coffee rather than being on the verge of confronting a dark force. "In the meantime you look for Senka and then head for the engine room."

"What for?"

"You'll know when the time is right. Trust me. Now get dressed, love. If you walk around the ship naked, I don't think you'll go unnoticed."

She dressed quickly, choosing the most comfortable clothing she could find, suspecting she would be moving around a lot during the next few hours.

"You still haven't told me how we're supposed to get out of here," Kate said. "Remember, I can't walk through walls."

"Nor can I." He walked over and hugged her. He smelled like cologne and sex. "But I can do other things."

He approached the closed door and turned the handle. The lock clicked, and the door swung open soundlessly. If the situation hadn't been so frightening, Kate would have clapped like a schoolgirl watching a magic trick.

Cautiously, Kate leaned into the hall. The guard had vanished, possibly headed toward the blast or to receive orders.

"Be careful, my love," she heard Robert whisper from behind.

Kate turned around to respond, but he had vanished again.

"I hate it when you do that, Robert Kilroy," she whispered as she stepped into the hall. "I really hate it."

She had no idea where to start. The *Valkyrie* was vast, and apart from her fleeting excursion into the lower decks the day before, she was familiar with only the first-class section and a couple of halls in second class. She didn't know where Senka was being kept or what the hell to do when she found her.

Luckily, she remembered something important. Before communication had been cut off, Anne Medine had said she would send information pertaining to the *Valkyrie*. Maybe it would provide a clue about where to begin.

The Gneisenau Room was two levels above where Kate stood. She would have to try to get there and pray nobody saw her, especially Moore. Kate perceived a subtle change in the balance of power aboard the *Valkyrie*. Feldman had stepped aside and allowed that English brute to make decisions as he saw fit. But she was certain that Feldman still played a vital role in everything happening aboard his ship.

She walked down the hall without seeing a single person. She was surprised that a couple of cabins were wide open with no one inside, as if their occupants had forgotten to close the door after leaving their rooms. Kate scanned inside them and found unmade beds, scattered clothes, and books and computers lying about. Then, she heard a dull, repetitive noise approaching.

She had nowhere to hide. Trapped, she scurried into one of the rooms and hid beneath the bed, waiting for the noise to pass.

A dull click-click-click, like a damaged gear shaft, came closer, and a pair of legs and the wheels of a laundry cart came into view.

The legs stopped in front of the cabin. Kate swallowed, certain she'd been seen. But the legs remained motionless as if their owner were unsure what to do next. Kate lifted up the bed skirt a hair for a better look. It was Mrs. Miller, Feldman's maid. She was wearing a verdigris KDF uniform. Her hair was in an old-fashioned bun, and she looked haggard and worn as if she'd been drinking. Her white apron as well as her mouth and chin were streaked with blood that had run from her nose. She was moving sporadically like a robot losing its charge.

The woman muttered something unintelligible in German. Kate watched as she approached the table in the cabin and gathered all of the books on top as well as the laptop and its cables. Next, as if it were the most normal thing to do, she tossed everything into the laundry cart. The computer cracked as it hit the metal. Mrs. Miller then left the cabin and paused outside the door across the hall. She jingled her keys a moment before she managed to open the door and enter.

This was Kate's chance. She crawled out from underneath the bed and went back into the hall. Passing the cart, she glanced at its contents and became pale. Piled up haphazardly, at least twenty laptops, cell phones, chargers, calculators, and digital tablets were mixed in with technical manuals. Some of the gadgets had cracked screens. It looked like a heap of trash ready to be tossed into the sea.

They were slowly eliminating any sign of the twenty-first century. The *Valkyrie*, or whatever lived inside the ship, had imposed her voice adamantly.

Kate headed for the elevator, which she thought would be less risky than taking the stairs. She pressed the button and waited nervously for the elevator to arrive. The humming of the engine and the rattling of the gears sounded like cannon fire in the ghostly silence that had overtaken the ship. The sirens had stopped sounding, and silence covered everything. If she hadn't known there were other people on the ship, Kate would have sworn she was the sole passenger.

I'm starting to understand how you felt, Carroll, she thought. *Alone, yet pursued by some dark, malevolent force.*

The elevator arrived with a cheerful ding. Kate clenched her jaw and figured it had been heard as far as the dance floor, so she quickly stepped into the elevator, closed the gate, and pressed a button.

As the elevator went up, she fell back into the cushioned seat. Her legs were too weak to stand. She noticed a folded newspaper and picked it up, her hands shaking. She was completely unsurprised by what she saw.

It was a copy of the *Völkischer Beobachter*, the official newspaper of the Nazi party. On the front page a wrathful Goebbels was speaking to a feverish crowd. In the corner was the date: August 1939. She dropped it like a poisonous snake and frantically rubbed her hands on the seat cushion, trying to get off the invisible filth.

The elevator came to a stop with a jolt.

Kate jumped to her feet and opened the elaborate elevator gate. Just as she was about to get out, she stopped, paralyzed as if hit by lightning.

In front of her, staring with glassy eyes, stood Isaac Feldman.

X L

Time seemed to stand still. Feldman looked at Kate curiously, wondering how the hell she'd gotten there. Kate, for her part, looked back hopelessly. Her game was up. Any moment now he would shout out, and a slew of security guards would be at his side. She remembered how brutally Moore had treated Senka, causing a pang of terror.

Feldman looked deplorable. He had only a few tufts of hair remaining, and the rest of his scalp was red and scabby as if he'd contracted ringworm. Hunched over, he was now shakier than ever, using an umbrella as a cane. His eyes were dull, and Kate noticed what appeared to be a cataract in one of them. His skin was wrinkled and dry as if the business tycoon had aged fifty years in the matter of a few hours. He was trembling like a leaf about to fall from a tree.

"Hi, Isaac," she murmured. "Listen to me, please. I beg of you. Let me explain."

"Do you know where my grandpa is?" His voice was as parched as an old newspaper. "I want to see my grandpa."

"Isaac, what are you talking about?"

"My grandpa. I want to see my grandpa right now," pouted the old man as a string of thick, foul-smelling spittle dribbled from his mouth.

The colossus known as Feldman, the business tiger who'd made people tremble, had lost his mind, reduced to an elderly man with dementia shuffling through the hallways of the *Valkyrie*. The ship had destroyed the only passenger still alive from the original 1939 voyage. His body was still alive but not his mind. With a shiver she wondered if Feldman's consciousness had become a black hole hiding in some remote part of his brain.

Kate approached him and held his arm. Carefully, she walked with him toward a chair and helped him take a seat. Feldman smelled strongly of urine.

"Have a seat, Isaac," she said in a soothing voice, watching behind her the whole time. If a guard were to appear, everything would be lost. "Let's make a deal. I'm going to search for your grandfather. We'll come back for you in a little bit, but you can't move from here or make any noise in the meantime. OK?"

Feldman did nothing but continue staring off into the infinity of space. His jaw hung open as if he were in a permanent catatonic state. Kate looked at him sympathetically and wrapped a blanket around his shoulders. The last time she'd seen him he'd been acting so curtly with her, which had made Moore treat her like a terrorist. But he was no longer himself. Everything that had made him Feldman was now gone. Unsteady remnants were all that was left, a Feldman who no longer recognized her voice.

When she was certain he would not move, she set off down the hall again.

Feldman stayed in his seat, trapped in the heavy netting of a deep dream from which he was unable to awake. He was burnt out like a lightbulb after a power surge.

The Gneisenau Room was deserted. The stations that should have been occupied by the research team were empty, and all of the monitors had been shut off. Above the table the small projector Cherenkov had used during the opening presentation was still there. Kate felt like that had been a million years ago even though it had been only four days.

Four days.

A cold sweat slid down her back. If it had already been four days since departure, then that meant the *Valkyrie* would be approaching the same place where its passengers had disappeared more than seventy years ago. An appointment with destiny, once again.

Time was running out.

In a corner of the room sat piles of folders with documents and temperature readouts that no longer meant anything to anyone.

The scene was one of desolation and absolute emptiness— the remains of a shipwreck forgotten by its own passengers.

Someone had knocked over papers, and the ground was layered with wrinkled pages covered in mathematical calculations. Dried blood stained many of the pages, like disfigured flower petals. Kate put her hand up to her nose, relieved to find that she was still not bleeding. For now.

She pushed past several reports and studies on electromagnetism that nobody would ever read again until she found a set of pages stapled together that was labeled "Attention Kate Kilroy." Although there didn't seem to be anything useful in the forty to fifty pages, she would have to try to find clues, but this was no place to do it.

She exited the room and went to the great gallery. Its name was far too grandiloquent for what it really was, but Kate supposed that the place was probably quite impressive to a passenger in the 1930s. It was a long, wide corridor with high, ornate ceilings that were dotted with stained glass depicting Germanic gods contemplatively frowning down at the wood floors below. Along the sides were spots for small shops where KDF had planned to put bars, jewelry shops, cafés, and several other types of businesses for the first- and second-class passengers to enjoy. Kate paused beneath one of the stained-glass pieces. Above her, a bearded and muscular Germanic pagan deity looked like he'd just eaten a meal that was too spicy. Kate approached one of the empty shop fronts. She found it was locked with all of its lights off, as were all of the others.

This was her first time in this part of the ship. Dust and plastic covered the floor, and wires still remained from the restoration efforts. It didn't seem like anyone had been there since the ship had embarked on this journey. Although the commercial walkway was much smaller than ones found on modern cruise ships, the *Valkyrie* had still been ahead of its time for the 1930s by implementing such a commercial center.

Kate turned a door handle, and the door swung open noiselessly. She walked through the shadows until she came to a corner where a stream of dim afternoon light filtered through a porthole. On the other side the fog had become denser, and it clung to the *Valkyrie* even more closely. The rain continued to whip violently across the ship, and the wind howled like a distressed soul.

She fervently leafed through the file. Just as she'd been promised, the list of passengers and crew was there. One of the pages had the name *Schweizer* underlined, the owner of the straw hat she'd found. Kate found it almost funny that she had been so scared of that, in light of all that had happened since. As she had expected, there was no blueprint of the ship or any clue as to where Senka might be found.

"Typical, Robert," she whispered angrily, tossing half the pages to the floor in frustration.

Then, she looked down at the last two pages in her hand. It was a copy of the *Valkyrie*'s logbook, the one Captain Harper—if he still even answered to that name—had consulted on the bridge. She noticed that Anne Medine had copied only the pages from the last two days. Her eyes jumped down to the final passage that had been made in the angular handwriting of Captain Kuss, the German who had led the original voyage in 1939. In the bottom right-hand corner, there was a small, dark stain, like someone had spilled a drop of ink on the page and tried to wipe it off with a finger.

20.47 GMT: 53 degrees 94' 17" north and 28 degrees 47' 09" west. Slight wind blowing NNW with strong gusts of wind interspersed. Ten-foot-high waves. Fog bank unchanged since the last changing of the guard. Direction and speed constant. Next to the boilers, a strange vibration has been detected. Oberfeldwebel Dittmar found no apparent irregularities. During the following inspection, five stowaways were discovered in the lower deck in boiler room number two. The captain left the bridge to attend a Gala dinner. Official duties were delegated to head of security Otto Dittmar. Changing of the guard performed without incident.

After that, the rest of the logbook was blank until the *Pass of Ballaster* had discovered the *Valkyrie* at four thirty that morning, empty and adrift.

Kate reread the passage many times. Stowaways on board the *Valkyrie*. This was the first she'd heard of this. Feldman had never said a word about it, and it wasn't in the file Robert had started. It made complete sense, considering how the logbook had been buried in naval archives up until a year ago, hidden beneath a stack of administrative documents from that era. But if Feldman knew about it, why had he not said anything?

Then, it came to her. Feldman must have been one of those stowaways.

Everything he'd done stemmed from there, hoping to discover what had happened to that family. *His* family.

He wanted to find the root of his origins. The anomalies, Cherenkov's research, Wolf und Klee—none of it made a difference to Feldman.

Approaching footsteps scared Kate out of her thoughts, and she scurried under a table like a rat. The steps stopped right in front of the entrance. Kate gleaned a dark, shapeless shadow outlined against the windowpane. Distressed, she looked around, but there was nothing she could use to defend herself and no way out.

She watched as the doorknob turned, and the frosted pane of glass embedded in the door rattled.

The air in Kate's lungs felt as if it were being sucked out.

Harvey Carter, the American physicist, stood in the doorway. A ray of light from above bathed his face in a dull shine. Before he had worn a whimsical raccoon pin, but now he wore a gleaming swastika, red as blood.

X L I

Carter stumbled into the darkness of the shop, muttering something under his breath that Kate couldn't make out. Although she couldn't see him clearly, she imagined that his shirtfront was covered in blood and he had that far-off zombie look. He was now one of them.

Without taking her eyes off Carter, Kate groped blindly around on the floor. Her fingers scratched over pieces of plastic and dust bunnies that had accumulated under the table. Then, her hands closed over a hard cardboard tube likely left behind by one of the decorators.

Kate gripped it tightly. Six feet in length, it was like a bat, and she waited patiently as Carter got closer to her. As he passed by her, she popped out from beneath the table and let out a shriek of fury, holding the makeshift weapon above her head. With all of her might, she struck Carter with the tube. The physicist screamed in shock, turned around, and instinctively raised his hands. Kate stepped back and raised up the tube again, but she bumped against the wall, which gave Carter enough time to jump back and put the table between the two of them.

"Kate, for the love of God," he bellowed. "Have you gone crazy? It's me, Carter."

Kate stood motionless upon hearing his voice. He recognized her. He spoke to her in English, not German. Her relief was so intense that she dropped the tube and felt on the verge of tears.

"Carter. Is it really you?"

"Of course," he assured her, rubbing his back. "Or at least what's left of me after you hit me."

The scientist limped toward the porthole and stood beneath the fading light. Kate could see he hadn't shaved for several days and he was wearing a simple white shirt. Huge dark bags drooped beneath his bloodshot eyes. But otherwise he seemed very much the same. He had no sign of blood on his nose or his clothes. What he really looked like was someone suffering a terrible hangover.

"Do you recognize me?" he said after a few moments, sounding skeptical. "Do you know who I am?"

"You're Carter, the physicist. You work for the University of Georgia. You're a vegetarian, and two days ago at dinner you told me you hate baseball and that you prefer football," Kate reeled off. She felt comforted by saying everything out loud. It was like reciting an incantation that was able to break past the cloak of darkness surrounding them.

Carter nodded in satisfaction. He groped around in his pocket and pulled out a pack of cigarettes and a lighter. He lit one and took a long drag before coughing out a large cloud.

"You're Kate Kilroy," he said in turn as he rubbed his throat in pain. "You're the reporter from that English newspaper. You hate peas, and you were wearing a beautiful blue dress two nights ago. You're also the only person on board who does not seem to have lost her mind."

Overwhelmed by a rush of relief, Kate hugged the scientist, to which Carter responded with a couple of awkward pats on her back.

Pulling back from the embrace, Kate pointed at the swastika pin gleaming wickedly on Carter's shirt. "What's that about?"

Confused, Carter looked down at his chest and passed his hand over the pin, frowning. "I can't remember very well. My memory has been all muddled up the last few hours. My head feels like someone jammed a ton of cotton into my ears. The lack of sleep is killing me."

"Lack of sleep?"

"That's the only way of avoiding what's happening," Carter said, sitting down and ripping off the pin. "Either way, I think I probably fell asleep for a little while during the last twenty-four hours. I don't recall putting on these clothes. I have no idea where I picked up the stupid little pin."

"You haven't slept for how long?"

"Seventy-two hours, more or less," the physicist answered, passing a hand over his stubble. "In the laboratory we detected a surge in the electromagnetic field that was interfering with the alpha waves, which in turn—" He stopped himself and made a dismissive motion. "Bah! That doesn't matter anymore. To put it bluntly, the human brain is no more than an electric field. My theory is that these conditions have been enough to interfere with human brain functions. I told Cherenkov, but the bastard wouldn't listen to me. He was far too obsessed with being able to empirically demonstrate the existence of his Singularity. Now the idiot has found what he was looking for."

"But what do dreams have to do with all this?"

"I can't explain it," Carter said, the extreme fatigue weighing down on his words. "It wouldn't even be simple to explain it under normal conditions."

"How did you find me?"

"The floor is covered in dust. You left a trail even a blind man could follow. I passed through the doors to the great gallery and noticed that they were open, and so I came looking to see who was here. I'm looking for Feldman. He's the only one who can help us out of this insanity."

"Feldman's no longer able to stop anything," Kate replied bitterly, relaying what she'd been through the past few days.

Carter listened attentively. When she got to the part about Senka's arrest, he shook his head.

"I can't believe that woman would be a neo-Nazi. It just doesn't make sense."

"I agree. That's why I'm looking for her. Something tells me she's the only one able to stop this ship."

"Seriously? How do you know?"

Kate didn't want to tell Carter about Robert. She didn't care if he thought her to be a lunatic, but she desperately needed his help, and if she brought up phantom lovers, he would think she was completely off her rocker. "I just know. Trust me, Carter, I beg of you. I need your help."

Carter sighed and raised his arms up.

"I suppose I have no other choice. You're the only person on board that isn't bat-shit crazy and still remains aware of the fact that we aren't a part of some fucking Nazi parliament."

"Will you help me look for Senka, then?" Kate felt hope burgeoning inside.

"I can do you one better." The physicist gave a wry smile. "I know where she is this very moment."

X L I I

Richard Moore was confused. Confused and angry. Sitting on a stool in one of the ship's bars—the only one fully stocked—he was looking at himself in the bar mirror with severe irritation. A thirty-year-old bottle of Talisker whiskey stood before him. The bottle was already half-empty, and Moore felt more than a little tipsy. He was drunk and enraged.

Everything had happened so fast. He did not know when this simple job had transformed into an endless nightmare.

Or when he'd lost control of the situation.

Moore was a worldly man. Approaching forty, he had the hardened body of a football player with muscles like pistons and without an ounce of fat. He'd joined the Black Rats, the infamous British army brigade, when he was only eighteen, and he'd quickly climbed the ranks. Year after year he strengthened his reputation as a hard-nosed, irritable soldier who held a fierce reverence for the hierarchy of power. Moore was happy with the military discipline imposed by Her Majesty's army. He'd found a home there that an alcoholic father and an ex-prostitute mother hadn't been able to offer.

If it had been up to him, he never would have left the Black Rats. That was his home. But one hot day in the summer of 2005, everything went to hell twelve miles outside of Kandahar.

It was a routine checkpoint on a dusty road near a handful of smelly villages made of adobe and donkey shit. Their mission was to perform random checks to fish out Taliban sympathizers. Moore was there with five men under his command, all behind two heavy machine guns and sweating nonstop. The wind made things worse as it swept down from the mountains carrying dust and sand. All that, on top of a full day in the sun wearing a Kevlar helmet, had given Moore a severe headache. It could have happened to anyone.

Anyone except him, he kept telling himself as he poured another shot. He took down the expensive single malt in one gulp and let his mind wander back to that horrible day.

The motorcycle that arrived at the checkpoint carried two men and a boy. Someone must have stopped them, but the subsequent investigation found that none of his men remembered doing so. When Moore saw that the motorcycle was only six feet from his armored vehicle, his training kicked in like clockwork. Before he could even see the face of the little boy, who couldn't have been more than three, he had already shouted "fire" three times.

Nearly eight hundred bullets were fired at the boy, the two men, and the motorcycle. Rationalizing later, he realized it had been hard to stop pulling the trigger after the tensions of such a long day. Somehow, it had been liberating, and for that he was ashamed. But Moore realized that sometimes monsters dwell within everyone, undetected, only to manifest themselves in the most unsuspecting moments. No matter the exact reason, one thing was certain: after Moore gave the command to cease fire, the Afghans and their motorcycle were no more than a mash of steel and shredded flesh.

One month later Moore faced a court-martial. Two weeks later, dressed in civilian clothes, with his memories of a life gone by tucked away in his bag, he walked out the door of the Black Rats' barracks without knowing where to go next.

That's when Feldman had entered his life. Just like in the army, Moore rose through the ranks of the business magnate's organization, moving from his first job as a bouncer in one of his casinos to finally winning Feldman's confidence and being named chief of security.

Everything had been progressing smoothly since then. During the past two years, Moore felt like he'd found a new home. That is, until they had boarded the *Valkyrie*. Now everything had gone to shit once more.

You have not done well, Richard, the voice whispered. *But you can still fix things.*

Moore shook his head and looked all around. He was alone in the bar, and the only light was right above his head. The rest of the bar was in shadows. The tables and chairs that supposedly would one day seat passengers were all covered in darkness.

"Who's there?" he said, standing up.

Someone loves you, Richard.

Moore looked around and stumbled to the back of the room. His headache raged so severely that he was unsure of himself, but he could have sworn that the darkest area in the shadows had just moved to another corner, running away from him like it wanted to play hide-and-seek. He walked to the other side, but he only managed to trip on a table and bump his shin.

"Fuck," he bellowed, grabbing his leg in pain.

He remained doubled over for a long while. He felt completely disgraced. For once in his life, he was giving into self-pity.

"Stress is starting to drive you mad, Richard," he said out loud to himself.

He walked back to the bar and continued to rub his shin but stopped in his tracks. He couldn't believe what was waiting for him. The glass he had just drained moments ago was now full again, with two cubes of ice floating lazily on top.

Moore scanned the room suspiciously, placing his hand on the pistol holstered under his arm. "Where are you?" he shouted, his speech slurring. "Kam oot madafuka!"

The pistol danced wildly in his hand, and large beads of sweat began sliding down his temples and back. As if he'd been punched in the gut, Moore leaned forward and threw up on the floor until there was nothing left. Panting, he stood up straight and went around to the other side of the bar and found the ice machine. With a single shot he blew it open. It was empty and off.

Looking at the perfect drink, he felt even more confused. He took it in his hands and meditated on the matter for some time before hurling it against the back wall and shouting. The glass shattered, and the wall was streaked with his drink.

Moore was huffing and could not stop sweating. Exerting a great effort, he turned back to the bar and sat down again. That was when an uncontrollable shaking overtook him. Hysterical laughter climbed up his throat, and muffled sounds began escaping his mouth, unable to hold them back.

Beside the bottle stood a new glass filled again with scotch and ice.

Don't be stupid, Richard. I only want to help you. Do me a favor and drink.

Hands trembling, Moore grabbed the glass and lifted it to his mouth. He took a deep, prolonged swig. It tasted good, fresh.

The liquor went down his throat until it felt like a burning punch in his stomach.

You need to redeem yourself, Richard. You can't let those bloody saboteurs get the best of you.

Moore shook his head and took another sip. The voice was right.

Until now they've been one step ahead, but now you've got one of the women locked up. Now's your chance to go on the attack. To look good in front of your superiors.

Moore nodded with a grunt of satisfaction. The voice was right. Now was the time to take action.

If he'd not been so blinded by worry, or so drunk, he would have realized that the voice had said "superiors" instead of Feldman. But he took no notice. His mind beat to its own rhythm as the voices screeched in unison in his head and tried to outdo one another.

You're the head security officer on board this ship. Your men look up to you. You're a role model. Don't fail them.

"No, no, I won't."

He poured himself another drink and emptied it in a single swallow. He was feeling better, and his thoughts were becoming clearer.

Who do you think they'll follow if you fail, Otto? Who will stop those Communist spies from taking over the ship?

Otto? A part of his mind realized that detail was out of place, but he could do no more. Before the alarms began sounding within his mind, a dark dizziness began demolishing his brain. As he drained the glass, his training with the Black Rats was systematically wiped out, along with everything else except her voice.

I'm sure she's a Jew, Otto. A Communist Jew. A dirty rat. An enemy of the Reich.

"Of course," Moore said, slamming a fist against the bar. Thunderous clairvoyance had suddenly replaced his horrible headache. He could see it all so clearly. The bar had begun to swirl with intensely vivid colors. Even his skin seemed to sparkle before his eyes.

There's another agent on board the ship, Otto. She's English and dangerous. You have to stop her. You have to do it now.

Moore stood up, holstered his gun, and rubbed his face vigorously. When he finished, the blood now running from his nose had been wiped up his forehead, giving him a demonic and savage look.

He'd been given a mission. There was work to do.

Another thing, Otto. There's a crazy old man and a younger man dressed in a cream-colored suit. Don't touch them. They're mine. I will take care of them personally.

Moore, fueled by inexplicable hatred, stretched his hand toward a peaked cap that hadn't been there moments before and placed it on his head.

Anyone who saw him at that moment would have cringed in fright. As he caressed his gun maniacally, he whistled something that sounded like the Nazi national anthem, "Horst Wessel Lied." The man who had once been Richard Moore stumbled out of the bar, transformed into *Oberfeldwebel* Otto Dittmar, as blood ran down his face. Around him the shadows were much denser than those in the rest of the ship. They moved ceaselessly, voraciously.

Waiting for those events that would inevitably come to pass.

XLIII

Kate looked at Carter as if he had just stepped out of a flying saucer.

"How could you possibly know where they're keeping Senka?" she asked slowly.

"The brig has to be close to where Moore's men are staying," Carter answered and shrugged. "Forty-eight hours ago, give or take, I passed by that area. I was falling asleep, and I needed something to do to stay awake."

"What do you mean?"

"I don't smoke," he said, holding up a wrinkled pack of cigarettes. "At least two days ago I didn't. Nicotine helps keep me awake despite the fact that it's tearing up my throat. The closest thing to a smoke shop on board is that goddamn guards' quarters. I got them to sell me half a carton for a hundred dollars. They're a bunch of miserable thieves."

"So what happened when you were there?"

"There are two rooms at the end of the hall beside the armory that are locked. There are also bars on the door. I'd bet what's left of my sanity that Senka is being held there."

"We'll never be able to get her out from there," Kate said, feeling like her world was collapsing. "If that's where she is, at least two guards will be on duty. We can't just stroll up and say, 'Hey, what's up? Would you mind opening up that jail cell and looking the other way for about fifteen minutes?'"

"There are other ways," answered Carter with a puzzling grin.

"What ways?"

The physicist stood up and motioned for Kate to follow him. They left the great gallery without saying another word and went back to the main deck of first class near the balustrade staircase. Before reaching the staircase, they stopped at one of the elevators and went up two floors to a hallway Kate had yet to see.

"This is where the laboratories are," Carter said through a frown as they walked down the hall. "Or at least this is where they were yesterday."

The room was dark and filled with shifting shadows. Carter turned the light on, and the fluorescent bulbs blinked to life to reveal long tables covered with scientific reports. It was cold and damp, as if nobody had been there for many hours.

"What are we doing here?"

"Grabbing a few things. Help me out," Carter said, handing her a pair of scissors. "You see that tinfoil bowl?"

"The one that has old meatballs covered in mold?" Kate wrinkled her nose in disgust.

Carter nodded. "You'd be surprised how careless scientists can be about certain things. But I need you to cut that bowl into small pieces. As small as you can make them."

Kate nodded, emptied the bowl, and began cutting. Meanwhile, Carter searched through the cabinets where the chemicals were stored. Kate suddenly recalled the Finnish man that hadn't recognized her on the dance floor, and she felt a chill. She knew that man would probably never again put on a lab coat.

"Got it," said Carter, holding two glass bottles filled with a clear liquid. Then, he grabbed a thick pair of gloves, two protective masks, and an empty five-quart plastic jar. He placed it all in a bag, wearing a confident smile. "We're set. Let's go get Senka back."

"What are we going to do," asked Kate, hands full of tiny pieces of aluminum foil, "throw confetti on them and spray them with water?"

"More or less," Carter said. "Trust me, I know what I'm doing."

Five minutes later, after passing through the service halls, they reached the deck where the guards' quarters were located. They could hear quiet conversing. Then, chilling laughter echoed from the cabin. It was a strange sort of cackle, dissonant like a poorly tuned piano.

One of the elevators was only thirty feet in front of them. Carter dragged Kate inside, and they both crouched down. Carter opened his bag, set the jar on the floor, pulled on the gloves, and filled the jar with a pungent-smelling liquid.

"This is hydrochloric acid," he explained as he added the aluminum shreds into the jar and closed the lid tightly. "It's very corrosive and has the bad habit of exploding when mixed with certain metals like—"

"Aluminum," Kate finished with a smile.

Carter nodded mischievously and then shook the jar. It started gurgling. The physicist bolted up and pushed Kate out of the elevator but not before pressing a button to close the door.

They hurried into a nearby hall closet and waited. Just when it felt to Kate that time had stopped, a deafening explosion shook the elevator well accompanied by a huge fire and a billowing column of thick smoke that stung their nostrils.

It was like kicking over an anthill. Security guards ran from their station, guns in hand, looking distressed. Kate caught a glimpse of them and was horrified to see that they no longer wore their usual blue fatigues but rather the KDF uniform with an eagle emblem sewn over the jacket pocket. All three men were pallid with dried blood on their faces. One of them was bleeding from his ear, which he did not seem to notice or mind.

Two of the guards ran up to the elevator door and tried to open it, but it was useless. They talked on their walkie-talkies and then climbed the service stairs as the third, perplexed, turned back to his station. Stumbling, he moved as if he had bad arthritis.

"We still have to deal with him."

"Yeah, but I have an ace up my sleeve," Carter said as he took out the other bottle from his shoulder bag. He also took out the two gas masks and handed one to Kate. "Put this on."

"What's the plan?"

"Concentrated ammonia. Even the poorest lab in the world carries it. It's nontoxic, but you should never breathe in its fumes. Now watch and learn. You're going to love this."

Carter raised his arm and launched the bottle toward the guards' room as if he were playing football in the backyard. The bottle spun through the air a few times before disappearing through the open door and breaking against the floor. Not fifteen seconds later the guard ran out coughing and rubbing his eyes.

Kate stepped toward the guard, confidently holding a bronze lamp ornamented with two little Valkyries. She lifted it up and smashed it over the man's head, knocking him out cold.

Without exchanging a word, they filed into the guards' room. The room was empty and had sustained no apparent damage, although the walls seemed to hum with a life of their own. It was as if the entire ship was angry and shocked that someone would interfere with the master plan. Kate suspected that the dark shadow would soon arrive. If she wasn't already there.

"Where are the fucking keys?" Kate circled her hands like a windmill over the table in the middle of the room and knocked over empty beer bottles, an ashtray, a pile of magazines, and a stack of radio transmitters. Even with the mask, some of the fumes had sneaked into her nose and throat. It was like breathing fire. "Where are they? Where the fuck are they?"

"I don't know." Carter's voice was muffled by his mask.

The fumes had gotten to him, too, and he doubled over and began coughing violently. He tripped over a few chairs that were strewn about and managed to get out of the room.

Anger once again boiled up in Kate. It could not be. So close and yet so far. But then, she looked to the door and resisted the urge to burst out laughing like a lunatic. The keys were hanging from the door lock like a handful of ripe grapes, ready to be picked. They had been in plain sight the whole time.

She opened the door. First, she saw long, shapely legs. Then, cotton panties and a shirt stained with blood. Finally, clumped blonde hair around the bruised face of Senka Simovic, who was looking out the door, baffled.

"Wer bist du?" Senka's voice sounded distant, as if she'd been drugged. Blood had begun to drip from one of her nostrils.

Shit. It's too late. She's completely deranged, Kate thought.

She dragged Senka out of the room in fits and starts. She stopped a moment and grabbed a pair of sweat pants from the top of a locker. They were about three sizes too large, but it was better than carrying around Senka in just her underwear.

The fumes were beginning to diffuse, and they were able to cross the guards' room without a hitch. Carter was outside. He was panting, and his hands were on his knees. He looked like he was about to collapse.

"We have to get out of here," he gasped, massaging his temples in pain. "They'll be back any minute."

"Come on, we need to get down to the cargo holds," Kate said.

She began walking and holding up Senka with an arm, but the Serbian woman stamped her foot on the floor and refused to budge.

"*Nein! Ich will nicht mitgehen. Ich weiß nicht, wer du bist.*"

"What the hell did she say?"

"She said she doesn't want to come with us," Kate murmured. "I don't think she knows who we are."

"She's lost, Kate," Carter said, unenthusiastically. "We should just leave her here. In her condition she won't be of any help."

Kate was trying to think of some way to bring Senka back to the present. Violence would accomplish nothing. They could beat her to death, but her mind would remain detached from reality. She looked at Carter, whose skin was turning an ugly sallow color. He'd avoided the ship's curse by staying awake all that time, but what had saved her?

Robert.

She blinked a few times and fought off tears, tears other than the ones caused by the ammonia fumes.

Robert.

Passion had turned into dull pain and then into something tangible.

Kate's love for a dead man had allowed her to keep sane in a world of madness.

Passion.

Without fully thinking it through, she held Senka's head between her hands and looked into her eyes.

What the fuck am I doing?

Kate tilted her head, closed her eyes, parted her lips, and softly kissed Senka Simovic.

Senka resisted as if a pack of wolves were attacking her, but she was far too weak to do much. She began to relax and kiss Kate back. Suddenly, the young redhead felt Senka's tongue playing in her mouth.

Kate pulled away from Senka and looked at her expectantly.

As Senka slowly opened her eyes, a radiant smile filled her face. Not even Senka could have known that the last time she'd smiled like that had been when she was seven years old, only hours before her village was razed.

"Hi, Kate," she whispered hoarsely. "What are you doing?"

"Trying to save our lives. We need to go. Now. Senka, I need you to—"

A muted thump cut her off. She turned around, and her blood turned to ice. The lobby was full of black shadows moving all about. Shadows that devoured the light.

She was there.

Carter was kneeling in the hall, bleeding profusely from his nose, and shaking uncontrollably as he stared blankly at Senka and Kate.

She had gotten him, too.

X L I V

Richard Moore, or the person formerly known as Richard Moore, climbed the stairs with footsteps like a metronome and lungs like two bellows. A strange, vibrant energy carried him forward with the force of a supercharged engine. He passed through the center of the hall of eagles. He approached the hidden door that led to the bridge. As he turned the handle, the first great wave from the storm slammed forcefully against the side of the *Valkyrie*. If the stabilizing engines had still been operational, the ship's balance would have been corrected automatically by the control board on the bridge. But none of that existed anymore. The wave's impact rocked the ship enough to cause Moore to lose his balance and fall with his full weight against the door he was opening.

Go to the bridge, Otto. The captain is waiting. It's urgent.

The voice.

The voice was seductive, intense, and powerful, and it filled every crevice of his mind while muffling all the other noises. Moore didn't like those noises—they scared him. They were telling him that everything was going horribly wrong. He preferred not to listen.

He entered the bridge. Captain Kuss, handsomely dressed in his finest uniform, was watching him with cobalt blue eyes. *Harper, his name is Harper. Harper, Harper, Harper,* the other voices corrected him before she drowned them out.

Don't listen to them, Otto.

Harper stared at Moore with disgust and then glanced at his watch.

"You're late, *Oberfeldwebel* Dittmar."

"I know, sir," answered Moore as he clicked his heels and saluted automatically. "I've been busy until now."

Harper brushed a speck of dust from his jacket sleeve before continuing. "I've been informed a blast was heard near boiler room number two. Something like an explosion, although there are no injuries. Go see what's going on, and then report to me. But hurry. I have that damned gala dinner in less than fifteen minutes. I don't want to waste any time."

"*Jawohl, Herr Kapitän.*" Moore clicked his heels again and ran off the bridge like a bolt of lightning. But he hadn't left because of the captain's orders. Her voice had returned, uttering only one word.

Run.

He rushed to the elevator that directly connected the bridge to the lower decks of the ship. It was the fastest way to move about the ship. Three of his men had been waiting for him, leisurely smoking cigarettes. Without saying a word they saluted him, and they all piled into the elevator.

A strange image materialized in front of Moore for a split second: two sheets of steel welded together before him that blocked his path and a huge red sticker on the obstruction with something written in English. Moore shook his head and reached out toward the steel, but his hand passed right through it. Then, the image disappeared.

He felt a slight throbbing in his temples, and his expression twisted. He could sense his headache was about to return.

The elevator rattled down for a very long time until finally arriving at the level where the boilers were located. The *Valkyrie*'s engines roared like a monotonous, loud buzz that drowned out all other sounds. The temperature was sweltering and stifling. Moore began sweating profusely.

He headed toward the chief engine operator, a fat, bald man close to sixty whose skin was glistening with sweat. He had a Prussian mustache that filled his entire face. As soon as he saw Moore, he stood formally, wiping his hands on a rag in an effort to clean them.

"There you are," he yelled, competing with the deafening sound of the engines. "We heard an explosion about an hour ago on lower deck three. At first we thought a mine had gone off or something because that area was deserted. Or it should have been. Anyway, we found them, and well, we didn't quite know . . . We thought it would be best if security checked it out."

Moore stared at him, and it happened again. It was like one moving picture on top of another. Moore looked at the chief operator with the *Valkyrie*'s enormous engines behind him. But the colors of that image began dissolving and swirling into each other. For a few brief seconds, the background became fuzzy and transformed into something else as it gained clarity again. Atop the broken gauges of the control panel, Moore could see a spattering of blood and guts and the broken bodies of three engineers lying on the floor, riddled with hundreds of tiny pieces of shrapnel. The vision was so real that Moore stepped back in horror. He opened his mouth to scream, but the image vanished like a soap bubble bursting. Everything was normal again. The indicator lights and valves were in perfect condition, shiny, lustrous, and without the slightest trace of human carnage.

It was only an illusion, Otto. You're very tired. The sooner you finish, the sooner we can go back to the bar for another drink.

"Where was the explosion?" Moore asked.

"Over there," said the chief engine operator, pointing obediently. "On the other side of that door."

They passed through the door and came into an empty, cavernous room. In 1938 the *Valkyrie* had been designed with coal engines in mind. This room would have been a huge storage hold for coal. Eventually, they installed more efficient diesel engines, leaving this space empty.

Moore blinked several times—what his eyes saw did not match with what his brain processed. In front of him, two ultramodern engines were smoking from damage, with their metallic, twisted remains scattered across the rest of the room. He closed his eyes tight, and when he opened them again, it had all disappeared. The room was completely empty except for a group of people sitting in a corner. Moore's headache got worse. He felt ill, the heat was making him dizzy, and he wanted to throw up. He would have killed for a stiff drink.

"You're bleeding, sir," said one of his men quietly, offering Moore a handkerchief.

Moore took it without a word and wiped his nose, breathing in the thick, metallic smell of the *Valkyrie*'s diesel engines. Anything that came down to this area inevitably returned smelling like the engine room. He walked through the empty room, afraid the visions would return at any moment. Perhaps he should visit the ship's doctor. It was not normal to see things that weren't there, things he couldn't understand. But the idea vanished from his mind, only to be replaced by bafflement as soon as he saw a group of people seated on a girder. They were watching him fearfully.

It was a family, or at least they appeared to be. There were five of them: two men, a woman, a girl, and a baby only a few weeks old, crying faintly as his mother rocked him.

Moore gazed at them. The young man and woman looked like a married couple. He was somewhat short with fair skin, some early gray patches of hair, metal-rimmed glasses, and intelligent-looking green eyes. He held his wife's hand. She was thin, with frightened dark eyes. Her oval-shaped face was framed by dark, curly hair. Every now and again she leaned over the baby, trying to soothe him. At her feet was a girl, who was maybe six or seven years old and dressed in a plain gray cloth dress and slippers that were too large for her feet.

They were frightened, weak, and hungry. Their panic was as palpable as the diesel smell. Moore instinctively realized they were afraid of him, and, suddenly, endorphins began surging through him like lightning. The sensation was so gratifying that he became addicted.

They were scared of him.

Of *him*.

Their lives were in his hands. He was like a god of the underworld. He swallowed and was almost unable to breathe. At last, his eyes paused on the last family member, and his euphoria turned to rage.

The man must have been nearly eighty years old. He looked feeble and wore a black suit that had begun to fray at the elbows. He had a thick gray beard. A few traditional ringlets fell from beneath his yarmulke and over his ears. His shoulders were covered with a blue-and-white-striped shawl.

A fucking rabbi, thought Moore.

A rabbi on board the *Valkyrie.*

The old man was the only one in the family who didn't appear to be scared. His granite eyes looked through Moore like fireballs. They were scrutinizing the deepest pits of his soul. A sardonic smile began to creep to the corners of the man's lips, as if he had noticed something very humorous about the head of security.

That was too much for Moore. As if launched from a catapult, he smashed his fist into the old man's cheek. The man fell back hard, his mouth bleeding profusely. The woman and her daughter screamed and tried to help the elder, but the husband held them back and glared at Moore. The husband knew that they couldn't win this battle.

The rabbi got slowly to his feet. He picked up his cap from the floor and dusted it off before putting it back on his head. Then, he walked toward Moore with the look of a man resigned to his fate. But there was something else, something fleeting, that rippled beneath his face that Moore was unable to put his finger on. A threat perhaps?

"What are those bottles of water?" Moore pointed to a pair of carafes on the floor. The little girl held another in her hands.

"We gave them water," the engine operator sputtered. "Here below it's so hot that you can easily become dehydrated. They must have been hiding down here when we set off from Hamburg. They could have died if we hadn't—"

Without letting him finish, Moore screamed in rage and kicked over the carafes. As the water spilled out, he grabbed the little girl's arm with one of his enormous hands. His brutal grip made the girl drop the bottle and cry out in agony. Moore picked her up and shook her in the air like a lion playing with its prey.

"Dirty Jews," he spat, continuing to shake the girl, who was writhing in pain. "You sick commie rats! You have no right to be on board a ship of the Reich! You sons of bitches!"

As he uttered the last word, he tossed the girl to her father's feet. The man reached out in an effort to cushion her fall. Moore, who was expecting that, took advantage and unleashed a brutal kick straight to the man's face as he leaned forward. The cracking of the bones in his nose could be heard above all else. His glasses lay shattered by his side on the floor and were soon surrounded by a puddle of blood.

The engine operator looked both uncomfortable and alarmed. "You can't do that here," he said. "Sure, they're Jews, but they don't deserve such brutality. They're human beings after all, aren't they?"

"Shut your fucking mouth!" Moore spun around and put his nose inches from the other man's. "You just worry about your own fucking problems. This is a matter of ship security, and no goddamn machinist is going to tell me what to do. I'll decide if they're human or not. Don't even think about giving this trash another drop of water until I have spoken with the captain. Got it?"

The engine operator puffed his chest up and looked defiantly at Moore. He was a man who was used to being in charge of his terrain, and that was where they were. He wouldn't tolerate such insolence there. Nevertheless, the gun hanging from Moore's waist and the rifles his men were carrying were enough to make him shrug. "Go to hell," the machinist growled and spat on the floor. "It's not my problem. We'll see what the captain says."

With a smile of cruel satisfaction, Moore walked out of the room without looking back at the family. They had all crowded around the bruised girl and her crippled father. The old man had closed his eyes and rocked back and forth while mumbling under his breath in Hebrew. Around him the air seemed to condense and thicken.

Fifteen minutes later, when he returned to the *Valkyrie*'s bridge, Moore felt peaceful. His sweat had dried, and he'd buttoned up his jacket again. He informed the captain about the stowaways below. Harper, with his gala jacket and white gloves on, was about to leave for the great hall. Even from the bridge, the distant buzz of passengers who had already arrived at the dining hall could be heard.

The captain listened to Moore's report idly, more interested in checking himself using a small hand mirror. He seemed to have some problem with his mustache. Finally, he sighed with exasperation and turned to Moore.

"My God, that's enough! There are Jews on board. So what? I'm busy, Dittmar. I have two hundred people waiting for me in the dining hall. So do something about it. After all, you are the head of security."

Moore felt a heady, dark sensation wash over him. He exerted a superhuman effort not to let his emotions shine through.

You have to take care of this yourself, Otto. Teach those dogs a lesson. Finish them.

Moore nodded without realizing it.

Show them who's boss around here, Otto. Show them who's in charge of the new order.

"Yes," he murmured with a dry mouth. "Yes."

The captain opened up the logbook. In angular handwriting he noted the time and date of the important events that had taken place since the last changing of the guard. When he heard Moore mumbling, he looked up and a drop of ink fell to the page. He blew on it, clearly annoyed, and passed a fingertip over it, but all it did was smudge the paper and stain his glove.

The captain had no idea that his entry would be the logbook's last and that before he wrote it, someone else had already read it in another reality that was slowly fusing with his own. But the *Valkyrie* knew well how to keep secrets.

"Let's go, Dittmar." The captain gestured to the door. "What are you waiting for? Make up your mind once and for all."

Moore nodded and saluted before he left. As he went down the stairs, an alarming grin possessed his face without him even realizing it.

A terrible, chilling notion had erupted from some black hole in his head. And he was going to act on it.

X L V

In the hallway leading to the guards' quarters, Kate watched as the shadows moved and felt a wave of fear swell within her. She couldn't look away from the black mass that had swallowed the entire hall in darkness. In the gathering gloom, the outline of Carter on his knees could be seen against the darkness behind him, which was lighter than the one gaining on them. Kate struggled in vain to understand.

The shadow crept across the walls and ceiling. Each lamp it approached began blinking and turning a deeper, dimmer yellow before the light disappeared entirely.

"What's that?" Senka asked, looking pale and shaking.

"I'm not sure," Kate managed to say, unable to tear her eyes away from it, whatever it was.

Kate.

She screamed and fell to her knees.

Kate. You conceited bitch. Did you think you could get away with making fun of me?

"We have to get out of here," Kate howled, struggling to stand up.

She grabbed a table, and a jar fell to the floor and shattered. Kate collapsed again and dragged Senka down with her. The two women landed in a tangle and gasped for breath. The air was too hot and thick to breathe easily. Once again the stench of burnt oil and rotting algae reigned, but this time it was stronger than ever. There was hardly any oxygen and small, colorful flashes of light danced before Kate's eyes. She suddenly realized they were about to die.

You're not going anywhere, Kate. He is not here. I've tricked him. He's lost and can no longer see you. You're mine.

Darkness began crawling toward her, devouring everything in its way. Kate was barely able to make out her own hands right in front of her face. The elevator at the end of the hall was too far to be a real option for escape.

You'll be fine in the shadows, Kate. I take care of everyone. Here in the shadows it's never cold. Never cold. It's never cold . . .

Something struck Kate's shoulder. She screamed in agony but did not budge. Her head was buzzing, and forming clear thoughts became nearly impossible

She was struck again. Only then did Kate realize it was Carter. The physicist was dripping blood from every orifice on his head and was slapping her hard on the back in an attempt to make her get up. Tears of blood splotched his face grotesquely and made him look like a psychopathic clown.

"Run," he panted, almost whispering. "Run."

Carter held out his hand. He was holding a naval flare that looked quite old. Kate didn't have time to ask him where he'd obtained it as the physicist tore the paper and pulled the ring in one swift movement.

In an instant the hallway lit up with such brightness that it hurt, as red sparks cascaded in all directions and cast off a dense, impenetrable smoke. The shadows flickered and trembled momentarily in fear of such a sudden and unexpected flash of light. The light broke the shadows into tiny pieces and illuminated the entire enclosure. A muffled groan quickly transformed into a bellow of fury. Carter was howling in pain as hundreds of tiny veins began bursting throughout his body like a string of firecrackers.

"Run," he shouted as he stumbled down the hall, away from the elevator and toward the heart of the shadows.

The darkness was churning. Kate could see it swirling around itself. Carter, screaming in defiance, stepped into the shadows. The flare began to flicker out as soon as he entered the first layer of darkness, and the shadows advanced once more.

Kate helped Senka get up, and both women began running for the elevator, which was glowing dimly at the end of the hall. Those thirty feet seemed longer than a marathon. The shadows were hot on their trail and closing in on them quickly. Something wet and cold grazed their hair. One damp finger brushed Kate's neck like the tongue of a dead fish, and she screamed in both terror and pain.

The elevator was only a few feet away. Just then, Carter's defiant howl became one of infinite misery before being cut off as if someone had pulled a cord. The flare finally exhausted itself, and the shadows in the hall returned, hissing greedily and all the more black, like a starless sky on a cold, distant planet.

Senka and Kate entered the elevator, and as Senka closed the gate, Kate pressed the button. The door closed, and with a jerk they began descending into the depths of the *Valkyrie*.

On the other side of the gate came the sounds of a sigh of indignation followed quickly by loud knocking. Something was roaring in anger, and the knocking was turning into a frenzied cacophony. A piece of metal broke off the gate, fell on top of the elevator, and bounced around on the roof. Kate and Senka exchanged a look before embracing in fear. Kate thought she could hear Robert's voice standing up to that dark shadow, but she couldn't be certain. Perhaps her mind was playing tricks on her. Only one thing was for sure: the shadow had stopped paying attention to them and focused on something else.

Suddenly, the noises stopped. The feeling of sluggishness that had dogged them was slowly dissipating as the elevator sank deeper into the heart of the ship. The air seemed to become more breathable, and Kate was able to stand up straight without feeling like someone was violating her mind.

"I think it went away," she murmured, trying to convince herself, as she labored to catch her breath.

"I think so," Senka answered, looking up at the ceiling doubtfully. She pulled on the sweatpants and tied her hair back in a ponytail. Gradually, they seemed to be regaining control. "But I don't think we can outrun whatever it is for much longer. We have to get off this ship as soon as we can, or we'll be found sooner or later."

"It's not that simple," Kate said. "We're in the middle of the Atlantic Ocean, in case you forgot."

"We could take one of the lifeboats."

"And drift around six hundred miles from any land and in the middle of a storm?"

"How about we scamper about this damn ship without a plan until that thing hunts us down, Kate?" Senka's Slavic accent was even more pronounced than usual. "Unless you have a better plan, we ought to go out to the deck rather than the storage holds. That's the equivalent of hiding in the basement of a haunted house."

"We have to go down to the boiler rooms. That's the only hope we have of getting out of this nightmare."

"Why do you think that?"

Kate stared at her. It wouldn't be easy to explain that she had just slept with her husband a few hours ago and that he was the one who had told her. Not to mention that her husband had been dead for weeks. Even though the line between rationality and irrationality aboard the *Valkyrie* had long ago been tossed to the wind, it was simply too intimate to share.

"When you got me out of the brig, you freed me from reliving a horrible experience," Senka finally said, a repulsive grimace contorting her otherwise beautiful features. "You have no idea what they had in store for me. I overheard them talking. Those sons of bitches. It's all I'm able to remember."

"What happened?"

"That's it. They were just talking about what order they were going to . . . Then, I remember being struck hard on the side of the head and then . . . nothing. That is, until you kissed me." Senka smiled openly even though her split lip made her wince. "So, either I'm crazy, or this ship is cursed. Both choices are equally scary. So if you want to go down to the cargo holds instead of venturing out on the ocean, maybe it's not such a bad idea after all."

It was Kate's turn to smile. The two embraced, silently affirming that they had one another's backs.

Then, the elevator stopped with one final rattle, and the door opened.

X L V I

What awaited them looked straight out of a Bosch painting. A draft of fiery hot air whipped across their faces as the two stepped out of the elevator, far too shocked to speak. Kate's inability to focus on any one thing was making her sick as everything whirled around her. She heaved, but all that came up from her empty stomach was bile.

The explosion of the stabilizing engines had sent a volley of lethal shrapnel across the machine room. The chief engine operator, tall and athletic, had been torn apart by the blast. The other four engineers had met the same fate, and now their bodies were sprayed across the room. The largest pieces of the remains looked like pincushions some sadistic giant had delighted in by poking them with splintered, twisted needles. Blood oozed out around the primary engines that continued to roar. It was hard to tell what smelled worse, the stench of burning oil and diesel fuel or the blood stewing on hot metal.

Both mental and emotional exhaustion dropped Kate to the floor. It was all just too much. She wanted to cry but couldn't even muster the tears to do so. Her emotions had been disconnected or perhaps stamped out completely. She wanted to close her eyes and sleep for a week. She wanted to wake up and realize it had all been a horribly vivid nightmare. But more than anything, she wanted to wake up and find Robert's hot body next to her in bed.

"Are you going to make it?" Senka asked, leaning over her with a look of concern.

Kate shook her head. "This place. So many horrors. So much bloodshed and death, Senka. I can't do this anymore."

Senka took a couple of strides toward the middle of the engine room and stepped within an inch of the severed head of one of the engineers, its neck studded with many bits and pieces of steel.

"We have to do something now, Kate!" Senka said, the urgency in her voice betraying a hint of panic. "No one is around, so whatever it is we've come to do down here, now's our chance to do it!"

Senka walked forward and stepped on a piece of lung that collapsed beneath her foot with a squishy sound. She didn't even flinch. She just stared straight at Kate, looking more and more confused.

Then, Kate understood.

She can't see it, thought Kate. *She can't see any of this.*

"Senka, tell me what you see down here. Doesn't something seem off?"

"The stench of metal," Senka said and shuddered. "I remember I smelled something just like it just before . . ." Her eyes widened in terror, and her head whirled all around. "Do you think it's here? Do you think that shadow's found us?"

"I don't think so," answered Kate, getting up off the ground. She felt like she'd aged tremendously, like her soul had been weighed down by a sack of rocks. Something had changed within her, perhaps forever. She was trapped between two worlds. "It's just the smell of the engines, Senka."

"So what are we doing down here?"

"We've got to stop the *Valkyrie* by any means necessary." She looked at her watch. The time of the last log entry had already passed. Whatever was going to happen—or, rather, whatever had already happened—was about to happen.

About to happen again.

"How are we going to do that? Do you understand any of this?" As Senka pointed to the multitude of gauges, levers, buttons, and indicators, her index finger brushed a dial that was soaked in blood and clumped bits of brain.

With both disgust and fascination, Kate watched how Senka didn't even realize that her fingertip was slicked with someone else's blood.

Robert, Kate thought to herself, *now would be a great time for you to say something.*

As she paced around hoping to discover an answer to their problems, Kate kicked something that jingled across the floor. She followed it with her eyes and assumed it was a piece of shrapnel. But the metal was far too long and perfect. Intrigued, she took a closer look. It was a long screw, maybe two inches in length. It was perfectly greased and shiny. She wondered where it had come from. Then, the screw trembled a moment before beginning to roll, moving slowly, as if being attracted by a magnet.

At first Kate thought it was because the sea had been rocking the ship. But she realized the screw was rolling in the opposite direction from everything else, which was sliding in an avalanche of iron, flesh, and unidentifiable parts.

It was hair-raising. It defied all of the laws of physics. With a pang of sadness, Kate thought of how much Carter would have liked to see it.

The screw rolled against a steel grate on the wall and stopped there. There were five other screws sitting on a jacket. The jacket had been set neatly in the crack of the grate, conveniently propping it open.

Thank you, Robert.

"Where does that tunnel lead?" Senka asked as she helped Kate move the grate. The reporter shrugged, and Senka, a bundle of nerves, started to smile. "I don't suppose there's any screw rolling around in that passageway that will tell us what to do, is there?"

Kate's only response was to start moving through the tunnel. The stench of burnt oil was stronger than anywhere else on the ship. The passageway narrowed down to a circular tunnel that only became more cramped and dark. Only then did Kate realize that neither of them had brought a flashlight. Their only option was to grope a path through the blackness.

The passage continued to narrow, and a severe wave of claustrophobia hit Kate. She could picture herself enclosed in that tiny passageway with hundreds of tons of steel and pipework above her head and only a plate of steel beneath separating her from thousands of feet of icy water. Ahead was only darkness, and behind Senka was blocking her only way out. The ceiling became dramatically lower and forced both women to continue by crawling.

Kate stopped. Her legs and arms were getting stiff. Her breath was getting shorter and more labored. Little fireflies of light pranced before her eyes in the darknesss. She shut her eyes. Sweat was rolling down her back and sides, and her clothes were sticking to her body like a second skin. She was hyperventilating so much that she was on the verge of fainting.

I'm going to get stuck in here. We'll be trapped, and that shadow will find us and devour us in this rat maze.

"Easy, baby." Robert's voice burst into her mind and had an immediate soothing effect. "There's just a little ways left. Have faith, Kate Kilroy."

Her nerves relaxed, and she opened her eyes to see the faint glow of a flashlight flickering in front of her. She crawled toward the light, but her nostrils were assaulted by a new stench that overpowered the smell of burnt oil. It smelled like decay and charred flesh.

Kate then noticed that beside the flashlight was a bulge that was not moving. As she got closer she realized it was a human body. Kate armed herself with courage and crawled the final few feet until she was within inches the figure's feet. She pulled on the leg, but the body did not move. The person was dead.

Trying to hold back her repulsion, Kate turned the face up. She was stunned to see the bloated, bloody face of Will Paxton. He was gazing at her with the same expression of shock and rage that would remain plastered on his face for all eternity.

"It's Paxton." Senka had crawled up to her side. Both women were quite skinny, yet they barely fit side by side in the narrow tunnel. "What the hell was he doing here?"

Kate grabbed the flashlight, which was nearly dead, and pointed it down the tunnel. They could make out the opening over the axle and the neat bundles of Semtex piled around the room as if some dangerous child had been playing there. The detonation wires hung out of each pile, ready to be connected.

"Paxton was the Wolf und Klee spy," Kate whispered in disbelief.

"Maybe," Senka murmured with a shudder, lost in her own thoughts. "Or maybe not. Maybe it was the *Valkyrie* that brought him here. Besides, the who is not as important as the why." Pensively, Senka examined the piles of Semtex for a few moments. Finally, she nodded and looked sure of herself. "He wanted to render the axle useless, that's for sure," she said as she handled the detonators. She took a bundle of explosives and handed it to Kate. "But he was using too many explosives. If he had succeeded in setting this off, he would have blown a hole in the hull the size of a bus. We would've gone down in five minutes. There wouldn't have even been enough time to deploy the lifeboats." Senka frowned and began piling a few bundles of Semtex around the axle. "It's strange," she said. "Someone capable of handling this kind of material must know how much to use. I don't get how he could have made such a dumb mistake."

"Perhaps he wasn't able to think clearly," Kate speculated. "Aboard this ship it seems like there are times when your mind is thinking backward."

"These three bricks should be enough," Senka said. "The blast will twist up the axle and probably create a hole in the hull, but it won't be serious. I'll set the timer to go off in fifteen minutes. What do you think?"

Kate thought and then gave a nod. They would be able to get out of the engine room in fifteen minutes and take the elevator up to one of the outside decks. Once there they would be able to hide in one of the lifeboats hanging from the side of the ship. With a little luck they would go unnoticed until the moment the Singularity ended, and everything went back to normal. In the event that the madness continued, they could always drop the lifeboat to the water and hope to be rescued by some nearby ship.

Senka pressed a sequence of buttons and stuck the end of a detonation wire in the wax around the Semtex. At the last second, compelled by a sudden epiphany, she grabbed Paxton's green cloth bag and looked inside. With a perverse smile she took out what looked like a metallic pin and connected it to the explosives. Then, very carefully, she dragged Paxton's body over the bundle in the middle of the passageway, so that if anyone wanted to get to it, they would first have to move the body.

"This is a pressure detonator," she explained and backed up on all fours. "If anyone tries to get to the bomb and moves the body, the whole thing will go off."

When they got back into the engine room, Kate was gasping for breath. She took the stale, rotten air of the storeroom into her lungs because she had to, but after all that time trapped in the service tunnel, it smelled like the sweetest air on the planet.

She turned to Senka and smiled, but her heart shrank to the size of a pinhead when she saw the terrified expression on her friend's face.

Before she even had time to think about it, Kate felt an insufferable pain in the back of her head, and darkness fell over her.

Moore felt so jubilant that he could barely stay still. For starters he'd been given complete authority to deal with the Jews. That alone was enough to make him ecstatic, and his mind teemed restlessly as voices continually whispered dark, devilish ideas.

But as if summoned from a magical lamp, when Moore and his three men exited the elevator, they ran headlong into the two Communist sluts. Their backs were to him, and they were apparently distracted. It had indeed been a stroke of good luck. The voices in his head had howled in a chorus of delight as Moore rammed the butt of his gun into the back of the redheaded bitch's neck. If they'd come five minutes earlier or later, the two women would have already placed their bombs and stealthily scurried away again.

They were very good, he had to admit it. The Serb had managed to break out of her cell in astounding fashion. The three men that had been on duty were missing without a trace, something that worried Moore slightly, until the strongest voice in his head told him to forget that minor detail. Since she told him to, Moore obeyed. She was his friend. His personal goddess. His guiding light.

The fact that these two women were moving freely about the ship constituted a security threat. But now it was as if they'd fallen from the sky, holding a bag full of detonators and some futuristic, earth-like material that could only be an explosive. Moore had taken care of the English woman, and one of the guards had put a stranglehold on the Serbian woman, who had fought back like a viper. The four men dragged the women into the empty coal storage room.

"More stowaways?" asked the engine operator. "It's like a goddamn infestation of cockroaches. Someone oughta be more careful in Hamburg."

"Worse." Moore pointed above the man's shoulder. "These women are Communist spies. Probably Jews. We no longer have any need for you, Chief. Head back to work. We'll take care of things from here."

Moore managed to make his last sentence sound so threatening that the chief operator turned pale and raced out of the room. The thought of what Moore might do to these stowaways made him feel sick, but whatever might happen, he wanted nothing to do with it.

Kate began coming to slowly, feeling like she'd polished off the entire wine cellar. She wanted to throw up and had a terrible headache, but now she realized that it hadn't been caused by the dark shadow.

Moore watched the Jewish family as if he were finding them all over again. The young father had managed to stanch his bleeding, but his nose would never look the same again. His glasses were no more than a twisted, broken souvenir. The man looked furious and frightened all at once. The mother was sobbing softly over the baby. The young girl's arm had taken on a blackish color, thanks to Moore's manhandling of her.

The only one who hadn't changed positions was the old rabbi. He stood on his two feet as if they were cement posts in the ground, standing indefatigably. An incomprehensible murmur, his prayers almost couldn't be heard above the thunderous noise of the engines. His eyes remained shut until Moore walked up to him, at which point he stopped and opened his eyes.

The rabbi did not blink. He simply moved his eyes over the group without expressing an iota of emotion. He appeared to be off in some distant land that was beyond all feeling, emotion, or suffering. Then, his eyes stopped on Kate. His lips curved up in the slightest of smiles that was nearly imperceptible before he uttered nine simple words that were spoken in a surprisingly firm manner for a man of his age.

"Hello, Kate. You're finally here. Now everything can begin."

He closed his eyes again and swayed rhythmically. He was far from everything that surrounded him, distant and peaceful.

"You know the Jew!" Moore threw up his hands and turned beet red. "I knew it. I knew you were a Jewish spy. Fucking Zionist conspiracy—admit it!"

Kate, still lying on the floor, shook her head but was too feeble and confused to speak. She looked at each member of the family with wide eyes before they fell on the eldest member.

"All right, if you won't talk, maybe the old man will." Moore spun around without warning and put a hard boot into the rabbi's knee, which crunched like firewood being split in the winter. The man collapsed to the floor. His face was full of color, but his lips were pressed shut, and he didn't make a sound. He kept his eyes focused on Kate, looking at her with such tender care and warmth that she could feel his genuine affection.

"Father!" The young mother gave a piercing shout with the baby still in her arms. She pressed him closer to her bosom, debating whether to protect the child or help her injured father.

She did not, however, have a chance to decide. Moore motioned one of his men forward, and he jumped in front of her and rammed the barrel of his rifle straight into the woman's stomach. She doubled over, her mouth gaping like a fish out of water. Automatically, she wrapped her arms around the baby. Off balance, she couldn't stop herself from falling, but as she fell she turned to protect the baby from being hit. Her ribs smacked against the floor, making an audible and unpleasant crunch. She yelled out in agony.

Her husband emerged from his stupor and punched the guard in his side. The guard, bleeding from his ears and nose, had been distracted by looking at the pale legs of the woman on the floor. He turned to keep from falling to the floor. He spread out his arms, and that was the precise moment the young Jewish man chose to make a grab for the guard's gun.

He had very little time. Maybe two or three seconds. If there had been just a few more seconds, the young Jewish man would have cocked the Mauser and pointed it at the guards. If he'd been a bit more experienced handling a firearm, he would not have hesitated before finding the trigger. If it had all been slightly different, the rest of the story would have completely changed. But his fate had been decided. The dark shadow laughed in the dark corner and smacked her lips over a story that had already played out a million times.

The young man lifted the barrel too late. A few shots sounded out, and two huge holes appeared in his flannel shirt. Tiny pieces of flesh and blood flew out. The man looked around in disbelief before he fell to his knees, the gun still in his hands. The red flowers bloomed out on his chest into one enormous dark stain that was only growing larger. His wife's scream was muffled by the uncontrollable sobbing of their daughter. The guard whose gun had been taken bellowed out in anger and repeatedly kicked the young Jew's body. Soon, everyone began shouting out at once.

Kate watched as the horrific scene unfolded, but shock kept her from saying anything. They had shot and killed a man right in front of her. Senka watched it in her own way and seemed to be in a state of deep concentration. If Kate had been calmer, she would have noticed that Senka looked like a fully charged battery waiting for action.

The only one who remained calm amid the chaos was Moore, who was still holding up his Walther PPK. The smile on his face had spread to unnatural and deformed proportions. The voices in his head chanted wildly. The last vestige of his personality had been destroyed. All that was left of Moore was his body. *Oberfeldwebel* Otto Dittmar had returned from the darkness with a new lust for life.

"Silence," he belted.

Somehow, his voice carried over the chaos. Slowly, everyone quieted down until the only sounds heard as the engine droned on were the wife's muffled sobs, the little girl weeping, and the baby crying.

"Since they wanted to come aboard so badly, we'll go ahead and let them stay." Moore's voice had become raspy, making him sound like a different person. "But it'll be in a place that fits your means. Let's not forget we're talking about dirty Jew rats."

They moved the prisoners toward the ship's walls, which were lined with enormous steel frames that looked like the giant ribs of some prehistoric animal. They forced Kate and Senka to help the young mother drag her husband's body next to his huddled family. The mother looked at her hands in horror. They were covered in blood. She frantically wiped her hands on her greasy clothes.

Moore took notice and gave a hollow, harsh chuckle. "Don't worry, bitch. It won't matter what you look like where you're going."

He twirled the pistol on his finger, pointed it at the young mother's head, and pulled the trigger without blinking. A small red hole opened up in her forehead, but the back of her head exploded like a piñata. Behind her, blood and bits of flesh sprayed the interior wall of the *Valkyrie*'s hull, leaving a strange design like a demented expressionist painting. The woman's limp body fell to the floor as it continued to convulse.

Next, Moore pointed the gun at the little girl. Kate's blood froze. She knew that little girl. Although it seemed like it had been a lifetime ago, it was the girl she'd followed. Even in hell she would recognize that raggedy dress and the bruises on her arm. But most of all she would never forget the sorrow plastered on her face.

"Esther," Kate whispered weakly.

The little girl looked at Kate as a tear rolled down her cheek. She closed her eyes and resigned herself to what was about to happen, as it had a million times before.

Moore fired, and the bullet entered the little girl's temple. Her brain matter sullied her blonde hair, and her body toppled as if she'd been struck by a giant hammer. Her legs tangled, and she fell at Kate's feet. A puddle of dark red blood began spreading slowly around her head like a fiery halo until it reached the tip of Kate's boot.

For the first time during all of this, Kate felt like she would die here. This was the end of the line. Shot by some lunatic who thought it was 1939. The shadow had won.

Moore again pointed his gun, this time at the elderly Jewish man, who was staring sadly at his dead family. His chanting came to an end, and his fists were clenched. Then, he raised his eyes and paused a moment on Kate.

"Don't worry, Kate." His voice was weak like a dying river. "Everything will be all right."

He turned to Moore, and his expression completely altered. He used what little energy he had left to straighten up on his wounded knee, and the elderly man transformed into a monstrous giant radiating waves of energy. The shadows hiding in the corners rippled in agitation as a chorus of unintelligible whispers grew in intensity.

"You!"

The elderly man's voice had become a roar as he pointed an accusatory finger at Moore. A light breeze stirred his mended coattails. As the moments ticked by, the wind picked up in strength. Kate rationally knew that it was impossible for a gust of wind to blow inside an enclosed space on board a ship, but she panicked nevertheless.

"You!" The elderly man bellowed once more and raised his other hand high above his head. He opened his fist, and a sandy-colored powder was taken by the wind and blown everywhere. The powder sketched serpentine patterns in the air before dissipating. *"Pulsa Dinura! Pulsa Dinura!"*

The powder reached Moore, and the shadows went mad as they swirled around Moore and the others like a hurricane, making sounds of bewilderment. The room pulsed with a beat of its own as the rivets in the wall began shaking.

"Pulsa Dinura!"

The sound was almost superhuman. As the old man yelled, he opened both of his hands and pointed all of his crooked fingers straight at Moore. Overwhelmed, the head of security raised his gun and fired three times. The first bullet hit the elderly man in the shoulder, which sent him spinning like a top. The second entered through his side and passed through his lungs before exiting and becoming lodged in the steel wall. The third bullet shattered his backbone, and he collapsed to the floor like a rag doll, dead before he hit the ground.

As soon as the man hit the floor, the hurricane ceased. The wind stopped, and the walls no longer trembled. Calmness returned. Fabric remnants and cardboard that had been stacked to the ceiling began falling all around them. Everything seemed eerily normal.

Everything except one subtle change.

The shadows in the corners were no longer moving or mumbling. They were blacker than the darkest of nights, thicker than a well of crude oil. They were almost solid.

They were almost breathing.

Pulsing.

On the verge of starting something.

Moore, covered in sweat, turned toward his men and pointed toward several steel planks that had been carefully stacked as ballast on one side of the room.

"Throw those bodies in a pile over there, and then cover them with those planks." His voice was calm, as if he hadn't just murdered four people in cold blood. "Have the chief engine operator give you a generator in order to do the welding. Since they wanted on board so badly, let them stay on board forever. Like rats behind the walls." He turned toward Kate and Senka, who were sitting totally still, spectators to the drama. "Throw them in, too, but alive."

"But . . . sir," one of the men stuttered.

Moore swiveled and stared at the man without saying a word. His pupils were two throbbing pools of dark hatred with a life of their own. The man shrank beneath Moore's look and whimpered. A tendril of blackness eddied about the ceiling above his head, and from one of the man's tear ducts came a droplet of blood. His head bobbed like a marionette missing a string.

"Do as I say." Moore's voice sounded like the rumbling of distant thunder. "Now."

His men began stumbling about. They pushed both women at gunpoint toward the lifeless bodies of the Jewish family.

Senka, who'd been passive this whole time, brought up her arm in one perfectly fluid motion. Her elbow struck the man's neck with a hard blow. He coughed, gagged, and brought a hand up to his broken trachea. Senka took advantage of his vulnerability by grabbing the barrel of the gun and pulling, which sent her toppling onto the other guard. Both fell and became a tangle of arms and legs.

Moore and the third guard pointed their guns at Senka. From such a short distance, it would be impossible to miss. Nevertheless, right at that moment a wave that was more powerful than the others hit the side of the *Valkyrie*. Without the stabilizing engines, the ship rocked with the force of the wave. At the same time a harsh sound like that of a locomotive crashing echoed throughout the room. Moore tried to regain his balance as one of his men fired a shot that hit the ceiling.

"Now, Kate," shouted Senka. "Run for the elevator."

The door leading to the main boiler room was only a few feet away. If she hurried, she could get there before her captors regained their balance.

Kate ran for the door. But then she saw him—a little bundle of blankets and hair, barely moving or crying.

The baby.

She recalled the tender look the elderly Jewish man had given her. Now she understood her duty. She finally knew what her role was in all of this.

She stopped in her tracks, and it saved her life. Moore's first bullet hit the wall right where her head would have been if she'd kept running. Instead, she'd turned around and lunged for the baby on the ground.

She picked up the baby on the run, grabbing him by the edge of the blue-and-white *tallit* that was wrapped around him. Without stopping, she continued full speed as a second bullet ricocheted off the floor near her feet. She could hear Moore raging just above the click of the firing pin as it struck the air. He was out of ammunition.

In the meantime Senka had reached the boiler room door. Moore was running toward the door with his eyes on Kate as he switched out the empty clip. Kate had wasted precious time by picking up the baby, and the head of security had recovered his position. He was blocking Kate's path to the doorway.

Out of the corner of her eye, Senka saw something moving to her right. The guard with the broken trachea was writhing on the floor and turning blue. But the other two had regained their balance and were now taking aim at Kate as the *Valkyrie* continued to sway back and forth.

The guards, who were half-brain-dead, weren't having much luck aiming their long Mausers as the floor beneath their feet kept moving. The first shot missed high and provoked a shower of sparks several feet above their heads.

"That's some real shitty aim, boys," Senka shouted from the doorway before heading for the elevator, giving the guards the finger as she ran. Moore was too focused on Kate and the baby to take notice.

As Senka zigzagged toward the elevator, she felt a sharp pang in her side. She probably had a broken rib or two from when Moore had kicked her. Each breath hurt, but she had no choice but to clench her teeth. If she could get to the upper decks of the ship, her chances would increase exponentially. She might even be able to lower one of the lifeboats before the explosives detonated and the whole place turned into an even bigger storm of pissed off guards. She wiped sweat from her chin and panted.

The elevator door was so close now. She was about to make it.

Trained for situations just like this, Senka heard warning signals go off in her head. She'd been zigzagging in order to make her a difficult target to hit, but now she noticed that no more shots had been fired. Then, she saw the chief engine operator and his team huddled in the corner, all with the same look of mute terror splashed across their faces.

She risked a look back and was instantly paralyzed. Both guards had stopped in the doorway that led between the engine room and the coal chute, and they stood perfectly still, leaning on their guns. Both men wore expressions of wicked amusement. A black cloud of evil swirled endlessly around them. It covered the entire back wall and had begun to fill the rest of the room.

The first tendril of darkness stretched out toward the engine room workers and enveloped them with a sound like a watery vacuum, immediately followed by shouts of agony. The painful chorus lasted a few moments before cutting off like a fading radio signal. And that was it. There was no sign of the men. The shadows snarled, satiated. Somehow, they'd become even darker.

Everything turned black. Only the lights of the elevator shaft remained lit, casting the scene in a sickly yellow light.

Senka let out a howl like a caged animal. They weren't going to shoot her. They planned to let the shadow take care of her. She would suffer a fate a thousand times worse. A bell rang behind her. The elevator had come down from above, and as the gate creaked open, she heard the murmuring of voices that told her Moore's reinforcements had arrived. She was trapped.

The memory of a distant day when she was a girl washed over her—a day she had seen black clouds of smoke spread high into the sky as her village burned to the ground. A girl surrounded by grim-looking men with rotten souls. A girl about to be dragged to the gates of hell.

Senka opened her eyes. Tears began welling up, but her defiant gaze didn't waver. She was no longer that little girl. She was Senka Simovic. A python, an expert in inflicting pain. A survivor. She wasn't about to let evil win again.

"Come get me if you have any balls, *kopilad*." She raised her hand and made a gesture of rebellion. "One against seven. Cowards. Bastards."

That was enough to incite the men, but instead of peppering her with gunfire, they charged like bulls. The shadow twisted around in surprise as if things were not going according to plan. It flew toward Senka, but she jumped a railing and headed toward the service tunnel that led to the propeller shaft.

The grate was still loose. Senka ripped it off in a single motion and climbed in as the guards nipped at her heels. At the end of the passageway, she could still see the faint light of Paxton's flashlight.

The sound of a gunshot in close quarters sounded like a cannon and deafened her immediately. A sharp pain pierced the small of her back. The first bullet ripped through her kidneys and lodged inside her. She stumbled and had to grab the wall to avoid falling over.

The second bullet punctured a lung. Senka noticed a pressure on her back that propelled her forward. A flash of heat suddenly stifled her as if she were in the middle of a fire. Her mouth bled slightly, but she refused to fall to her knees. Not yet.

When she was close enough to Paxton's body, she collapsed. She felt a third and fourth gunshot and something hot cut through her leg. Her vision was turning fuzzy. Digging deep into her last reserves of energy, she turned around to look toward the tunnel opening.

Guards were marching single file after her, the lead man brandishing a smoking barrel and a hazy expression. Behind him all that could be seen was darkness like a starless night on a distant and hostile planet. They'd nearly reached her.

The shadow had overtaken the men, devouring them as it went. A black, impenetrable cloak swooped over Senka, sounding like excited, evil whispering. Senka glimpsed into the gathering gloom and made out the face of a blonde woman. She wore the most malevolent expression and watched Senka from the bottom of the ferocious cloud. It was the same face she'd kissed to exhaustion. A face that cast a wicked, vulgar smile. Something cold and bitter gripped Senka's heart.

Senka. You are mine. Come with us. Now.

Senka spat out a mouthful of blood with a blank look and gave the shadow one last grin as it approached. "I'm no longer scared. Go to hell, bitch."

She grabbed Paxton's leg and pulled it, triggering the bomb. Right before the ball of fire obliterated her, Senka was able to hear the sound the shadow made.

A sound of shock. Of pain.

The fireball erupted and devoured everything in its way. Finally, Senka Simovic had been set on the path to peace.

X L V I I I

"It's over, Jew," Moore snorted in satisfaction as he approached Kate with wide strides to maintain his balance. He cocked his gun and pointed it at her.

Without warning, though, a huge fireball emerged from the service tunnel in a flash of light so intense that it split and destroyed the shadows. At the same time, the fireball splintered throughout the tight space of the passageway and spread over the huge axle. The pressure was so powerful that it gave way like a sail to the wind. Forced out of place by the explosion, the axle scraped against the metal that surrounded it, causing an awful screech. By the time the axle came to rest, it had scarred the inside of the ship.

The diesel engines of the *Valkyrie* continued working at three-quarters power as warning lights began flashing on the control panel. Normally, in a situation as serious as the loss of an axle, the chief engine operator would immediately order the shutdown of the engines without even consulting the captain. But all that remained in the engine room were shadows, so no one pressed the necessary button to make an emergency stop. The engines continued churning, behaving as if the axle hadn't been rendered useless. The pressure continued to build up on the gears until what could have been an easy repair became an all-out disaster. Camshafts flew through the air, and the engines, which had been overloaded, began grinding horribly as dozens of parts burst apart and became twisted. Finally, a metallic cough indicated that the engines had stopped working and were completely ruined.

The *Valkyrie* was adrift in the middle of an intense, strengthening storm.

The explosion spread and hit the weakened walls that separated the engine room from the coal hold. Hallucinating, Kate was seeing double as images from two different times superimposed themselves on her vision. Behind Moore, almost like a magic trick, she saw the stabilizing engines that had been destroyed by Paxton overlaid with the image of the dead Jewish family.

The force of the blast also caught Moore by surprise and sent him flying through the air. Three or four alarms began going off simultaneously, and the sprinklers began raining down on the fire that spread through the engine room. The shower of chemicals was so strong that Kate could hardly see a few feet in front of her own face.

It was the moment she'd been waiting for. Limping, she slunk along one of the walls, trying to put distance between herself and Moore. She headed toward the other end of the space, where there was a closed hatch. Kate didn't know where it led—perhaps it was some rat's nest or another room like the one she was in, but she had to try. With the baby pressed to her breast, she lurched forward faster until she arrived at the entryway. With her free hand she tried to turn the handle, but it wouldn't budge.

She could hear Moore huffing behind her as he charged about like a bull in search of Kate. He was getting closer.

Robert, move your ass and help me out of here. Now!

Kate closed her eyes and used all her strength to turn the knob. Just then, it released and began turning as if someone, or something, had helped it along from the other side. The door creaked open to reveal a long corridor lined with pipes along the walls and ceiling.

Thanks, baby, thought Kate in relief as she entered without looking back.

As soon as she passed through the doorway, the door closed quickly behind her with a thunderous boom. The doorknob turned in the opposite direction as before, and the bolts clicked into place. Through the window Kate saw that Moore had arrived at the door and was trying to open it. The English head of security turned red, and his muscles clenched hard. A thick vein the size of a finger swelled up in his neck, but the knob refused to budge.

Furiously, Moore punched the window. He stared hatefully at Kate, who was watching him from the other side of the door with a mocking smirk. Slowly, Kate stretched her arm toward the door. Moore watched her with disbelief and fascination. Kate lifted her hand and closed her fist gradually. Then, her middle finger went up right in the face of the stunned former soldier.

In careful German, overenunciating her words so that Moore could read her lips, Kate shouted, "Rot in hell, you crazy bastard," as she raised her fist again and gave him the finger.

Moore's face turned several different colors, going from white to red to purple. He began shouting as he kicked and punched the door. But all he managed to do was make Kate smile. Moore stopped and pointed his gun at the glass and shot three times. Fine cracks like cobwebs appeared, but the glass didn't break. It was a security hatch that had been designed to isolate an entire section of the ship in case of a leak and, therefore, was also designed to withstand a vicious amount of force. Kate made one last mocking gesture before running down the hall toward a ladder. She needed to find a way out of this claustrophobic hell.

She needed to get off the *Valkyrie* by any means necessary.

•   •   •

Seven decks above, in a hall that was enveloped by shadows, the potted plants shook as the *Valkyrie* bobbed in the rough sea. The lack of balance from the stabilizing engines was much more noticeable on the upper decks of the cruise ship. The only light in the hall came from the ghostly illumination of the occasional lightning bolt. A large bronze jar rolled around on the floor, clanging against the baseboards each time the sea slammed into the ship.

It was the only noise that could be heard in this phantasmagoric space.

Then, the sound of approaching footsteps echoed throughout the deck. Someone was walking with calm determination. Despite the fact that the entire floor was completely dark, the person was moving easily through the shadows without any need of a flashlight, walking freely, as if he knew every twist and turn on board and whistling a jingle.

A bolt of lightning flashed outside. Everything briefly lit up, revealing a young man, perhaps thirty, with tousled black hair. He was dressed in a fancy, cream-colored Italian suit. As he walked, the shadows scurried out of his way as if he were surrounded by some special aura.

The man approached a corner of the hall where there was a low table surrounded by several couches. On one of them sat a bundle of blankets that were piled up haphazardly. The man watched the bundle closely and then took a seat in a free chair, taking care not to wrinkle his jacket. Then, he turned to the pile and spoke.

"Hello, Isaac," he said.

The bundle stirred, and an aged hand covered in liver spots emerged from beneath a woolen blanket. Behind the hand peeked the lost face of an old man whose eyes were watery with cataracts. He was completely bald except for a few hairs on the back of his head that were about to fall out. He was covered in sores, and a string of drool dripped down his chin. Upon hearing the voice, he blindly directed his head toward the man.

"Isaac, my name is Robert Kilroy. I'm Kate's husband. Or, rather, I was. All I know is I shouldn't be here, and you have something to do. The woman I love is in danger, and so is your soul."

Feldman drifted in his own galaxy, trapped in a dark castle with no windows or doors.

"It's far too late for the other crew members, but not for you two." Murmuring unintelligibly, Robert was talking more for his own sake until he leaned toward Feldman. "I need you to come back from the darkness, and I need you to do that now."

Feldman's only response was a weak yelp while he put his hand up to his face, as if the faint light Robert emitted was a nuisance.

Patiently, Robert grabbed Feldman's shirt collar and pulled him up in his seat. He smelled like urine, but Robert was undeterred. With one hand he began undoing Feldman's collar and tie. Then, he stood up and gave the old man a light slap on the cheeks.

"Isaac, look at me. Look at me." He slapped him again lightly and slid his hands under his armpits to make him stand up. Feldman huffed in anger. "We don't have time," Robert said. "So I'll have to do it this way."

Robert brought his lips closer to Feldman's gaunt and sickly face. Relaxing, Robert closed his eyes and pressed his lips against the old man's forehead and held him in a tight embrace. They were like two dancers who hadn't heard the music stop.

Someone encountering this scene would have been extremely surprised. A tenuous glow was becoming brighter and brighter with each passing second in the room. The source of the brilliance was Feldman's shriveled body, which levitated a few inches off the ground, held up by some invisible force. His arms were stuck to his sides, and his head was tilted back. Light shone from every pore of his body, beaming through his clothes and radiating from his extremities. On the floor below him was a blanket, embroidered with "KDF," that had slid off his shoulders.

The light continued to glow brightly. The shadows whirled about in fear and cried out in pain. The glow emanating from the elderly man melted the shadows as if it were acid. Any shadow in the path of that light was shredded and fell to the floor. The lights in the hallway trembled weakly, and the filaments in the light-bulbs began glowing faintly, like smoldering embers. Vanquished by the powerful glow, the shadows fell back down the hall.

And then, Isaac Feldman opened his eyes.

• • •

At the same time, seven decks below, a dark and ancient presence lifted its head and took notice of the unexpected glow. The entity deliberated over its toy, a muscular man in uniform who was pounding furiously on a door as his target made disrespectful gestures on the other side of the glass. The timeless creature hesitated. For the first time in an endless cycle, something had changed. The creature felt disconcerted, and it did not like the feeling.

It took one last look at its prey and roared angrily as it flew off toward the upper deck. Toward the defiant light.

Isaac Feldman blinked several times, perplexed. His cataracts were disappearing, something that would have made any ophthalmologist faint in disbelief. It took only a minute for them to vanish completely.

"What . . . who . . . what's going on here? Who are you?" Feldman's voice still sounded weak. But the relentless businessman was gaining his fire back from beneath the shattered ruins.

Robert responded by looking Isaac Feldman in the eyes. Without a single word uttered between the two of them, Feldman understood everything. Every last bit of the truth became clear.

There was no doubt. Feldman was going to die within the hour.

X L I X

Kate found that climbing up a ladder while holding a bawling baby was much more difficult than she'd expected. She needed to use one of her hands to hold the little boy, leaving only one hand free to hold on to the bars as she climbed up. Her head still hurt, and she suspected her swollen ankle might be broken. Every time she put weight on it, a flash of pain crept up her leg.

The ladder was part of a service duct that seemed endless. It was illuminated every few feet by a flickering light that trembled like drunken fireflies. The heat was absolutely stifling. Kate was unable to do anything about the sweat running down her face except close her eyes, which only made it worse.

Each time she shut her eyes, a new image greeted her upon opening them again. It felt like someone with a remote control was wildly changing the channel in her head. In one moment Kate was able to see a well-lit tunnel with pipes that were painted bright colors and the glinting metal of the ladder's rungs. But in the next, the lights were covered in layers of cobwebs, and the pipes were broken and riddled with rust. Every time that happened, the steel ladder was substituted for a rotting, swollen wooden one that was on the verge of crumbling like sand.

All of it should have disturbed Kate, but she found herself calmer than ever. Her fright had faded and was hidden in some remote corner of her mind, far too weak to come out. She was in a state of tranquility that she hadn't felt since before she'd been handed Robert's remains in an urn.

Confident, she saw everything clearly, and she knew she wasn't on the *Valkyrie* by coincidence. She had a specific role to play. Kate no longer felt like the events controlled her. The story had already been written, but she knew that, thanks to Robert's help, she could change the ending.

She'd taken the initiative and confused the shadow.

The movement of the baby against her chest broke her thoughts. He was still wrapped in a blue-and-white *tallit*, and a gold chain hung from his neck, lost in the rolls of his baby fat. Kate didn't need to look to know that the end of the chain had a small Star of David—the same one Feldman had shown her a few days before.

She paused a moment to catch her breath and looked at the baby's scrunched-up face. She stroked the top of his head down to his chin.

"One day you're going to be a very important man, Isaac," she whispered to him sweetly. The boy began hungrily moving his mouth toward her finger in search of nourishment. "That is, if this shadow doesn't get us. I think your grandpa set free something quite dangerous."

His last words continued ringing in her ears: *Pulsa Dinura*.

Kate knew exactly what it meant.

A few years ago she'd worked with Robert on a story about ultraorthodox settlements in Israel. In the course of their investigation, they came across the fact that in certain parts of Jerusalem a few very unusual groups had retained the values and customs that reigned in central Europe in the nineteenth century. The groups were quite hermetic and turned their backs on the state of Israel. In order to maintain their rich cultural identity, they harbored Kabbalists who practiced the Jewish equivalent of black magic. For those practitioners their most powerful weapon was the *Pulsa Dinura*.

Invocation of the Shadows.

The only problem was that such power required a spell caster of equal magnitude to control it. Someone who was able to see the future and prevent letting the shadows take over. Very few people in the world had the knowledge, which took decades of study, to do it, and even fewer ever called on the dark power. These ancient and prudent individuals knew better than to wake such a monster if it were not absolutely necessary.

The man who had invoked *Pulsa Dinura* now lay dead on the boiler room floor, several floors below, having been killed by his own handiwork. The monster he'd summoned, free for the first time in eons, no longer had a master. It found itself ravenous and full of hate and pain.

Kate had never believed in such mysticism. As far as she was concerned, it was no more than folktales and legends for those who lived in a fantasy world of superstition. Tales that were quaint but imaginary. But now she believed.

A thunderous boom sounded from one side of the *Valkyrie*. The ship tilted sharply about ten degrees, and the lights flickered out for a moment, leaving Kate in total darkness. Amid a chorus of metal scraping, the *Valkyrie* slowly righted itself as Kate clung to the ladder to avoid falling. The ship was pitching and heaving. Without the propulsion of the engines, the *Valkyrie* was no more than a hunk of metal and wood floating on the vastness of the ocean, mercilessly rocked by the waves.

Kate looked down and immediately regretted doing so. Below her was a drop of nearly one hundred feet with boiling hot pipelines all around. One wrong step and she would end up being no more than a pile of broken bones at the bottom of a pit. She clutched the child closer and began climbing up the ladder again until she was forced to stop once more to catch her breath.

She looked up to see a hatch door no more than six feet above her head. She blinked several times before sighing hopefully. That had to be the exit. But Kate could only see the door when she was in 1939, so she was forced to wait for the rocking motion of the ship to sync up with the correct moment in time.

The next time the door entered her vision, she jumped for it. Her ribs smacked hard against the door, knocking the wind out of her, but it opened. She balled herself up to protect the child and found herself rolling on a carpeted floor before hitting a wall.

Kate was dazed, and it took awhile for her to stand. When she did, she recognized the passage as belonging to first class. She walked down the hall with the baby held tight and looked around. Most of the hall lights were still working, but some hallways were no more than pits of darkness. Kate avoided them, making a wide circle in order to get to the outside deck of the *Valkyrie*.

Her goal was to get to the walkway that surrounded first class, find one of the lifeboats, and hide inside. It was better to risk her life in the middle of the ocean on one of those boats than to spend one more second aboard this cursed ship. On the other hand, the *Valkyrie* was not going anywhere. The storm had become a beast. Bolts of lightning flashed all around. The thunder was loud enough to shake everything. There were no windows where she was, and Kate was unable to see the sea, but she figured the waves had to be monumental, judging from the way the ship was swaying.

Everything appeared deserted. The floor was covered with confetti and empty bottles rolling from side to side. It looked like the celebration there had ended just minutes ago. Rows of KDF paper flags along with swastikas lined the ceiling. But nobody was in sight.

Several claps of thunder rumbled outside. The ceiling above her head shook, and the chandeliers jingled. Kate looked up in confusion. It was not thunder she heard. It sounded more like a continuous series of staccato explosions. It stopped. Those had been gunshots.

Her resolve began slipping away. What was going on up there? Who was shooting? Who were they shooting at?

Something moved behind her. She spun around and felt a chill down her back. Shreds of shadows were whirling in the corners, each fragment stretching out to link with another and form ever-larger blocks of darkness. A nervous whispering could be heard, getting louder by the second. It was already taking up the entire end of the hallway and was slowly growing as it advanced. The shadow seemed to be waiting for something.

Kate heard footsteps approaching. She looked around but saw nothing that could be used as a weapon, and she could not recede into the shadows. Suddenly, a trapdoor above her head opened, and a drop ladder crashed down in the middle of the hall. Through the opening, gusts of frigid wind brought in sheets of rain that soaked the carpet below. A man came down the ladder, taking care not to slip. He was wearing military boots, a wide-brimmed helmet, and a uniform with the insignia of the British Home Guard.

The weathered-looking, thickset man of about forty jumped to the floor and turned to look at Kate. His face twisted into a look of surprise.

"What the hell are you doing here, ma'am?" he shouted. "The Germans are up there. The entire southern section of the port has been razed, and more airstrikes are coming. This is a combat zone."

Kate looked up through the trapdoor opening. Through the rain and lightning, she could make out about half a dozen men huddled around an antiaircraft gun that was launching heavy artillery into the sky. Above the howling wind Kate could hear the distant drone of aircraft. When far-off explosions echoed over the ship, the sailors crouched behind their weapons, hands on helmets, in search of a nonexistent safety.

"It's seriously not safe here." The man's tone was paternal and conciliatory. "Go back on land and search for shelter. If the Germans bomb the ship, we'll all be dead. You and your baby."

Kate shook her head as if she were on board a train that had been derailed. Everything was spiraling out of control.

"You need to get off this ship, all of you." Kate grabbed the man's jacket and spoke carefully. "There's something on board this ship that is far worse than a German bomb. Get out of here, or it will finish you off."

"Ralph! Bring that goddamn ammunition right now." A voice, tinged with terror, came down through the hatch opening. The soldier who responded to the name Ralph looked up and then at Kate. His face was full of doubt and panic.

"Get out of here," he finally sputtered, pushing Kate out of the way politely but firmly. "Right now. If you don't, I'll have you arrested. Now if you'll excuse me, I need to get ammunition for our guns."

The man walked straight toward the shadows. He removed a flashlight from his pocket, awkwardly fumbling to turn it on, as he entered into the tatters of darkness swirling at the end of the hallway. Far too busy with his flashlight, Ralph did not notice how the impenetrable darkness closed in all around him. The explosions from outside drowned out the impatient sounds the shadow was making.

After a few steps Ralph disappeared entirely. That watery vacuum noise was followed by a gurgle and the sound of something falling to the floor. The ship rocked again, and out of the shadows rolled Ralph's burnt-out flashlight.

The growing shadows advanced toward Kate. She closed her eyes, breathed deeply, and pursed her lips before turning around and running away from the evil presence. The shadows had already climbed up the ladder and visited those on the outside, entangling themselves around the unsuspecting men on the deck.

As Kate ran she could hear screaming and the hiss of the darkness as it grew louder and moved closer.

L

Moore was furious. The Jewish whore had barely escaped. There was no way of opening that door. He howled with rage and pounded on the door with his bare fists. Waves of unnatural anger washed over him, and all he was capable of doing was making unintelligible noises as he banged against the steel. The door became splattered with his blood as his knuckles split open, but he continued to punch.

Otto.

The voice. Her voice—a soothing balm to calm his feverish state. With her everything made sense. Moore stopped hitting the door and let his hands fall to his sides. Blood dripped from his knuckles as he tilted his head and listened. He drank in each and every word.

The other bitch is history, Otto, but this one's different. She's dangerous. You'll have to work for it.

Moore frowned. He sensed blame in her voice, but there was something else. Urgency, maybe? He was reminded of his mother's tone when she would head off to work at the factories, yelling out her good-byes as she checked her watch.

She has something, Otto. Something that makes her special and dangerous. You have to find him and get rid of him.

Moore shook his head, confused. He had begun to bleed from one ear, but he paid no mind. He felt a light push within his mind, and he was suddenly able to picture Kate's cabin door shining like a neon sign right in front of his eyes.

"No," Moore yelled, hitting the door once more. "I want to find her now. Open the door. I know you can do it."

The pressure within his head became more intense, and Moore let out a howl of pain. A portion of his brain died instantly, and Moore lost all feeling in his face and right arm. But he didn't care. A wave of orgasmic feelings ran up and down his body like a series of electric shocks. It was the most wonderful feeling he'd ever experienced in his life.

You'll have that, Otto. You'll have it whenever you want it. All you'll have to do is wish for it. But right now you have to obey me.

"Yes." A bit of spit dribbled out of Moore's mouth. "Yes, I will."

Inspect the cabin up and down, Otto. That's where you can find what's protecting her. If you get rid of it, she will be defenseless.

With the determination of a shark tracking the scent of blood, Moore headed for the elevator. He noticed that the shadows surrounding him lost some of their intensity. He sniffed at the air like a restless hound and tried to determine what had happened. It was her. Moving. Receding. Moore could feel her doubts and concerns. The connection between his mind and the shadow was so powerful that he was able to perceive the thoughts and feelings of his new mistress with total clarity. They were not thoughts in the literal sense, or at least, Moore wasn't able to perceive them as such. Still, they were clear, complex impulses that flowed through his mind and viciously laid siege to his rationality.

She's worried about something, Moore thought and shivered. *Something's happening to the ship that isn't in her plans.*

He had no time to contemplate his discernment of her master plan because an impulse forced him to walk toward the elevator. As his boots kicked through the scattered remains of the explosion and as the sounds of sirens and bells echoed throughout the ship, the voice in his head continued to provoke him.

In her cabin. You have to go there. Search him out. End him.

Moore entered the damaged elevator, and as it rattled up, Moore wiped the blood from his face with the back of his hand. A mixture of grease and blood covered his skin like a macabre disguise. His shirt was completely ruined. By reflex he threw it to the ground. He was naked from the waist up. He checked the magazine in his gun and waited patiently for the elevator to come to a stop.

The doors opened up on the *Valkyrie*'s main deck. The pits of darkness had multiplied all around the ship. It was as if some fungus had attacked the ship and was meticulously colonizing every last corner of it. Some areas were darker than oil, while others were still full of light and life. The shadows spread without any intelligent design. Rather, the darkness was something organic, growing around what it encountered.

The only thing certain was that when the shadows reached somewhere, they took root and stayed there.

They prowled and waited for something to happen. Lurking.

Moore stumbled through the halls. The waves outside were getting stronger, and the hallway bucked like a wild stallion. From time to time he heard something crashing in the distance. Not even the slightest noise, however, could be heard coming from the areas that had been touched by the shadows, which were like black holes that consumed sound along with light. Somehow, Moore knew that absolute stillness reigned in those bleak patches.

Nothing moved in the shadows. Ever.

His ears picked up the muffled sounds of the cooks struggling with the stovetops when he passed by the kitchens. In one corner he watched as several tendrils of darkness seeped into the room like thick smoke, slipping through the vents. The lights grew dimmer until they vanished altogether. The last thing Moore heard as he rounded the corner were screams of surprise and agony coming from the kitchen staff as the shadows established their empire.

After five interminable minutes he arrived at the hallway that contained Kate's cabin. Moore didn't even bother to grab his set of master keys jingling from his belt. He simply placed his hand on the doorknob and turned. He knew it would be open for him.

He walked inside the cabin, while the shadows huddled in the hall behind him. They were anxious but dared not pass through this particular doorway. Moore looked around before he opened the closet and emptied it systematically. He tossed Kate's clothes over his shoulders after thoroughly inspecting each garment. When he finished with the clothes, he started in on the suitcases, and once he was through with those, he tore down the framed pictures off the wall.

Next, he turned to the bed and tore off all the sheets. He sank his knife into the mattress, cut a huge hole, and proceeded to rip out all of the stuffing. He did the same with the couch and Kate's suitcase, completely destroying it. Once finished, he stood straight up in the middle of the room and heaved for breath. He felt dizzy. His eyes hurt, and shapes were shifting all around him.

He had the feeling that something was moving on the other side of the bathroom door, but when he opened it no one was there.

Feeling defeated, he dropped down onto what remained of the mattress. His eyes fell on a black ceramic urn that he hadn't seen before. The waves must have caused it to roll into a corner and be hidden by a curtain.

Moore's heart began to race as he walked across the cabin and crouched down to pick up the urn.

He shook it next to his ear. Something was inside. With great trepidation he uncorked the container and looked down inside. It was sand. He sank his fingers into the contents and then removed them. No, it was ash.

That's it. You've found it.

Her voice sounded triumphant, jubilant, and relieved. Another pang of trepidation shook him briefly, but he had no time to react. The voice, eager and breathy, glided into his head once more.

You have to get rid of those ashes, Otto. That's his only physical connection. Without them he has no way of holding on to this side. It's his bridge. You have to get them off the ship right away.

L I

Kate went to the outdoor walkway and immediately lost all hope. The sea was churning with an unknown and vengeful fury. The waves, as tall as a four-story building, were lashing the sides of the *Valkyrie* with the strength of a freight train. Each time one of those frothy behemoths slammed against the hull, the entire ship quivered as if a boiler had exploded inside. The teakwood floor was buzzing and cracking with every wave. In some places the wood had splintered or burst, and half a dozen of the port-side lifeboats had already been swept away.

Kate heard something that sounded like several bottles of champagne being uncorked at the same time. She carefully poked her head over the railing, clutching the baby against her chest as she looked down. Approximately thirty feet below, screws about six inches in length were shooting out like rockets. Despite all of the renovations, the seventy-year-old rivets had begun to burst as each surge of the ocean weakened the entire ship's structure. Kate watched as an entire steel plate the size of an enormous window was ripped off and dragged into the sea. Petrified, Kate realized the storm was going to destroy the *Valkyrie*, this time for good.

Above her, the last of the lifeboats hung from the side of the ship. Kate glanced out to the sea and vacillated. Staying on board the *Valkyrie* would be an almost certain death. On the other hand, going out on a tiny boat in these conditions was something akin to suicide.

But she had no other choice.

She walked toward the lifeboat and started devising a way to unfasten the boat from the side. As she did so, the side door closest to her suddenly burst open, and there was Moore, holding something against his chest in one hand and his Walther PPK in the other hand. Blood gushed from his ears, mouth, and nose. The right half of his body was paralyzed as if he'd suffered a stroke. But his look was one of fierce determination. Kate saw a glimpse of the demons that were feeding on the enormous man's last reserves of energy.

"You," Moore yelled. "You're mine now."

Kate stepped back and felt the railing against her back. The rain and waves were soaking her, but it no longer mattered. She was trapped.

"You know something?" Moore stared at her with something like respect. "I never would have thought a dirty Jew like you would give me so much trouble. You've got nerve, and you're smart. But I also have those qualities. And I've also got this." Moore smiled and pointed his gun, so Kate could see the barrel's opaque glint.

"I don't like weapons," Kate retorted and cradled the baby closer. "Or those who use them to kill innocent people."

"Don't you?" Moore moved two steps closer without lowering his pistol. "Guns have two sides, one good and one bad. I'm standing on the good end. You're on the other end, the bad one. The rest is just extra."

Kate realized that he was slurring his words as he spoke, as if the lights had been turned out in a section of his brain. Only then did Kate notice that Moore was holding the urn that held Robert's ashes. Her heart began beating wildly.

"Well, well," Moore said, seeing what Kate was looking at. He raised the urn above his head and gave a low chuckle. "You know each other. Well, say good-bye to this charred fucker because he gets off here."

He extended his arm to hurl the urn overboard. Kate gulped, frozen in place like a statue. Everything was moving in slow motion in an uncontrollable sequence of events that would ultimately end with Robert's ashes in the sea.

From the swirling shadows behind Moore emerged a figure brandishing a wooden chair, which he smashed across Moore's back. The chair broke apart, and Moore crashed to the deck. Isaac Feldman was heaving like a train. He dropped the piece of the chair he was still holding and spat on Moore's body. He put his hands to his knees and tried to catch his breath, visibly shaken. Lifting the chair had taken a superhuman effort.

"You're . . . fired . . . bastard," Feldman panted. When he finally caught his breath, he walked toward Kate with a bright smile on his face.

She couldn't believe her eyes. Feldman no longer seemed to have one foot in the grave. He'd made a remarkable recovery. He was no longer the healthy, formidable old man who had left Hamburg, but he also was no longer the senile and drooling shell of a man she'd encountered a few hours earlier, wrapped in blankets. No. The Feldman that stood in front of her brimmed with life, radiating a brilliance of his own as if he'd been refitted with new batteries.

"Isaac," she whispered and felt a wave of relief flood through her. "I don't think I've ever been so happy to see a familiar face."

"Listen, Kate." Feldman stepped toward her and picked up the urn from the deck. "We don't have much time. Robert sent me. You have to get out of here. The cycle is about to finish."

"Cycle? What cycle?"

"It's hard to explain." Feldman's voice was imbued with sorrow. "But you've got to believe me. If Moore had managed to toss those ashes overboard, we would have been defenseless against her. She's angry but scared. For the first time everything's different."

"Who is she? What's changed?" Kate fired off. "Why is the urn so important? I don't understand, Isaac."

"It's got something to do with *Pulsa Dinura* and the ashes of a dead man, but I'm not sure. It's all so complicated. Robert's presence has changed the cycle of events that's been repeating itself on board this ship since 1939. Now we can stop it. But you've got to—"

A bullet pierced the small of Isaac Feldman's back. He looked down at the red stain that was spreading across his abdomen. He then fell to his knees, drowning in his own fluids, before collapsing to the deck and shaking like a fish out of water.

Moore got up from the deck, his hair soaked in the blood that continued pouring out of the wound on the back of his head. He looked dizzy, but he groped along the floor for the urn. He kept his eyes and his gun trained on Kate, who was too scared to move. His aim had been incredibly accurate the first time.

"It's over," he said with a gritty voice. He sounded like an old jukebox that was slowly losing power. "To hell with these ashes and to hell with you, fucking Jew."

He struggled to open the top of the urn. In order to do it, he had to put down his gun. Kate took advantage of the brief moment in which Moore took his eyes off her and got up on the railing near one of the lifeboat clamps.

Moore looked up, having twisted off the urn's lid. He picked up his gun again and glowed with a savage triumph. The lid to the urn rolled on the deck and plunged down into the sea. Kate followed it with her eyes as it disappeared into the waves. Then, Moore raised the urn over his head and slowly tipped it overboard without taking his gun off Kate.

The ashes whipped out like a curtain of dust, fluttering in the rushing wind and vanishing into the sea. Moore looked away from Kate for half a second as he finished emptying the urn, and Kate knew that was her only chance.

The clamps holding up the lifeboat were one of the few modern concessions on board the *Valkyrie*, due to safety regulations. The lifeboats were lowered via electric pulleys. Once on the sea, there were switches that would release the cables tying the lifeboat to the ship. The switches were located inside small Plexiglas boxes that were to be broken only in case of emergency. Kate hit one with her elbow and prayed she would be strong enough to break it in one try.

Her elbow broke through the thin layer of glass and cut her skin. But her elbow also hit the switch inside. Moore looked up at her upon hearing the crack. That was enough of a distraction for him not to see as the end of the lifeboat swung down and fell on his head.

The impact was so violent that all of the ribs on his right side were pulverized and his arm shattered before he even knew what was happening. The blow sent him flying over the railing, and he had no time to use his good arm to grab hold.

With one final scream of rage, Moore wildly flailed his good arm to grab hold of something, but the damage had already been done. He only had time to give Kate one last look of wrath before plunging headfirst into the cold black waves of the Atlantic.

After a moment he disappeared completely, as if he'd never existed.

Kate jumped back to the deck and fell to her knees, the baby still in her grasp. He had woken up and was fussing tirelessly from the biting cold. The rain hadn't let up, soaking both of them, and now Kate's elbow would not stop bleeding. She took a look at the wound and turned pale. The cut was much deeper than she had suspected. She would need to make a tourniquet or she would lose too much blood.

She walked closer to Feldman's body and began undoing his crocodile-skin belt. She looked over his body with infinite appreciation and sorrow. If it hadn't been for him, she would be dead. She reached out to close his eyes.

And then, Isaac Feldman blinked.

Kate thought she had imagined it, but the first blink was followed by a second and then a spasm of bloody coughs. The old man was alive, hanging on by a thread, but alive.

"Isaac," she yelled and loosened his shirt. "Isaac, look at me. It's me, Kate."

The man's abdomen looked war torn. The bullet hole was about the size of a baby's fist. Moore must have used a special type of ammunition. The wound was no longer pouring as much blood as it had been at first, but there was nothing that could be done, not to mention Kate had no idea where to even start. She was certain that not even a medical team with all of the proper equipment could have saved him. Isaac Feldman was about to die.

"Kate." Feldman's voice was no more than a faint whisper.

His hand, covered in blood, closed around Kate's arm and trembled uncontrollably. Kate's tears mixed with Feldman's blood, but neither one realized it. The old man's life was escaping in spurts.

"Kate," he repeated and coughed violently. "Robert's . . . ashes . . . He's the only one able to stop the shadows. The spirit of a good man. The . . . *Pulsa* . . . *Dinura* . . . If you hadn't . . . brought . . . them . . . we'd all be . . . Where . . . are . . . they?"

Kate looked to the ground. The urn was on its side, empty. Moore had thrown all of Robert's ashes to the wind in the middle of the North Atlantic. All that remained was the ceramic vessel filled with nothing. The bastard had won despite her best efforts.

"They're right here," she lied and succumbed to her tears. "Don't worry, Isaac. With these in my hands, they won't harm us."

She watched as the shadows advanced on both sides of the deck. The darkness was being cagey. It was moving patiently like a pack of wolves stalking a lone traveler with a fading campfire. Kate's flashlight flickered and took on a deathly glow.

She was approaching.

"Let . . . me . . . see." Feldman was almost unable to breathe.

Kate thought he was talking about the ashes until she saw where his eyes were directed. With a weary smile she raised the baby, who had stopped crying. She pushed the *tallit* away from his face, so that the elderly Feldman could get a good look at the chubby, rosy-cheeked baby, who was looking curiously from side to side.

"Isaac Feldman, I'd like you to meet Isaac Feldman," she said as a chill ran through her. What she was doing was theoretically impossible, and yet it was happening right in front of her. A paradox that was impossible to understand.

Feldman's eyes lit up, and for a brief moment, he became the old tycoon. "I'm a beautiful . . . baby . . . don't you think?"

"I wish you long life and happiness," Kate whispered as she swaddled the baby, hardly able to see anything between the shadows and her teary eyes.

"You've got to set him where"—he began coughing harder than before, and Kate thought he might be done for—"where they can find him when they come . . . when the *Pass of Ballaster* arrives. It's the only way to . . . end the cycle. If the shadow gets him, an infinite hell will begin for . . . for everyone. Including you. Don't let her get to him, Kate. Save him. Save me. Save . . . us . . ."

Feldman's head fell to one side, and his muscles relaxed for the last time. Kate closed his eyes and sobbed. She then took his belt and wrapped it around her arm to stop her elbow from bleeding. Next, with a trembling baby at her breast, a dead body at her side, and an empty urn at her feet, Kate watched the wall of shadows as it glided over her like a pack of thirsty vampires.

And then Kate heard her give a victorious howl as the last embers of light burnt out, and the shadows enveloped her entire body.

L I I

Impenetrable shadows. Darkness thick and full.

At first nothing happened. Then, slowly, a tiny spark of light timidly pierced the darkness, an absolute darkness as deep as anything a human can imagine. It was an ancient darkness, sagacious and wicked. But that single modest spark, that ember, began growing all around the silhouette of the woman who was kneeling on the floor and clutching a small bundle close to her chest. Gradually, the shaky light grew stronger until it was as bright as a handful of fireflies after a storm.

Kate let herself breathe out after she realized she'd been holding her breath for some time. Frightened, she looked up. Around her a starless night had fallen. There was no hint of even the slightest ray of light with the exception of the clarity that seemed to be emanating from all around her. Thanks to that, she was able to see twenty yards in every direction. Beyond, something imperceptible and dense was whirling around, furious but unable to traverse the halo that was protecting her like a bubble.

She looked overboard. The storm that had been relentlessly besieging the *Valkyrie* up until a minute before had suddenly vanished, as if by magic. The surface of the Atlantic was as glassy as a mirror. Everything was a pool of darkness that extended beyond her sight.

She looked around. The *Valkyrie* looked the same as ever. Almost.

The ship looked the same, but there were dozens of subtle changes everywhere. The side paneling destroyed by the storm had returned to normal. The lifeboat that had struck Moore was also back just as it had been before, except now it had a new type of varnish, one or two shades lighter.

Kate got to her feet, disoriented and confused, and only then did she realize that Isaac Feldman's body had disappeared. It was no longer there.

Nothing made sense. Kate figured she must have walked several feet before the shadows had overtaken her. She walked up one way and down the other, but she could not find any trace of Feldman or even a drop of blood. The deck was immaculate, like it was fresh from the shipyard.

She tried to relax. The atmosphere was thick, hot, and heavy. There was no trace of a breeze, and the only wind being generated was from Kate walking. It was completely silent; the ship was lifeless and motionless. Kate was certain it was the work of the shadows.

Suddenly, she stopped when something clicked in her mind. *It's like being in a photograph, trapped in a moment in time.*

The thought hit her with the force of an uppercut. She was trapped.

The question was no longer *where* but *when*.

She took a step back and bumped against something bulging out of the wall. She turned around and saw it was one of the life preservers. Her relief quickly gave way to nausea.

Right below the ship's name and below the KDF logo was a proud eagle with spread wings, holding a blood-red swastika between its talons.

Kate couldn't breathe. She was choking. Her right foot bumped the urn that had contained Robert's ashes, and it rolled with a hollow sound. The vessel, still carrying trace amounts of ash along the inner lining, produced a faint light in the face of the shadows and grew ever weaker. Kate looked at her hand. Her skin seemed to be glowing on its own as if each and every one of her cells had turned into a tiny power plant providing energy to a besieged city. Kate was producing the light, not Robert. It made no sense.

Something stirred in the shadows. It was a dark stain that stood out against the starless black background. It advanced toward Kate, exuding anger and misunderstanding.

You can't resist me! He's not here anymore! You don't have the strength to stand up to me.

A tendril of darkness flew at Kate. Before it could reach her, however, it struck against the halo of light surrounding her and burst apart in a volley of ash and smoke as the shadows howled in agony.

You can't!

Her voice boomed out like a thunderstorm above the restless moans coming from the army of shadows in her wake.

You can't, fucking bitch! It's impossible! He's not here anymore!

"Of course, he's here, you dirty bitch," Kate lied and tensed her muscles. "You just don't know where."

Without a second thought Kate raced directly into the shadowy darkness.

Crossing through the cloak of shadows, she first felt a glacial chill so intense that her lungs felt like they were on fire, and her pores froze over. Still, she didn't give up. She knew her time would be over soon enough.

The shadows moved quickly behind Kate, who knew that the only thing saving her life was the halo of light that surrounded her. The only thing saving her and the little child who had nodded off inside of his *tallit*.

"We have to find a lifeboat, Isaac," she murmured soothingly to the baby. "We've got to get off this floating tomb as fast as we can."

Kate.

She stopped in her tracks. It was not possible.

"No." She pursed her lips and continued walking.

Kate, listen to me. It's me.

"This is a trick." She shook her head and tears began to flow. "Robert, you're not here anymore. I watched him throw your ashes into the sea."

Kate, it's me. I swear.

Robert's voice came loud and clear into her mind, fraught with urgency.

You can't see me now, but you've got to listen to me. It's very important.

"Go to hell, bitch! You can't play me like that!" Kate turned around in fury and shook a fist at the surrounding darkness. The sound of her footsteps was drowned out at the edge of her aura, and her voice did not carry much farther. It was like trying to fight off a hurricane.

You love cherries, especially when they're cold. You don't like me to rub the small of your back when I give you a massage. We have some pictures hidden in a copy of Alice in Wonderland *on the eighth shelf of our living room. You always said that if your mother ever saw those pictures, she'd have a heart attack. You once slapped an ice cream cone on my head for saying your red hair looked like a fire. The last time we saw each other at home you told me that you loved me and kissed me on the neck. I know you miss me every minute of every day. Like I miss you.*

The silence was deafening. Kate wept openly, and her lips shook.

It's me, Kate. I'm still here. I haven't left you. That's why she can't do anything to you.

"But . . . how is that possible, Robert? I watched him throw your ashes overboard. You—"

You know how, Katie. You know perfectly well.

Upon hearing those words, Kate closed her eyes and began crying out loud, but it was out of happiness.

"Robert . . ." she whispered.

We don't have much time. The cutoff is approaching, and the cycle will close. You've got to leave that baby on the dance floor. Right now.

"Leave him?" Kate almost sounded outraged as she unconsciously pressed the child closer to her body. "I can't do that!"

Listen to me, Kate. It's the only way. The cycle has changed. Isaac Feldman has finally died aboard the Valkyrie. *He was the last survivor of the original voyage left for the cycle to close off. Now the shadow will have to leave. Its mission has been carried out. All that's holding her is that child. She wants it, so she can keep going. If she gets him, the cycle will go on. As long as he's with you, they will chase you wherever you go. You'll be letting a terrible nightmare loose on the world.*

"So . . . what choice do I have?" Kate's voice quivered with emotion. It seemed like a horrible atrocity to abandon a helpless baby on this floating nightmare.

He has to get out of here on his own. Go on with his life. Be what he's going to be on his plane of reality.

"But he's just an infant! How can he get out of here on his own?"

Like it was written. As prescribed by his fate. Look.

Kate heard a noise behind her, and she spun around. A beam of faint light pierced the shadows like a hot knife through butter. The dark clouds dispersed, and Kate was able to see three men dressed in clothes from the 1930s as they climbed on board the *Valkyrie*. The youngest of them was a rascal with acne and a face full of fear. Kate knew that many years later that young boy would become an old man whose walls would be covered with pictures and souvenirs.

The tallest of them swung his lamplight over the walkway. They were discussing something between themselves, but Kate couldn't hear a word of what they were saying despite not being that far away. It was like they were in a huge crystal bubble that separated them from the rest of the world.

The head officer cupped a hand to his mouth and shouted something in the opposite direction from Kate. She could not hold back any longer and shouted back in response.

"We're here! We're here!"

The result of her words was surprising. The three men all spun around at the same time and looked terrified as they stumbled into one another. The way in which they all fell to the floor was so funny that Kate would have burst out laughing if the situation were not so serious.

They can't hear you, Kate. Or at least not the way you want them to. To them you're like a ghost. You always will be if you don't get out of here in less than ten minutes. The cycle is about to close, and if you're on board when that happens, you'll be trapped between two worlds forever. You'll be no more than a ghost for all eternity. And him, too.

"Will they find him?" Kate looked down at the baby, who was sleeping soundly.

Of course! As long as he's in the right place at the right time. Now run!

Kate didn't need to be told twice. She quickened her step and walked toward the door that led to the great hall. She twisted the knob, which gave way with a loud creak. The door opened wide, and she waited for the sailors to follow her footsteps.

She walked over the thick blood-red carpet and came up to the imposing staircase. The chandelier was as dark as the one in the lobby, and Kate had the feeling that every last speck of light had been sucked out of the place.

She walked past the set of proud eagles. They were both eternally screaming out in defiance with swastikas in their talons. Kate felt no fear as she split the shadows, crossing through the dining room and entering the dance hall. Trays with hot food were still steaming. No more than twenty minutes could have passed since the shadows had taken over that area. No signs of life had been left behind.

Passing by a service closet, Kate opened the door and took out a blanket with the KDF logo stitched along the edges. She wrapped up the little one in the blanket, and that was when she felt something. In the dark and silent atmosphere of the room, something was moving behind her. Something wicked and confused.

Give him to me. Givehimgivehimgivehimgivehimgivehim. He's mine, bitch. Mine like this entire place. Don't get in my way.

Kate carefully placed the sleeping baby on the floor and turned around with her right fist clenched. She was not sure what she was doing, but she'd never felt so calm and serene in all of her life.

"It's just you and me now, right?" she whispered to the shadows. "Good. If you want him, you'll have to come get him. But you'll have to get through me."

I've been saving a sweet slice of suffering just for you.

Her voice was filled with wrath but also fear. Having gotten used to eons of cycles without a change, she was disconcerted by this new, unique moment.

You'll wish a thousand times over that you had died.

"You know what? I'm tired of all this death and darkness shit. So if you're going to do something, then do it already or else go to hell."

The air in the room started to freeze up. Then, a dreadful shriek filled Kate's ears as an enormous wave hurled itself toward her, devouring everything in its path like a tsunami of evil.

Kate waited a moment before opening her fist and tossing Feldman's Star of David necklace at the wall of darkness that was hovering over her. As the necklace left her hand and penetrated the darkness, Kate felt time come to a standstill. The six-pointed star surrounded by Kabbalistic symbols disappeared into the darkness, and a second later, it burst apart in a blinding flash of light that illuminated the entire dance hall. It was as if some photographer had used the most powerful flash on the planet.

The rays of light pierced through the shadows and completely dissolved them, and a gurgling noise faded. For a fraction of a second, with her eyes half-open, she could make out an enormous shadow set against a background of bright light. The shadow, so much like a person yet far from human, writhed in pain. The brightness of the explosion continued to strengthen, and the cries of agony grew louder. The light became so brilliant that Kate was forced to shut her eyes. Finally, the last remnants of darkness vanished completely.

At last, seventy years after it was unleashed, the *Pulsa Dinura* had reached its end, and she ceased to exist.

L I I I

Once the luminous glow had begun to fade, Kate opened her eyes. The spectral flashes of lightning began flickering in through the dance hall's windows. The storm had redoubled its efforts, and the entire hull of the *Valkyrie* was creaking and trembling against waves thirty feet tall.

The floor swayed relentlessly beneath Kate's feet. The ship moved like a pendulum, and the furniture shifted about like dice in a cup. An expensive seat made of oak and leather cracked when it slammed against a pillar. Seconds later the tremendous cacophony of glass shattering into infinite pieces boomed out of the great hall. The huge chandelier, unable to withstand the rocking of the ship any longer, crashed to the floor. The *Valkyrie* was disintegrating amid the storm.

She looked all around. There was no sign of the baby.

In another moment and place in time, a terrified British naval officer was picking up the baby off the dance floor. The only difference was that he wouldn't have any jewelry around his neck this time. From there, the future would be altered. That child would live, but he would not be the same. The cycle had changed.

A wall of foamy gray water slammed into the dance hall windows, breaking them. Kate had just enough time to run out of the hall before it was flooded with thousands of gallons of water and broken glass. The lights flickered, and after a final spark, they went out for good.

Kate crossed the landing with the eagles and had to step around the broken remains of the crystal chandelier. Frayed wires above her head cast intimidating sparks with each movement of the ship.

In order to get outside, Kate needed all the help she could get from her good elbow and her knees. With one of her arms out of commission, she found it incredibly difficult to hang on to the window frame and leap onto the ship's deck. When she managed to, Kate's eyes opened wide and she gulped.

The *Valkyrie* was drifting through the storm with no one at the helm and its engines powered off. The waves had lashed the ship off course. In a storm like this, it was no more than a question of time before a particularly strong wave obliterated the hull and sent the *Valkyrie* to the bottom of the ocean. The wind grew more blustery, and it was hard to tell if it would take hours or just a few minutes, but one way or another, the ship was doomed. If she didn't hurry, Kate would go down with the ship.

Fighting against the ceaseless wind and rain, Kate gripped the railing and walked forward step by step. Each movement forward was a serious accomplishment. The salty water was splashing against her knees more frequently, and Kate realized that the water level had risen quickly. It could only mean one thing—the ship had sustained a leak somewhere, and the *Valkyrie* was sinking.

While the leak hastened the *Valkyrie*'s end, it also saved Kate's life. Flooding the *Valkyrie*'s cargo holds, the water was weighing the ship down and causing it to be more stable as it sank. For Kate to lower the lifeboat down to the water without hitting the side of the ship, it was imperative that the ship not rock too violently. If the lifeboat slammed into the ship, the force would break the boat apart, casting Kate into the ocean to drown.

She finally reached the closest lifeboat. Next to that boat, in some vicious time warp, she had found a straw hat, the first sign of the nightmare that was to come. Kate shivered at the memory.

She raised the glass protecting the pulley and activated the boat's descent. The electric engines hummed to life, and the boat began its trip to the water. When she was about to step into the vessel, her foot bumped something. It was Robert's urn. Kate picked it up and entered the raft.

Then, she breathed deeply a few times, and screwing up her courage, she pressed the button to release the two pins simultaneously.

With a click the lifeboat was released from its securements, and it dropped to the water. Kate grabbed hold of her seat to avoid being bucked off. The tiny lifeboat was tossed about in the middle of waves that looked like enormous hills all around her.

A treacherous wave slammed the side of the boat and flooded it. Kate struggled to keep her head above the waves. Seawater got into her mouth, and she spat out what she did not swallow. Then, she heard a thunderous crunch behind her, and she looked back. Through the fog of the storm, she watched as the majestic stern of the *Valkyrie* tipped up above the waves and sheets of water poured from the bronze propellers. The ship was sinking and producing a symphony of sound. Metal crunched and scraped. For a moment the ship remained vertical and was tossed about by the waves, and all of the lights turned off on board. Kate flinched and waited for the final blow that would finally send the ship to the depths of the ocean. But the *Valkyrie* sank tamely below the waves, as if an invisible hand were pulling it from below.

The ocean surface bubbled a few times, and a couple of life preservers appeared in the dirty, oily whitecaps that crowned the waves, but suddenly, everything had come to an end.

The *Valkyrie* was no more.

L I V

Eight hours later

A cold morning sunrise slowly usurped the darkness. The sea had been tossing the lifeboat around for hours, leaving Kate bruised and unable to sleep. She was exhausted, terrified, and dying of thirst. The fog had vanished, and the sunshine had revealed a wide expanse of empty ocean that was still stirring from the aftershocks of the storm receding on the horizon.

As soon as the boat had quit swaying, Kate risked letting go of the seat she'd gripped tightly for hours. She took a couple of shaky steps to the other side of the boat and pulled open a rubber cover to reveal a modern emergency beacon. With tired eyes she followed the instructions and pressed a button to activate it. The beacon turned on with a blip, and a red light began blinking on one side. Then, far too exhausted to care, she collapsed against it and closed her eyes.

Even though the *Valkyrie* had drifted quite a ways during the storm, Kate knew more or less *where* she was. She was near the commercial routes that crossed the Atlantic. What she did not know was *when* she was. She contemplated what the hell she might do if she wound up trapped in 1939.

She looked up and weighed her possibilities. All in all, living in 1939 would not be such a bad thing. It would have its drawbacks, of course, but . . .

Smoke. Smoke was on the horizon.

Kate got up and looked for a pair of binoculars in the boat's emergency kit. In the distance she could make out a black spot moving against the rising sun. She put down the binoculars and searched through the supplies until she found a flare gun. She placed a flare inside before pointing into the sky and firing.

With a hiss, the flare ascended into the air and exploded high above in a lovely cloud of red. Kate fired two more flares before opening a colored smoke flare she found at the bottom of the emergency kit. The lifeboat was immediately enveloped in a red cloud that had to be visible miles away. She picked up her binoculars again and looked toward the ship. She sighed in relief. The spot in the distance was coming closer.

They had seen her.

The wait felt like an eternity. It was an enormous, imposing cargo vessel that was sailing alone. It made Kate feel miniscule and left her in a state of doubt. But eventually, the ship was close enough for her to make out the colors on the hull. On the deck above she could see hundreds of stacked Maersk containers.

Overcome with joy, Kate looked around the bottom of the lifeboat. Tucked back in a corner, dripping wet, was Robert's urn. Kate picked it up tenderly and brought it to her lips for one last, soft kiss. Then, she held it above the waves and let go. Entranced, she watched as the urn slowly sank down to its final resting place at the bottom of the ocean.

Good-bye, Robert.

Robert, who had helped her survive this horrible experience.

Robert, whose spirit had somehow nestled into those ashes.

Robert, the man who had been able to remain by her side even after Moore had tossed his ashes out to the winds.

Robert, the man who had defied the shadow's plans.

Kate smiled and delighted in her secret. She watched as the boat that would rescue her descended to the water. As she waited Kate gently placed a hand over her womb.

Because there, inside, grew the fruit of one last fit of passion. Because she knew that the child of a dead man was growing inside of her, the child of the man who had come back from the shadows to save her life.

A child of love. A child of light.

The last passenger on board the *Valkyrie*.

ABOUT THE AUTHOR

International bestselling author Manel Loureiro was born in Pontevedra, Spain, and studied law at Universidade de Santiago de Compostela. After graduating, he worked in television, both on-screen (appearing on Televisión de Galicia) and behind-the-scenes as a writer. His Apocalypse Z trilogy—*The Beginning of the End*, *Dark Days*, and *The Wrath of the Just*—took him from the blogosphere to bestsellerdom, earning him acclaim as "the Spanish Stephen King" by *La Voz de Galicia*. Loureiro continues to reside in his native Pontevedra.

ABOUT THE TRANSLATOR

Andrés Alfaro is a translator, teacher, and musician who focuses on Central American literature, especially that of contemporary Costa Rica. He received his MFA in literary translation from the University of Iowa. His translations have appeared in *The Buenos Aires Review*, *MahMag*, *Hispanic Issues*, and *Trinity Journal of Literary Translation*. He currently resides in Iowa City, Iowa.